All Things Impossible
Crown of the Realm

D. Dalton

Crown of the Realm (All Things Impossible #1)
Third Edition published May 2019
First Edition published May 2009

www.allthingsimpossible.com

Cover art and map by Cassandra Canady.

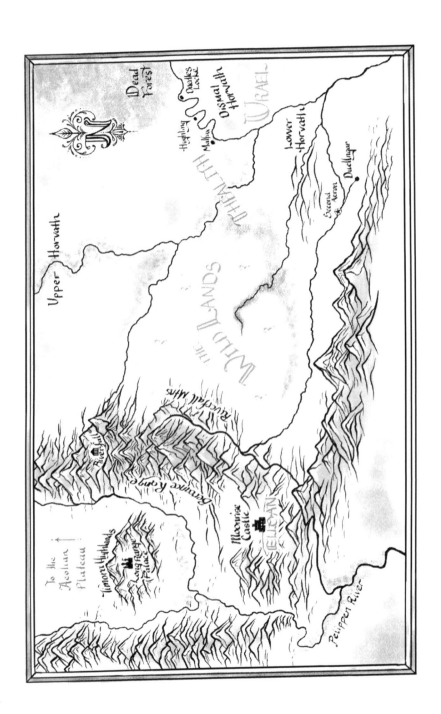

PROLOGUE

Betrayed. By his own parents. Prince Edillon opened his mouth to roar, but the words constricted in his throat. He couldn't breathe. His lips were parting but no air was passing through.

The elf reeled for balance as his gaze fell up to the sky. The sun was incandescent. He felt weightless, soaring, and he found the strength to inhale again.

He bunched his fists and stamped the heels of his boots against the paving stones. *"How dare you?"*

His auburn-haired younger brother, Alsalon, pressed against his side. Edillon was on the cusp of adulthood, but his brother was barely into adolescence. Tears rolled down Alsalon's cheeks as the two of them faced off against their mother and father. They were in the palace's largest garden, full of towering trees, atop one of its towers.

Edillon screamed, "How can you do this to us? Because we won't leave you!"

"You will!" King Valladen's voice left echoes fading throughout the garden. Edillon realized that his father had never looked so regal before, or so sorrowful. His fair hair shimmered like the sunlit prairie, lighting the platinum crown on his head, and his sea-blue eyes stirred with the power of a thousand storms. Edillon gulped. He would not see this again.

He wondered if he could ever be that extraordinary, and he hurled out a prayer that he would never have to find out. He'd been chasing his laughing brother around Grandfather Oak and through the trees. And now...

Valladen raised his hand toward the path through the trees. "You will escape, my sons. You have a chance. Meet your guards, and do not tarry."

Edillon collapsed to his knees. His throat ached with words he could not force out. His dark-haired mother stole his gaze. She was weeping too, but no panic marred her beauty, only grief.

Alsalon rushed forward into their parents' arms. "I don't want to leave you." He was trying to blink away his tears, but Edillon saw him trembling.

"Family is all I have." It took all of Edillon's strength to wheeze those words. His gaze was too heavy to lift.

"You have an entire kingdom of family, son," his father whispered.

"No!" He pounded his fist against the grass. "Please! We'll all run. Everyone in our lands can run. If we can make it, so can you. Father...Mother, *please!*"

Valladen smiled gently, but his eyes creased in sadness. "I wish it could be so."

Tears scorched Edillon's cheeks. "Give them the kingdom. It's not worth this. Please."

Valladen rested a hand on his head. "It is our kingdom that needs to be saved." He stepped back. "You must succeed. Your duty is to deliver our people. I regret leaving this to you, but fate has spoken."

The prince bit his tongue so hard he tasted blood, but he said nothing. Dying thoughts echoed, *How could they give up? How dare they leave this impossible task to me!* But they floated away as numbness overtook him.

Their mother spread her hands out toward them. "I pray that your lives are eternal, full of love and joy."

Edillon remained kneeling and staring at the grass. How could she say something so hollow? How could she *lie?* But his voice was low as he answered, "I accept your blessing, Mother."

Now he had lied too.

She stepped back to stand beside their father. "Go, my sons."

He stumbled to his feet but kept his gaze downcast. Against his will, he nodded.

"We love you," Valladen whispered.

"We love you too!" Alsalon tripped as he dashed forward and buried himself in their arms again. Valladen and his wife did not return the embrace, and instead, swept him back toward Edillon.

"Forever will you sing the first songs," they recited.

"Forever—" the brothers' voices faltered at the same time.

"Now, *go,*" Valladen commanded.

They bowed low and long before turning away. Edillon did not look back, but his brother kept his face turned over his shoulder as they disappeared behind the trees.

***

Alone in the tower garden, the queen sagged against her husband. "Oh, my love, this is all they've ever known."

Her slender frame seemed so fragile to Valladen as he wrapped his arm around her. "I know, Thia." He buried his face in her hair and held her as he watched where the boys had disappeared. The shadows of the trees moved across the paving stones as the sun drifted overhead.

Daylight's warmth waned against his skin, and the air heated to a damp, slimy feel. Shadows stretched and bloated, snaking out across the garden. Valladen glanced skyward. The sun was still shining, but it appeared as if a greasy film had been pulled over it.

The garden faded to gray, to those ashen seconds between dusk and darkness when colors leached away from the world. The storm-readers' light.

He studied the muted garden as the tree branches lowered and their now-gray leaves withered. He felt his own heartbeat slow. At least Thia was still warm against him.

A voice as smooth as silk sliced through the oily air, but to the king's ears, it sounded like the scraping of a whetstone. "You surrender your lives."

Valladen turned toward the direction of the voice. "We do." The words hissed through his teeth as the polluted air drew the very breath out of him. He held his wife closer.

A chuckle spilled out from the shadows. "Very well." The voice slid closer. "I want you to know we already have your people on the run across your lands, which are burning so brightly."

Valladen narrowed his eyes, trying to pierce his gaze into the shadows. "Your victory here is only a small one. Our children live freely."

"Until we find them," the voice retorted. "And we will. Call it payback for what you did to our children." The voice calmed to a thoughtful tone, "You know, we earned our agelessness, unlike you. And you never respected that achievement."

"Your rise to immortality was a mistake of history. One I thought we had corrected." The king straightened his shoulders. "Now stop gloating and do what you came to do."

Thia took his hand as Valladen dropped his crown to the ground. It rang out as it crashed onto the stones. She kissed him. In that kiss, he was unsure of the exact moment he expired.

CHAPTER ONE

"Ready?" The shout carried in the wind.

"Ready!" Derora Saxen hollered and then caught her helmet as it slipped sideways. She bit down on a curse, but it was too late and her hand was already snatching up the lance from the boy. He flinched and scuttled back.

She grinned as the polearm slid into balance at her side, and she angled it at her opponent. Her gaze flitted to the center of the field, watching for the flag.

Swish! She imagined the sound of the flapping banner but couldn't actually hear it over the blood pounding in her ears. She leaned into the saddle as the horse under her heaved and surged forward.

Her grin widened.

She shifted her lance's tip up to hit higher on her opponent's chest as she studied his charge. He realigned his lance too, but it wobbled in the last half-second.

She struck first—a solid blow that reverberated through her arm and torso. Her competitor's lance clipped her left shoulder exactly when he lost control of his mount.

She grunted as the horse beneath her spooked. It bucked, and she scrambled for purchase on the pommel with her left hand as the entire saddle slid to the right.

She threw her lance out wide and cleared herself of the galloping animal. As she was falling, she caught sight of her opponent also tumbling off his mount.

The ground hit harder than the lance, and the impact echoed throughout her body, forcing out the breath left in her lungs.

Groaning, she rolled onto her back. She propped her head against the dirt to see where her horse had charged off without her. Spikes of pain shot through her arm and chest as she sat up and winced.

Someone at the edge of the meadow was chasing after her pony while the rest of the dozen or so kids stared at her and her opponent in awe.

She eased off the cheap pot helm to reveal dark hair and green eyes. She was seventeen summers and never bothered to comb her hair; instead she diverted her potential to things she enjoyed, like swords and horses.

She brushed some dried leaves from her shirt, wincing as she raised her arm. Then she stood before anyone could offer a hand up. She steadied her breath as she glanced around the small meadow where they practiced. Their battlefield was hidden from sight of the village of Riversbridge, and it was where the youth met to escape their daily chores.

She massaged her shoulder as she walked up to her opponent and grinned.

He rubbed his chest as his smile spread. "Der dares again."

She narrowed her gaze. "What?"

He adopted an innocent expression. "Nothing, Der. Dare. Your name is said the same way for a good reason."

She rolled her eyes as she turned toward the direction the ponies had run.

He wheezed. "We need spurs."

"No, we need actual warhorses, Donley. These ponies ain't that." Der stiffened at the burning glare of the red-head two months her junior marching at them.

"The both of you need armor, or at least padding in your shirts!" Avice scolded. She had already folded the blanket they used for a flag. She was the seamstress's daughter and provided the three blankets: one as the flag, and two to soften the blows on the ends of the blunt wooden lances that Donley had cut. They were lucky neither of the so-called lances had broken yet, since Donley hadn't refined them and, in fact, they were little better than planks.

Der turned away from Avice to her father's plow pony that one of the children had led back. He jigged and hopped to the side, whinnying. She reached up and scratched between its ears. "It's all right, boy. See? We're done. You did well today."

Donley stretched. "Mine spooked too when I fell off. You'd reckon they'd be used to it by now." He glanced over at his younger sister who was holding their pony's bridle.

Der chuckled. "But they're not as bad as they used to be."

"Don't worry about the silly horses." Avice slapped Donley on his shoulder. "Are either of you hurt?"

Donley forced a smile, trying not to wince.

Der patted her pony's neck. "I'm fine. Don took the worst blow today."

Around them, the children settled across the grass as they pulled out their lunches. Der wrestled her sandwich free from her saddlebags and sat on the ground. She raised it to her nose and inhaled the scents of cheese, lettuce, and mutton—she had even sneaked in some pepper.

Then she caught the wide-eyed stare of a child. The freckled girl wasn't even blinking. She was about seven years, wore a plain green dress, and had dried mud ringed around her bare feet. She also had no food in her hands.

Der passed down her sandwich. The girl grinned and snatched it up like a prize. Der nodded and then waited for the others to eat while trying to ignore her stomach's grumbling.

She shaded her eyes as she glanced up at the sun. "We've spent enough time out here."

Their parents would know where they had been, of course, but they never asked. Der figured they remembered their days in the meadow. Except for her folks, who in the village hadn't played here when they were young? She made a face, thinking of her generation and if they would ever ask their children what they did in the meadow.

Donley wiped the crumbs from his clothes as he stood, but Der was only half listening as he dismissed the gathered youth. She walked back to town with her pony trailing behind her. Someone had tied the reins on the saddle, but the pony still followed as though she were leading him. The cool breeze teased her cheeks, and she could hear the dried leaves crinkling on the trees. She didn't notice as the others around her dispersed and took different trails. This way, they didn't parade back together all at once.

She wandered between the houses. Their village boasted nothing as large as an inn, and it was mostly self-sufficient. It had to be. There was no castle or lord's manor guarding it, nor was there any road leading to it.

Der stopped in front of the blacksmith's. The forge was a square building that Donley and his father had built four and a half years ago. Over the entrance hung the sign of a hammer striking an anvil, the symbol of the Blacksmiths' Guild. She tied the pony outside.

She pushed through the door. Kelin hardly had time for the meadow these days.

She ran a hand over her sweating forehead; the extra heat was pleasant in winter but not in the summer. Here in autumn, it was still a little warm today, she decided.

Sigard, the old master smith, waved to her as she walked in. Then he hunched back over whatever he was working on as he pulled a chisel from the pockets on his leather apron.

She found Kelin sweeping out the back. "Almost done for the day," he trilled, pushing his broom as fast as he could. The young man had a hardy build, and his hands seemed too large for the stick of the broom he was holding. His dark curly locks hung damp against his forehead, and he hadn't shaved in days, as usual.

"You're done early then." She grabbed the spare broom.

"Had to happen someday." He dropped his gaze. "I think Sigard's trying to get rid of me." He sighed. "I've been packed and ready for two weeks, but every morning, I still come to the forge instead."

She rested her chin on the top of her broom. "And we're still only play fighting in a field, not making a damn bit of difference in the world." She prodded him with her broom. "And you're missing out on seeing that world."

He frowned. "I'll have to go. Someday too soon; the guild doesn't come to me for the examination."

Then they worked in silence, sweeping out different areas. Kelin presented his broom to Sigard and pointed to the floor.

"Huh. You and th' girl work fast. Well enough." He waved the pair off.

Outside, Der untied the pony and let the reins slacken as they walked toward the arched stone bridge.

Kelin's house stood on the other side. The water wheel attached to the mill behind the dwelling rolled along with the current. They crossed the bridge at least eight times a day, and hardly noticed the worn stones underneath their soles anymore.

She stopped in the bridge's center and looked up the hill in the direction of her family's farm, where she could make out the wheat leaning with the breeze in the distance.

A whinny shattered the village's stillness. Der spun toward the sound—she hadn't recognized it and she knew all the ponies in the village. The stones of the bridge vibrated beneath her as several horses thundered between the buildings. Her pony flattened its ears and she heard Kelin gasp in surprise.

Three riders stopped before the bridge. They had swords, bows, and wore leather armor. Cloth masks covered their faces. Der felt her heart racing. These definitely weren't the few traders that visited.

She dropped her pony's reins and walked toward the strangers.

Behind them, she could see Donley, Avice, and the others from the meadow staring. The townsfolk too, and mothers grabbed their children, pulling them back. Sigard stepped out of his forge carrying a hammer.

In the middle of the way, she saw Oric, the village's skinny, self-proclaimed lord mayor, freeze in place.

The rider in front—a large, heavy man—dismounted. He wasn't fat, built more like a bear instead, and he towered over her as her feet carried her forward. The other two riders also swung off their horses and left their hands near their swords.

Der inhaled, licked her lips, and forced out, "Are...are you lost?"

The heavy man glared down at her. She thought she saw the hints of a sneer underneath the mask.

One of the men behind him pulled the cloth down from his face and offered a smile. "Didn't mean to startle anyone. We're hunting the outlaw." He moved close to Der.

She kept her gaze locked on the man in front of her. "Outlaw? There's no law here to break. Not even a knight lives out this way."

The third man twisted toward the one who had spoken and chuckled. "Told you this was the most backwater part of the kingdom."

"Which is why he'd come here—"

Der turned her attention back to the heavy man, who hadn't moved. Something sparkled, half-hidden beneath his tunic and armor. She reached for it and pulled out a polished, black medallion of a serpent's body supporting a striking head on each end.

She'd never seen anything like it. "What's—"

The smile fled from the second rider's face. He drew his sword and thrust it into the large man's side.

Der didn't move as the man gasped and fell. His collapse yanked the medallion from her grasp.

Kelin was shouting and the man was seizing on the ground, but the snake had her hypnotized.

"We didn't know!" someone shouted through a fog.

A power able to overflow the chalice of all her dreams descended all around her. She flinched at an overriding sensation of astonishment, shock even, but it wasn't hers. The impression of a voice crashed down with the weight of mountains, *I'm surprised to see you again after all this time, enemy mine.*

She threw her arms over her head to protect herself. But she knew it wouldn't save her; the voice was enough to snuff out her life as easily as a candle flame.

Distantly, she heard the uneven rhythm of hooves as the riders bolted. She pulled her sleeve over her hand and wiped the fingers that had touched the medallion.

She blinked her eyes back into focus at the movement in front of her.

Sigard was bending over the body at her feet. He removed a pair of tongs from his apron and lifted the snake pendant and its chain out from underneath the corpse's head. He raised his voice, "Kelin, Don, Der, go dig a hole. Then build a fire hot enough to melt this."

"What about the forge?" Kelin waved toward the building.

"I ain't taking this inside!"

"Did anyone else hear a voi—something?" Der rubbed her hands together and held her arms flat across her stomach.

"Hear it?" Kelin looked at her. "We all just *saw* it."

"No..." But the protest died on her lips.

Oric inched up to the body. "What is it, Sig?"

The old smith tightened his jaw and shook his head. "Just trash to burn and bury."

CHAPTER TWO

Night had fallen by the time they'd collected a supply of hard firewood that would burn hot enough. Deep in the forest, they'd dug a pit, lined it with stones, and made a bed of tinder.

Der watched Kelin lower the medallion onto it with Sigard's tongs. She shivered in the cool air. A few others had come to watch, but most had remained inside with their doors closed.

Donley's father had taken the body out on the rig he used to haul trees and had left it for the wilderness to devour.

Her stomach had been twisting all evening, but she found she could finally breathe out as the fire rose. Donley stacked on more logs. She stared hard, but the flames blurred together and she couldn't see the snake any more.

She heard footsteps crunching on dried leaves behind her, and looked to see her father approaching. Riodan cut an impressive figure for a farmer with broad shoulders and a sharp chin. His once dark hair and beard had faded to salt and pepper.

He beckoned. She glanced back at the fire and its glow on Donley, Avice, and Kelin's faces. She couldn't remember seeing them so pale before.

Der felt the flames bright on her back as she turned and approached her father, but he walked ahead into the darkness.

She followed him across the river and up the hill to their barn. He picked up a torch, pressed it against the outside wall, and struck his flint with his dagger until it caught. He lifted it and looked at her. "I know you've always wanted what I never did, so this is your chance to prove it to yourself."

She shook her head. "It's not that. I just want to come up with the plan that saves the day."

A flicker of a smile graced his face. "Unfortunately, this isn't such an opportunity, but you're the only one I trust." He opened the door and disappeared inside. She followed as if she were tiptoeing barefoot over chips of glass.

He gave her the torch and walked ahead. She saw their pony dozing next to the wagon they'd be using to pull in the bushels from the fields starting this week. The barn was wide and tall, housing all their farming tools, and still had enough space to store grain for the winter.

Overgrown shadows of sharpened scythes undulated in the torchlight. She shivered; she wasn't used to the barn like this.

Riodan bent low in a corner, picking at layers of loose hay. He uncovered a wooden chest. Der saw two crests emblazoned on it, which must have shone brilliantly once. She recognized the crossed yellow rose and sword as the shield of Saxen, but she did not know to whom the falcon belonged. Her father rested his fingers on the symbols for a moment, then he wiped away the dust and opened the chest. To her surprise, it was unlocked.

He raised a sword from it, and she hopped back as if he were lifting it from a coffin. The blade needed care, as witnessed by a slight glaze of rust, but the metal hadn't dulled with age. The design was simple, and Der saw the Saxen shield on either side of the guard.

He held it out to her.

She gripped the handle and, not expecting the weight, almost dropped it. Der cursed herself; she knew how much a sword weighed!

She raised it up to meet her gaze. It was a blade of quality, and it far surpassed the shortswords Sigard had made at Riodan's request to protect the farm. Her hands had weathered many callouses from practicing with them.

As she stared at the sword, Riodan reached down and lifted a belt and sheath from the chest. He closed the lid and set them atop the box. His voice was low, "I will write a letter to Count Calloway tonight, and you will take it tomorrow."

Her lips parted and her eyes widened, but she said nothing.

"We don't know anything about this outlaw," he continued, "but if priests of a malevolent deity are after him, I *do not* want him hiding here."

Der tried to gulp, but her mouth was suddenly too dry. "A dark god? *Here?*" She blinked to focus her vision. "That's what the medallion meant?"

Riodan nodded. "Our village militia is young and largely trained by you, and I wish I were joking. We need the count to know we're defenseless."

"I heard his voice..."

He frowned. "The priest spoke to you?"

She shook her head. Then her blurred and rust-scarred reflection on the sword captured her gaze, and she hoped it was the unsteady light making her appear so pale. She realized, *The only way I will get answers is if I go. About this outlaw, about this god...who must have mistaken me for someone else.*

But that thought settled uneasily. Gods weren't supposed to get such things wrong.

She bobbed her head. "I'll take the letter."

Riodan exhaled. "Good. Just..." He set a hand on her shoulder. "I know—old father moment—but stay safe, be smart, and it's all right to kick a bastard in the shins if you need to."

She huffed a chuckle but didn't feel it in her smile.

He lifted his hand. "I'll see you in the morning."

She nodded and watched him leave the barn.

Der tried the belt on, and as she expected, it was too big. She slung it over her shoulder and tested drawing the blade that way. The sword kept slipping lower as she increasingly leaned farther back to reach it until she tripped over her own feet. *This isn't going to work*, she decided.

She lifted the belt over her head and returned everything to the chest. Then she dragged it over near the door.

The darkness didn't slow her as she ran down the lane toward Riversbridge. She had long since memorized every stone and bump on the path.

The only sounds were the river's babbling and the singing crickets, while the only light was from the stars. No one could afford to waste candles or oil, so the townsfolk went to bed when the sun ducked under the horizon...at least on normal evenings. She'd hoped the fire had already melted the medallion and that everyone had returned home by now. It was a trek to and from her farm after all.

She skidded as she misjudged the distance to the side of the miller's house and smacked hard against it. She pushed herself upright and darted around to the rear where she banged on the wall until someone on the other side hit back. Taking the cue, she jogged to the front of the house.

Kelin hung in the door wearing a nightshirt. "More riders had better be here."

"Even better!" Der bounced on her toes. "I'm leaving!" She heaved for breath and tried to recount everything her father had said in one shot. She rocked back to the balls of her feet. "And you're heading out for the guild in Duelingar—"

"Not tomorrow, Der! And maybe I'll go even later because I'm missing my sleep!" He shut the door on her nose.

***

Kelin rested against the closed door and listened to Der jog away.

He counted his breaths, and then slipped outside himself, quivering against the chilly breeze. He was still in his nightshirt, and his boots were untied.

He wandered to the forge and scowled when he saw candlelight underneath the door. He was hoping it would've been empty, so he could smash things against the anvil. He was owed that after today.

When he pushed it open, he found Sigard glaring down at his tabletop. Two candles glowed next to him. The old smith swiveled his gaze over to him. "I doubt you've seen a ghost."

"No." Kelin stepped inside and closed the door.

"It ain't like you to do *more* work than you're asked." Sigard waved his hand toward the cold forge. "So why are you here?"

Kelin caught him staring with scrutiny, even suspicion. So he demanded, "Why're you?"

Sigard shrugged. "Sleep is a younger man's game."

The silence prodded Kelin on, "Der's leaving." He moved farther inside. "It seems the whole of the kingdom is out hunting this outlaw, and she's walking into it." He sat on the anvil. "I could go with her, but...why bother? It's not like guild recognition means anything out here. This is home. It's always been safe here."

"Today was safe, was it?"

Kelin stiffened.

"What would've happened if those other riders hadn't ran him through?" Sigard growled. "Der's forged for things that Riversbridge can't offer, but she ain't faced a man tryin' to kill her before."

Kelin's fingers pulled up a horseshoe. He'd had to make quite a few of them lately with the jousts going on in the meadow. Her idea too. Now she was leaving...

They'd been infants together. They'd grown up as brother and sister. She *was* his sister more than some of his younger, actual sisters. He said, "Her father may be sendin' her off, but Der wouldn't go if she didn't want to."

Sigard nodded. He tapped his fingers on the table as his expression became distant. "Long, long time ago, when Midan the Merciful's armies of Pallens fought in the Centum Wars—"

"I already know about Pallens."

"Right, so after the fall of the empire, our ancestors fled to this continent—"

"Where are you going with this?" Kelin's patience slipped a little further away from him.

"I'm just sayin' that Derora has the right to leave, and fight, and starve, and be crippled or hacked to death if she so chooses. The empire was slain, but her ideals are still limping along." Sigard pointed at him. "What about you? What do you stand for?"

After a moment, Kelin shook his head. "I don't know."

Sigard's chuckle was rough. "I remember when you first became my apprentice and you flinched at the sparks when the hammer struck."

The younger man scowled. "Not anymore."

"Of course not. But the world is full of sparks." Kelin watched the smith rise and walk over to his prized possession, a large safe he had crafted years ago. It was a symbol of pride more than anything. At least, that's what Kelin had always thought, but he was no longer sure.

Sigard fished the key from his pocket and removed the lock with delicate precision. Kelin tried to peek over his shoulder but the old man was too large.

The smith turned around, holding a sword across his palms. It had a long handle and a smooth, slightly curved blade with a plain square guard. Only one edge was sharpened, but it was keen.

Sigard's expression remained grim. "Your hammer isn't enough to hit the world with. You'll need a proper blade too."

Kelin pointed. "You didn't sharpen the backside."

"It's not supposed to be." Sigard tensed. "I hadn't intended to give this to you, but you'll need it more than I ever will." His eyes glossed over as he sighed. "I saw a sword like this once, long ago in the capital on a brightly clothed warrior from a distant land..." He snorted. "Anyway, I wanted his sword, and I am a smith, so I made one."

"It, uh, looks like a sound blade." Kelin tilted his head. "But how do you wield it?"

"It is a sound blade—I wouldn't make anything else. As far as wielding it goes, ask Der. Now get out of my forge; you'll need sleep." He tossed a plain sheath, designed for the curved blade, onto the table.

Kelin walked home with his arms loaded. Riversbridge was as still as an undisturbed pond. It gave him time to think of how suddenly his life was changing. But it wouldn't, he told himself, he'd come right back.

CHAPTER THREE

"Arise."

Der blinked her eyes open and wondered when she'd fallen asleep. It had seemed so impossible.

"Morning," she croaked through a dry throat as she eased out of bed. It was the room she'd shared with her brother and sister all her life. Emil had become a lord's scribe years ago, but now she couldn't find Chera in the morning light.

Riodan nodded and left the bedroom. She dressed rapidly and breathed out as she cinched on the sword. She'd cut a length of leather from the belt and had sewn it back together to make it fit. The blade felt awkward with the weight on one hip, but she liked it. She picked up her boots and backpack, then tiptoed into the kitchen.

She inhaled. Every morning she came out to the airy and sweet scent of dough rising. Her mouth watered at the thought. It baked while she was in the fields, and when she and her father returned for breakfast, its promise had become divine.

But the room was empty of scent, without even the dream of it. She cast her gaze to the wood-burning stove—it was cold.

Her father stood near the door to her bedchamber, while her mother, Rhoesia, sat at the table next to her older sister. They were both pale as they watched her. Der stared into Chera's eyes, the same green as her own, although her hair was lighter like their mother's. Beside them was some of yesterday's bread as well as mounds of vegetables, wrapped cheese, and smoked meat.

"Put socks on." Riodan pointed at the boots she was carrying.

"Yes, sir." She set her backpack down and reached into it. Her sword banged on the floor as she bent. She cursed under her breath and imagined what he must be thinking.

When she had both socks and boots on, she straightened out the rest of her clothing, including the sword belt. Then she turned to face Riodan. In the predawn light, she saw him more as the knight-in-training he used to be than her dad. His inspecting eyes did not disappoint the vision.

He held out a sealed scroll. "You must swear to deliver this to Count Calloway."

He did not release his grip as she grasped it. She met his gaze. "I swear I will deliver this to Count Calloway."

She felt him hesitate to let go, but he gave up the scroll's weight. "When you get to the count's, use my name. They'll know it, or at least they should—I spent half my life there."

Rhoesia forced a smile as she stood from the table. She swept the food into a cloth bag and passed it along to Der, who slipped it into her backpack. Her mother also handed her a coin-purse. "I know there's not much use for money out here, but you'll need it in the city."

Der opened her mouth to decline, but then wrapped her fingers around the purse.

Chera stood, holding something white and square in her hands. Der squinted. A staff bursting with bright flowers decorated the handsel. Her sister whispered, "It's the walking staff of Amiery, so you'll have good fortune on your travels."

"Thank you." Der folded the handkerchief into the coin-purse and then tied that to her belt.

"I was nervous enough when Emil left." Riodan walked to the window in the house's front room and looked out. "I don't know anything of the current court. We may be friends with old enemies or enemies with former allies." He pointed through the grayness to where the sun would rise. "Out in the world, you'll need everything I've taught you to survive long enough to learn what you'll actually need to know. I only pray I've taught you enough." He pulled her into a brief embrace. "When your sister was born, when I held her, I knew what I had wasn't a life I could cherish." He blew out a sigh and stepped away from her. "Farewell, my daughter. You have my permission to return when you will. Until that day, may Carenth grant you many blessings and Zine many victories."

She nodded, feeling a tightness in her chest. She didn't know what she could say, so she turned, opened the door, and stepped outside.

She walked down the path from the house and glanced at the barn, where the farmhands and her father would hustle to work soon enough.

Riversbridge was quiet and the world dim. She ventured onto the stone bridge and stopped halfway across to listen to the water. She could make out its gentle flow in the early light.

How she had ignored this simple beauty for so many years! And she would not see it again any time soon. And she was all right with that, she realized as she walked off the bridge. But she'd miss her family and friends. She thought of Donley, Kelin, and Avice safe asleep in their beds.

But a grin accumulated as she walked, and her step came with some spring to it. She started to whistle *Victory Over the Bridge*, thinking it vaguely fitting.

Her song died in mid-note as she passed the last house. "Kelin! What are you doing here?"

"Oh, I thought I'd finally walk up to Duelingar for the guild examination." He paused, as if he'd been rehearsing. "Aren't you going the same way?" He twirled a walking staff, and she caught him eyeing the sword at her side. He shifted his own backpack, and she heard metal scraping against metal inside. She also saw a sheath tied to its outside, encasing a blade she'd never seen before. He leaned forward and wheezed, putting his weight into the staff.

"Indeed I am." She couldn't help but smile.

"Might I journey with you then?"

"Of course, but," she pointed, "why are *you* carrying a sword? I want to see it."

"When the sun's up." They began to walk. "I wonder how many riders are out there, hunting in groups, only they're stalking a man instead of a deer."

"Don't know." Then she added, "Let's not forget about ogres, dragons, or even vampires. Perhaps even a few chemmen."

"Chemmen? Everyone knows that the storm-readers aren't real." He stopped mid-stride. "But were they?"

Der shrugged. Brief remnants of campfire stories about creatures that drained life or something flitted across her mind. "I think they were killed off in the Centum Wars." She chuckled. "The elves would know. Perhaps we'll meet some! Or dwarves too. Wouldn't that be incredible?"

"Need to get to the city first," he chided. Then his tone darkened, "*Without* running into anyone else."

They struck out across the meadow. On the far side, the trees thickened around them until they were no longer able to see the village.

CHAPTER FOUR

It was two weeks until they caught sight of Duelingar. Once they'd found the road, they'd encountered no one on it until this morning, and then there seemed to be too many people for anyone to try anything suspicious.

Tall gray walls, dotted with turrets, surrounded the city. It was as if the earth had risen and declared this place under its protection. Beyond the walls, they could see hundreds of busy, stacked buildings, and three small castles at its center.

"It's too big," Kelin murmured. "There can't be this many people in the world."

"Let's go meet them." Der sped down the lane as several other roads merged into the one they were on.

As they closed in on the city, the details of individual stones on the walls came into focus. The gates themselves boasted two portcullises and manned towers on either side.

A soldier stuck out an arm before they could step under the first portcullis. "Hold it."

Kelin nudged her. "Der."

She blinked and stretched her neck up at the guard in front of her. She had almost walked into him. Below the open helm, she made out a weather-stained face.

"Just the two of you?" He nodded between her and Kelin as he scratched a nostril underneath the nose-guard.

"Yes," Der answered.

"What's yer business?"

She reached for her backpack for the rolled-up letter but hesitated. It wasn't meant for a gate guard. Kelin stepped forward. "I'm a blacksmith going to take the guild trials to become a journeyman."

The guard sucked in a hissing breath. "You got proof of that?"

"Why should we show you?" Der asked.

He chuckled. "I hope your smithy skills are as sharp as your tongue."

"Not a smith," she muttered.

He glanced down at her sword. "Do you even know how to use that?"

"They're just kids, sarge, let 'em through already." Another guard leaned on his halberd behind their would-be interrogator. He pushed himself forward. "That sword don't look too bad. Let me see it, I might buy—"

Der's jaw dropped. "Buy?"

"Sure." The guard beckoned. "I can offer a decent price too. Come on, let's show it."

She scuttled back and closed a hand over the hilt. "No, no, it's family."

"Oh, I understand." He nodded. "You're just carrying it. It's too big for you anyhow." He stepped aside to let them pass. "Watch yourself, girl. Other people 'round here might not ask."

Kelin paled. "Is this about the outlaw everyone's after?"

The guards' expressions darkened. The second one looked at Der. "Not about stealing a sword, no."

"What's it about?" she asked.

The guard glanced at the sergeant, who shrugged. He said, "There's been a smidge of trouble out west." He grinned a little, but it didn't match the nervousness across his face. "And our orders are to keep out that trouble."

Kelin frowned. "The Wild Lands are the only thing west of here. Nobody lives there."

The guard forced a laugh. "Exactly." He waved at them. "Go on through."

They nodded to both guards and slipped underneath the portcullises. The noise of the city swept over them, and Der swiveled her head around and even up. The buildings crowded against each other, wall to wall, and countless faces shoved past each other.

Kelin's jaw hung open. "I've never seen a building with two floors before, and did you see that one? It has four. Four!"

Der had to raise her voice over the street. "I see it. I see it!"

He wiped his forehead. "Who needs all that space? What could they use it for? Where could the guild be in this madness?"

She turned in a circle, then looked at Kelin and shrugged. She pointed. "Most people seem to be heading that way."

"Uh...sure." His words dragged as he spoke, but he followed her as they set out deeper into the city.

Soon, the wedge of people had funneled them into a corridor—not an alley, but something with buildings' high walls on either side and tighter than the avenues by the gates.

Der gasped for breath. Her shoulders squeezed together as the crowd bounced them around. Too many people—too little space—too loud!

The flow pushed Kelin and her out into a wider street, and Der found she could inhale again.

Kelin grabbed her shoulder, but she was already staring. She felt her mouth dry at the sight of the pillars holding up the white marble edifice. The other structures were of wood, darker stones, and thatch; nothing like this!

Above the rows of white stairs, she could see statues of the gods rising over the visitors inside.

She swallowed, but at least these were gods she could name.

She tapped Kelin's shoulder and pointed at the temple. "Maybe they'd know."

"Know what?" His expression turned pensive. "But we should thank Amiery for our journey here being outlaw-free."

They wove their way through the people and across the street.

"Look!" Der snatched Kelin's arm. Her mouth slipped open.

A mounted knight in brilliant blue armor towered over them as he passed. His mail shone, as did the hair on his horse and even the leather on his polished saddle.

"Is that a dragoon knight?" she squeaked. "It has to be." She stopped while biting down against a smile. "Do you think he's after the outlaw too?"

"I hope so," Kelin answered and quickened his pace. "He's actually qualified." Der jogged after him. She felt excitement rising as they ascended the temple's stairs.

The gods' statues stood taller than she had thought, at least well over ten feet. She recognized some of them from the stories. There was Ahtome with her scroll and sickle, the goddess of harvest, fecundity, and knowledge. There was Zine, patron of war, justice, and mercy, and finally, Amiery, god of travel and music. And in the center, Carenth, father and king.

The statues were white but painted in glowing colors from the stained-glass windows that were almost the entire temple's rear wall.

Der had witnessed nothing so exquisite before. She grinned. There was a connection in this place all the way back to Pallens. They still followed the same gods two thousand years later. "I wish I could see the paladin empire."

Kelin blurted out a laugh. "Well, you can't."

Her grin deflated. "I know, I know." She surveyed the temple and noticed there were openings in the walls to the sides, making the space feel much larger than it was. The outlets were much smaller than those between the pillars out front, but it wouldn't be hard to squeeze through. When her gaze drifted back to the entrance, she saw the dragoon knight had dismounted and entered. Several people in white or gray robes clustered around him.

Kelin elbowed her. "I'm going to thank Amiery."

"Yeah..." she trailed off as he left her side. She spun in the opposite direction and leveled her eyes on a young man about her own age in a gray robe. As she inched toward him, she felt her smile withering.

"Excuse me, uh, priest..." She petered out as she stepped in front of him, not knowing what his title might be.

He opened a smile and spread his hands. The sun hadn't tanned his round face, and he was only a little taller than Der. "I'm not a priest, not for a while yet. Only an acolyte."

She parted her lips to speak, but her throat tightened. She told herself that this man had taken vows, it'd be all right. "So. I'm having a bit of spiritual crisis."

His grin widened. "You needn't worry. Such is common, my child."

She stared at him—he wasn't any older than her. She said, "Yeah, so, one of the dark gods, uh, the snake one...? He has me confused for someone else."

The acolyte's face froze behind his smile. "Are you talking about Sennha?"

"Am I? Double-headed serpent?" She tried to imitate the medallion's shape with her fingers.

The acolyte nodded as the color fled from his cheeks.

"A man wearing, uh, *Sennha's* symbol came to our village."

He grabbed her upper arm. "A priest? A fell priest?"

"I guess so..." She took a step back to dislodge his hand. "I touched the pendant, then I heard his voice."

The acolyte hissed. "What did he say?" His expression filled with urgency. "Was he trying to enchant you? The cultists have suddenly become so aggressive, and we *need* to know why."

She forced herself not to look away. "No, I heard the *god's* voi—"

The acolyte spun and dashed off, blundering into people as he kept staring at her over his shoulder.

"That was the reaction the other riders had too," she said to the empty space before her.

She whirled and jogged over to Kelin while hearing the rising voices on the other side of the temple.

Kelin raised his eyebrows at her as she grinned at him. "I think I'm going to be kicked out," she glanced behind her and caught the dragoon veering toward them, "or arrested." She pointed at the nearest opening in the wall. "We should go."

She grabbed his sleeve and jumped.

CHAPTER FIVE

Der kept an eye out for priests—no matter whose—as she and Kelin trekked between the buildings.

"What did you do?" he demanded.

She smiled and shrugged. "I did not keep my mouth shut."

He rolled his eyes.

They headed toward the city center where they could stand in view of the three castles. From what Der could make out between the eaves and overhanging roofs, they were small and squat—the city's walls looked thicker than theirs—but they appeared sturdy.

The world was quieter here, she noticed, and Kelin's pace was slowing too. There were people, but it wasn't the crowds by the temple or the gates.

"Which one?" Kelin asked.

Der glanced to the castle to the west and then the north. "Er…"

He heaved a deep sigh.

"Oh." She caught sight of the banner hanging off the wall of the castle to the east. The falcon was the same as was on the chest that had held her sword, and her father had said he'd trained half his life there. She smacked her forehead and pointed. "It's that one."

She started toward it, leaving Kelin to chase after her. The castle didn't seem to grow any larger as they approached.

They stopped at the closed gates. They were smaller than she had imagined, standing at only a couple feet taller than she did.

She stepped back and noticed a soldier in the shadows staring hard at her from the walkway on the wall above. She waved at him. "We're here to see the count. I've got a letter to deliver—"

"Court's closed." He didn't move. "Come back tomorrow."

"This is important. Our village—"

"Court's closed."

"My father used to live here—"

Each word snapped like a breaking branch, "Court is closed."

Kelin tapped her shoulder. He nodded back toward the rest of the city.

"But—"

He hauled on her arm, pulling her away.

***

Over an hour later, and after being more lost than Der would like to admit, they gazed up at a metal plaque of a hammer striking an anvil. Stone steps led up to a heavy wooden door, which was propped open. Above the building, thick plumes of smoke fought for height before the wind tore them apart.

Der raised a hand toward the door. "You first."

He remained where he was.

She looked at him and then at the building. "You're not moving."

He bunched a fist at his side but sighed. "This is the rest of my life, Der. What if I ruin this?"

"You can't ruin it if you don't go inside."

"Der!"

"Isn't this what you wanted?"

"I... It was always just what was there." He shuffled backward. "Let's find an inn, we'll go to the count's first thing in the morning, then we can return tomorrow." He exhaled. "I'm only here because I followed you— *What are you doing?*"

Der shoved him up another step. She had to squat low, dig her shoulders in, and heave. Moving him was like rolling a boulder uphill.

She pushed again and they stumbled through the door into a well-lit entryway. Racks of weapons, horseshoes, and scythes lined a stubby hall. A man wearing a leather apron spat into his palms as he stood behind a metal desk. He wiped his hands on the apron and looked up at them. "What do you want?"

Kelin licked his lips. He stared. Der prodded him with an elbow. He managed, "I, uh, I'm an apprentice, and I, uh, want to take the trial exam. For journeyman."

"Oh." The man held out his hand. "Your master's letter?"

"Right!" Kelin threw down his backpack, and it clanked when it hit the floor. The scraping of metal against metal sounded louder than thunder in the quiet hall. "Here." He proffered the bent document with shaking fingers.

The man's eyes brushed over it. "All right, we can fit you in today. Got a few others taking the journeyman trial too. Go on straight back through that door there. And, you," his gaze drifted over to Der, "you'll have to wait over there." He waved at a small archway, then he looked back down to his desk and didn't glance their way again.

She grinned at Kelin. "Best of luck, my friend."

He gulped. "Yeah. Thanks."

She watched him inch through the door. Then she poked her head through the arch into a medium-sized room with benches lining the walls. A window on the back wall allowed in some light and breeze. Two other people were already waiting. She stopped and stared at the nearest one.

He was a dwarf. Der had never seen a non-human before, but there was no mistaking the height and the black beard tucked into his belt. She tried not to gape too obviously as she unbuckled her sword and edged down onto an empty portion of a bench. She set her blade across her lap.

The dwarf grinned—as far as she could tell between the beard and heavy mustache anyway—all she saw was the hair move and assumed there was a smile underneath. She inched back a smile of her own.

"Yer no craftsman," he said in heavily accented Common. "Buyin' or tradin'?"

She placed her backpack between her boots. "Uh, no. I'm waiting for my friend. He's taking a trial."

The dwarf nodded, seemingly satisfied with the answer. He swung his feet out over the floor. Der peered at the metal triangles on the tips of his boots and laughed as she imagined kicking someone with those.

She coughed. "Excuse me."

He smirked. "Yer not from th' city, are ya?"

She grinned uncertainly. "How did you know?"

He chuckled, and it sounded like gravel rolling down a hill. "Yer tense and yer eyes keep rovin'. Also, them is practical clothes."

"Oh." She locked her gaze straight ahead.

He leaned in her direction and wagged his thick eyebrows. "Ya know them city walls, they is dwarf work. 'Tis why they's held so long."

"How old are they?" she inquired, still trying not to stare.

"Two centuries young."

"Really?" Her eyes shot wide.

"Indeed. This city was built by dwarves fer trade; 'tis why th' Blacksmiths' Guild is here and not th' capital." He leaned back and banged his helmet against the wall. "Name's Gnirun Heavyaxe o' Clan Heavyaxe."

She shook her head. "Haven't heard of it, sorry."

"Oh." He slouched. "I thought all humans 'round here knew th' name."

"I'm sorry," she said again.

"Bah." He shrugged. "Not yer fault ya ain't been educated."

"I can read!" she shot back, louder than she expected.

"So?"

"Um..." She wasn't sure how to counter that.

The other human in the room chuckled. "Not most farm-folk can, master dwarf. I do not mean to intrude, but I thought I might bridge this river." His voice was silken and soft, not to mention instantly trustworthy. He looked at Der with laughing brown eyes set under dark hair. "Most dwarves do not seem to be aware that many humans cannot."

"What are ya here fer?" Gnirun demanded, staring hard at the man.

"Myself? I am a merchant. I'm visiting the guildmaster about a late shipment. Alas, he's busy and I must wait."

Gnirun snorted. "That th' shipment with th' elvish goods in it? Ain't comin'."

"I beg your pardon?" the trader asked through a tightening smile.

"Ain't comin'." The dwarf kicked his dangling feet. "Something 'bout that lousy outlaw everyone's huntin'. Dwarf news, doubt most humans got word yet."

"He robbed it?" The merchant knotted his fingers together. Knuckles creaked and popped.

The dwarf stopped kicking and his voice deepened, "Don't know 'bout that, but I can say th' shipment ain't comin'."

The merchant's face fell into his hands. "No! That's the one shipment I wait five years for! Every five years! Do you know how hard elvish goods are to find?"

"I do." Gnirun started swinging his boots again.

"Elves?" Der pressed her hand against the bench, leaning forward. "Honestly, elves?"

She tried to imagine them. Their secret kingdom lay beyond the Wild Lands and an uncharted mountain range. But the Wild Lands repulsed attempts by settlers and people told stories about its natural magic pushing them back or cursing those that remained. Thealith, their kingdom, was the westernmost human kingdom, existing in the Wild Lands' shadow.

"Yeah, elves," Gnirun repeated. "They cut off trade. All o' it."

The merchant jerked to his feet and offered a half-bow. "If you will excuse me, I must discuss this with my colleagues and clients." He swept out of the waiting room.

Der raised her eyebrows. "Um, I don't want to be rude, but he trusted you."

The dwarf pointed to his helmet. "Heavyaxe."

"Oh." She shrugged.

He chuckled. "'Course, ya don't seem o'erly concerned yerself."

She held out her hands. "How does what happens in the elvish kingdom affect me?"

He cracked another grin. "Fair 'nough, girl."

She pursed her lips. "So, um, master dwarf," she tried using the trader's term, "you know a lot..."

"Sometimes I wish I didn't." He slapped his thigh. "Bah, I'd like to get back home, truth be tol'."

"You sound like my friend."

"Friend sounds smart then."

They both laughed. He sighed, "I'll be headin' back ta War'Kiln soon enough. But alas, I'm out here on errands 'cause everyone wants to deal with th' lord. Only ta make 'im wait!"

Der wasn't wholeheartedly listening, instead trying to frame her own questions. "Do you know what this outlaw did?"

"Murder," Gnirun spat. He swung his head toward her. "Of elves."

"Oh." She frowned. "Then how does Sennha fit into all of this?"

The dwarf snorted. "Don't think he does, child. He just likes ta jump into the pot ta claim chaos an' vict'ry."

"You don't think he's connected?"

"Nah." He kicked his feet. "His sycophants seem ta be actin' up though. Hm."

Der nodded, concentrating. "Does he have any enemies? Like historically?"

Gnirun looked perplexed. "Not one in particular I can name, no."

She turned toward movement at the entrance and saw the man in the apron from the hallway enter. He bowed to the dwarf and announced, "The guildmaster has rushed to make himself available for you. Please, this way." He stood and swung a hand open wide.

Der caught the dwarf rolling his eyes as he slid off the bench. He stopped in front of her and raised a finger. "Mind yourself 'bout this outlaw. Not that you'll meet 'im, but e'ryone's agitated these days."

She nodded. Then he and the man departed, leaving her alone in the room.

She slouched back into the bench. Then she pulled her knees to her chest and stared up at the ceiling.

Kelin eventually slid into the hall, looking around before focusing on her.

She raised her head away from the wall, blinking as she reined her attention into the present. "How was the trial?"

He sighed. "Boring. All I did was show the things Sigard packed for me and answer a few questions. I didn't know the one about limestone though."

"Limestone?"

"Why we use limestone to remove slag. That's all though. I passed without a second glance. Then I had to pay the fees." He gave her a tight smile and lifted his backpack. "At least my load is lighter."

"Ah. What's slag?"

"Impurities in the molten metal."

"Oh. Right." She pushed herself to standing and cinched her sword belt around her waist. "Now what?"

Kelin shrugged. "Find an inn. We'll go back to the castle at dawn, I promise." He patted his belly. "But for now, I want supper."

Der noticed her own stomach rumble at the mention. "Good idea, but..." She felt for her belt purse and listened to the musical jingle of coins inside. There weren't enough notes, she decided. "But I don't know how long this needs to last."

CHAPTER SIX

Der woke up hugging her backpack. She spat a leather strap out of her mouth and yawned. She approached cogitation as she listened to the inn's other patrons snoring. Then she unwound herself from her pack and the thin blanket she'd found in a pile by the door last night. She slapped on her sword and dagger, then looked around the room.

She was the first awake. Around her, other sleepers remained splayed across the large, flat panels overlaid with hay that served as a communal bed. She'd slept in her clothes and her boots.

She poked her head out the door. "Ah." She grinned and picked up the bucket of water. Clean water was worth waking up for first. Back inside, she splashed the icy water on her face and gasped. She thought, *I knew it would do that.* She pushed the bucket against the wall for the next person.

The next person was Kelin, who groaned as she tapped him in the ribs with her foot.

"Wake up."

He glared up at her with one eye open, and then rubbed his scraggly face. "It's too early, Der."

She grinned.

Then she ambled into the dark common room, stretching one arm and carrying her backpack in the other. She stopped in front of the staircase leading upstairs to the private chambers and leaned against the wall, enjoying the moment of silence with the promising scent of bread wafting from the kitchen. How much she missed her morning bread!

She flinched as she caught sight of gray and white robes as a young man and a middle-aged woman entered the common room. They were in deep conversation with their heads bent toward each other. She fought to keep herself from gasping as she recognized the acolyte. She eased backward up the stairs, keeping to the shadows.

She scowled—they weren't Sennha's cultists! They were the opposite and most likely coming in for a morning meal. She was overthinking this.

The words "we *need* to know" echoed in her mind.

She crested the stairs and backed down the short hallway. Someone had come through and replaced the few candles in their sconces this morning because they were lit and tall.

Der glanced side to side at the nearly identical doors until she bumped up against the hallway's dead end. She held her breath, listening.

Then she smirked, snorted, and let her shoulders slump. She felt her face warm in embarrassment for allowing her fear to best her.

But she still didn't want to go downstairs.

She twisted to see if there was a window she could climb down and find Kelin that way. The wall, however, was solid.

Two sets of footsteps creaked on the stairs.

Der grabbed the nearest door's latch. It rattled but was locked. The footsteps were rising higher.

She jerked toward movement on the other side of the hall. Someone was opening a door.

She grabbed that latch and yanked.

The door stuck halfway as the young man opening it froze.

"Please," she hissed, glancing down the hallway. She could hear their voices clearly now and see the tops of their heads. "The religious hardheads—" Her mind snapped to blankness and she struggled to force out, "You know, the ones wearing temple robes—"

He opened the door and she dashed through it. She spun as he guided the door closed. He was a svelte young man about her age. Platinum blond hair spilled out from under his green cap. A long, thin sword adorned his side.

He glanced toward the door, his hand landing on the hilt of his sword. "They're disguising themselves?"

Der frowned. "Don't think so." She couldn't place his accent; it wasn't anything like hers or the others she had heard over the last day.

"You said the cultists were dressed in temple robes."

Her forehead wrinkled in confusion. "N—"

A knock thundered on the door. A twin banging echoed from across the hall on another door.

Her jaw clicked closed.

The young man waved her to the side. He turned and cracked the door open.

"Excuse me," Der recognized the acolyte's voice, "We're in search of—"

"Is it me?"

"What? Uh, no, sir. Sennha's followers have been—"

"Then good day." He pressed the door shut.

Der breathed out. She shuddered as they knocked on the other doors; she couldn't perceive the conversations, but their tempos were grunted and short.

Then she noticed the young man staring at her. She offered a tight grin. "Thanks."

He nodded in reply. Then he cocked an eyebrow at her.

Her smile faltered.

Silence descended.

Der twisted her foot against the floor. She slouched. "I hope the count opens his court early because I'm absolutely ready to get out of the city."

After a moment, he replied, "Me too." He stared hard at her. "I tried to find it last night, but I wasn't sure which castle it was. The sun was fast setting, and the mood of this city is quickly darkening."

"It's the one with the falcon banner," she volunteered.

He blinked as if in surprise. "Thank you."

"Welcome." She shrugged. "Why don't you come with us?"

He frowned.

She heard heavier footsteps outside, along with the shuffling sounds of other people waking up.

"Der?" she heard through the wall.

She grinned.

"Dare?" her rescuer repeated.

"That's me." She watched him as she moved toward the door.

"Oh." He bowed his head. "Caleb." But he glanced away.

Der pushed open the door, swiping her gaze up and down the corridor.

"What are you doing up here?" Kelin eclipsed the doorway. His face was red and his voice was harsh.

"Making a new friend."

Kelin narrowed his gaze at her. "And this has nothing to do with the priests downstairs? They're getting chased out by the innkeeper, by the way." He looked over at Caleb, unsure.

"We should get going to the count's," she chirped and grinned at Caleb. "But, you know, take our time getting out the door."

She started to catch Kelin up while she delayed at the top of the stairs and tossed his name to Caleb, who exhaled but waited with them.

Out on the street, Der searched for temple robes, but she didn't see any. Still, she hesitated—they had to be close. There weren't too many people on the street yet, but those she saw dressed normally, at least normally to what she saw yesterday.

She turned in toward the hill that hosted the castles. There stood a maze of winding streets between them, but she was glad to have a direction.

"Have you heard anything about this outlaw?" she asked as they began to walk.

Caleb grunted, "Who hasn't?"

"We hadn't." She jogged to keep up with his stride. "Then a priest of Sennha showed up in our village hunting him."

He scowled and leaned away from her.

Kelin demanded, "When did you learn the god's name, Der?"

"At the temple, when, uh…" she petered out. She set her boot down and her stomach erupted with a chorus. She reddened as she was sure the others had heard it.

Kelin caught her eye. He nodded.

"Here." Caleb swiped a white package out from his belt pouch and handed it to her. She sniffed it and welcomed the scents of meat and cloves. Then she unfolded the cloth to reveal a sausage the length of her palm.

She broke it into two pieces and tossed half to Kelin. Spices melted together across her tongue when she bit into it. She stopped walking to enjoy the sausage.

She opened her eyes and grinned at Caleb. "Thank you!"

He hinted at a small smile and dipped his chin in a slight nod before dropping his gaze.

"Where in the city did you buy this?"

He hesitated. "It wasn't from this city, my apologies."

"Then can you make it?"

He blinked, looking confused. "Well, yes, but not in the moment."

"Of course not *now*—" She felt her face warming with embarrassment. "But later..."

"When and where?" Kelin chuckled. "Is the count going to let us use his kitchen and larder?"

Der's cheeks flared. Kelin laughed, and she caught Caleb fighting off a smile. So she gave in and let out her own snigger. Then the three of them were snickering together as they walked through the streets.

She noticed the avenues became more familiar as they neared the castles on the hill. Caleb glanced at her sideways as she twisted toward the falcon banner.

The castle loomed larger as they approached. She felt both of them trailing after her as they entered the castle's shadow. She scowled. No guards overlooked the walkway from above, and it was quiet.

She exchanged glances with Kelin and Caleb. Then she swiveled around and knocked on the gate. The sound echoed.

She frowned, then pushed on it. The side she pressured swung open with ease. She glanced back at Kelin, who retreated and shook his head. Caleb was silent, but she could read the apprehension on his face.

She let an ear tilt toward the gate but didn't hear anything. She waved a hand through the open portal. Nothing.

She twisted her head and shoulders through. It was much dimmer as the walls of the castle choked off the sunlight, and she saw that the walkway over the gate ringed the entire courtyard. Iron-banded wooden doors barred every entrance beyond the yard. Over to her side was a pile of canvas covering what she guessed was either lumber or bushels of wheat.

She stepped through. She heard Kelin cursing beneath his breath as he followed. Once inside, she sniffed and wrinkled her nose. It didn't smell like the barn, she reckoned, but something potent was *off*.

But maybe the silence was playing tricks with her. She tiptoed deeper into the courtyard and cupped a hand around her mouth. "Hallo the castle!"

Her shout bounced back to her from the courtyard's far walls.

Caleb slipped through the gate, leaving it open behind him. She thought he looked even paler than before.

Kelin frowned. "But...someone *has* to be here."

Caleb shook his head. "The count must be in the capital. Dammit." He turned back toward the gate.

Der shook her head. "The soldier said to come back today. Surely, he'd have said if the count were in Second Acron."

Kelin's face looked more and more ashen by the moment. "Perhaps not..."

Der glanced around the desolate courtyard again. "Or maybe he's just murdered."

Kelin tapped his boot against her ankle and scowled at her.

Caleb stopped and swung his head toward her, his eyes widening.

She forced a smile. "Uh... Do you know where he'll be in the capital? We've never been there."

He nodded with glacial slowness.

Der turned and grabbed the gate. It swung easily with one hand—it was open, unbarred, and the carved holes in the ground that fitted stakes at its base were empty.

"Who are you?"

They spun. A woman on the far side of the walkway aimed a crossbow at them. She was wearing a plain brown dress with a matching shawl covering her hair.

Kelin gulped. "We..." He inched toward the gate, bumping into the canvas-covered pile.

Caleb eyed her with cold suspicion but said, "I'm searching for the count's master cook. However, I see no one is here. I assume the lord took his retainers with him to the capital."

"The gate was also open," Der called as she wiggled it back and forth.

The woman raised the crossbow toward the sky and glared down at them. She approached on the walkway. She lifted her chin and looked at Caleb, then to Kelin, and finally to Der. "My lord demands we be hospitable. You may remain for a meal, and I suppose you could stay in the stables tonight if you must."

Kelin's smile bunched together. "That's very kind, my lady, but..."

Der sniffed again. She knew that scent, but she hadn't expected it *here*.

It was the same as that deer they hadn't dragged home in time because Donley had sprained his ankle. Even the sheepdogs had avoided it.

Keeping her eyes on the woman, she bent and ripped back the canvas.

Several feet and legs stuck out from the uncovered corner. The skin facing the sky was green and pale, but pooling blood had bruised the bottom halves of the visible flesh.

Kelin's hand clawed at her shoulder as he hauled her toward the gate. Caleb was already flying through it. The woman shot her crossbow, and the bolt skidded across the courtyard's stones where they had just been.

Der looked up as they emerged from the castle to see the woman running over the open gate. She was cupping her hands around her mouth and yelling. Der couldn't make out the words, but everyone on the street turned to stare.

She, Kelin, and Caleb froze.

Her eyes slid to the left, then to the right. Curious people surrounded them, creating a roadblock of onlookers and leaving them no way to run.

Der found the sounds of the footsteps seemed louder than usual. Suddenly, everything was deafening and colors swam more sharply in her vision. She felt her throat drying, her legs went leaden, and her clothing seemed too tight.

She focused on four men closing in. They dressed in mismatched heavy leathers: some brown or black, and others even a deep red.

They drew swords. One of them nodded to the woman above, and Der's shoulders pinched together as she realized they were trapped.

She eyed the approaching fighters—she couldn't see any insignia, and they weren't in uniform.

Then she saw the sweat shining on Kelin's forehead. He looked over at her and swallowed. "We can make it, right?"

She didn't answer. Her hand fell to her hilt as the men advanced. Beside her, she caught Caleb glancing behind toward the castle, but Der could no longer see the woman.

Her head swung back to the warriors. This wasn't how things were supposed to go. Then again, she'd never been in a fight before, not like this, so maybe she didn't know how things actually fell into place. She inhaled and steeled herself.

She stepped forward and locked her gaze onto the fighter at head of the pack. "I'm not sure whose misunderstanding this is, but it's not ours. We're just leaving."

He sneered. They didn't slow.

Der tried to jerk her sword free, but it stuck about halfway out just as the nearest warrior raised his blade toward her throat.

As she heaved to draw her sword, she had to confirm to herself that this was happening. Part of her still resisted. *Why* was it happening? Whatever she and Kelin had fallen into hadn't been meant for them.

She held her sword low, trying to hide its shaking. "We're simply leaving."

The man out in front was only a few feet away. He raised his sword and swung. She stiffened, and that took up all the time she had left.

Caleb yanked her back and lunged with his sword. The slender blade bit deep into the man's gut, and he looked up in surprise as he sagged forward.

The world snapped back into speed, and Der fell in line beside Caleb. "You just—you just—"

The rest of the pack closed in on them.

Kelin skittered up behind Der and Caleb, drawing the curved sword and dropping his backpack.

Der thrust at the nearest one, but he blocked and forced her to parry his immediate counterattack. She struggled to keep up with his pace, never imagining she could move so quickly. But she would die if she didn't.

As their swords clashed, she felt tremors echoing throughout her entire body. She realized two things in that white-hot instant: her father's blade was too big for her, and she wasn't nearly as good as she thought she was.

Her opponent lunged. She barely managed her parry and forgot to riposte. He thrust again. She blocked and hit back this time, trying to keep from lurching off balance.

Beside her, Kelin tripped over his pack as he pedaled backward. He cursed and struck out wildly with his blade.

He drew first blood on the man's leg. His enemy must have expected a complicated move from the single-edged, curved sword, and he almost missed batting down the straight thrust, and Kelin was able to pierce his leg.

But Kelin lost his grip on his sword and hopped backward, leaving the blade in his attacker's thigh. The man lunged, and Kelin scarcely dodged. He dipped down and ripped the hammer out of his backpack while ducking under his attacker's next swipe. He ground the hammer into his opponent's groin.

The man screamed and grabbed himself. Kelin snatched his sword back out of his attacker's thigh and plunged it into his chest. Then he stared and gasped in shock of what he had done.

On the other side of Der, Caleb had already felled the man in front of him.

You struck at your *opponent*, Der remembered, not his weapon! In the next few furious seconds, she got several flicks through, and blood flowed from shallow cuts on his arms.

"Bitch!" He chopped at her arm instead of her torso—she wasn't expecting that! She parried, but it was late, and she failed to push his blade far enough away. It sliced down her forearm.

She yelped and dropped her sword. Her opponent's face lit up, but she seized the brief pause to punch his mouth with her left hand. While he was surprised from the hit, she snatched her sword and plunged it into his neck. He sank to his knees and then to the ground, taking the blade down with him.

Der gasped at the sight of her own bright blood on her arm. But it didn't hurt much, and she could flex her fingers. She glanced around in the sudden, deafening silence. "Is that it?" She knelt and scooped up her blade.

Caleb stuck his bloody sword back in its sheath. "Run!"

Der stared back down at her wound. She blinked. It was getting hard to see straight. Her arm was both burning and felt as though it were floating several inches above where it was. "Huh..."

He grabbed her shoulder and pulled. "Run!"

She let him drag her along, but a hand snatched her ankle and held her in place. She looked down at one of the fighters. Blood was pooling in the street near his stomach, but his grip was still strong. His face pinched tight in pain and he squeezed his eyes shut as he heaved for breath.

She stuck the point of her sword at the man's throat but stopped. They were no longer in combat—

His eyes sprang open. Blood leaked from his lips as he hissed, "The sword of Sennha will cut you down!"

Caleb threw his hands on top of hers and slammed her sword down through the man's neck. She flinched when she felt it strike the street below.

"Run!" He bellowed into her ear.

She opened her mouth, but nothing came out. Caleb pulled again, and the motion shook the dead man's grip from her ankle.

Der looked up and saw a wall of people around them, gaping and pointing. They blurred together with the buildings until everything was a seething blend of color. In the distance, she heard the city's bell ringing in alarm. She started to sway. Back home, a bell meant a flood or a fire...or a funeral, she recalled with a shiver.

She'd never killed before. It had happened so fast, she had to react, just had to survive. Now she was standing over the bodies of the slain. But they had been fighting, *breathing* less than a minute ago.

She reeled from a sudden slap across her face and swung her sword up in reflex. Caleb swam into focus. He tightened his grip on her non-bleeding arm and dragged her behind him.

Kelin tripped over his backpack as he turned to flee. Caleb let go of Der, and the three of them thundered down the street. Shouts and yells echoed after them.

Der glanced over her shoulder. More men with swords were giving chase. She couldn't figure out if they were city guards or more of Sennha's followers.

What were the cultists even doing there at the castle? But the question faded in the wake of their sprinting footsteps.

Caleb spun into an alley. Kelin tried to make the turn and crashed into Der. She gasped and rebounded off the wall. But she regained her balance and hauled Kelin after her.

Caleb was already at the end of the short alley. Der tripped and stumbled for balance as she moved to follow him when he turned back around. She watched him glance back toward the thoroughfare. He ducked deeper into the alleys and they followed. Then he stopped, raised a knee, and cupped his hands above it. "Up."

Der shoved her sword back into its sheath. "What?"

"Up! Now!"

She put her foot in his hands, and he flung her up onto the thin, wooden planks above.

She rolled back to the edge and lowered her good arm down to Kelin. With her pulling and Caleb pushing, he clambered onto the roof.

She froze as the wood bent beneath their weight.

Kelin jerked tense. "If we even breathe too much—"

Der cast him an uneasy glance and threw a hand down over the edge.

Caleb shook his head. "No! Other hand! Other hand!" Then she saw the bright red painting her skin and she realized she had thrown down her injured arm without thinking about it.

She heard heavy footsteps pounding down a nearby alley. Caleb grabbed her bleeding arm and jumped. She gasped at the weight on her injury and felt his hands slipping on her blood. But he was up onto the roof with amazing speed.

Der dropped back away from the edge, clutching her injured arm. She wheezed.

"Don't move," Caleb mouthed.

Below them, they heard the rhythm of boots slowing to a stop. Someone growled, "Damn this maze. They came this way. Look for more blood. You three, that way! The rest of you, follow me!"

CHAPTER SEVEN

Der pressed her arm against her shirt; the bleeding had largely been staunched while they lay on the roof. Frantic footsteps had echoed up from below, but they had faded. The sun had grown bright overhead, and now began its trek down toward the horizon.

"I left my pack," Kelin said. "It's in the street." He held up his hammer and sword, staring at the dried blood on them.

Caleb rolled his head toward Der. "Can you hold up your arm?"

She winced and lifted the limb.

He pulled a dagger from his belt and cut along the seams of his sleeve until it came free. "You should have used your other hand to pull me up."

She shrugged, and then hissed, "I didn't think. This is the hand I use."

He inched over and held her arm up from its underside. He whistled softly. "You're lucky. He shaved off your skin but didn't sever anything you can't grow back. But you've bled a lot, and you're wearing most of it."

She laughed as it finally hurt, and it *hurt*. The pain sprinted from her arm to her head, and she thought she would faint as his lissome fingers tied the cloth around the wound.

She said, "You could've easily outrun the two of us."

He tightened his jaw. After a moment, he answered, "Leaving people behind just isn't something I can stomach."

Der held her arm. "Me either." She played through the fight and the dying man's final curse in her mind. "Why were they after the count?"

Caleb frowned. "They seemed to know he wasn't there."

"Then what would Sennha's followers gain by taking over an empty castle?" she asked. Then she shivered, feeling the weight of that voice in her mind again. It had been so *real*.

Caleb snapped, "Well, his will is not in the manner of flowers and holding hands, so nothing charitable."

Der felt her chest tighten. But that feeling—it had been almost serene; it could grant every wish. She stretched her gaze up to the sky. "He certainly seems interested in this outlaw for some reason."

Caleb pushed his hat down against his platinum hair. "Or he's simply profiting from tragedy."

Kelin shifted the weight of his pack. "I wonder who this man killed. I mean, the reward must be something powerful."

"In this kingdom, I heard it was a noble title and land," Caleb said.

"In Thealith?" Kelin shook his head. "But we don't do that." He glanced at Der. "It has to be inherited."

She was frowning. "But wait, that means there are rewards for him in other kingdoms...?" She looked at Kelin. "We never heard about this back home."

"Der," he sighed, "we wouldn't hear if our king had died. Makes you wonder why your father moved out there."

She started to shrug when they felt a thump from below and the roof trembled beneath them. The tip of a drill chewed through it. Kelin yelled and Der grabbed the handle of her sword, but her fingers were too stiff to close around it. Caleb pulled out his dagger.

She stared at the twisting drill. "This is not how I expected to be arrested."

"Quiet!" Both Kelin and Caleb barked.

"Why? They obviously know we're here." The drill had stopped and retreated, and someone below pushed a flag of paper up through the hole. She reached out with her left hand and clumsily forced it open. "'Look below.' What does that—"

On every side of them, axes broke through the wood. As abruptly as they appeared, they were yanked back.

The wooden planks groaned then snapped as the roof collapsed, leaving the trio scrambling to hold onto something for the ride. They crashed hard against the floor below.

Kelin coughed amid the dust. Der twisted to impact on her left shoulder in order to protect her injured arm. Caleb landed on his feet, dagger ready and his other hand reaching for his sword. The axes that had cut the wood were angled toward them, but the dwarves holding them did not seem alarmed.

"Up, young ones," a gruff voice ordered. A dwarf stepped forward out from the ranks.

"Master Gnirun Heavyaxe?" Der hazarded. She couldn't pick him out from any of the others.

He squatted and touched his helmet. "You was expecting another dwarf, mayhap?"

Caleb replaced his dagger in his sheath and uncurled his fingers from his hilt. "We weren't expecting any dwarves, sir. Are you aiding us?"

Gnirun laughed. "'Course! My kith saw what happened."

Caleb remained in a fighting crouch.

The dwarf lord shrugged. "'Nough things is stinky these days." His gaze dropped to Der. "And the girl was kind ta me when we met."

She grinned at him.

His expression darkened. "And didn't I warn ya, child?"

She nodded as her smile faded.

"Oh." Caleb adjusted his green cap and straightened his shoulders. "I apologize for being defensive."

Gnirun smiled beneath the beard. "Bah."

Kelin helped Der to stand. "Please. She's wounded."

She held out her arm. Caleb's bandage had bled through. "I'm fine," she wheezed, leaning heavily on Kelin for balance.

Gnirun waved his hand away from the hole in the ceiling. "Let's get out of the weather."

Caleb didn't move. "Where are we going, sir?"

Gnirun glanced over his shoulder and grunted again. He marched into the next room, reached down, and hauled on a large metal ring in the floor. A trapdoor opened to reveal a dark stairwell. He looked up at the young man. "We's goin' ta supper."

Caleb remained tense.

The dwarf grinned beneath the beard and started down the steps.

Der leaned against the wall as they descended. The warmer air felt steamy as it kissed her skin, and it was spiced with smoke.

Kelin squinted ahead toward the promise of light around the stairwell's bend. But they turned out to be torches. "I always thought dwarves had magical lights, or some glowing animals like in the stories." He shrugged.

Gnirun chuckled. "We might has our ways, but torches work, don't they?"

Caleb frowned. "However, torches require much air, and it would become uncomfortable to breathe."

"Oooh, aren't you th' wiseass of the company?"

"I'm just observing that it would fill with smoke." He glanced around. "This does not seem to be the case."

"We..." the dwarf paused and narrowed his bushy eyebrows, "ain't sure on the right words. We change the air from the outside."

"Ventilation?" Caleb suggested.

"Vent. Wind. Yes, vent."

A few feet behind them, Der stumbled into the wall. Kelin caught her shoulders. She forced a tight smile. "I'm all right."

He shook his head. "Yeah, and you also said you were all right the time you broke your leg falling off a log into the creek and then tried to *walk* home."

Caleb turned around. "Der, please. Save your strength. You're wounded."

"I'm fine."

Kelin grimaced as he took most of her weight. "Der, it was an honorable fight."

She hesitated. "I guess if you put it that way..."

"Here." Gnirun passed under a stone arch that the three of them had to duck beneath to enter a bright dining hall. Sconces holding torches were anchored to the walls, and each one had a glass case around it with a tube that snaked into the ceiling. The air here was surprisingly sweet with only a tang of smoke.

Caleb scraped his head on the ceiling and ducked as if someone had thrown something at him. He grabbed his cap and swore under his breath. The dwarves walked forward under the low height, and Gnirun ambled to the nearest of many tables.

The wooden tables and benches were simply hammered together. When everyone sat down, Der blearily stared down at the nails. She blinked. Each nail displayed an individual stylization on its head. She nudged Kelin in the ribs and pointed. "Could you do that?"

He shook his head. "Wouldn't know where to start."

Their knees came up too high for comfort, but the table could certainly take the weight. Across from them, Caleb poked at something sticky, while Gnirun stomped off to a door on the other side of the dining hall and yelled into it. The other dwarves left.

Gnirun returned and stood at the head of the table. "Surgeon's comin'—as soon as someone finds 'im anyway." He sat down next to Caleb and nudged the slender man so hard with an elbow that Caleb wheezed.

The blond coughed as politely as he could. "Your generosity is overwhelming, master dwarf."

Gnirun shook his head. "'Course not! Humans is bein' too jumpy these days with the outlaw nonsense, an' hurtin' good folk." He stroked his beard. "You migh' not last inna cage right now."

Der stared at the dwarf, concentrating. Beside her, Kelin shifted his weight, and Caleb remained motionless.

Another dwarf staggered through the far door as if someone had pushed him. Unlike the others they had seen, this one was not bristling; instead, his long black hair and beard were braided neatly.

He barked something they couldn't understand, to which Gnirun held up his hands.

Der shrank away from the surgeon. "He looks angry."

Gnirun shook his head. "Just his little rule, no blood on the eatin' table."

"Good rule," Caleb murmured.

"It washes off with everythin' else," the dwarf countered.

Caleb pulled his hands into his lap. "How are you doing, Der?"

"I'm all right." She extended her arm to the neat dwarf. It didn't really hurt at the moment, yet it didn't really feel like her arm was there either.

The dwarf turned his face up at her. "Hurt, but no more bleed." Then he used what looked like a paintbrush to vigorously rub an orange, noisome paste over the wound.

The pain began as a sizzling, swelling sensation, and then it shot up her arm and echoed throughout her body. She had never been in so much agony before! She felt hot tears draining out of her eyes, and she banged on the table with her other arm.

"Let it out, girl, let it out," Gnirun whispered.

She roared out all the air in her lungs. She pushed her pain into anger and screamed.

Caleb clapped his hands over his ears. Kelin looked on, helpless.

Der's head sank to the tabletop, and she was panting and whimpering.

Gnirun nodded to the surgeon, who dropped a small glass vial on the table, picked up his bag, and departed. "See? Ain't so bad. That will form a barrier. Just don't peel it. It'll fall off when your skin's healed. Understand?"

She nodded.

Kelin patted her back. "You'll be fine."

"A glue?" Caleb asked.

The dwarf shook his head. "Don't know that word. Shell?"

Caleb frowned. "Not exactly. Adhesive."

"Sticky?"

"Yes, and it gets hard when it dries."

"This stuff then." He rolled the vial over toward her. "Mix a l'il with your drink until it's gone. Wards off infection. Won't dull the pain none though. And don't use it all at once."

She gripped the vial in her left hand. "Thank you."

Through the far door, a couple more dwarves entered, carrying several black cast iron pots between them. Without a word, they dropped them on the table lining a wall and stamped out.

"Go getcha some food." Gnirun pointed to the pots.

Kelin bowed his head. "Thank you. Hey, Der, I'll get yours."

She nodded.

He and Caleb approached the other table, which held a stack of hammered metal plates and a pile of two-pronged forks. Kelin filled two plates with steaming meat, and some green gooey substance. "I think this is the afterlife of mashed peas."

Caleb set his plate down on the dining table. "What kind of meat are we enjoying, master dwarf?"

Gnirun grinned. "Cooked."

"Ah." There was only a hint of a grimace.

Der groped the fork in her left hand and managed to slice into the meat sideways with it. "I'm hungry enough to eat a horse and cart."

"There may be a chance of that," Caleb murmured.

Kelin fumbled his fork. "What?"

The dwarf shrugged. "And how is horse different from cow? Or a badger or a mouse? It's all meat."

Der continued chewing. "He's got a point." She swallowed. She dug into the meal while Kelin tasted whatever the mushy green stuff was. Caleb just poked his plate with his fork.

Gnirun nodded. "Let's talk about th' fight. Now, my folks who seen th' ruckus say that the group 'proached. Why?"

Kelin shrugged. "I didn't even think about that."

Der scowled. "They murdered people in the count's castle. I'm sure of that."

The dwarf grunted. "We'll let th' lords here know." Then he shifted his eyes to Caleb.

Caleb placed his fork beside his plate and held his gaze.

Der drummed her left-hand fingers on the table. "But why would Sennha's followers risk all this?"

The dwarf shrugged.

"Are they after the outlaw too?" Kelin asked. "Could that figure in here somehow?"

Der wrinkled her nose. "But he's a villain too. Shouldn't they be helping him?"

"I highly doubt they's friends." Gnirun grunted a chuckle. "Perhaps they're seekin' his bounty as well. 'Tis an interestin' thought." He lifted his hand. "But eat now, and we'll show you from the city."

CHAPTER EIGHT

The breeze rustled the remaining leaves on the trees. They weren't on the road but were paralleling it from about twenty yards away, using the forest as cover. They had promised to keep their lips sealed about the dwarven passages under Duelingar, but Der assumed a few other humans must know too.

"I hope you're not planning on wearing that to meet the count," Caleb said.

Der looked up from picking at the dwarven glue-bandage. "What?" She stopped walking.

He hesitated. "Well, besides all the bloodstains, ah, they're a little ripped."

She started picking at her tunic instead. "But they're the only clothes I have." She leaned on the crude walking staff they had cut for her. Caleb wore her backpack, but she had refused to relinquish her sword, even to the point of using it on them if they tried to take it away from her again.

Kelin bunched his hands over some stains on his tunic. "We could probably buy some."

"No," Der grunted. "Our money needs to last."

"Der." Caleb frowned. "We need to make a good impression. It may be the only time in your life you do something like this."

"That may have been the only time we get meet dwarves too," Kelin chimed. "But that was amazing! And those tunnels!"

Caleb sighed. "It certainly came in handy for us. However, Der still can't wear that to meet the count. Trust me, please."

"Why not?" she demanded. "We can wash them first."

Caleb raised both eyebrows. "Put it like this, if you removed every stain, you'd be out of clothes."

Kelin blew out a sigh. "I've dealt with this before. Der, do you remember when you went to visit your brother? You hadn't washed your clothes after the pig fiasco, and the guard wouldn't let you in?"

"Pig fiasco?" Caleb echoed.

"My clothes were still decent, just a little dirty." She coughed and tried to recover her breath while leaning on the staff.

"Right," Kelin agreed after she finished wheezing. "And the same thing will happen here, only your brother will not be around to save you from being tossed into a cell."

Caleb looked quizzical. "What happened?"

Der shrugged. "I kicked the guard in the knee and went in anyway. What? It wasn't like I was invading the manor by myself."

Kelin cocked a half-grin and glanced at Caleb. "I've tried to explain this, honestly."

He nodded. "I think I understand. What happened with the pigs?"

Kelin chuckled. "The pigs had taken up position in—"

An arrow kicked up the dirt inches from his foot.

Der stared at it. They all did for an endless second. She swallowed and tried to force herself to believe that the arrow really was there.

Caleb shoved her. "Run!"

Five marauders leaped out from the foliage ahead of them.

Der stumbled forward, trying to draw her sword and sort out her feet. She felt the wind from another arrow tug at her hair. She gasped and her vision exploded in bright colors as she tried to yank out her sword. Her eyes drifted up in her head and she fainted.

"Der!" Kelin hollered. He gaped. The woman from the castle was rushing toward him, bow in hand, but he couldn't linger on her. All of them had swords, and their eyes burned with a deranged fire and determination.

Caleb ripped off the backpack and rolled it in front of her head as he slipped his sword free with his other hand. An arrow punctured the pack and stopped, missing her by inches. "Kelin, move!"

"But Der!" he yelled.

"Kelin!" He sidestepped to avoid staying in the same spot, and another arrow flew past him. "This is the only way! Now, *run!*" He charged the archer.

Caleb dodged the next arrow by moving just as the woman released her hand. She was fast, and was already nocking another shaft. He sprinted as hard as he could. He yelled and jumped just as she leveled the bow at his chest. Sunlight glistened on the arrowhead's barbed point as he raised his sword.

His blade struck home through the cheap leather armor. The bow sagged in her slackening hands.

For Kelin, the distance between him and the attackers seemed impossibly far. He was not certain he was going to make it, or even if he wanted to, but the image of Der passing out made him sprint faster. He brought up his sword in one hand and his hammer in the other.

Nearby, Caleb kicked to his side as a man tried to flank him. His foot landed squarely on his face, and he caught sight of a double-headed snake pendant wrapped around his arm.

The cultist swung his blade with all his weight behind it but only cut through air. Caleb had dropped to a knee and he thrust his sword into his attacker's gut.

Kelin had finally closed the distance. He bowled over the nearest cultist, cutting him open as the man reeled backward, the cultist's sword whistling through the air.

A few feet away, Caleb's blade fiercely clashed against the fourth attacker's blade. The cultist's sword flicked across his shoulder.

Caleb hissed but managed not to drop his sword's point. He retreated a few steps, and the man rushed forward into the opening space. Caleb parried a few times and then feinted high. The man tried to parry it and exposed his hip. Caleb didn't miss.

The last assailant rose up behind him. Kelin hurled his hammer. The handle bounced off the man's cheek, but it stunned him long enough for Caleb to thrust his sword home.

It was over in the same amount of time it had taken Kelin to close the distance. He leaned forward, trying to recover his breath. Then he stared at his new friend. Caleb had been so fast! Kelin thought he had missed half the fight when he'd blinked. "Where in the corners of hell did you learn to *do* that?"

Caleb sheathed his sword and pointed with his free hand. "Get Der!" He spun on a heel and dashed into the trees.

Kelin heard anxious whinnies and stamping hooves. Three saddled horses burst out of the forest.

Caleb emerged, leading two others, even as they fought against his pull.

"Are those their horses? Have to be, right?"

"Get Der!" He jammed his foot in a stirrup and swung up into the saddle.

Kelin hesitated, staring at the wild-eyed horse in front of him. It was so much bigger than the ponies he was used to. He passed the backpack up to Caleb. Then he turned to his horse, rolled Der up by the pommel, and pulled himself onto the saddle. It felt cramped and awkward. Caleb wheeled the horse toward the highway and kicked its flanks.

Kelin grappled with the reins as his own mount broke into a canter, its hooves pounding against the mud and grass as they flew down the road.

CHAPTER NINE

Der propped herself up against the wall, staring at the plate of food on the blanket in front of her and wondering when dinner had happened. She shifted against the stiffness of the bed's straw mattress. Twilight seeped through the window. She chewed on her lip. "I didn't faint. I tripped and hit my head on a rock or something."

Kelin looked up from his own plate of mutton, vegetables, and bread. "You have no idea how much blood you lost, do you?" He kicked off his boots and sat beside her. They'd found an inn at the crossroads. It had plain wooden walls and a candle sitting in the glassless windowsill. A heavy leather curtain hung over the opening. They'd paid for a private room, but it was cramped and contained only one bed.

She shrugged. "Not enough to keep me down." She tasted a bite of her mutton.

He frowned. "You can pretend you're invincible to yourself all you want, but don't you dare lie to me."

She half smiled.

"I'm serious, Der."

"You always are."

He dropped his eyes. "Caleb saved your life. He's incredible. I don't think I could have." He twisted his fingers together. "I'm sorry."

"Kelin, you would have."

"Thanks." But he shook his head.

"Where is Caleb anyway?"

Kelin glanced toward the door. "Out getting clothes; he said the innkeeper's daughter is a seamstress, and I desperately hope that she already has some made, or this could take a couple days."

She nodded.

He blew out a sigh. "I should have stayed home."

She chuckled. "I think you just want to go see Avice."

He sighed but a grin wound around his mouth. "Maybe. But I am thankful you haven't said anything."

She smirked. "No, although I was about to poke you in the back with a sword to make you do it yourself."

"You would have to." He stole a small piece of bread from her plate. "Did I ever tell you that Avice thought you and I should...? Well, you can guess."

Der blinked, tilted her head, and blinked again. "Oh. That's not something I'd expect her to say." She leaned away from him. "We grew up together—your mother watched me more than my own when we were little."

"I know, I know."

"And why would I *ever* get married? Especially with all the great adventures out here. What about you? What do you think?"

He pressed his fingertips together. "How do I put this politely? You're more of a drinking partner. And you know I want to settle down somewhere with my own forge, a small garden, and make a life for a family."

"You mean, like, children?" She gave him a look as if he had started speaking another language.

"Yes, Der." He dipped his head into his hands but smiled. "This is why I say you're more of a drinking partner, because after talking with you, I want a drink."

She frowned. "Speaking of..." She raised an empty mug. "Is there any more?"

"For you, there's water. And I checked, it's clean."

"Thanks."

A whispered knock rapped on the door before it swung inward. Kelin clicked his mouth closed. Caleb entered, holding a small pile of folded clothes. She caught his gaze. "Oh good, Der, you're awake. How are you feeling?"

"Tired and dizzy."

He set the clothes on the bed. "An honest answer."

She dug her shoulder blades into the wall in an effort to find a position where her head wasn't spinning. "Do you think they'll—anyone—will find us here?"

Caleb exhaled slowly. "I hope not."

"But they were waiting on the road..."

"Yeah, for anyone," Kelin said. "To rob them."

Der shook her head. "No, for *us.*"

Caleb pressed his lips together. "I saw Sennha's mark. Perhaps someone who saw us in Duelingar gathered together more cultists and waited for us, but it's also likely they were just waiting for anyone. They are bastards like that, but there are bigger bastards out there."

"Like the outlaw?" Der pushed herself up straighter. "That makes sense. Why would they bother hunting us when he's obviously such a heftier prize?"

Caleb lowered himself onto a corner of the bed and sagged. "Because they're after me."

She frowned. "But I thought they were hunting the outlaw."

He looked at her and raised an eyebrow.

Kelin glanced down. "Oh."

It took Der another moment. "Oh."

Kelin grunted. "So, Der, are you going to arrest him?"

She shook her head. "No-o. Not if those evil men are hunting him too." Her expression warmed and she looked at Caleb. "And you barely know us, so I have to honor this trust in us."

A brief struggle crossed his features, and his face fell. "You shouldn't die because of me." He paled as he spoke, and his hands fell limp against his thighs. "But you... I'm just surprised that strangers can be so kind. And I've rewarded it with injury and fleeing. What if our wounds become infected? There's nothing I can do. I don't know any songs of healing."

"Songs of what?" Kelin echoed.

But Caleb wasn't listening. "They lied." He drew his knees to his chest. "They sold such a convincing untruth to all the spies and nobles."

"You're saying the cultists lied and set up this bounty on you?" Der frowned in confusion.

He glared ahead. "No."

"Oh, you mean their god."

"What?" Caleb shook his head. "No, something a bit more tangible."

She squirmed—the voice had been tangible enough. She inhaled and straightened her shoulders, then she looked at Caleb. "What can we do to help you?"

Kelin gently shoved her shoulder. "What could we possibly do?"

She folded her arms. "I'm sure we can figure out something."

Caleb seemed to fight a small smile before it faded.

"Wait, wait." Der raised a hand. "Master Gnirun said this involved the elves. How does that fit?"

Caleb rose and straightened his tunic. Then he reached up and poked the cap. It slithered off his head, pulling his hair over his face as it slipped free. He pushed back his platinum locks to reveal his ears. They were the same size as a human's but came to a simple point.

The two villagers gawped at the elf, speechless.

He dropped his chin to his chest. "Yes, I'm the outlaw, but I've done no crime. I'm hiding...running...and I'm terrified." He sucked in a shaky breath.

"What happened?" Kelin whispered.

Caleb shook his head and stared at his hands. "I was so weary that I was becoming clumsy. We had fled our home, all the way out here. Nothing was safe. And, and...I lost sight of my little brother, and I fell. So far. I was already cold before I hit the water."

"I'm so sorry," Kelin whispered.

Der tapped her chin. "What are you running from if it's not the cult?"

He shook his head as he pressed the cap against his face. His knees quivered and he sank to the floor. "I'm not sure how I wake up each morning, or how I fall asleep at night." He gasped as if he were drowning, pulling the cap away. He stared at the hat in his hand like he'd never seen it before. "It can't be real. It's too foreign. I...I can't make myself understand."

Der eased closer to him. "Understand what, Caleb?"

He wiped his eyes against his sleeve. "I can't say it." He twisted toward them. "How do you live with death? How can you go on when your loved ones are forever gone? My parents..."

Kelin squirmed in his seat. "It takes a while..." He glanced to Der for support.

She pulled the handkerchief out from her belt purse and gazed at her sister's needlework. The flowers shone in the candlelight. What would she do if something happened to her family?

She pushed the thought away and passed the cloth over to Caleb. "Here."

Without a word, he took it into his hands and wiped his cheeks.

She said, "It helps to talk about the good things, what they did for you, and how your life is better from loving them. At least...that's what my dad said to me."

"Um." Kelin slid off the bed and sat on the floor next to Caleb. "You have to realize that life didn't end for the rest of the world, nor for you."

Caleb shook his head. "I *know* that, but I don't believe it."

"Because it's not something that comes immediately. My mother told me that their memories become alive in you, so they're not really gone."

Caleb huffed.

Der cleared her throat. "We know your parents were good people because you're a good person. You wouldn't have risked your life to help us against those cultists—twice—if you weren't."

Caleb shook his head as tears slipped from his eyes. "This is just making it real again." He hid his face behind the handkerchief. Then he seemed to sink in behind it as he stared down at the floor. He dropped the cloth. Der glanced to see what he was looking at. The boards were thick, scraped, and stained by many years of use, and he was studying every crack in them.

She licked her lips. "Uh, you'd said something about meeting someone at the count's...?"

He looked away, but his shoulders relaxed. "The master cook."

She cracked a grin. "We wouldn't mind seeing him too." She patted her stomach.

"Der, this is serious!" Kelin tossed whatever food was left on his plate at her lap. "He's the—"

Der wiped carrots off her trousers. "Don't yell it!"

Caleb replaced his cap on his head and pulled his hair over his ears. "Quiet, both of you." He scraped off the vegetables from the bed. "And, Kelin, throw the pillow next time, please."

Kelin narrowed his eyes at Der. "We are beyond pillows."

Der nodded. "Yeah, ever since that time I hid toads in his."

Caleb opened his mouth, "Wh—" But instead, he looked away with a hint of a smile. "If you two are friends, then I don't want to be your enemy. Now, let's try to sleep. You may use a carrot in place of a pillow if you wish."

He offered Der the embroidered cloth back. She shook her head. "Keep it."

CHAPTER TEN

Two days later, they stared up at towering walls, mouths open. Kings long dead had built Second Acron to parade what extravagance the kingdom of Thealith possessed, and it contained only a silhouette of the dwarven practicality in Duelingar. The stone walls reached higher, blocking much of the sun, but they were thinner. The buildings were also taller, and many were painted in bright, blinding colors. However, they were all shadowed by the great gray castle clinging to the highest point of the city like a dragon on its treasure.

Der had never seen a sight like it. She leaned on her walking staff as they trudged up the road. A few extra coins jingled in her belt purse. They'd sold the horses to a caravan when they'd first seen the city in the distance. The capital had only gotten bigger as they approached.

The guards waved them through the gate with hardly a second glance. Der picked at her new outfit instead of her bandage. "That was easy."

"Thankfully," Kelin muttered.

She went back to pulling at her tunic. These clothes fit much tighter and didn't have pockets, which she did not like at all. They were also much brighter than what the villagers were used to. Caleb had changed hats into a simple black one with a single feather.

She, Kelin, and Caleb skirted along the edges of the curving avenues. She fought to keep from staring. This city was far more expansive than Duelingar. Some of these buildings even had six stories!

They passed by a short, wide fountain at a crossroads. Several people were filling ceramic pots and wooden buckets.

Der slowed her pace to watch as long as she could—she'd never seen a reverse well before. She pointed. "Look, it spits the water up."

"Keep walking," Kelin ordered. "Heads down, remember?"

Caleb brushed his chin while staring ahead at the city. His skin was as smooth as ever without a hint of scruff. "I visited this city before."

Der raised her eyebrows and waited for him to continue.

"I wanted to practice the Common tongue."

"Well, you're obviously fluent," she remarked.

He offered a small smile. "I insisted when my parents didn't agree..." He closed his eyes. He stopped walking. "Thank you. I was alone and lost, and now, I'm only lost. So thank you."

Der smirked. "Welcome."

They kept climbing higher up the hill crowded with manors. She wheezed as she leaned into her staff.

"Hey, look!" She waved her unwounded arm at a stone mansion covered in creeping ivy. A large banner hung over its walls. "That's the falcon; we're here."

"Yeah..." Kelin shifted his weight from one foot to the other. "This is it. We're going to deliver the letter, and you're going to go wherever, Caleb. Hopefully somewhere you're not being hunted."

His shoulders slipped forward and he exhaled. "I won't forget your kindness."

"Yeah." Kelin kicked at a smooth cobblestone underneath his boot.

No one spoke, and the sounds of carriage wheels and clomping hooves filled the spaces between them.

Der rolled up her sleeves and started to march toward the mansion.

Caleb pulled her back by her shoulder. "Der. A moment."

She stopped and raised an eyebrow.

Kelin frowned at the manor. "It doesn't look crowded. Just a couple of guards and people."

The elf sighed and ran a hand over his face, staring hard at the mansion. "Remember the last time?"

"Trap?" Der asked.

Caleb nodded. "Those devil-worshipping bastards may have been spied on by those offering the reward. Or are working for them."

"And that is who?"

He frowned and shook his head.

"Oh. You think whoever else is out there told them to watch the count's." She nodded without looking at him for acknowledgement. "However, they can't pull that same ruse here, not with all these people, so instead, they've got people here already—" She cut herself off.

"You may not be wrong," Caleb muttered. He looked as if someone kicked him in the gut, and he withdrew farther into the shadows of the buildings.

Der snapped her fingers. He flinched. She offered, "Why don't we go and meet your contact for you? The cultists—or whoever—have a far less chance of recognizing us. And, just to be clear, you're not being hunted by Sennha, are you?"

Caleb shook his head. "No. I haven't angered any devils recently."

Kelin paled. "I don't like this, Der."

Caleb slouched against the wall. "I don't either. There's too much we don't know."

"We'll learn it as we go," she prompted.

He wrapped his hands around his waist. "I don't know. But, oh, you're right." He banged his head on the wall. "How could I have been so stupid? I should've thought of this!"

Kelin glanced down the street. "Can we find another inn? Or maybe rest at that waterwork we passed a few streets ago?"

Der grinned. "Yeah, we could tell your contact to meet you there. We'll all meet back there. This plan will work."

Caleb stared at her. "My fate is in your hands." He shivered and looked away. "The head cook is cloaked under a spell, so he will look human. Tell him that...tell him that—*damn.* I can't think of anything to say that isn't obvious. Wait!" He scrambled to unwind a necklace with a golden chain that had been tucked beneath his tunic. "Give him this. Tell him he dropped it or something. And...and...Der, give me your letter."

She freed the rolled-up letter from her backpack.

"Thank you." He ripped off a corner.

"Hey!"

"Not so loud!" Kelin hissed. He glimpsed around, but the rushing people on the street didn't deign to give them a single glance.

"I'm sorry, but I need parchment." He pulled out a tiny stylus from the folds of his belt purse. He penciled a quick sketch of the fountain on the scrap of paper and a few words in letters the humans didn't recognize. Then he rolled it up and stuck the paper through one of the necklace's chain links.

It swayed as he held it out to them. "Be careful."

Der didn't hide her smile as she snatched up the chain. "We will." She pulled the necklace into her belt purse.

Kelin scowled.

She turned to Caleb. "Thank you for your trust. We'll all meet back up at the waterwork." Then she tossed her walking staff away, and it clattered against the cobblestones as it landed. Kelin cursed and chased after her.

At the entrance, the guards waved them through without hassle. They ambled through a tunnel-like corridor, and emerged into a walled courtyard.

Count Calloway sat in a high-backed chair overlooking the yard below. He was a large, dark man, once a fighter who had lost a siege to years of fine food. He wore a saffron cloak and golden armbands.

Now Der understood why they hadn't been made to check their swords. Nothing but a bow could reach him.

They were in line behind a couple currently speaking with the count. She glanced over her shoulder and saw more people shuffle in after them. Sooner than she was ready for, the couple in front of them bowed and turned to walk back down the tunnel.

She stumbled a little as she bowed and then strained her neck to look up at the count. "My lord, uh, I'm delivering a letter from an old squire of yours, Riodan Saxen."

The man high on the tall chair stirred. "I haven't heard that name in quite a while. He moved out to the country, didn't he?"

She gulped, staring at him. "Yes, my lord, he's my father."

"Is that old blacksmith still with him?"

"Yes, my lord," Kelin answered through stiff lips.

The count chuckled. "So, girl, you're his daughter, eh? Why didn't you have yourself announced?"

Der flushed. She thrust up the letter in front of her. "I have—"

"Just because your father would rather be a farmer than a knight doesn't mean you aren't noble, girl," the count boomed.

She wrinkled her nose.

The count leaned forward. "Are you embarrassed, child?"

Der tried to keep her shoulders from creeping up toward her ears. She glanced at Kelin for support, but he leaned away from her.

The lord hummed tunelessly to himself. "Yes, yes, your mother was a maid here, and—" he interrupted himself with a laugh. "Oh yes, she wouldn't give young Riodan a breadcrumb no matter how hard he tried."

Der's forehead bunched together in thought. She'd known her parents had met in the count's service, but she'd never asked about it.

"Yes, until one night he was inebriated, incredibly, and was sauntering around naked as the day he was born. He went to the window where the maids slept and threw rocks through it. Then he sang the Song of Mendelin and Tara. Extremely off key, I may add. Woke up the entire castle."

Der's jaw dropped.

The count's smirk faded. "So, child, what news do you bring? Let's have this letter."

A small robed man, with ink splashed across his fingers, stepped forward. But Der was still staring up to the count. "Naked?"

She let the letter slip from her grasp and into the scribe's. In her heart, she knew this moment was important. She'd completed her quest. However, all she could think about were images she was trying to burn out of her imagination.

"Indeed." His tone changed, and his imperious voice drifted down. "What is this missive regarding?"

Der blinked, trying to say something other than 'naked' again.

"Security, my lord," Kelin cut in; his words only wavered a little. "Our lands are unprotected. There are no soldiers or men-at-arms to defend us if anything happens, and this outlaw has already brought chaos to our home."

The count nodded. "I am not surprised, although I believed our western settlements to be more at peace. Still, dark times are unfolding. We have border raids to the east with Urael and, of course, this outlaw. And now they say he's in the cult of Sennha. Damn scum."

Der coughed into her hand. "But what if he's an innocent man who has just been framed for whatever murders have happened?"

The count snorted. "You're young, child. An innocent man need not fear, but this outlaw obviously feels he has to hide. This is not the action of an innocent man."

Kelin bowed and trod on Der's foot just as she was inhaling for another sentence. He burst, "Your wisdom is, uh...sage, my lord. I wonder if we could, in your mercy, beg some food from your kitchens. We've come a long way to deliver this letter, and we're very hungry."

The count nodded once. "Very well. For the lady." His gaze lingered on Der, then he looked beyond them. "Bring in the next." A guard broke away from near the stairs to escort the villagers.

Der heard Kelin's sigh of relief as they ducked forward into the folds of the manor. The guard led them to a dark dining room without a word. When they asked for food from the nearest servant, he wordlessly handed them some leftover mutton and vanished back to his duties. The guard departed and left them alone at a large table.

Der whispered, "I—I'm too nervous to eat."

Kelin looked down at the soup, and she heard his stomach grumble, but he pushed the bowl away. "Me too."

She rose and headed toward the kitchen. He followed behind her. Der waved at the first person they saw and stepped in front of the man. She assumed he was some sort of under-cook because of his apron. She announced, "I need to speak with the head cook, please. Right now."

The cook eyed them with severe doubt but shrugged. "This way, but he won't be happy to see you. He's not been the most patient man as of late."

"Let me guess, since about the time the news of the outlaw started," Der gauged.

The cook fired a look at her. "Yeah, I guess. There he is." He pointed and strolled off.

The master cook was a short, round man whom Der would not have picked out to be any sort of spy, or even an elf. He was not attractive by human standards, and the stains across his apron made him appear a beggar. His scowl deepened when he saw them approaching. He crossed his arms, leaning a large, wooden spoon against his shoulder. "Who are you?" He started tapping a foot.

Der groped her belt purse. "Uh, I..."

Kelin hastened to say, "We wished to compliment you on the food; the leftovers we had were excellent. My mouth is still watering."

The cook sneered. "I have things to do." He spun on his heel.

Der let the gold necklace slip to the floor. "Wait! You dropped something." She lowered herself to a knee and scooped the necklace up, staring hard at the paper stuck into it.

The cook eyed her with unashamed suspicion but plucked the jewelry from her fingers. He cupped his hands as he read the note, and she heard him suck in his breath and hold it. His head snapped toward them.

Kelin clasped his arms against his chest. "Never thought a kitchen would be so cold."

Around them, Der felt cool, damp air flowing in. The lights were dimming, and the world was fast fading to shades of gray.

"Run!" The cook knocked over bowls from the counter as he whirled around. He was gone before the dishes hit the floor.

Der hauled on Kelin's arm. "Come on!" Tendrils of fog curled into the room. She charged through the expanding mist and yanked her sword halfway out of its sheath before it got stuck.

The last thing she saw was Kelin's terrified face before the world went black.

CHAPTER ELEVEN

Der awoke in blackness. She blinked to be certain that her eyes were open, but she remained blind. So much for her plan... She hoped the elven spy had gotten away, and that Caleb had been far from the manor.

Darkness curled around her skin. It was thick and heavy, and she couldn't shake it off.

Lengths of chains weighed down her wrists and neck as she stirred. She tasted copper in her mouth at the realization.

Her breathing amplified, matching pace with her furious heart. Pain needled its way down her injured arm as she squirmed. It was instantly forgotten as the chains tightened their coils like pythons, moving on their own.

In reflex, she jerked her hands up to her neck. The chains wound tighter, and she began to choke. She fought against the terror rising in her throat, but panic crashed over her like a tidal wave. She yanked against her restraints. She tugged, thrashed, and kicked. The chains kept constricting, kept squeezing their cold metal into her skin.

She heaved against the collar as it tightened more against her neck. She fought for a single breath and opened her mouth to yell with all the air she had left.

She cut off her scream, biting her tongue so sharply that it bled. Now she held onto the air she had and was too afraid to breathe. How tight could the chains cinch? Would they kill her?

Straining to control each muscle, she forced herself to stay still. Slowly, carefully, she inhaled a tiny bit.

Slowly, carefully, she let the breath back out. She made herself remain motionless when all she wanted to do was kick and scream.

As she tried to breathe, ever so slightly, despair sank through her fright, just as the coldness seeped through her skin. Who had chained her here? What did they want?

Silent tears treaded down her cheeks, but she didn't sob. She didn't dare.

***

Der didn't know how long she had waited in the darkness on the verge of choking when the door to the cell opened.

It shut immediately. She flinched and then scolded herself for doing so. She was tough in the face of danger and wasn't going to show any fear. She could stand pain—she'd worked on a farm for her whole life, after all. And she implored herself to believe that she wasn't lying right now.

She didn't attempt to crane her neck to look at whoever may have entered, if anyone even had. She'd heard no footsteps.

A masculine voice shattered the silence, "Answer my questions, and I will grant you a quick death." He must've touched the chains, because they rustled and the pressure around her throat eased.

She swallowed, afraid to speak, but the chains didn't move at her motion this time. She gulped for air. "Who—"

"Did the prince escape?"

She coughed. "What prince?"

There was no reply.

"Oh." She sagged. "He was a prince. An elven prince." She tried to picture it but didn't have the energy, and the gravity of Caleb's identity remained distant. She summoned her strength and sat up straight. "Well, unless you bastards—whoever you are—have him, then yes, he did. That was a stupid question."

There was the wind of an indrawn breath. "I do not think you understand what hell has swallowed you."

She spat a laugh. "I really don't! I don't even know who you are."

"Of course you don't. Now, I can save you from pain beyond your imagination, or you can continue with this stultifying bravado, and I will leave you to burn."

Finally, her mouth began to dry.

"What do you know about the elf you were traveling with?"

She parted her lips to say something about Caleb leaving them behind on the road, but she realized that she didn't know how to tell anything but the bedrock truth. In fact, she even hesitated when trying to compliment her brother's atrocious cooking, let alone attempt to deceive an enemy that had her chained to the floor.

She tried not to stir as she spoke. "Just that he was the outlaw, framed by whoever you are, and going to meet someone at the count's. I didn't even know that he was an elf for most of it, and I didn't know he was a prince at all."

"Is that everything?"

She sighed. "It is." She flinched as she imagined hearing the whispery rasp of steel sliding free of a scabbard, but there was no sound from across the room.

She slammed her eyes shut and squeezed them tightly, readying her good arm to swing the heavy weight of the chain. It might be the only chance she'd have.

She lifted the links, which still didn't move on their own, just as the door shoved inward. This time, it was left ajar and light filtered in. Two men whisked through the opening.

She squinted and could make out the slim shape of the voice's owner stand at attention next to the door. She studied the speaker, despite the dim light, but he appeared no different from the two that had just entered.

They were tall and lean, but they looked human. Or at least had the veneer of it. Their dark hair was styled in the same glued-to-their-heads appearance, and they moved in dark, flowing clothes that seemed too thin to withstand everyday use. She stared hard, trying to find a mark or defining trait on the speaker. He wore a sword while the other two did not.

Then she heard Kelin's screams through the open door. She froze, and trembled at the pain squeezed out of his wails. But she also felt her own blood steaming. She lifted her handful of chain, readying to throw or hit with it. She wanted to hurl it now, but she gritted her teeth; she needed the right moment.

The two newcomers turned to the speaker. There were some snapping words in a language she did not comprehend. The original speaker saluted, bowed, and exited the room.

She ignored him. Kelin was the only thing in her mind. The screaming cut off as the door to her cell slammed shut.

"He's alive!" she breathed.

A candle flared into life. "For perhaps the next hour." This man pushed his words through a much heavier accent than the other. She almost couldn't understand him.

She brought her chin up toward her captors.

The one holding the candle leaned over her. She blinked when she saw his eyes; she had never seen orange eyes before.

She wanted to recoil but forced herself to remain still. "What are you?"

A slow smile crept across his countenance. "We are chemmen, little mortal."

"But—but the chemmen don't exist." Fear singed her throat anew.

His grin became crooked as his face hovered over hers. "History has failed humans, I see."

Der heaved the chain up with all her strength, aiming for his nose. The man didn't have time to move. Inches away from his face, the chain wrenched her wrist back and against the wall.

The collar tightened again, and she wrenched for air she was no longer getting.

The chemmen didn't exist! Old campfire stories loomed up in her mind. But now those unimaginable horrors of ancient stories were all too easy to imagine. She saw blackness tickling the edges of her vision as she struggled to gasp.

A chuckle stung the air. The speaker snapped his fingers, and the collar unlocked itself and fell from her neck. She crashed forward to her knees and one hand while grabbing her throat with her other hand, hacking and panting.

Both of the chemmen stood back and waited. The one who had spoken snapped his fingers again, and the chains around her wrists pulled her upright against the wall.

The speaker floated in front of her. "Where is the prince?" he asked in a voice laced with honey.

Der tried to glare. "Told you. Don't know anything."

He swept closer, almost pressing his face into hers. "I'm certain you're aware of more than you believe. Tell us whatever you're thinking about the prince right now."

She swallowed and had never considered how such a small, usual thing could hurt so much. She narrowed her gaze at the speaker and realized she'd be damned if this slick bastard was going to best her so easily. She bit down on another cough. "Why? I'm going to get it anyway because I've never heard of a nice torturer."

His smile withered. He growled something to the other chemman in their language, and the second chemman stepped forward with a large metal tray that he set on the floor.

Der heard the thunder in her heart as she stared. There was a small razor, glass funnels, and a glass cylinder full of clear liquid on the tray. She didn't understand any of it.

The first chemman lifted the razor between his thumb and forefinger and regained his smile. "I believe fear drives people to say things before torment. Such as the fear of disfiguration, the loss of your fingers— one at a time—losing your nose, your ears, and so on.

However, I believe that people need to know the kiss of pain first to truly fear the worst."

He ripped off the dwarven bandage. Then he sliced the blade across her arms, collarbones, and through her clothing into her stomach, ribs, and legs. She barely recognized the touch of the metal itself, just pinches where it cut. He was quick and silent. She felt her own hot blood leaking across her skin; however, this wasn't hurting too badly, and that left her even more confused.

The chemmen lifted the glass funnels with their fingertips. The devices were needle thin on the narrow end. Der wasn't sure exactly what they were doing, but her mouth dried out all the same.

They inserted the thin ends of the funnels into the dozen or so small cuts and pressed them in deeply enough to stand on their own. Then they poured the liquid from the jar into her body, and whatever it was began to *burn*.

The chemman who had not spoken seized her chin and tipped up what was left in the jar into her mouth. She tried not to swallow, but he held her mouth closed until she did. Pain flamed up inside her chest.

She tried to will herself to vomit as she wrenched against the chains. She tried to yell but found she couldn't. Her body went into spasms. She knocked most of the glass tubes out of her skin in her thrashing.

The first chemman stepped back with enthusiasm etched across his face. "This is acid, girl. Do you know what acid is?"

She tried breaking free, but the chains kept her clutched against the wall. The burning roared louder throughout her body with every heartbeat, and she couldn't extinguish the flames.

He chuckled and continued in a singsong voice she could barely register through the inferno, "Acid melts things, even metal and stone, and you are experiencing what it can do to a mortal coil. This is too weak to kill you quickly. After all, I did say we'd start with smaller pains."

She coughed again and failed to see her blood splash across the floor as pain continued to rip through her body with fury. She felt nothing in her mouth anymore or where they had cut her. The acid had burned away sensation in those areas, but everywhere else more than made up for that.

The chemman drifted above her face. "Imagination failing? The acid is burning holes through your body. It's dissolving your bones and muscles. Now," his voice became coaxing, "I can stop this. Can you still hear me? I can make it all stop with one quick stroke of my knife. Pray tell me, where did the prince go?"

Der opened her mouth but could no longer say anything even if she wanted to. She flopped against the wall like a dying fish, but she made herself look him in the eyes and cough blood onto him.

CHAPTER TWELVE

"I did it again!" Caleb stumbled into a tree and smashed his fist into it. "I left them. I left people to die *again.*" Dried leaves tumbled onto his head from above. Around them, the forest remained quiet.

He saw it again. His parents remaining behind in the garden. Kelin and Der vanishing into the manor. Over and over.

"But, my prince," the elf from Count Calloway's service pleaded, "you survived."

Caleb rounded on him. "They were my friends, Soheir! They were my friends! I stood with them and I didn't run from Sennha's lot, but at the suspicion of chemmen, I crumbled." He pawed at his face. Part of him was trying to convince himself that he hadn't known them long enough for them to be trusted companions, but he'd been through more with them than had been than anyone else he could call friend.

The dark-haired Soheir faltered to a stop. He had dropped his mortal disguise and now he was tall and thin. "My prince, but—"

"But what? I betrayed them. I betrayed my friends! And...my parents." He fell to his knees. All of this was too much, too fast. Part of him continued to deny the reality of it and demanded he wake up. Yet, every morning he did rise, and everything still had happened.

And he had run away. Again.

The other elf bowed and continued to hold himself low as he spoke. "We feared terribly for you."

The prince doubled forward, nearly resting his forehead on the dirt. "Don't you know what will become of my friends? They could be in Darkreign!"

Soheir knelt beside him. "I regret what you have suffered, but we do not have the time to spare. Let them go. Release them from your mind. No one returns from Darkreign."

Caleb stared at the soil and leaves as his vision blurred. "Not even those who were banished there? Because history has lied to us." Tears bled from his eyes. "I left them behind—in the hands that murdered my parents. I'm wicked!"

"You are not," Soheir whispered.

Caleb slouched. "Yes, I am." He hammered a hand against the forest floor. "All I've done is left good people to die."

Soheir hesitated. "Like you, I am unaccustomed to understanding such desperation. I fear that we have long forgotten how to consider it." He gazed up at the overcast sky. "But may I say this? Make their deaths be not in vain. You must live for all of them. You will take on the mantle of king."

Caleb shook his head. "I don't want it. I was never meant to have it."

Soheir pulled the younger elf up by his shoulders. "You are what is left of the king and queen. Do something to bring them justice! What about those who still live? What about your brother?"

"Get away from me!" Caleb flinched away, staring wildly at everything except Soheir. He grabbed his head in both hands. People had died. There would be no justice for that.

Could he ever get used to this numbing sensation?

He looked to the trees of the surrounding forest and listened to their autumn leaves crackle as they moved on their branches. He shivered as a blast of air flowed past him. Winter was teasing, dragging its icy fingers through the wind. Only a touch on the breeze, just enough to know it was on its way.

He had always seen the world as falling asleep, resting for next year's bounties and blooms. But now, all he could see was the world growing colder and the life being choked out of it. He wasn't sure if spring would ever come.

He gulped. "What about my brother? Have you any word of him?"

Soheir shook his head. "Up, my prince. We must hurry. I have no illusion that they are far behind us."

King Dis stood over the chemmen soldier's corpse. He flicked the body's stub of a truncated wrist that had healed over years ago. No change, and now this warrior was dead.

Dis frowned. It still wasn't fair. This brave and faithful soldier had offered up his own body to be filled with the late elf king's blood to see if his hand would regrow like the elves could do naturally.

He'd died in agony. Dis lifted the shortened arm, and sighed loudly. Absolutely no change. What a waste of that smug king's corpse.

Scowling, he left the room and climbed the moldy stairs to his borrowed throne room. He swept past Vlade, slouched back in the obsidian throne, and then looked at the chemmen commander, who was standing over a large table laden with maps.

"You had him. You had the older prince!" Dis slapped his armrest. "And you give me two humans instead."

It wasn't *the* obsidian throne that rested in the heart of Darkreign, but a shrunken similarity he'd brought with him to this cramped, bog-smelling court of a long dead, minor king. Behind his throne was the obsidian mirror, and that was not a replica. The polished mirror over the black stone was one of the most important pieces of treasure the chemmen owned, and the king was never far from it.

Dis caught Vlade glowering at him in the mirror. The commander's dark hair outlined his sharp features, all of which brought forth his orange eyes. They could have been brothers, and in a way, the king muttered to himself, they were.

Vlade shrugged. "He is intelligent prey."

Dis pressed his shoulders against the obsidian throne's back. "And?"

The other chemman closed his eyes and exhaled. "We almost had him twice, but the cultists failed in Duelingar, and those humans interfered with our trap in Second Acron."

"He is intelligent then, to throw the humans at us as his shield." The king clicked his fingernails on the armrest.

Vlade glanced down to find that he too had been drumming his fingers against the table. He scowled. The chemman pulled his hand away.

Dis frowned. "Then you've learned nothing."

The commander's reply was as sharp as a knife's edge, "There was nothing to learn."

The king ground his teeth. "So, we have two humans who don't know anything, and the princes have escaped your grasp yet again. You, the elite, you, our hero who has planned this assault ever since our banishment, lost two boys. Your discipline is fading."

Vlade sighed. "We have lost nothing, since we never had them in our possession."

"You should have gotten them *all* the first time!"

Vlade snapped, "The harder the fight, the better the victory."

Dis snarled. "A sentiment shared by those who enjoy the hunt, not the meal. I prefer to know where and when the next meal is. When will you have the crown prince?"

Vlade brushed some dust that drifted down from the ceiling off his sleeve. "I wasn't aware that you were planning to consume him."

"You know what I meant." Dis rolled his eyes. The commander's insouciance was especially irksome at the moment. They'd had their total victory snatched away from them, and he didn't seem to care. The king dug for something to repay his annoyance. "Hero. That makes you a dangerous thing, Vlade, because you are too different from us."

The commander raised an eyebrow. "As king, you are different too. As his majesty is aware."

"Not like you." Dis settled back into the throne. "You and I should never disagree. The chemmen have only one voice."

"Yours, naturally," Vlade drawled.

"No, we are one voice. Except for maybe you."

"And yet, you are king. Your words are our words."

Dis glowered. "You spent too much time chasing other races, Vlade; you've picked up disobedience from them."

Vlade gave him the dry look of a man who knows exactly from whom the army takes its commands. "I do not suffer disobedience."

"No, I just suffer you." Dis smiled coldly. "Because you are our hero."

The other chemman basked in his smirk. "And what else? You know."

The king's expression dropped to a scowl. "There is nothing else. We do not keep secrets."

Vlade took a single step forward, watching the king's eyes. "Because I get your will done. I may not always follow your orders, but only because you don't know how to accomplish your dreams. I do."

Dis curled his fingers around the edges of his throne with white knuckles. He turned away but ended up staring at the commander in the mirror. "This is what you wanted too."

"How could you know? You've never asked me what I want."

"The sword, Vlade, I know." Dis relaxed. "Our plans were sailing so well too. We did it. We slew the hateful king and queen." A wistful, playful smile appeared. "And, after what those two did to us... Yes, now we need to kill their offspring and the elven witch."

Vlade shook his head. "We need not hurry. The elves are suffering in disarray and despair. I never imagined that they could crumble and flee their kingdom so easily."

"Good." Dis rolled his orange eyes. "But it made our task that much harder."

The commander barked a laugh. "And such a glorious sin it was for them, abandoning their homes. But now they finally fear us like they should."

The king waved his hand dismissively. "Yes, I agree, of course. But we need the princes, Vlade; that was our plan. We can't kill their hope in front of all of them if it's not in our hands." He smirked. "As we used to say, to win the war today, kill tomorrow."

Vlade rolled his hand over the maps. "Yes, yes, that used to mean destroy the crops, water, livestock, and the children. Used to, Dis, used to."

"It still does." His smile spread. "Hope, Vlade, because tomorrow is always about hope. I will not leave them a tomorrow."

"But you will leave me to accomplish that. As always." Vlade sighed. "I have duties to attend to, my king." He turned and started to walk, but then glanced behind his shoulder. "One odd thing, why did you find it necessary to post a guard in the girl's cell? Did you think she was capable of suicide?"

Dis frowned. "What do you mean?"

"The torturer told me that the guard said your orders had been to make certain she didn't kill herself."

"But," the king licked his lips, "they used the chains. The magic doesn't allow them to do that. It only brings them to the edge of death. We can't question dead men."

"Those weren't your orders?" Vlade raised his eyebrows.

"No. Yours?"

The commander shook his head. "But I suppose it makes a sort of sense, with her surprising ancestry." He clicked his heel against the stone floor. "Perhaps the guard misunderstood an order."

Dis shook his head. "Yes, probably. Odd, though."

CHAPTER THIRTEEN

Kelin waited in the damp darkness for Der to rescue him. She had always sprung him from trouble before. Admittedly, it was usually her fault they were in said situations, but she had always been there for him, and he'd always followed her. He refused to see any difference now. She'd come.

After all, she'd saved his life before.

The smithy had caught fire. It was an ever-present danger in a structure with wooden walls and a thatched roof. He'd been trapped between a burning wall and the forge, which was roaring like a beast of legend. He could still hear it now. Molten metal was splattering everywhere, spraying silvery drops that started more fires where they impacted.

He'd spun around again and again, but he could not find a way through the burning timber. Sweating tears, he remembered coughing and folding forward on the ground. His skin had felt so hot.

Der had defied the flames. There had been no path through the fire, but she made one by bashing apart the flaming wreckage with a small log.

Then she had stood over him, reached down, and yanked him to his feet. The air had stung because it had felt so cold when she pulled him outside.

In that icy air, there had been the concerned faces of Avice, Donley, Sigard, and his parents. He'd been all right. They'd rebuilt. He'd been all right.

But maybe this was too much for her, he thought, and the tendrils of doubt curled tighter. He struggled for a damp breath as he tried to make out the walls that seemed to be closing in on him.

He fought against oncoming tears. It wasn't only because of the pain or the humiliation, but because he missed home. He yearned to smell the scents from the forge again, to hear his brothers' and sisters' laughter, to see Avice's face. He wanted to go back there, shut the door, and never come out.

In a few years, he'd be the town blacksmith. Sigard would join the other old men sipping beer and telling each other heartfelt lies. He'd build a new home behind the forge that didn't flood every other year like his father's mill. That way, he wouldn't raise his own children with their ankles often wet.

He released the tension in his muscles. He would never see that. He knew it as much as he knew his blood was red. After all, they'd shown him quite a bit of it.

He was going to die here. A comforting notion, he mused, as he let himself slip a little closer into darkness. It would be such a relief.

No, Der was going to come, so he'd better be here.

He wanted to be furious with her. In fact, he begged himself to give into that rage. And he refused. If he were angry with her, she might not rescue him.

He wound himself into a tighter ball on the stone floor. His eyes rolled back in his head. *Here we go,* he thought, *it's happening again...*

He knew it was useless as they dragged him from his cell and into another chamber. He was a large man, and yet, these two stick-thin guards had carried him without apparent effort.

The third man, already waiting inside, turned around and smiled. "You were almost able to make history."

Kelin licked his lips. "What?" It was nearly impossible to understand the speaker through his accent.

"You almost got to be the one to tell the world that we chemmen still exist."

"What?" He stared ahead. The storm-readers? They were from the stories about the Centum Wars, but that's all they were, stories.

He dropped his gaze. He was too exhausted to try denying it.

The chemman's smile broadened. "Of course, everyone will know soon. Let's begin, shall we? Tell me about the prince."

"Prince?"

He moved so quickly that Kelin barely had time to tense. The chemman plunged a thin knife right through his chest and retracted it in one smooth motion. Kelin gasped. He gasped again, but suddenly he couldn't get enough air.

"Mortals need both lungs, don't they? Well, from now on, you'll have to live with one."

Pain took over from there. While he was still reeling, they forced his mouth open and ground in it with a large file. His flesh and teeth broke away in blossoms of agony, and his hindered lung exploded in anguish when he couldn't gasp any longer.

In moments, his teeth were just pieces that wouldn't fit back together.

It wasn't anything like a dream. He knew every second intimately.

The chemmen dropped heated gravel onto his chest. It felt cold then hot, searing, and even liquid fire. Smoke wafted up from the burns, and he smelled his own flesh cooking. And he could not draw one full inhale.

The pain was unending. And through it all, he couldn't breathe. That's what broke him. He doubted he could withstand the other torments, but every time he tried to inhale, it felt like hammers inside his chest. Weeping, he gave in and told them what little he knew, even details he didn't think he would have remembered. He spat and blubbered it through the tooth shards and bloody gums. He told them everything, and still they tortured him.

***

Der knew she was dying. A person wasn't meant to survive that. She flicked at the gray lumps of flesh falling off her body as she fumbled for control of the swollen sticks that were her fingers. They hadn't bothered to chain her again, and had left a candle burning.

She exhaled and lay back on the stone floor, drifting in and out of consciousness and pain. She'd never imagined that it would end like this. Part of her refused to believe it. Then the agony cut in and made this fate all too real.

She was ashamed of herself and couldn't explain why. But that humiliating rage burned underneath her skin just as much as the acid.

She would have to be greater than this, she told herself, and smarter too. She had known it was a trap—that's why she went in Caleb's stead. Next time, she vowed, she wouldn't be caught.

At least he had the wisdom to be silent about himself. She clawed at that logic, because it was practical and had probably saved his life, but she found herself resenting him.

Der pushed herself up to sitting and swayed, watching the colors dance across her vision. She wasn't going to die like this.

She yanked herself to her feet and growled against the pain as she stumbled forward and collapsed

123

against the door. She flailed against the wood to keep herself from sliding down to the floor.

After scrabbling for an endless moment, she gained her balance. She heaved a shoulder against the wood and tried to find the door's handle. She watched the lump of her hand bang against the latch. At least there was one, she thought, so this space was probably not originally a cell. But the notion passed. She couldn't control her fingers and just bashed them against the cold metal, splitting fresh cuts open across her skin.

It wouldn't turn. No matter how long she thrashed, she could not manage the latch. And she had no idea if it was even locked. Grunting, she leaned back against the door and wheezed.

She pushed herself away and glared through the haze that permeated her vision. She wobbled as she tried to maintain her balance. In her experience, she hadn't encountered too many problems that couldn't be solved with a meaningful, well-placed kick.

But she wasn't sure if she could even feel her feet. She braced herself to line the kick up nonetheless.

It wasn't fair. She sagged and lowered her foot. It was hard to remember all her heroic dreams now. She had been robbed—because *those* were meant to have happened, not this!

She stumbled forward. Anything but this. She swallowed and felt a weight sink all the way through her stomach.

Tears stung her eyes as she tried to picture how it should have been, but the agony of the acid anchored her inside the cell.

She hadn't deserved this. And neither had Kelin! He ought to be safe in Riversbridge.

She sensed heat flowing to her face and began growling beneath her whimpers. She wanted to lash out against Caleb, the chemmen, and fate itself.

Wheezing, she raised her foot when the door swung open on its own to reveal a chemman. She kicked at him just as he gasped.

He reeled back toward a second storm-reader who was carrying another tray. Der hissed as she saw the clear liquid sloshing in its jar.

She jumped and swept the jar off the tray with the flat of her hand. It smashed against the head of the first chemman.

The glass shattered and the acid splashed over his face. He screamed. It began as a roar, but as soon as the acid flowed into his mouth, the scream became a squeal, and then a low, horrified moan.

She kept kicking as he went down, clawing at his cheeks.

The second chemman shoved her. She swung her foot at him and missed. Then she rebounded off the wall and tried to press against it for balance, but her hands were sluggish to respond.

The first chemman twisted upright and ran off down the hall, stumbling with every step.

The second storm-reader kicked her legs out from under her. He rolled her on her back and pounded his fist against her ear. She yelped and batted at him with her arms, but she couldn't shake him off.

The chemman leaned over her face. "You—"

She heaved upward and bit his throat.

She lanced through his windpipe. She chewed and tugged until she felt her teeth grinding against each other.

The chemman tried to gasp but had nothing left with which to inhale. He stuck his fingers deep into his opened throat to stem the flow of blood.

He spasmed and rolled off her, and within a few frantic seconds, he was dead on the floor.

Der stared at the ceiling and heard herself gasping and hacking. She attempted to stand but collapsed again.

The heat of rage melted and she was left drained. Still coughing, she curled up. What now? How could she even find Kelin?

She lugged herself up onto her elbows. Then she pulled herself to her feet by crawling up the wall. After that, she lurched toward the door leading out of her cell and would have screamed if she had enough energy left.

A third chemman rested against the doorframe. She hadn't heard him approach. Unlike the other two, he carried a sword at his side in a plain sheath. His orange eyes were wider than she'd expected, and she realized that he was staring at her. And not just staring, but watching her with the disbelieving surprise of seeing a fish walking on land.

She crouched for a lunge, but the chemman raised a hand.

Der leaned her weight against the wall. She coughed out blood, and she wasn't sure whose it was. She tried to recreate that red rage, but she felt her anger sliding out of her grasp, leaving her hollow and dizzy.

The chemman cocked his head. "What was your next move?" His Common was remarkably unaccented compared to her torturers. He pointed at the corpse.

"Rescue my friend," she growled.

He snorted and folded his arms in a single, swift motion.

She slipped against the wall and sank almost a foot. She fought to form the words, "Well. If you're no' goin' to kill me, I'll be on my way." Her tongue felt like a dead weight, and she heard how slurred she was.

The storm-reader arched an eyebrow.

She shoved herself at him with all the momentum she could summon.

He moved to the side of the doorway and she stumbled past him. "I do not think you understand what hell has swallowed you."

She staggered to a halt. She wasn't entirely sure about *when* things had happened, but she'd been very certain about the events and what had been said. "That was you?"

He nodded. Then he grabbed her ear and pulled. Outside in the corridor, the air didn't stink as much, mostly smoke from the torches lining it. Then again, everything smelled acrid after her torture.

She hammered her hands against his arm to no avail. She dragged her feet in vain. She coughed and her tongue limped against the side of her mouth as she managed, "Who are you?"

He didn't answer.

She batted at his hold on her ear again and forced out, "I'm...dying 'cause of you!"

He stopped. "Not because of me." His orange eyes turned on her with an intelligence she recognized as outmatching her own.

She ground her teeth. "You *knew*. And you didn't do anything!"

The chemman shrugged. "Your life is not as important as the information you may have had."

She opened her mouth, but he moved faster than her words and slipped two fingers into her throat. She gagged and tumbled back, but he tugged her upright.

"Now, if you speak another word, I will leave you to die."

She glared and inhaled sharply, and then Kelin's face fizzled in her mind. She glared harder but nodded.

"Be mindful of how little time you have." He led her down the hall while she tripped and stumbled to keep up. She stared hard at his back, wondering if this play was some method of getting even more information from her. Then again, she hadn't withheld anything.

Shortly, he spun her around by her ear and she found herself facing an unremarkable wooden door. The chemman opened it.

He pushed her through. Der lurched to remain upright but tripped over something heavy and heaving. She crumpled over it and split her chin on the stone floor. Then she realized that the lump she'd fallen over was wheezing.

And not very well, it dawned on her. Kelin's breaths were shallow and whimpering. What did they do to him? In the meager light from the hall, she couldn't see much external damage. As best as she could without the full use of her fingers, she pushed the dark, curly hair from her friend's face.

He shuddered and squeezed in a tighter ball. She leaned against him. "No, no, no, it's me, it's Der." Her voice sounded as if it were being strangled before she spoke. Forming every word hurt, but that chord of pain went unnoticed in the symphony of agony.

He mumbled something and tried to avert his gaze.

She looked up at the chemman in the door, who had his eyes trained down the hallway. "Kelin, get up."

He didn't respond.

"Kelin..." She pushed herself back. "Kelin, listen to me."

When he failed to answer this time, she slapped him. "Kelin Miller! Get on your feet! If I can be walking, so can you, now *get up!*"

His eyelids fluttered. "...aer...?"

His speech was so mangled that she didn't recognize the sound. She guessed it was her name. "Yeah, it's me."

"Come." The storm-reader beckoned but continued to watch the corridor.

Der tried to lift Kelin up but could not even get her fingers to grasp anything. "Please. We have to go."

"Now," said the chemman.

"A moment!"

"No."

Kelin muttered something incoherent. His breath was just a shallow wheeze.

Der looked up. "I can't carry him."

The chemman shrugged. "Leave him."

"No!"

"Then I'm leaving you." He turned away.

"Why did you even help me in the first place?" Her head was spinning so much she thought she would fall over if she weren't already on the floor. She paused for a large breath and forced herself to concentrate. "You're a traitor."

His expression remained calm. "There are no chemmen traitors. So they say. To you, I'm the hero."

"You're not a hero," she snarled, surprised at the venom in her own voice. She'd convinced herself of heroes, and they were nothing like this stranger.

"Only if we flee. Otherwise, I may have to kill you and say I stumbled across your escape." The chemman stepped inside and hauled Kelin off the floor. The motion was too simple, as Kelin was much heavier than the storm-reader. Der began to wonder what other differences the chemmen had from humanity than eye color. He shoved Kelin into her arms.

The chemman stalked down the corridor ahead of them. But Kelin weighed Der down, and she only made it a few steps before they both fell.

Kelin wheezed, "'On't make it." He gasped for air.

She tugged on his shoulder. "Better to die trying." She managed to lift him up with his help. She pressed her back against the wall.

He sagged and was slipping down against her weak grasp.

She looked at him, noticing he still had some color left on his face. "I'll get you out."

He shook his head. Der, staring at him, could not read if he understood or not. Then he dropped most of his weight on her and she, trembling all over, lost her fragile grip. He fell again.

She crawled over to him, watching the sweat drip off her nose. "Up. Get up." She tried to lift his shoulder. "Help…" she trailed off when she looked up and saw she was speaking to nothing but the air.

They were alone. Then again, this had been farther than she'd secretly expected to get. She glanced around but had no idea which way to go. She felt the pain closing in as she pulled herself back up.

Distantly, but not as far away as she first thought, she heard a cacophony of shrill whinnies. Horses? Here?

The chemman rounded the corner into the hall, his heels clicking against the floor. Der glared at him. "Help him up."

But the storm-reader just stared.

"I can't carry him, please!"

The chemman's orange eyes were the widest she'd ever seen.

Bile stung her throat.

The storm-reader went for a knife on his belt, and she saw he didn't carry a sword at all.

She tried to pull Kelin back down the hall away from the chemman, but his weight was already making her knees tremble. She told herself that their new ally would get them out. She watched the chemman's knife reflect in the torchlight as he pulled it free.

She held her breath and waited for him to collapse with a sword in his back. She'd never believed in stabbing in the back, but with Kelin's and her lives in immediate jeopardy, she could find nothing wrong with it. Any second now.

But the chemman didn't fall.

She eased herself in front of Kelin and crouched. The storm-reader took a swipe at her head, but she fell to the floor where she grabbed the chemman's calves and lunged with her shoulders.

The storm-reader went down and crushed Der underneath his weight.

The chemman hopped back to his feet like a cat. She went for his knees this time. He stepped out of her reach and caught her with a small cut on the back of her head. However, he had retreated near to Kelin, who kicked out with a gasp of pain.

The chemman turned to slash at Kelin, and Der jumped. With just her palms, she tried to wrestle for control of the knife. She saw the blade cut into her hands several times, but she couldn't get her fingers to work enough to capture a grip.

So she kicked. The chemman stumbled back and she shoved him even farther in the same direction. He bounced off the far wall.

She tensed, waiting for him to spin around. Instead, he slumped forward, his own knife protruding from his chest.

She didn't immediately fathom what had happened. She let herself slip to the floor, breathing out as she sank.

"You aren't useless," an imperious voice drifted down.

Der hissed as she raised her head enough to see the chemman with the sword. Her lips framed a question.

"Any deaths must be on your hands. They will investigate." He leaned down and hauled Kelin to his feet. Without another word, he dragged the blacksmith down the corridor, leaving Der to limp and stumble on her own.

Soon, they left the torch-lit corridors and tiptoed into murky, darker paths. There was only enough light to reveal more darkness ahead. She tried to let her fingers glide along the rough stone walls, but she couldn't feel through her swollen digits. The walls looked more like those of a cave than a dungeon.

Kelin muttered something, but she didn't make out the sounds. She dipped her head close to his chest, listening to him struggle for even the shallowest of breaths.

The chemman stopped. He gestured ahead with his hand and then turned.

She furrowed her brow in suspicion but managed, "Thank you."

He nodded. The darkness closed its cloak around him as he walked away.

Der leaned against the wall, too tired to move. Kelin rolled on his back. She sighed, "Can't stay here." But she felt her bones sagging and the physical weight of pain pinning her to the floor.

Kelin grunted. "Up!"

"Wha—?"

"Look." He coughed. "Up."

Above, a thick puncture in the rock let in moonlight. But it was over their heads.

"Help me." She pushed herself up on the wall.

He shook his head.

She scrabbled for purchase on the rock. With a small jump, she wedged her hands against the stone. She had practiced pull-ups in the barn all the time, but then, she had the full use of her hands. She never had to lift her weight using mostly her wrists before.

She struggled and kicked before she was rewarded. The sweet tasting breeze brushed her cheeks. The moonlight was blinding.

She kept pulling and wriggling until she was free of the crack. Damp grass rubbed her ankles and legs, and it was softer than any blanket.

She twisted and thrust down her arm. "Kelin, please." The moon caught the remnants of the dwarven bandage—she had completely forgotten about that injury.

He thumped his head against the wall and fought to form the words, "'On't fit."

"Then you're going to lose weight really fast."

Reluctantly, he rolled forward, pulled himself up, and grabbed her hand. She heaved and gritted her teeth. She didn't let go, and by now, the pain in her muscles was so great they were almost numb.

Der watched his chest shudder with every hacking breath. His feet were off the floor, dangling. He couldn't fit. Panicking, he started kicking.

"Exhale, Kelin, exhale!" she hissed, straining against her agony and his weight.

His mouth opened and closed soundlessly.

Since she couldn't hold onto Kelin's arms well, she made certain he grabbed her around her neck. Then she pushed and pulled so hard she thought she heard one of her knees crack.

She wrenched him free.

They collapsed onto the cold ground. Der twisted to see the hell they'd escaped. Across a stone-filled creek, it was just an unremarkable abandoned castle, half-rotted away.

"Made it..." Then there was darkness in her vision. It wasn't a tunnel, it was a wall, and she hit it.

CHAPTER FOURTEEN

Der awoke to a campfire brightening the inside of her eyelids. She smelled its smoke as she listened the pops and crackles.

But she felt its soothing warmth as she forced her eyes to open and the fire blurred in her vision. She couldn't decide if it was because of the motion of the flames or because her eyes weren't working.

She also wasn't aware how long she'd been here—wherever here was—but she knew she was hungry. Funny that, she mused, because she could not remember when she'd last eaten. A day? Two? A week? Well, probably not that long.

A shadow eclipsed the firelight, and a small face hovered over hers like a full moon. Der flinched when she saw orange eyes.

She stared. He was just a child—he couldn't be more than six years old! Light brown hair topped his head instead of the black hair she'd come to expect.

When he saw that she had focused on him, he grinned at her.

She flinched again. The child stuck both his arms out as far as he could reach and waved his hands so rapidly that she felt a small breeze. She noticed two long knives hanging off his belt, bouncing to the rhythm of his hands. They were too big for the boy and came to rest below his knees. *I'm dreaming,* she concluded.

"Hey, lady, get up! You'll be a lot better once you have some of Mama's cooking. It's the best in the whole world!" He never stopped waving.

Der opened her mouth but couldn't even make strangled sounds anymore. She couldn't imagine how she had been able to speak during the escape. Maybe that had been the dream instead.

"Hush, little one," ordered a breathy voice. A slender woman pulled the boy aside by his shoulder. She sat down beside Der. Her red hair was so long it flowed down her back and onto the grass. "Can you understand me?"

She brushed some hair from Der's forehead as the young woman nodded. "Good. We are not safe here, so we'll have to move soon. I can heal your friend with song, although he will be without most of his teeth."

Der closed her eyes and let her head sink into the grass. The pain resurged, burning her body from the inside. She heard the woman rise and leave. She'd never believed in the chemmen, never really considered that they'd existed. And now she was dying because of them. But at least Kelin would live.

***

The rustles of dried, fallen leaves in the wind echoed in her ears the next time Der awoke.

She'd lost her father's sword. Tears escaped as soon as the thought arrived. He'd given it to her, and she hadn't even been able to use it against this foe. It was just gone.

She wished the soil would rise up and envelope her, but surprisingly, she felt strong enough to push herself up onto her forearms.

She stared at the campfire. It could have been the same one as before, but she wasn't sure. At least it was more in focus than...yesterday? Last night? Had she slept all day, or was this the same night?

She didn't see Kelin or the boy, but then again, she may have dreamed him or just imagined his eyes. The long-haired woman knelt next to the fire, stirring a small pot. It was engraved silver. Der thought it should be hanging on a wall in a castle somewhere instead of turning black in a wilderness campfire.

After the distraction of the pot had faded, she saw that the woman's ears also curved up to tips. So, another elf.

The boy tiptoed up from behind her, but the elf spun just before he pounced. Der watched her wrap her arms around the child and kiss the top of his head.

Then she felt her eyes surrender to the weight of their lids and they closed.

***

"Got you!" Someone grabbed the back of her neck. Every muscle in her body tensed so tightly that Der thought they would explode. Wheezing erupted from her torn throat. The boy hopped in front of her, grinning.

The woman rattled something off in another language and the boy's shoulders dropped. He stepped toward the elf, but she pointed back at Der. Scowling at the ground, he recited, "I'm sorry."

Der opened her mouth to speak, but only incomprehensible sounds hissed out. She settled for nodding.

He tapped his chest. "I'm Thalon."

"Yes, you are." The elf glided over to them. "And now it's your turn to tend the pot." She pushed him along.

Der swallowed and focused. "Thought," she rasped, "thought not safe...here."

"Of course it isn't. But it is more dangerous to move than to remain."

She scowled and bullied her slipping strength. "Who...are you?"

The red-haired elf's face softened. All the elven features that Caleb had striven to blur, this woman wore as a badge. Der could not imagine her ever being mistaken for a human like he had been.

She patted Der's arm. "All in good time. The forest is hiding us tonight. The chemmen are near. Therefore, no matter what, do not leave the reach of the firelight."

Der nodded. "Why do I feel better?"

The woman glanced at the ground. "I did the best I could, but your injuries are too severe for my songs of healing."

She gulped. Wasn't that what life was anyway? Always staving off death until you couldn't.

"You would have passed away in great pain otherwise."

Der snorted and flinched as she mused that at least she wouldn't be in pain right now.

"Child, you need to show bravery for your friend." She sat back on her heels. "You may call me Laurel. You've met my son, Thalon."

Der glanced over at the boy, and this time she noticed that while his ears were still rounded, they arched upward into almost tips. An idea crystallized in her mind.

"And you've met my husband, although he will remain without name to you." She held a hand open toward the fire. "We have prepared soup for our meal, and you will have some whether you can stomach it or not. Your friend needs to see you eat."

Der tried to pull herself upright, but her muscles barely responded. It felt as though she hadn't used them in months. Every movement had to be wrenched from deep within and individually forced. The distance of a couple feet was a ten-mile run through sand.

Kelin was sitting in front of the flames; he was pale and pinched but breathing steadily. He wore a dark cloak on his shoulders, and she knew he hadn't escaped with it.

She tried to sit upright, but she leaned toward the elf as she stared. The elves and the chemmen were enemies, and she'd had a child with one! Her trust of this elven savior had bottomed out. She turned and heaved herself closer to Kelin.

He looked at her from underneath his heavy curls and began to cry. She sat there too stunned to even reach out to him.

She stuttered, "W—we...we made it. You'll be all right."

His voice sounded thick and slurred through his sobs, as if his tongue weren't working properly, "We—didn't—know anything. We're not a part of this!"

She sat there, helpless.

He grabbed his torn tunic. "My chest hurts. They stabbed me and—and I couldn't breathe, so I panicked, and—and—and I still couldn't breathe." His tears drowned out his voice.

Der put a hand on his shoulder and flexed a finger. It seemed to be working. "You're breathing now."

"They took my teeth, Der, my teeth!"

She nodded. "I know."

He turned to face her. His eyes were wide and unfocused. "I—I don't know if I want to thank you for saving us."

She frowned as she focused on untangling his broken words; she had to guess at a few. She wanted to hide from his gaze but made herself meet it. "You still got all of your fingers and toes—and your life. A few days of rest, a good surgeon, and you'll be better."

"Do I want to be? Am I going to be able to eat anything other than soup?"

She stared down at her own hands and wondered how by Amiery's Wandering Staff, Ahtome's Seed, or anything holy, they were still alive. Of course, it wasn't to last, not for her. She didn't know what to say.

Laurel came to the rescue with a bowl. The soup wafted of tomatoes. The dish was engraved silver like the pot, and so was the spoon leaning over the rim. Der stared at the porringer, but maybe elves always dined with such finery. It fit with the stories she'd heard growing up.

Kelin accepted a bowl too. Der saw him relax his shoulders a smidgeon as he tried a sip. Then he winced as his cheek bulged, and he hissed in pain.

"Teeth?"

"Yeah, but..." He tipped the bowl up against his lips.

Der pushed the spoon around the side of hers. The scent made her stomach growl, but why did it matter? She was still going to fade away.

"I don't know what you did, my lady, but I feel better." Kelin held the dish out in front of him. It was already empty.

Laurel offered a tight smile. "I'm sure the wilderness air helps too."

He turned to Der. "They say that the poorest man in Pallens eats on silver." A humorless smirk flitted across his face. "And we're so horribly poor right now."

Der let the bowl fall from her fingers. Soup splashed onto her boots.

Laurel picked it up. "The Empire of Pallens has been gone a long time now, Kelin."

Der snapped, "How did you know his name?"

"Because my husband knows."

"And just who is your husband? He's one of them—" Her eyes ripped toward the boy. The child grinned as he tossed sticks into the fire.

The elf moved between her and Thalon. She pointed at her own eyes, redirecting Der's gaze. She cleared her throat and spoke as if announcing something, "What happened back in Pallens' time may be history to you, but it isn't for the elves and the chemmen."

"And?" Der raised an eyebrow.

Laurel leaned back. "What do you know of your captors?"

Kelin scowled. "Um. They were called storm-readers because they could summon storms."

The elf shook her head. "No, not unless they use magic like everyone else."

"Not sure why they're also called chemmen though."

"One by themselves, one by other races," Laurel answered. Her green eyes passed over to Der. "And lucky for you, it's a limited immortality like mine.

Neither of us age, and although we elves heal more extensive injuries and diseases than they do, both of us can perish by the sword." She pushed her red mane behind her shoulders as she held Der's stare. "Or teeth."

Der didn't flinch. "But where are they from? What do they want?"

Laurel eyed her askance for a moment. "They used to be human, the chemmen. Their kingdom was on the same continent as Pallens."

"Then what are they doing here?" Der demanded. "How can they *used to be* human?"

Laurel pursed her lips and glanced back to Thalon. "Derora, this isn't your war."

Der thrust out her gray, swollen hands. "Then I'm glad to be dying for what isn't any of my business."

Laurel frowned, but her tone was mild, "Yes, Derora, you are just another casualty of a war that began millennia before you were born." The elf moved to tower over her. "Do not make the mistake of thinking the two of you are the only ones who have been shown how the chemmen ask questions."

She leaned back and stood straight again. But Der had seen it. The briefest flicker of fear in her steeled gaze.

Laurel sat between them and Thalon. Kelin remained staring at the fire, and Der couldn't even guess what was on his mind.

She looked back to the elf. "So why did you marry one?"

"That truly is none of your business." Laurel kept her expression firm. "But we wanted a child. One he didn't have to give to the cause."

Der narrowed her eyes in confusion.

"Mama." Thalon yawned as he stretched. Laurel rose and walked over to him. She sat next to him and he crawled into her lap. He was snoozing before he was fully settled.

Kelin stared at the ground. "What they did to us with, with such dispassion. It was just another day at the mill for them."

Der fought against a sneer. "Oh, I think they enjoyed it."

Laurel swept her fingers through the child's hair. "How much do you know of the Centum Wars?"

Der frowned and shrugged. "Fall of Pallens."

Kelin added, "War of Hell on Earth, when the gates to hell were open. So they say."

Laurel frowned. "The War of Hell on Earth, combined with the fall of the empire, did so much to destroy the knowledge of the previous wars before them. Including the storm-readers'." She exhaled. "And so much of what Pallens truly was." A small smile played on her face for the first time. "We were everything the chemmen were not—different races, different languages—even though they'll tell you that everyone spoke Palls, don't believe it—different foods and music..." She closed her eyes. "Sometimes I still pretend to smell the salty air from the ocean." Then her mirth receded and she tightened her grip on the boy in her arms. "This was the Pallens Front War."

The humans shook their heads in confusion.

"The wars had given the chemmen opportunity to invade a few of the empire's new provinces—lands that had chosen to join the empire because their own kingdoms had crumbled into chaos."

Der scowled. "I didn't think people *asked* to join empires, not even Pallens."

Laurel sighed, with that same hint of a smile. "Midan had long given the people the choice. Even to depose him, which they never did."

Der blinked.

"Where was I? The chemmen had invaded. It was in these outreaches of the empire that the storm-readers learned the legend of the water of life."

"So they found the source of the water of life? Like in the story?" Der tried to imagine the divine forest with its spring. In her mind, she always added towering trees to it, making it larger than life.

Laurel shook her head. "They learned of the legend, but it is more accurate to say that they made their own."

"What?" Kelin gasped. "Eternal life is not something that can be just made! It can't be...right?"

The elf pulled her sleeping son's head against her chest. "In every life, there is a drop of this divine water, so that we may breathe and our hearts may beat. Anything with this drop of water is alive: an infant, a forest, a bird."

Kelin shook his head. "But how did they do it? Their whole race... They *must've* found the source, right?"

Laurel shook her head, her eyes sorrowful. "The water of life is not made or unmade. It is part of the cycle of this everlasting world. When something expires, their water passes on to a new life being born."

Der felt her stomach sinking. "And the chemmen..."

Laurel pressed her lips together. "They learned how to find the drops in people. One drop from one person, and they needed hundreds of thousands of drops."

"I don't understand." Der held up her hands. *I don't want to*, she thought.

"But." Kelin gulped. "It'd be too much. It couldn't be done."

Laurel sighed. "And the world's population still has not recovered to what it was before the wars."

Der bowed her head under the coalescing weight of Laurel's story. She tried to picture the bodies, piled high, rotting in the sun.

But she couldn't imagine so many people being alive, let alone all in one place. She attempted to envision what that many people looked like, but her mental picture faltered because she had no idea how big of a crowd that was. Riversbridge didn't even have a hundred people.

She could hear the words and she could repeat the numbers, but she could not understand them. She let her head fall forward into her hands and watched her vision spin. "How does an elf prince fit into this?" she muttered.

"Indelleiria was Pallens' greatest ally. They didn't send troops, at first, but they sent their spies and saboteurs. So, too, came the dragoon armies."

Kelin grunted. "That was too much for the elves, wasn't it? To have another immortal race, and one so wicked."

"It was. There are other immortal races besides the elves, you know, but none who made themselves like the storm-readers did." She rested her head on the side of her hand. "Indelleiria should have done something sooner, but they couldn't dare themselves to interfere while the storm-readers were mortal."

"What did the elves do?" Der asked, frowning.

"They, with the help of an elven sorceress, banished the chemmen to a place for those too hard to kill, too dangerous to live. Darkreign. It had been a prison for thousands of years, but this was the last banishment there."

The humans shook their heads in confusion.

"It is not of this world." She hugged Thalon. "But the chemmen forced paths open and returned to this realm." A tear sparkled in the corner of an eye. "We were unaware. That peace wasn't to be had, even after all this time. We thought, surely they were gone..." She kissed her son's head.

Only the crackle of the fire sounded around the camp.

Der exhaled and let the fascination out with the air; she was still too exhausted and injured to be mesmerized. The elf's stories had stolen whatever strength her healing had restored.

Laurel pushed her hair behind her shoulders. "I pray tomorrow's dawn brings more life than death."

But Der wasn't listening anymore. What was the point? She was done for. She wiped a tear from the corner of her eye and wondered if she'd just whisked away her drop of life.

CHAPTER FIFTEEN

She was supposed to be sleeping, but Der had too little time left to waste it snoring.

She grimaced at the normally comforting sounds of dawn. The chirping insects and birds could be masking the predators that hunted them. Even if the forest were hiding them as the elf claimed, Der still saw shifting eyes out between the trees. Animals, she knew, but...

She listened to thunder crackle. It didn't sound far. She shivered against the gloomy light of morning; it was as if the world had washed to gray. The storm-readers' light.

"If you cannot rest, then don't lose your time pretending," Laurel's voice wafted down from above.

Der tried to speak but could produce no sound. She gulped down her rising panic.

She mentally screamed at her hands and feet. They sat there like lumps. She tried to kick, but nothing happened, so she felt herself kick harder in her desperation, and again, her legs did not respond.

"Shh, child," Laurel whispered. "Concentrate on breathing. Slowly, slowly. Inhale slowly."

She tried her best and could hear the air pumping in and out of her mouth. After some time, her heart slowed.

The elf knelt beside her, and Der felt something cold, harsh, and wet rub against her skin. She jerked away. Laurel grabbed her and pressed the damp cloth down. "Don't struggle. It's a healing salve." She dragged it over the young woman's throat.

Der's eyebrows creased. "Don't—"

She heard a snort. "You'll die without it. And it's less dangerous than trying to avoid an infection without it, and far less dangerous than not being able to control your muscles when trouble calls."

Der tried to push one more protest through her lips, but the icy-hot stinging sensation had drained her strength.

There had always been healing potions and salves, but no physician or mage had ever perfected the formula. The body wasn't meant to heal that quickly. When something forced it, there was the chance that the body couldn't handle the strain, and the person would die.

She closed her eyes, feeling as though she were levitating. The pain faded to a humming in the background. When she came back down, she coughed a few times. "Better."

Laurel shook her head. "Still not enough, but it will buy you time."

"Time for what?"

"We are going toward Indelleiria."

Der gasped and pushed herself up to her elbows. "That's where Caleb was, well, running from."

"We're going *toward* Indelleiria." Laurel brushed some hair from her face. "There is an outpost of the kingdom hidden in the Riverfall Mountains."

"Uh-huh..."

"We can't go to Indelleiria, child, because you, your friend, my son, and most certainly my husband cannot go there."

"Why not?"

The elf shook her red mane. "None of you would be able to find it. One must be invited to cross the borders of my motherland." She tossed a couple sticks on the fire. "But I must go, because my husband and I have learned information that can save many lives, but only I can—"

An arrow landed in the fire.

Der stared. There was an arrow in the fire.

Flames sprouted along it, but she couldn't look away. More arrows bit into the soft soil around her, and yet, Der watched the burning shaft.

She heard another arrow whizzing and a harsh gasp, and she suddenly didn't want to look away from the burning arrow. She didn't want to see the body falling. But she had to.

Laurel's red hair blended with the flames as she fell behind the fire.

There was no light in her eyes. It was a lucky shot, directly through her chest. Der watched a single tear slide from her eye and vanish into the soil.

She gulped. They were found! The chemmen had found them! She wished she could have been surprised.

She heaved herself up and tried to shake off her dizziness as she crawled toward the sleeping forms of Kelin and Thalon.

"We gotta go!" She thrashed Kelin's shoulder. "We gotta go!"

Thalon raised his head. "What's—Yow!" An arrow plunged into the ground two inches in front of his hand.

"Kelin!" Der jerked the blacksmith's arm so hard that she felt something pop in her elbow.

"Hey!" Kelin yelled, sitting up on his own.

"Mama? Mama!" Thalon tore away from his blanket and scrambled toward his mother's body.

Kelin snatched at the boy's clothing, but the child was too fast.

"Mama?" Thalon stood over her. His shoulders slouched. As he turned back to them, tears spilled from his orange eyes. "She's dead."

Der's hand groped her hip for a sword that wasn't there. She didn't have her sword.

This wasn't a dream, a game, or a combat drill in the meadow; the enemy was here to kill them, and she had no weapon!

She stained the air with curses as she scrambled to find a sharp rock. When she looked to see if more arrows were hailing, she saw figures moving through the trees. "They," she faltered and tried to launch her voice again, "they're human!"

She rose and stumbled toward them.

Kelin goggled, turning to run. His words were garbled, but recognizable as he boomed, "What the *hell* are you doing?" He grabbed for her arm.

She threw off his hand. "Get Thalon back!" Without listening to his reply, she charged.

There were only three attackers, and two had their swords ready. The third shouldered his bow and went for his sword. *That was stupid,* she thought. On the other hand, he was armored and she wasn't. Maybe he wanted to preserve his arrows. She sprinted at the nearest one, trying to force herself to fly faster. He stepped back and dropped into a crouch, angling his sword at her stomach.

He swung widely. She ducked under the blade and sprung up with her shoulder straight into his groin. He dropped his weapon, staggering backward.

Der dove for the prize. Her fingers curled around the hilt.

The man she'd assaulted grabbed her neck and yanked up. She didn't care because she had the sword. She stabbed sideways at an awkward angle, trying to get the blade into his armpit. She felt something catch on the sword and he fell away, cursing as he hit the ground.

The second man thundered toward her, and she saw the third going after Kelin and Thalon. Her attacker was already swinging his sword at her well before he was close.

She moved her blade toward him, grinning. Despite everything, she found herself coming alive again.

The man's face went rigid behind his scowl. His feet carried him forward, but his expression didn't move. She swiveled around his wild swings and heaved her sword at his back. He collapsed, his last breath hissing out between his teeth.

Kelin shoved Thalon behind him and backed away from the man rushing at them. The boy reached up and handed him one of his knives. "Here!"

Kelin snatched up the blade, but it looked far too short against the sword bearing down on them.

Thalon's hands dug into the back of his belt. "Move to the side," he barked. "Wait for him to swing and move to the side!"

"How do you know—" But there was no more time. They ducked away from the whistling weapon.

Kelin glanced down at the boy's face. Then he twisted his entire body to the side of the blade, and suddenly, he was inside the sword's reach. He didn't stop moving and rammed the knife home in the attacker's throat.

The man went limp against his hand. A double-headed snake medallion slithered out from his robes. "Dammit!"

Wide-eyed, Der staggered over, gasping for air. Kelin waved his bloody knife in her face. "Do you realize how lost we are now?"

"Uh..." She blinked and then looked around. "We need to salvage what we can from the camp." She glanced over, one of their attackers was still alive, squirming on the ground and clutching his bloody armpit. But he wasn't getting up, not yet.

Kelin howled, "This is beyond us, Derora Saxen. The elf's dead!"

"Salvage!" she commanded. She sagged against the trunk of a tree. Then she dropped to her knees and fought against vomiting, but she didn't let her grip on the weapon slide.

Kelin moved between her and the cursing man. "Are you even strong enough to carry that?"

Her voice was low and steady, "I'd rather die standing, Kelin." She pulled herself to her feet and forced her way toward Thalon. "We have to run." She looked back to where the surviving attacker was still rolling on the ground, spiritedly cussing.

For the first time, she studied the man. He wore cheap leather armor over his torso. She saw he had a large, flat nose that must have been broken many times. She bit her lip. "We can't just leave him." She looked back uneasily at Kelin.

Hoofbeats broke through sudden stillness. No one moved for a frozen second.

"More of them!" Kelin breathed.

Der swung her head back and forth, searching.

There! She pointed. Behind them was a steep bank. She grabbed Kelin with her free hand, who in turn pulled Thalon along as they ran. They slipped over the lip of the bank, tumbling through dirt and exposed roots toward the water below.

Thalon struggled against the Kelin's hand, even though it had wrapped completely around his arm. "No! We can't leave her—"

"Sorry," Kelin panted. "I'm so sorry—"

Der let go of him and lost her balance. She crashed into the creek on her knees. Icy water seized her and she gasped for air. She blinked stupidly as the weak current slurped by her.

We're in the Wild Lands, she thought. *We have to be. The Wild Lands. No one comes here.*

No race had settlements that survived in the thick, dark heart of the continent. It was said that dragons lived here without fear of questing heroes. Der wasn't certain about that, even though she wanted to believe it, but she had no doubts lesser beasts thrived. It was also said that animals had no fear of humans because they never had known any.

She stared upward at the trees. She could see as plainly as the sky was blue that these were ancient and alive. The branches seemed to hold aloft the fabric of time.

She growled. So, if the Wild Lands were such an unconquered and uninhabited domain, what were the chemmen, cultists, and now more cultists on horseback doing here? *Why was it so godsdamn crowded?*

Kelin and Thalon slid down into the creek behind her.

She wobbled to her feet. "We need to go."

The child grabbed her arm and shook his head. He pointed up.

Hoofbeats pounded above them nearby.

Thalon let go and pressed his small body next to the steep bank. His hair tangled with the roots hanging from above.

Kelin craned his neck up the embankment.

Der opened her mouth, but the muffled sounds of stamping horses and voices drifted down the slope. Soil slid down into their clothes against the back of their necks, and tendrils of roots brushed their hair as the humans pushed themselves tighter against the earthen wall. Overhead, thunder began to drum.

Der shook her head and raised her sword. She whispered, "One's still alive, and the other bodies are still warm. They're gonna figure we ain't far. We've got to get out of here, quiet-like."

Kelin chewed his lip but nodded. He knelt to face Thalon. "Der and me, we promise to keep you safe."

The boy was trembling. "But my dad, he'll..."

"We have to go, Thalon."

Tears tumbled down his face. "But, but..."

Der watched Kelin force a smile at the boy, and he said, "We'll help you find your father."

She nodded in agreement as she scanned the surrounding forest. Then she picked a random direction, and they began to slink down the creek.

CHAPTER SIXTEEN

The day toiled into night, and the skies had grown dark early. They hadn't encountered another soul. Although they knew that was a good thing, it still left them feeling even more lost.

The shadows rose as the sun faded. The surrounding trees shook in the wind and thunder. It hadn't stormed on them yet, but the angry sky hadn't let go of its grudge either.

Der, Kelin, and Thalon hunched together in the exposed roots of a massive tree. Kelin's dark cloak stretched out above them. The sounds of the forest sliced through the wall of silence between them.

Der stared out ahead. It was about all she could do. Her hands were as heavy as rocks, and the pain was returning. Healing salves were said to fix bones and mortal wounds, so what was so wrong with her that she couldn't be saved?

Beside her, Thalon's whole body shuddered. "She never hurt anyone!" He beat a fist against Kelin's thigh and sobbed. "She never did bad things! Why did she have to be killed?"

Kelin banged his head against a large root. "I know. She was kind to us. It—it was just bad luck." He put a hand on the boy's shoulder.

Thalon howled louder and thrashed in place. "She didn't do nothing wrong! She was kind to *everybody!*" He tried to dry his eyes with his fists. "She was the nicest person in the whole world. There was this one time when this man tried to rob us, and Dad was gonna kill him, but she wouldn't let him. She made the man dinner, and he became our friend." He sniffed. "Why? She wasn't a fighter or anything! She didn't do anything wrong! She was the most kindest person!"

"We know, we know," Kelin soothed.

"None of this is fair," Der whispered. She looked down at her hands. "It should have been me."

Kelin shook his head at her.

Thalon struggled against Kelin's arm. "The bow should have broken! The arrow should have missed! *She didn't do nothing wrong!*"

"We know." Kelin squirmed. "She helped us when we had nothing to give in return. She was the most generous person we've ever met."

The boy wailed against his chest while the wind rose to a scream around them.

Der glanced above the cloak, watching the flashes of lightning. "I wish it would either storm or pass."

Kelin nodded, trying not to disturb the crying boy. Thalon cried until slumber took him away.

After a while, Kelin lifted him and pushed him into Der's lap. "Your turn."

She pushed the boy back at him, and pressed against the trunk of the tree. "My first reaction with a baby was to put my hand under its nose so it could smell me!"

"Good thing he's not an infant."

"But I have no idea what to do with him." Her expression softened. "The most rearing I've done is I helped old Aergo to raise his sheepdogs since they were puppies."

Kelin let Thalon fall into her arms anyway. Then he smiled. "You really did that, didn't you? With a baby?"

She nodded. "When Mother dragged me to see Ashine's new one." She spared a thought to reflect that she had already grown used to his slow, warped speech.

Kelin chuckled and then dropped his gaze down to Thalon. "I feel for him. He's half-chemmen. Nobody's going to want anything to do with him."

"He didn't choose it."

"No, but think about it," Kelin ordered. "If he were older, would you want to be around him?"

"No one would know. We didn't even believe in the storm-readers."

"No, but everyone will now."

She sighed. "We promised to find his father. I don't know how, but we need to."

He gave her a long-practiced glare. "Do you want to go back to that place?"

"Want, no. But…" She gazed out at the clearing. The winds howled, the thunder cracked, but it wasn't raining. The sky couldn't decide what to do either.

Der shivered and drew her arms around herself while she wheezed for breath. "My hands are already slowing. I don't know how long they'll answer me."

She looked at him and saw how fear had hollowed out his eyes.

"Please don't die," he whispered. "You can't. We won't survive if you…"

She turned her face away. "Let's try to sleep. Maybe things will be better in the morning." Above the cloak, the thunder rumbled on.

***

Der jerked awake to someone's fist jabbing her shoulder. "Wha—"

"Riders!" Thalon hissed.

She blinked and tried to push herself backward into the tree. "What?" It was daylight again, but the sunlight wasn't pushing through the trees' lower branches much.

Kelin was pulling the cloak down from the exposed roots. "Lucky they came that way. Hide already!" He yanked it down and squeezed up beside them.

Then there was nothing to do but wait. They each held their breath. The hoofbeats grew louder, knocking loose the damp leaves above their heads. Then they stopped.

They heard the stamping of hooves, but no voices.

Der rolled her head to the side to try to catch a glimpse through the roots.

"They're not riders," she whispered as she pushed herself to her feet, still hugging the tree. The other two crawled up beside her.

Three white unicorns looked up from their play. Their coats were so brilliant Der had to squint to see them. Their golden and silver horns made the cloudy light dance around them like a bright noon. She forgot about her pain at the sight.

Kelin frowned. "And a black horse. A really, really enormous black horse."

Thalon gulped and shook his head. His orange eyes were wide. "Doesn't look like a horse!"

Der blinked, and sure enough, there was a massive, midnight black horse standing behind the unicorns. It was hard to focus on both at once. The horse was everything the unicorns weren't. It was huge. It was muscular. Its hooves were larger than her face, and suddenly, she couldn't get that measurement out of her mind because that horse flattened its ears and stamped the ground.

The unicorns cantered off into the forest, moving as fluidly as a mountain stream. But the black horse stayed and glared.

Der slipped her hand toward her stolen sword where it was propped up against the roots. "Thalon, start climbing the tree."

Kelin shook his head. "Do you see how big that thing is? It'd knock the tree down!"

The horse snorted and flipped its mane. The ears lifted. It looked after where the unicorns had gone and then back at them.

It stuck up its nose and raised its tail. Then, as daintily as an equine can, it tiptoed into the forest by the direction it and the unicorns had arrived.

Der let her fingers relax on the pommel. "Well, that may have been one of the strangest things I've ever seen."

Kelin grumbled, rolling up his cloak. "We should go." He kicked a root. "Thank the gods we're not burdened down with supplies, like food."

"We'll find berries. Remember, red ones are only poisonous half the time. Blue and black ones are usually all right."

"Then you're eating them first, Der."

"Uh, there might be some wild onions. I mean, there are at home." She picked up the blade while hiding a grimace. She forced a tight grin. "Thalon, do you have any idea where your father is?"

The boy held up his empty hands.

She opened her mouth, but instead of a reply, she threw up whatever was left in her stomach. Then she lost her grip on the sword and collapsed onto her knees, hacking and retching.

She grabbed her chest as pain surged through her body.

"There's blood in this, Der. You're vomiting blood." Kelin paled as he pointed.

She tried to push herself up and stumbled forward. "I'm all right."

"No, you're not." He threw his cloak on the ground. "You're dying. We don't know where we are. We don't know where we're going. *And* we're being hunted by cultists and chemmen!"

Finally, after a day and a night of rumbling skies, it started to pour.

Kelin stuck his hand out in the curtain of water and laughed. "Oh, and now it's raining!"

Der rested her head against the tree. "Our best idea is to find and remain at our camp. I think the boy's father could find us there."

"Who couldn't?" Kelin snapped. He sighed. "I won't say you're right, but that's probably our best chance."

"Riders!" Thalon squeaked.

"Are the unicorns coming back?" Kelin asked, stepping away from the tree.

"No." The boy pointed. "It's the black horse with...shit."

The massive horse led the way, but this time, he carried a bareback rider in red who held a lance. Other horses with riders followed closely. Their armor didn't shine but instead mirrored the colors of the forest. But their drawn swords, those shone, even through the rain.

The riders fanned out around them. Each one had a helmet with a lowered visor, so they could see none of their faces.

Thalon ducked behind Kelin and clutched his belt.

The black horse stepped in front of them and twitched its ears. The rider's size was to a man what the horse was to other horses. He couldn't have ridden a normal horse. He wore blood-red plate armor and was carrying a great sword and a battleaxe on his saddle and a massive shield on his back. He lowered the lance at them. The rain ran off its sharpened point. At least it was just rain, Der told herself, instead of something much more precious.

The red rider cleared his throat. "We've seen many people out here who don't belong. Chemmen, cultists, and now you, so I'm only going to ask once for surrender."

Der forced her chin up. Beside her, she saw Kelin and Thalon looking at her. She winced at how bright the boy's eyes were. She said, "Uh, this might take a while to explain." Then she started swaying and groaned. She leaned forward. "Oh no..." With a tremendous heave, she vomited right on the black horse's massive hooves.

CHAPTER SEVENTEEN

"Are you putting me on trial?" Vlade roared. His voice echoed in the cramped throne room.

The chemmen king leaned away from the spittle, glancing sideways at the obsidian mirror. He wished not to look at Vlade, but the commander's reflection was all he saw. He tightened his jaw. "No, not as such, but something unimaginable happened on your watch, so you must be held accountable. *Seven* of us died."

Vlade paced in tight circles. "I was overseeing the capture of the calvar. A pen got loose. In such tight quarters, be thankful that only four soldiers fell." He stopped pacing and picked at a deep scratch he'd received from one of the beasts.

Dis leaned forward. He found that he was drumming his fingers. "And seven of us are dead. Three by these humans." He glanced at the mirror again and watched his face, as if reassuring himself that he was still here. He knew chemmen would perish in this campaign, but none so close to him as this!

It didn't matter, his reflection told him, they had more than enough bodies. Darkreign only had so much space, after all. "Seven, Vlade, seven of us."

The commander held up three fingers.

The king squirmed in his seat. "She's *human*. Well, mostly."

All the thunder rumbled back onto the commander's face. "We were once too."

The king tightened his grip on his armrest. "We make no mention of that!"

"It doesn't change the truth, Dis." He began to pace again. "And losing the princes has set us back. If you do not remember so well, it was I who orchestrated this war."

Dis breathed out. He looked at the mirror again, it was all right. He turned to the commander. "Yes, and your brilliant strategy seems to involve many people escaping us. First, *both* the princes. Then you lost the crown prince *again* in the human city. I'm surprised you killed the king and queen."

Vlade stiffened. "None of that has damaged my plan! It is merely delayed."

"What?" The chemman king pressed his hands together. "You don't think the elves won't use this time you've given them?"

"They cannot stab a ghost!" Vlade slammed his boot down. "They run in panic, which buys us time. They can do nothing, and soon they will realize how helpless they are. That is the moment I will savor."

The king continued to scowl. But he believed the commander. The chemmen could always rely on one another. It was their race against the entire world.

Their unity was the thing that staved off extinction after what the elves had done to them. It had brought them life, then peace, and now they could have their vengeance at last. Despite how much Vlade left a nasty taste his mouth, he knew he could trust him with his life. He had to.

His fingers slid across his identical calvar scratch, even though he had been near no beasts.

They'd been bound by an ancient magic, but it was no matter, he had always told himself, because they carried the same purpose. They all had—every one of them.

Dis avoided looking at the commander's face. He coughed and then cleared his throat. "When do you continue your hunt for the princes?"

"In the morning."

"Morning?" Dis's voice weighed heavily.

Vlade gritted his teeth. "My experiments continue."

"Are you still trying to enchant that noisemaker? *This* is urgent."

"It is not a noisemaker! It is the absence of sound!" He pointed at the wall toward the west. "It will pound fear into their hearts. They remember!" His tone slowed, and he snarled, "As if you aren't experimenting and scheming on your own."

"For the betterment of all of us. I don't want to lose a hand for all of time." Dis ran his fingers over his face. "The sword was lost, Vlade. Do not lose yourself too. We have victories to march toward."

"This is just another element of my plan." With that, he spat at the king's feet and marched out of the room.

***

Der stared blankly at the half circle of elves. She counted five of them seated on one long, simply crafted bench. She guessed they must have made it out here in the Wild Lands. But why? Then again, all of her thoughts seemed to be a distance from her. *At least the sun had come out*, she observed as she shaded her eyes.

The humans weren't bound or chained, but they understood the consequences of trying to escape. Next to her, Kelin was clenching and unclenching his fists, and shifting his weight from side to side.

Each symmetrical face before them was etched in stone. There were three men and two women. Two of them were wearing steel, including the red knight. She sighed and slouched. She had always wanted to meet elvish knights, but now she wished she could postpone the introduction.

She couldn't decide on any ages for them. They looked young, but every time she tried to think of years, the number just fell away. She knew she was staring. The women were the most beautiful people she had ever seen. One had dark hair which went well past her waist, and she shone in a dress that sparkled and shimmered like sunlight playing on a mountain lake.

Der didn't get a good look at the blond woman before she caught the glare of the male elf seated in the center. He wore an emerald embroidered shirt and dark trousers. His collar was turned up, and unlike the others, he glowered at her and Kelin with eyes burning so brightly they could have started a fire.

A chilly wind swept through, teasing leaves across the forest floor. Der felt her throat dry. The red knight rose to his feet. He seemed even more massive away from the horse. She thought that elves were supposed to be petite, svelte, and all those other things, like Caleb had been. This one wasn't. This one looked like an ancient oak. A strong jaw and stern features defined his face, which was set against short, clipped blond hair. His ears appeared to stick out farther than the others because of his haircut. His pale blue eyes glared down at them.

"I am Sir Jacob, knight-captain of the Silver Dawn Dragoons. Since this is a time of war, if you are found guilty of aiding the enemy, your lives will be forfeited, just like the man left behind at your camp. So now, you will tell us your tale of how you came to be here, and this council will tell you what we believe. Then we shall have a discussion. Introduce yourselves before you speak. I will admit that this is anything but a proper trial, however, this needs to be done and done quickly. Is all this understood?"

Kelin stepped forward and bowed. He never fully raised his head and instead gazed intently at the ground. "Lords and ladies, I am Kelin Miller, and this is Derora Saxen, both of Riversbridge." He licked his lips. "Actually, that should be Lady Derora Saxen of Riversbridge of the noble house of Saxen of Thealith."

The elves stared impassively.

Der whispered, "I wouldn't have said that."

"I know," Kelin hissed.

The neatly dressed elf in the center cleared his throat. He sharpened his glare on them. "There shouldn't even be a trial at all."

The knight-captain returned a blank but stern look to the other elf. "Dragoon law, sir. They have to have a trial because they have no allegiance to speak for them."

Der frowned. "Where's Thalon? You know, the boy?"

The dark-haired female elf shook her head. "Child, no questions now."

Der shook her head right back. "You didn't kill him, did you?"

Gasps circled throughout the council.

"Your life will be ended if you don't obey the rules of this trial," the cleanly dressed elf snapped. "So, please, go right ahead."

She scowled up at him. "Then I'd like to go to my grave knowing you didn't murder a child."

His upper lip rose, but before he could speak, the other elven woman raised a hand as smoothly as flowing silk. Her sapphire eyes appeared sympathetic. They also shone oddly, even at this distance, but Der couldn't make out any detail in them. Strawberry blond curls caressed her cheeks. Her dress was simple, unlike the other female elf's, and it revealed her beauty without drawing attention to itself. "The child is well." Her voice was the sound of bells singing in the wind and Der flushed in sheer wonderment of it. It wasn't just musical, it was a full symphony.

She and Kelin just stared. They were helpless. They couldn't have even run for their lives after hearing her speak.

The elf in the center turned his glare onto her, but she didn't seem to notice. She coaxed, "Tell us your story, please."

Kelin bit his lip. "Uh..."

Der shrugged. "Like back at the village? Where do you want us to start?"

The red knight and the graceful elf exchanged a glance. She nodded slightly. Sir Jacob returned his gaze to the pair and said, "Think of this from our perspective. We find you out here in the Wild Lands with a murdered elf not five miles away and with a child of...of mixed heritage. Why are you here? What events led you to be out here with this boy?"

Der opened her mouth, but the elf in the center scoffed, "If they will not tell us, then let us not waste our time."

Der glowered up at him. "We met them after we escaped from the chemmen."

No one moved in the silence that followed.

The red knight blinked. "Excuse me?"

"Laurel saved our lives," Der breathed. "She's the elf who died. But she said that she couldn't do enough for me—not after what the chemmen had done—and then Sennha's cultists attacked."

An argument exploded among the elves in a language Der and Kelin did not understand.

The elf in muted armor held up his hand and spoke in Common. "We are agreed. No questions. This is protocol." He looked back at the humans. "Continue."

Der shrugged. "Well, we met your prince. In Duelingar. Um, Caleb."

She heard the strain—heard words humming on the other side of their lips—but there were no more outbursts. The dark-haired woman tilted her head. "There are no princes named Caleb."

The knight in muted armor said, "He wouldn't have used any name that we would recognize."

The elf in the center scowled at them. "You can't believe they actually met—"

Kelin started, "The chemmen used their spies to hunt for him, calling him an outlaw, and we took his place in a trap—"

"And that doesn't matter!" Der yelled. "None of this matters! We didn't know who he was or where he was going. But, Laurel, she knew something really important. We don't know what it was though, so you're outta luck." She shrugged as she glanced around. "That's it. I'm done."

The neatly dressed elf in the center snorted. "Very well. I am Duke Farallon of the Aeolian Plateau, sworn to the royal family of Indelleiria." He glowered at them with nothing but disdain. "Your story is outrageous. I don't believe it."

The elf in muted armor inclined his head. "I am Sir Amthros, knight of Indelleiria, sworn to the royal family. We were passing through the Altice Domain, or Wild Lands as you say, on our return to Indelleiria. We were forced to evacuate our nobility and leaders after the murders of the king and queen. During our passage, we learned of the outlaw ruse and suspected that the missing prince may have been nearby. We discovered ourselves to be on the path of devil-worshippers, who had been driven out of the city to avoid execution. They were exposed when blood was publicly spilled."

The dark-haired woman beside him spoke, "I am the Duchess of the Aeolian Plateau, Lady Sabielle." She nodded at Duke Farallon. "So it seems that the cultists murdered the elf whom you knew. But you, in your haste, escaped us."

Der gasped. It hadn't been more cultists on horseback. It had been the elves! She rubbed her neck as she wondered: if they'd been caught back at the camp instead of near the unicorns, would it have made any difference?

The duchess frowned at them. "And you claim the chemmen have tortured you, with only light marks on the both of you?"

"No." The duke snapped his fingers. "It's far more likely that they are in league with our enemy, either the cultists or bought by the storm-readers."

Der inhaled sharply. Kelin stamped down on her foot before she could say anything. He held up a warning finger. She snorted but kept her mouth closed.

The duke sneered and leaned forward. "You have been agents all along. You tried to lead the prince to his death, and while you failed with that, you succeeded with the elf in the forest!"

Der's jaw dropped. Kelin flinched.

Sir Amthros raised a hand. "That is not the consensus of this council. Perhaps they were unwitting agents."

Sir Jacob nodded. "Yes, and there is the child."

Duke Farallon shook his head. "Surely the poor woman was taken against her will."

"The chemmen have never—" Sir Amthros began, and then silenced himself.

Der poked up her hand. "Uh, no."

"You're not allowed to speak." Lady Sabielle stared down her nose at them. "Your part of the discussion is closed."

Der jabbed a finger at the duke. "But he's getting it all wrong and you spoke during our half! I listened to the way Laurel spoke her husband. She loved him. And he was away from her side spying for information for you when she was killed."

"*You're not allowed to speak!*" Duke Farallon roared. "Even if you were, good sense does not allow us to trust you."

The graceful elf inclined her head to the duke. "She's not lying."

He gritted his teeth. "It doesn't matter; she doesn't know the truth—she just knows what she believes." He swept his hand out toward them. "And she *believes* that this elf and a chemman had a loving partnership. Do I have to explain this to you?"

"Then what about Thalon?" Der yelled.

Farallon whirled on her. "You may not speak! That's enough! We will carry the rest of these proceedings in our language." He curled his upper lip. "Not that it will make a difference."

Sir Amthros shook his head. "That is not tradition. Everyone must hear, especially the accused."

"They'll still understand. She'll just translate."

"Translate what?" Der lifted an eyebrow.

Stony silence answered her at first, but then a murmur spread through the elves.

Der leaned back toward Kelin. "I don't think we're reading from the same book here. I mean, elves are supposed to be arrogant, but to expect that we know their language, are they serious?"

He shrugged.

Lady Sabielle slipped in a few words in their language, and another intense argument erupted. They bickered for some time before finally turning back with upset faces. Most of them looked at Der, as if waiting for her to speak.

She and Kelin exchanged shrugs.

"You don't know?" Sir Jacob asked in the dumbfounded silence.

"You don't speak our tongue?" the duchess queried, staring hard at Der.

Der snorted. "Obviously not."

Silence floated on the air, and no one on the council moved for a moment. The graceful elf leaned forward. "Do you not know your heritage?"

"Yes, I do. My family's from Riversbridge. Parents from Second Acron."

The elf smiled softly. "You are part-elven, most likely one sixteenth, which isn't much at all, but most other people like you still know our language."

Der's eyes shot wide, and she retreated a step only to trip over a root, falling hard on her tailbone. She didn't notice. She gaped up at the judges. "That's a nasty joke."

"The truth, little one."

She fired her gaze at Kelin, who looked as shocked as she was. He offered her a hand up.

"Not true," she muttered, reaching for her head. "I have rounded ears."

"With noticeable, well, notches, and you have the cheekbones." Jacob shifted in his seat. "Um. Push your hair back."

She complied. The rear top corner of her ear was slightly pointed, but the ear still rounded over it. She ran a finger over them but felt nothing special.

Kelin offered a sympathetic smile. "It's not a bad thing, Der."

"Then why didn't Ca—the prince say anything?"

Sir Amthros's face twisted. "Possibly because the way your hair is and his recent trauma could've clouded his mind."

Duke Farallon threw up his hands. "So much for protocol. I suppose now it is discourse. We are still having a trial here, my lords and ladies."

Sir Jacob nodded stiffly. "Yes, we are. Now, I would like to hear the details of how they engineered their escape. That is the most elusive part of their tale for me."

Der still rubbed the tips of her ears. "What? Oh, right."

Beside her, Kelin looked up to the knight with red-ringed eyes. "They took my teeth." He grabbed his chest over his lung. Wheezing, he stumbled through the tale of their rescue. He stuttered, "A-A-And it happened, lords, it did—that a chemman helped us escape."

"Oh, right, then they met this other elf whom none of us know!" the duke exclaimed. "Does anyone honestly believe this?"

Sir Jacob shrugged, but his gaze remained trained on Der. "Did he even give you a name? Or did Laurel?"

They shook their heads. He had just been the chemman who had aided them.

"Were there any sentries or guards he instructed you to avoid?"

Der frowned. "I killed the one we came across, like Kelin said."

"Why were you not recaptured by the storm-readers after your escape?" the duchess asked.

"I don't know, my lady." Kelin bowed his head.

Der frowned. "I remember Laurel saying something about asking the forest to hide us, but I don't understand what she meant."

"Forest sanctuary," the strawberry blond elf replied. "If she hadn't been expecting any humans, she would have asked the forest to obscure them from only chemmen, which would have strained her and the forest less. This would explain how the cultists got through."

Farallon snarled, "They're not even wounded. Not by the chemmen at least, maybe by those cultist lowlifes."

"Come now, my lord duke," coaxed the duchess. "Healing salves have saved many a mortal wound."

He snorted. "Perhaps, wife, but they do not behave as if they'd been tortured. I've seen the results of what the chemmen have done to men—good, seasoned warriors. People who have survived the chemmen are afraid of their own shadows, and yet, these two mortals walk away smiling."

"I am not smiling!" Der balled a fist and stepped forward. "I am dying." She struggled for balance. Her wounds felt as though they had been dipped in acid anew.

The duke growled and shook his head. "Don't you see it? They were made to escape. They're agents of the chemmen. So they need to die."

Sir Amthros raised his hand. "Perhaps, but they appear not to know. If they are unaware, then they are innocent as far as this trial is concerned."

"If they are, they're stupid. A chemman would never aid an elf," Farallon snapped. "The story makes no sense."

The knight continued, "I agree that elements of their tale don't fit with what we know of the storm-readers, but that doesn't mean they are guilty of aiding the enemy."

"But they're mortals! She didn't even know her heritage," the duke spat.

"Let us not resort to personal attacks," Sir Amthros advised.

"But it is personal!" Der jerked her thumb at her throat. "It's our necks."

For a brief instant, she thought she saw Sir Jacob's mouth quirk.

"Yes, that is true," the knight of Indelleiria admitted. "But where's the evidence of your tale?"

"I'm not lying."

"I never accused you of that."

"Oh." She deflated.

Farallon slapped his knee with a loud crack. "The clever bastards! Their escape was impossible! They let them go. They could be watching us right now. It's why they didn't capture them in the forest."

"The chemmen have no traitors," the duchess declared. "If they met one that helped them, it was only to further their endgame."

"But they had a child," Der pleaded. "That doesn't make sense either according to your story."

"It doesn't matter!" the duke shouted. He looked to the rest of the council. "Even if they are unwitting, they still could be a danger to us. This is war, my lords and ladies."

Sir Jacob's face was stern, a perfect mirror of his tone of voice. "Their story may or may not be true. Alas, they have no one to vouch for them."

Der said, "The prince can."

Everyone stared at her, including Kelin and especially Duke Farallon. She glanced around. "What?" She raised both of her eyebrows. "We know him, so he could—"

Farallon coughed. "How dare you suggest that!"

"Would you stop interrupting me?" She glared. "He was my friend, all right? And I want to ask after my friend."

As everyone watched, the duke's face metamorphosed into a brilliant shade of red. He gasped as if he had just emerged from drowning. "Do you not understand that you are on trial for your wretched life?"

She took a deliberate step toward him. "Oh? Because it sounds to *me* that you've already decided." She felt herself teetering on the edge of a cliff. "You call this a trial? Out here in nowhere? I admit that I don't know much, but it seems to me, my lord, that you don't either." She had stumbled over the precipice and found that she could fly. "This little theater show of a trial ain't what's important." She looked around to all the judges. "What's important is saving Caleb's life." She glared at the duke. "So if you're in such a rush, just get this trial over with and move along."

Kelin slammed his hand over his mouth. "Der!"

In the silence that shook the forest around them, Sir Amthros nodded to her. Another intense conversation in Elvish shot off like an arrow. An eerie sensation flowed by them as they listened. No one shouted, but everyone spoke urgently, and they seemed to take equal turns.

Kelin grabbed her arm. "You guard that tongue. You may be dying, but the worst can still happen to me."

Her mouth hung open. She shifted her weight. "You'll be all right."

"They may not decide that, and I don't want to repeat this trial in front of the gods, all right?"

The argument stopped. The elves turned back to face them. The knight-captain's tone was tempered with patience. "You have not lied." Der watched his gaze slide over to the graceful elf. He continued, "Your tale is strange, and a larger truth may yet be found, but for now, your lives will be spared. You both are prisoners of the Order of the Silver Dawn Dragoon Knights."

Kelin sagged with relief and Der managed to exhale. She faced the judges. "Laurel was trying to find you. She—"

"All of this is out of your influence. Take what we give you."

She shook her head. "This isn't justice."

"You're right," the knight-captain replied. "It's war."

CHAPTER EIGHTEEN

"Saxen!" Der whirled to see Sir Jacob standing astride the black horse. She was still trying to get used to the camp. It was far more spread out than what she had envisioned, and she hadn't counted all the tents yet. Or the number of elves.

She glanced sideways but offered a smile to the knight as she rubbed her arms together. The chill was sharp this morning and it was piercing her as much as the pain with which she'd awakened. Last night, she and Kelin had slept on blankets that felt like clouds in a simple canvas tent. She hadn't seen Thalon yet, and Kelin had grabbed her leg and held on when she tried to sneak out.

She rose onto the balls of her feet as Jacob approached and did her best not to hunch her shoulders. "Yes, um, my lord?"

"You look pretty bad there, kid."

She shrugged.

The horse snorted and tossed its mane. The knight shot him a sharp glance.

"No," he stated. "You look bad. And we've seen more than our share of bad." He thumped the steed on his shoulder.

She shrugged again while her gaze shifted to the black warhorse. "Why does your horse run with unicorns? I wouldn't think they'd like horses."

He rolled his eyes. "Because he thinks he's a stud." He dodged a hoof that just happened to stamp down right where his foot had been.

Der stretched her neck, scanning the camp.

The knight sighed. "That look on your face, I see it all the time on the recruits' faces back at the citadel. You're lost."

She stiffened and then shook her head. "I'm not... I'm just, uh, exploring the camp. And I had orders from that other knight, uh, Sir Amthros."

He chuckled, and she swore the horse sniggered. "Fine. What are you 'exploring' for?"

"The surgeon's tent." She glanced around again while thinking, *and it gave me an excuse to search for Thalon.*

"Oh." The knight's face twisted as if he'd eaten too sour a lemon. "Peyna." She stiffened. His expression relaxed. "Don't worry, he just doesn't like mortals."

"Does anyone here?"

"Thanks," he drawled. He put a huge hand on her shoulder and spun her around. "Peyna's tent is that one over there, next to the big spruce. See it?"

"Yes."

"Be careful. If you set off any mental sparks, his head'll catch fire."

"He's hotheaded?" she ventured.

"No, he just hasn't had an original thought in twelve hundred years, so his mind is like dry firewood. I don't think he'd left Long Range Palace in a few centuries. Hell, only the total desertion of it evicted him, and he's not happy about it."

"Thank you."

"Yeah, good luck, kid."

Her pace wasn't as self-assured anymore.

The surgeon's tent was square and larger than the others around the camp. Somehow, it wasn't what she expected. The whole camp wasn't what she expected. She didn't know what she had anticipated, but it wasn't this. She wasn't sure if she'd thought they'd have special collapsible buildings or something, but she didn't expect ordinary-looking tents, campfires, and horses. It was too normal.

She looked up at the looming canvas hall in front of her. She took a deep breath. "Is anyone here? Master surgeon? Master, um, Peyna?"

The tent flap flew open, and she stared up at a tall, stiff-faced elf. He had frozen green eyes and thin black hair. "Use the word physician, please; it exists in the common language."

She blinked. "Uh, yes."

"Well, come in." He turned away, not even holding the flap up for her to step inside.

She pushed through the folds of the cloth. Expecting the interior of the tent to be muggy, she gasped at the chill in the air. She saw netting sewn into the tent walls where the breeze flowed through.

She also saw two cots beside a low table with knives and other various tools arranged on it. She lifted one of the tiny black blades. "Is this..." She ran her finger across the edge. "Is this *glass?*"

"Put that down!" the physician snapped. Startled, she did so. He straightened his shirt as if patting down ruffled feathers. "And yes, they are, actually. Obsidian. It's a volcanic glass, and it is sharper than any steel blade. However," he glared at her, "it is also quite fragile."

"Oh, what's it for?"

He sniffed. "I have to cut away the necrotic skin around your wounds. What did you think, child?"

Der had never whimpered in a fight—that's what she wanted to believe anyway—but she felt herself wincing now. She tried to cover her scarred arms. "I'm rather attached to my skin."

"It's dying, child, and so are you," Peyna snorted. "Therefore, you will let me get rid of it. I will save your life, and I'd prefer if you didn't argue with me about it."

She backed behind a cot. "But I don't know what you're doing!" She tiptoed farther away, but he followed. The physician thrust a hand atop her head. He spoke a single word and she fainted.

***

"No! No! Are we going to have mushroom patties?" the cook exclaimed as she pulled Kelin away from the fire with surprising strength for her slender build.

"Sorry!" He dropped the spatula. She swiped it from the air.

The elf from the trial waved a hand behind her strawberry blond locks. She eased the mushrooms off the base of the pan with the spatula. Kelin leaned around her shoulder in order to watch her repair the food. He had been smashing the mushrooms onto the skillet, trying to get them to cook quicker.

She turned toward him and flashed a smile. "I've fixed it. As much as I can, at least."

He blushed and looked down. He ran his tongue over his teeth again. It still amazed him at how it was anything but an elaborate process for them. He had been convinced he'd have to spend the rest of his life speaking slowly and eating only soup. But the physician had given him something to swish around his mouth and then spit out. It had tasted horrible, but instantly, he'd felt movement beneath his gums. The elf had handed him a miracle as if he'd passed him a damp rag. His teeth didn't hurt at all now.

She shook her head and grinned. "I don't know how you survive if you can't even heat mushrooms."

He wheezed a small smile in return. His shoulders dropped and he sighed, but he found that his back wasn't so tight anymore. Maybe it was because he'd escaped with his life twice in as many days, or maybe it was the fact that Der wasn't around right now. He would kiss the goddess Ahtome's sandals if she could keep out of trouble.

He cleared his throat. "We usually have 'em raw, and not fancy like this."

She chuckled. "This isn't fancy. This is camp food. We have to feed everyone, not astound them."

"It's fancier than anything I've ever eaten."

The cook cocked a grin. "I hope not." Up close, her sapphire eyes were multi-faceted, the same as a cut gemstone. None of the other elves had eyes like that. And he liked her; he couldn't help it. She had been the only one to look, or even smile, at him since the trial.

He sighed. No longer was he a journeyman blacksmith. He wasn't certain he'd ever wanted a life where adventure tugged at the corner of his soul, not like Der anyway. But here he was. She never thought about things; she just charged ahead. It was always left to him to think and pay—

"—Attention to the food!" The cook hurled several crumpled lettuce leaves at his head.

Kelin blinked stupidly. The mushrooms were burning. He dodged her next throw. "Sorry!" Then he flinched as he caught movement off to the side.

Sir Jacob glanced down at the lettuce bouncing off his armor. "So, supper will be late?"

Kelin stiffened and reddened. He turned back to the pan and began scraping up the mushrooms.

"What are you doing here, sir knight?" the cook asked, brushing a thick curl from her face.

The knight-captain grinned. "Well, my lady, I wanted to see what was for dinner."

Kelin angled his head to the side as he listened; they seemed to speak his language like natives.

"Right," she replied. "I was not expecting you, especially since you haven't taken the time to have a conversation with me on this horrible journey yet."

His grin froze. "Uh. Now, my lady, I've been a little busy hunting storm-readers." He blinked. "That's not something I thought I'd ever say again."

"Nor I," the cook whispered.

Jacob glanced over at Kelin and grinned. He slapped the human on the back, and as large as Kelin was, he barely absorbed the blow. "And how is this prisoner doing?"

Kelin grunted. "I thought prisoners were supposed to be tied up and under guard."

The knight uncorked a grin. "Not mine. They work. And if you want to run away, please, I'm sure some animals in the Wild Lands could use a meal or two." He looked the young man up and down. "Or maybe a whole week's worth."

"Hey—"

"Speaking of working..." He beckoned toward the shadows.

From around a tree, Thalon inched forward, orange eyes roving back and forth. Jacob beckoned again, sharply this time. Thalon slinked up to them. The knight bent down and set his fingertips on the boy's shoulders. "A dishwasher."

"Thalon!" Kelin grinned in relief.

"Kelin!" The boy ran at him and tried to tackle his knees.

Kelin leaned down and hugged him. "I'm so glad you're safe."

"The red knight stuck me inside this tent, and it was dark and I couldn't leave."

Jacob coughed. "It was for your own good."

"Well, you could have left the child a lantern," the cook chided. She snatched the boy's hands. "Now, let's get you to work. You too, Kelin." She removed the mushrooms and skillet from the coals.

"But—" Kelin began.

"Now." She tapped a spoon against her hand. Her strict voice was in stark contrast with her sparkling eyes. Kelin ducked his head.

"Here." The cook smiled and guided the child to a tub of water. "There's a rag and some soap."

The boy lifted a thin wooden plate and dropped it when it folded in half.

The cook laughed, and it felt as if they were standing in a rain of rose petals. She picked up the plate and popped it back out. "They're meant to do that, little one. See? They fold in half so they can travel better."

Kelin said, "I was under the impression that elves ate on silver and gold."

Jacob raised an eyebrow and bit down on a laugh. "Where did you get such an idea? Someone would have to be in an odd situation to be eating on precious metals on the trail."

Thalon dropped his eyes and snatched up the washrag. He scrubbed so hard that soap bubbles flew up past his nose and ears.

"Yeah," Kelin replied. His gaze was focused elsewhere. "But it feels like I'm in a different world."

The knight-captain shrugged. "We're actually not too far from your kingdom."

"What? We're not? But there were unicorns and chemmen and—"

"Oh yes. Wouldn't risk traveling alone toward it though."

Kelin pressed his arms against his stomach. "How could the chemmen be so close?"

"They can be as close as they want if you don't believe they exist."

He shivered. "So they could have been in the Wild Lands all this time, just watching and waiting?"

"No," a small voice piped up. Thalon met their gazes. "My dad told me they were all locked away, so we were safe."

Kelin bit his lip, remembering what Laurel had said about Darkreign. But how long had the storm-readers been *free?*

The cook knelt down beside the child. "Yes, they were. They couldn't hurt you. They couldn't hurt anyone."

"My dad said they couldn't get out!" He threw a plate down into the bucket of clean water.

Jacob sighed. "I suppose they found a way. They were always maliciously inventive."

Kelin shook his head. "I thought I knew history well, and I didn't even know the chemmen were real."

"I'm not surprised," the knight replied. "Let me guess, you only know about the War of Hell on Earth and the fall of Pallens?"

"Yeah," he answered. He'd known there had been other wars, but until Laurel had mentioned it, he'd never heard of the Pallens Front War. "And the only stories we know about the Wild Lands are about lots of monsters."

Jacob nodded. "That's right. There are monsters out here, just not here on the edges."

"Like dragons?" Kelin asked.

The knight frowned in thought. "Probably—out by the mountains. We won't encounter anything now that we've got, ah, special protection in this camp. Not even the storm-readers can find us at the moment."

Kelin sighed in relief. "Why are they called the storm-readers? I thought that's because they could create storms, but apparently that's not true."

The cook answered, "Because they perceive the subtleties lost to the human eye. They see best in the gray light of dawn and dusk, and of course, before a storm."

Thalon's head bobbed up and down. "Mama always said it was a special talent that I could see into the shadows." He looked up, his eyes as bright as the stars. A tear slipped through, followed by another and another. "I want her back!"

CHAPTER NINETEEN

Der awoke in a bushel of blankets. They were soft, warm, and hugging her. Outside, bugs were humming, and it was dark. Several candles were burning in the tent, and the cool air blowing in through the mesh wall touched her cheeks. She inhaled and flinched, expecting pain that was no longer there. No, she told herself, there was still some, but it was so much less. A headache, mostly.

The physician sat in the tent's open entrance, a mug in hand. His skin was pale in the full moonlight and his voice was drawn, "You've missed time."

She tried to lift a trembling arm. It was as heavy as an anvil. "Am I...?"

"You are well, child." He took a long sip. "You didn't yet understand what they had done to you. You didn't even feel the pain."

"I could definitely feel it."

He shook his head. "No, not since you had no idea *how* you were dying. The acid had numbed what could have been pain beyond your imagination. It was extensive. However, I am competent." He took another drink. "I also removed your scars."

She rested back on the cot, frowning. "Even the one I got when I chased that bear? And when I say chased...well, it was about half and half."

Peyna rolled his eyes. "I don't understand how you warriors can be so attached to them. They're so ugly."

"Uh, because they are what didn't kill us." Her head was spinning and felt like a large hoof had trod on it. But he'd called her a warrior, and she smiled at that.

"Elvish skin doesn't scar except in rare circumstances. You're part-elf, so that helped. You shouldn't suffer from poor eyesight or pain in your bones until you are very old." He snorted into his mug. "If you live that long."

"Huh?" She rubbed her arms again; they were smooth to the touch. "It's just that—"

"Are you questioning my work?"

She shrugged. "The other elf couldn't do much."

"The one who had the bastard child?" He sniffed. "She was no healer. I am a master. Do you understand the difference?"

She shrugged again. "All right, I guess that's that. Anything else, o master?"

He set down the mug on a small table. "I also gave you our language, which you should have already known. It will, however, take your mouth time to learn the correct pronunciation."

"What?" She blinked and then blinked again. "I know Elvish?"

"In what language do you think we're conversing?"

Der was too dumbfounded to respond. She dropped her head into her hands. She was convinced it would roll off. It seemed to throb more now that everything else didn't ache. She sat up but almost lost her balance in a rush of dizziness.

"Lie down, child; you still need your rest."

She clung to her forehead. "Wh—" She swallowed and tried again. "Why does it hurt?" Her voice was a croak. "Getting worse."

"Drink this." He rose and set a small waterskin on the edge of the cot. "You'll feel better, not well, but better."

"Healing's not supposed to hurt." She sipped the cool, sweet water.

"You'll find it often hurts more as you heal." He sat down on the opposite cot. Shadows rimmed his eyes. "Your head feels pain because it learned so much so fast. The rest of you will be sore because I had to scour your body, like cleaning rust out of a pot. The chemmen are damned thorough when they decide to damage someone." He clicked his tongue against the roof of his mouth. "Never you mind. I shall send for something for you to eat."

"No."

"No?" he snapped, sounding much more as he did when she first met him. "Girl, you have to eat."

"Don't send for it." She managed to swing her legs over the lip of the cot. "I'll get it." She struggled to snatch her boots as she watched them blur in her sight.

"Don't come back here for scraped knees when you fall."

"Thank you." She staggered for the tent's exit. Once outside, she leaned against a tree, her boots hanging in one hand. Her vision still wasn't steady. She took a moment to put on her footwear and then picked herself back up.

She moved in a calculated lurch to the next tree. Her feet slipped and squelched in the mud, and she rested against the trunk for balance.

When she windmilled into the cooking area, she collapsed over Kelin. She slapped her chest in an attempt to point to herself. She paused to make sure she was speaking Common. "Food."

She thought in Elvish and had to translate into Common. She could *think* in another language! Then she realized she could read it too. Symbols flashed across her mind. Elvish had a complicated writing system: an alphabet of forty some letters and a separate syllabary. She didn't even know what a syllabary was! It made her head pound all the more.

"You look like the walking dead, Der." Kelin leaned away from her. "Are you all right?"

"Better 'n ever," she mumbled.

"Der!" Thalon dropped his dish and dashed over. "You're better?"

She nodded.

He wrapped his arms around her. She ruffled his hair and smiled, feeling comforted by a familiar face. And it surprised her how familiar the boy seemed, especially because she'd met him only a day before the elves. She bent down and returned the hug.

"You seem more alive," a sweet voice called. Der looked up to see the cook gliding toward them with a steaming bowl in her hands. She proffered the dish. "You and Kelin take your time to eat. You too, Thalon."

Der stared at the cook and nearly forgot to accept the bowl. Up close, this woman was too beautiful. She coughed out, "Great. Uh, thank you." She sagged, and the cook nodded before disappearing back toward the fires.

Kelin scooped up the dish in one hand and helped Der with the other. "How do you feel?"

"Bad," she managed.

"Ah." He grinned.

She collapsed like a foal with unsure legs. There were a few others already eating in the area; she recognized the duke but not the other elves. They weren't sitting near them, and no one glanced in their direction.

Kelin sat beside Der and stuck a spoon in his mouth. "Mmm. Sweet poems spring to mind. I wouldn't be upset if the chemmen killed us now so long as I'm still eatin'."

Der dipped her spoon and tried it. "The taste certainly delivers on the scent's promise."

Thalon nodded and dug into his own dish.

She sighed, staring at her stew. "So, uh, I think Caleb—the prince—is all right somewhere. I think they'd be angrier if he weren't."

Kelin frowned. "I hope. But they're elves, Der. They're not going to act like us."

She shrugged.

"Of course, this may also explain why you're such a freak on occasion."

"What?"

He pointed to her ear.

Beside them, Thalon tapped his own and half-smiled. "So you're like me."

She shook her head. "It's not my fault."

Kelin closed his eyes. "I can see it too. Your mother. She is the most handsome woman in Riversbridge...in the whole county."

She punched him in the shoulder.

"Ow! Why are you angry at me? What? Stop staring at me. It's not like I think about your mother! I'm just saying I think she is part-elf." He rammed another spoonful into his mouth.

She was left frowning. "Yeah, maybe, but—"

"But you'll learn that you won't get sick as easily, you'll heal better, and live longer. How is that bad?" a towering voice passed over their heads. They looked up to see the immense form of the knight-captain.

"Well, I am human," Der said. "I grew up being human."

"Yeah, tell me about it." He took a seat beside them. "Elves are weird."

The three of them took turns staring at him and then each other.

"Uh," Der marshaled her words, "you're one of them."

He laughed, and it was deep and rich. "Noticed that all by yourself, did you?"

"Yes."

"You may call me sir."

"That sounds just like my dad," Thalon commented.

"Fine," she replied evenly. "You're too normal, sir."

His face lit up with a grin. "I don't know whether to be insulted or not. I'm anything but normal, *especially* by elven standards."

"That's it." She nodded. "So why are you an outsider too?"

His grin slid into a more cautious expression. "I'm not from Indelleiria."

She frowned up at him and narrowed her eyes.

"Why should I tell you?" he inquired when she didn't release her stare.

"Because I asked."

Kelin coughed into his hand. "Der, no."

But the captain chuckled. "All right, since you asked. I was born to the nomadic elves of the north— way north. I joined the warrior ranks at a tender age, not by choice, and I was forced to kill people who had done me no wrong."

Der's eyes widened. "Damn."

"Yeah, so next time, don't ask."

She shifted her weight and shoveled some stew into her mouth.

Kelin took another bite, and exclaimed as he chewed, "Elves aren't nomadic. I heard that they build cities and huge, legendary palaces."

The knight chuckled. "Out of the four of us, who do you think knows more about elves?"

"You, sir," he ceded.

"Oh, don't let him bully you." The cook smiled as she arrived on velvet feet. She glided into a seat next to Thalon.

"This food is wonderful, my lady!" Kelin exclaimed.

"You helped make it."

"Yes, well...it's incredible!" He grinned and nearly overturned his bowl.

Her hand snapped out and corrected his dish. "Then don't feed it to the ground."

Jacob grinned. "You know, my lady, that's usually the reaction soldiers have to your food."

"It was yours too, I recall."

He cleared his throat. "In my defense, it is amazing food." Then he turned to Der. "So, Derora, what do you think?"

She narrowed her eyes. "I'm wondering why the camp cook was at our trial."

He sighed. "I meant about the food, kid."

"Oh."

Thalon finished his supper. He looked up to the cook and said, "Thank you."

"You are welcome." She smiled.

Kelin stared down onto his bowl. "Der's not wrong though. No offense, my lady, but why were you there?"

Jacob leaned in and put a hand up to his mouth. "Because she might not cook for us if we didn't indulge her a little bit."

Der stared at him with a flat face and one eyebrow raised.

The cook chuckled with the tinkle of bells. "I know our ways must seem strange to you. But please, call me Evelyn. Or Lady Eve if you insist. Does that help?"

Der did not relinquish the raised eyebrow. "Yes, my lady."

"It is an honor to know your name." Kelin bowed slightly.

"Now we're becoming friends." Her smile melted their defenses. "I'm curious, is Common the only language you know?"

Kelin bobbed his head. "Yes, it is." Beside him, Der shrugged and nodded.

"Times have changed, haven't they?" She nodded to Jacob. "Our captain here grew up speaking a mix of languages, and I remember having to teach him his own tongue."

Jacob stiffened.

Guilt flashed across her face for a fleeting moment. "I also remember when each little kingdom had its own language. It's certainly easier to speak with them now."

"My grandmother spoke Common," Der stated. "I met her once when she visited when I was a child."

The cook laughed and shook her head. "I'm talking about the last of the Centum Wars, dear. That was before your grandmother's time, I'm sure."

"It depends," the knight mused. "One of her grandparents was quarter elven. Not the Wars, of course, but they live longer."

"But those wars ended two thousand years ago," Kelin protested.

"It's because of the Wars that Common was invented," Jacob said. "Well, forced into existence. And too quickly to be easily learned, in my opinion. Palls is still used a lot too, I think."

"Palls?" Der repeated, then thought, *the language of Pallens.*

The cook's eyes faded to focus on a distant destination. "I wonder what the world would've been like today if Pallens had not been slain."

Kelin coughed. "You're referring to King Midan being killed by the Blackhound, right?"

"Correct," the cook replied.

"So why do we speak Common instead of something else?" Der asked.

Lady Eve smiled. "Most races speak their own tongues, as you know, but humans had no unified language."

"You mean there aren't other languages between the elves?" Kelin inquired.

Lady Eve shrugged. "There are dialects, but it's not too removed from the usual. But back then, *everyone* needed to communicate. All the races, and all the different tongues within them. Palls was the medium for a long time, but along with it was the shadow of Pallens, and some people felt in using it that they were submitting to the empire. Thus, Common came to be." She smiled. "It hasn't been allowed to change either, unlike many other tongues. It has to remain stable, because if it changes, we would lose the wide communication path between all peoples. Sometimes, like your antecedents, people just kept on speaking it instead of their mother tongue."

"That's incredible," Kelin breathed.

"Yes," the cook grinned, standing. "Thank you for listening. It's pleasant to find humans who will hear their own history without argument."

Kelin blushed and stammered his thanks.

Thalon held up his bowl. "More please."

"Of course." She took the child's hand. "Come with me." She paused and looked at Der, and her bejeweled eyes unfocused. "I wish you could've met my son. He was just a little older than you when... Well, I'm sure you would've gotten along famously, or died trying to anyway." She led Thalon as they retreated toward the cooking fires.

Der tensed to stand. "Wha—"

"Sometimes she says things," Jacob interrupted. He stared ahead at the fires. "Even she doesn't know what they mean. Don't worry about it."

Her frown deepened. "But—"

"Derora." His voice creaked warningly.

She sighed and picked up her spoon.

Jacob shrugged. "There's a lot more history to the languages."

"Uh," Kelin started. "Are you a soldier or a scholar?"

He chuckled. "Do you want war stories instead?"

"Yes!" Der blurted, a little more enthusiastically than she intended.

"Maybe later." The elf laughed.

"Since they want war stories, why not tell them about the one they're in?" a deeper voice slid out of the shadows. Sir Amthros stepped into the light.

Jacob dropped into Elvish, "Where have you been?"

Der stared at the ground, trying to keep her face blank.

The other knight indicated behind them. "Attending the horses."

Jacob switched to Common as he looked back at the villagers and asked, "What do you know about this war already?"

"Not much," Der replied. "The king and queen are dead. Caleb said they murdered his parents, and if he's the prince..."

Amthros nodded and sighed. "Yes. A tragedy that we cannot fully comprehend. That's why everyone fled Long Range Palace."

Kelin squeaked, "*The* Long Range Palace! I've heard so many tales."

Amthros's face darkened. "None like this."

Der leaned forward into the ensuing silence. "I only know the song of Mendelin. That's the one where the prince dies, right?"

Jacob nodded. "Yes, but it's more story than fact. And, ah, with the way things are happening, let's not talk about dying princes." He turned back to Kelin. "Yes, Kelin, Long Range was magically guarded, and despite that, the chemmen invaded it." He frowned down at his bowl.

Amthros bowed his head. "That was our most sacred ground, and they defiled it with ease. Do you comprehend how impossible that is?"

The villagers shook their heads.

He sighed. "It would be hard to explain. Besides, it isn't your concern." He stood. "Pray excuse me, I have other duties." He nodded to them and departed.

Without anything to say, they returned to eating. But behind them, the Elvish conversation among the duke and his entourage had risen to new levels.

Der looked up at Jacob. "So, well, why don't you take the palace back?"

The other discussion froze.

Jacob shook his head. "Hush, Derora. You're not running this war." He glanced at the duke across the way. He spoke in a low voice, "It's not that simple."

"I realize, but—"

Farallon snapped off a loud comment in Elvish to the people around him. Then they all glared at the four of them. Der growled in her throat. "Captain, they're talking about us." She immediately added, "They have to be, I mean, after all we can't understand them. So what are they saying?"

Jacob set down his bowl. "They're calling you typical humans. That means ignorant or stupid, depending on their mood. You fell for the chemmen ruse, you didn't know you're part-elf, and he's calling me a fool for explaining things to you."

Der tensed to rise, but Jacob's massive hand slammed down on her shoulder. Food sprayed all over her face and shirt. She blinked in surprise, wiping a mushroom off her eyelid.

The knight remained looking at his own bowl and pulled his hand back. "Learn to fight better first, and then learn *when* to fight."

She felt Kelin staring at her. His eyes were wide. "What?" she hissed at him.

He glanced between her and the knight. "You're not..."

She rubbed her shoulder. "I think he'll break something if I try it again."

Jacob snickered and picked up his bowl.

She leaned over and whispered in conspiratorial levels, "So we have to take him out first."

The knight grinned. "Just try it."

"Kelin, you're getting along with the cook, I need you to give everyone food poi—"

"That's it," Jacob interrupted. "Finish up. You've got chores to do."

"We do?" Kelin asked, surprised.

"Yes, I just need to go and find out what they are." He didn't move to stand yet but instead attacked his bowl with his spoon.

Kelin smacked Der on the arm. "Thanks for that." He scowled. "You know he is not letting you get away with your tricks."

She stuffed more stew into her mouth. "What tricks? He can hear what we're saying."

The captain pretended to ignore them.

"Just you...what you do."

But she wasn't watching him. Everything around them had gone quiet. She nodded ahead at the duke, who was glowering at them.

Kelin shivered. "No one believes us, or our story."

Jacob shrugged. "They believe you believe it, at least." He set his spoon down. "You've only heard of the chemmen by legend and don't know the layers of deception they often involve."

Der stabbed her bowl with her spoon. "I think—"

"I know what you think, kid."

"Well, how did they set it up? We were never coerced or given orders—"

"Sir. How did they set it up, sir?" he corrected.

"Sir."

The knight-captain grinned tightly. "I have no idea." He set his dish down. "Before you open your mouth again, it's time for me to go. Some of us have actual work to do. Don't think that I've forgotten about your extra chores." He nodded to them and left.

"Thanks, Der." Kelin rolled his eyes.

She ignored him and chewed her meal, eyebrows narrowed in thought. "He interrupted me at least three times."

"Sometimes, it's the only way to get a word in."

She glared at him and then looked away. "I'm going to ask him if we can have our daggers."

"That's enough," Farallon spat in Common. He stood and stalked toward them where he grabbed Der's collar and hauled her to her feet. He pushed her all the way back to their tent, with Kelin and other elves dogging along on his heels. The duke threw Der inside and followed her in.

She could feel the heat from his glare down at them. After a long silence, his voice dripped, "You disgust me." Der glanced at Kelin, but Farallon snapped, "Not him, girl. You. He's just a regular human you dragged into this. You didn't even know what you are. Part-elf indeed! You were captured aiding a chemmen child. And now you're laughing and making jokes, and asking for a suitable weapon as if nothing's wrong!"

"A dagger's more of a tool," she replied conversationally.

His dark eyes flashed like lightning. "You correct *me?* You can't speak back to me! You were tortured by the chemmen, *and still you understand nothing!*"

She sat there, listening, and stared up at the duke with a cool gaze.

"Then again, how could you?" The sneer on his face almost made him look human. He flared his nostrils. "You can barely fight off a mortal, so how did you face the chemmen? You're a mistake, a fluke! I should send you away. Oh, they'll find and kill you, but you won't be my problem anymore—"

Der punched him in the nose. She didn't hint at her intentions or reveal any tenseness. She just landed a solid strike.

Kelin gasped and half-stumbled, half-rolled away from her. The duke yelped, more out of surprise than anything. He grabbed his face as he staggered back out of the tent.

The cook and the knight-captain came running with Thalon doing his best to keep up. Several other watching elves pressed closer.

The duke pointed. "She attacked me!" He inspected his nose with a gentle prod of his finger. "She broke it." His voice was dull and simple. He sounded as if he didn't believe it happened.

The captain glanced over at Der, who was sitting cross-legged with her hands in her lap, trying to smother any expression.

Farallon whirled back toward her. "I will throw you to the wolves for this!"

"Sir!" The captain's voice was as stiff as a stone column. "They surrendered to me and are therefore prisoners of the Order of the Silver Dawn Dragoon Knights. They are under my charge, not yours."

The duke whipped his volcanic glare to the knight-captain. *"What?"*

Jacob stared straight ahead. "Any punishment to them must go through my order, and as the sole representative, that duty is mine." He took a deep breath. "Sir, may I advise you to go see to your nose? I will see fit punishment delivered here."

Farallon shook with anger. He hurled a fuming glare at Der but then stormed away. Lady Eve held a hand over her mouth, and her shoulders were shaking with suppressed laughter. Kelin looked as though he were melting. The rest of the elves followed the duke with backward glares at the prisoners.

Jacob turned his stern countenance toward Der and approached. She scooted back. He reached out—

Kelin winced—

Der's eyes widened—

Jacob's hand extended—

—and he batted her nose.

Der went cross-eyed. "That's it?"

The knight winked. "Just, for the love of all that is sacred in this world, don't do it again."

Kelin scrambled forward. "That's it?"

Jacob grinned, and Evelyn laughed aloud. He chuckled, "I wish I could've seen it."

The others smiled, a tad apprehensively. The captain shook his head, still grinning. Thalon ventured a chuckle.

"Can we have our daggers, sir?" Der asked.

"No."

Kelin sagged. "I can live with that, but I'm not sure if we can live with the duke."

Jacob nodded. "I don't know what's going to happen next. But for now, just go to sleep."

"What about those extra chores?" Der inquired.

The mirth on his face dissolved. "I think the less of you seen tonight, the better." He ran a hand through his hair and whistled. "I hope that there aren't any other surprises."

Lady Eve shook her head with a half-smirk. "I thought you knew better than to say such things."

***

Two hours later, shouts of alarm echoed throughout the camp. The elves ran to the edge of their campfires' lights. Der, Kelin, and Thalon jumped out of their tent and raced with them. No one glanced at them, much less tried to stop them.

Ahead of them, a figure had appeared like a ghost out of the blackness. He held up a sheathed sword away from his body. He dropped it.

"Dad!" Thalon yelled and charged forward. Kelin grabbed him. The boy struggled, but Kelin scooped him off the ground.

Archers lined up their arrows at the chemman's chest. Jacob held a massive battleaxe steadily. It was a double-headed axe with intricate inlay, and he had it on a short pole without a tremor in his arm.

Der realized that she couldn't recognize this chemman as their savior. He was the same height as the others and had the same dark hair, but she had never witnessed so much anger in anyone's eyes. It was definitely different than she'd seen with the other storm-readers. It had to be him.

His gaze rested on them and then on Thalon. He spoke, "My name is Thistle, and I've come for my son.

216

In exchange, I bring you information. I am not the only traitor in this war. Who do you think sold out your king and queen?"

CHAPTER TWENTY

Another stick snapped like a breaking bone. The burly man winced and cursed his heavy foot. His five companions locked their glares onto him.

They hunched in their dark cloaks and resumed trudging across the clearing. They had tried to blend into the night's darkness so much that they stood out like shadows at noon.

Fear of their priest had whipped them to hunt elves in the dead of night. And worse, the king of Thealith had renewed his purge of devil-worshippers from Second Acron and Duelingar. Had they stayed, they would have likely been lynched.

"We're lost!" The stick-stomper thrust his hands into his armpits. "And it's cold."

"Shut up, man. You ain't done nothing but whine all this time!" the sole woman in the party huffed. She yanked her hood farther over her face. "You ain't the only one that don't wanna be out here."

"I *know*. But they're elves! We'll never find them. Why the hell did it have to be elves?"

"Shut up!" another hissed.

He stomped ahead, bellowing a deep laugh. "We ain't found a single trail to follow! Not a single one! We're twenty leagues away at the very least."

"We've got to be closer than that," the smallest member declared. He was thin, short, and often clumsy, but he had removed the heart from his own daughter's chest despite her screams on Sennha's altar, in exchange for erasing his memories of his dead wife. "Our god guides us."

"Does he now?" the man snorted.

"How dare you!"

"Never mind, the both of you." The woman snapped her fingers. "Has anyone seen Anton?" She spun to look for their missing member.

Shrill whinnies echoed like banshees throughout the trees, and hoofbeats thundered toward them. With a glance at each other, they turned and sprinted. The hooves pounded faster than they could flee.

***

Jacob's axe glinted in the firelight. His other hand was up, ordering everyone to hold their ground.

Der glanced at Thalon in Kelin's grip. She whispered, "If things don't work out here, we may have to take the boy and run."

"Der!" Kelin shook his head.

Thalon squirmed and stretched forward with his hands. "They're gonna kill him!"

"He can't lose both parents, Kelin, no matter what." Der balled her fists while glancing around, trying to find the best way to escape.

The chemman raised his hands higher.

"What about a traitor?" Jacob asked in a deathly severe voice.

Amthros leveled his sword. "He's bluffing to buy time. We should kill him."

"Time for what? He came to us," the captain barked.

"He's chemmen! He's one of them! Whatever he's doing is part of their agenda."

Farallon stormed through the crowd, followed by the duchess and the cook. Lady Eve slid in behind Kelin and Der. She took Thalon's hand. The boy sobbed into her gown, and she stroked his hair.

"I knew it!" the duke exclaimed. "They're following the humans." His nose was in one piece, but not one color. A thunderhead of a bruise decorated his face.

"Who is this traitor?" Jacob demanded.

Thistle stared evenly at the dragoon. "If you don't know who it is, you will lose this war. If I tell you now, you'll kill me. I'll wait until I'm away with my son."

"Then why show yourself?" Jacob's eyes narrowed to slits.

Thistle snorted. "Because you would kill me if I just took him."

"We'll kill you regardless," the duke sneered.

Thistle bowed his head. "I am not in league with the other chemmen. My son should be proof enough."

Silence followed in the wake of his words.

Farallon struggled to breathe. Then he roared, "He's using trickery! There is *no low* they won't fall to!" Behind him, Lady Sabielle clung to his arm to keep him from charging.

Evelyn stepped in front of him, guiding the crying boy. "This child has witnessed his mother slain. Now you wish to murder his father before his eyes too?"

"He is a chemman," Farallon growled. "They murdered our king and queen—my dear friends!"

"This one did not."

"One is the same as another! Who says that this one is even this child's father?"

"Would you know better than me?" Her voice, always with laughter brimming below the surface, had gone cold.

Amthros glared down the length of his sword at the storm-reader. "He has witnessed who we are. I advise we execute him immediately."

Thalon began to sob, and Evelyn turned the boy's head away. "You will do no such thing."

"Then perhaps you should remove the child from this audience." Farallon snapped his fingers.

Jacob bowed his head toward the duke. "We need to leave. Now. He found us despite our forest sanctuary; how long until other chemmen do? If the forest is too weak, we need to move."

Sweat glowed across Farallon's forehead and his face had gone ruby.

"Where will we go?" Lady Sabielle asked.

"Right where we were planning, which I will not repeat here." The knight-captain's eyes flitted back to Thistle. Beside him, Amthros was shaking his head.

"No!" Farallon lowered his voice to a growl, "I absolutely will not use the—*ahem*—in front of him."

Thistle raised an eyebrow. "The tree paths? The chemmen have known how to use those since before the banishment."

Gasps exploded from the elves. Thalon wailed as a torrential argument cascaded. The dam had burst, and the ensuing flood was furious. Blades and metallic arrowheads reflected the moonlight, and everyone's voices howled louder. Thistle remained unmoving.

One voice towered above the rest, "Shut up, the lot of you!"

Der marched forward, fists balled at her sides. "This man saved my life! He's lost his wife. Despite all that, he's still trying to save your sorry skins, and you want to kill him for it, in front of his own child. You're all—"

Jacob coughed. "Derora, did you lie to us when you said that you didn't know Elvish?"

"Oh." She gasped. "No, the healer, Master Peyna..." She waved her hand in the direction of his tent. "It doesn't matter! In all the legends I've ever heard, you elves are supposed to be better than humans. But here you are, arguing about execution of someone who only wants his kid back. This man saved our lives. Now that doesn't make him a hero to anyone else, but it's *another* piece of evidence that demands you don't just murder him." She narrowed her eyes. "You really aren't any better than the rest of us."

Silence descended.

Der inhaled again. "We—"

Farallon's growl trickled with disgust, "I will rip out that tongue, child."

Der readied a fist as Jacob grabbed her shoulder.

The duke broke from his wife's hold. "I am the highest ranked nobility here! Sir Amthros, you are a knight of Indelleiria, and you, Sir Jacob will—"

"I am not under your charge, my lord," Jacob interrupted. "Silver Dawn has never been a part of Indelleiria."

"Oh, but you'll listen to her." He jerked his gaze toward Lady Eve.

The knight paused to glare. "The lady has earned my respect." He turned back to the storm-reader. "You may surrender to me, or them. Your choice."

Thistle nodded to Jacob and stepped away from his dropped sword.

Farallon spun on his heel and stomped off. Sabielle and the others remained, staring. Amthros was glaring at Thistle, tensed but unmoving.

Der inched forward. "Um, sir...?"

"Der," Jacob snapped. "Line up with the chemman, and you're shutting the hell up."

"Yes, sir," she muttered. She raised her hands, allowing them to be tied together, and she gritted her teeth through her new gag.

Thistle, also with his hands bound, raised one eyebrow. "I appreciate the effort."

"'Anks," she attempted.

The knight-captain marched up to them. He looked at Der, shook his head, and blew out a sigh. "You are both prisoners of the Silver Dawn Dragoons. From now on, the rule is that you may only speak to answer a direct question asked of you. And you will be kept away from the duke." He leaned in closer. "Of course, I am the only one of my order here, so keep your ears and eyes open."

CHAPTER TWENTY ONE

The elven caravan stopped before an ancient tree. None of the other trees were even close to its size. Its green leaves glistened, while those surrounding it were already losing their yellowing ones.

Kelin grabbed his forehead. "This headache is too much."

Der had been working on her gag for the last hour and had finally spat it out. "But you said it in Elvish," she whispered.

"Languages aren't meant to be learned this way," he groaned.

The party marched in front of the ancient tree. Duke Farallon bowed low before it. When he spoke, Der did not comprehend any of his words. They were deep, guttural, and rolling like the winds through an endless forest.

Nothing happened.

The duke knelt.

Der leaned toward Thistle. "What are they doing?"

The chemman shook his head and watched straight ahead.

The ancient tree rumbled. With a sound like bones snapping, it began to rise. Leaves trembled against their branches, and roots thrust up in an explosion of soil. The tree twisted and rose until it appeared to be perching on its thinnest roots.

"It's on its tiptoes," Der murmured. "Would you hark at that?"

Beside Farallon, Sabielle knelt, and then, one by one, all the elves dipped low.

"Why are they—" Der bit her tongue when she saw that Thistle had also bowed. Glancing around, she realized she was the only one left standing. Even Kelin and Thalon had taken the hint.

"Oh." She dropped to a knee.

The wind lifted and she felt a drumming coming up from beneath the soil. Her head bobbed up at the sound, just in time to see a huge knot appear underneath its intertwining roots. It darkened and became more solid, swelling to three times the size of a man.

"It's a tunnel," she breathed.

The duke and duchess stepped into the knothole and vanished. Lady Eve, with Kelin and Thalon in tow, was next. Two by two, the elves entered the tree and disappeared. Then the horses went.

Der and Thistle were almost last, with two guards marching behind them. She hesitated, because up close it definitely wasn't a tunnel. It was a knot—a dark, twisted wooden knot.

Thistle stepped into the tree and vanished. Der stuck one toe forward and watched it pass through the wood with the resistance of smoke. She closed her eyes and hopped ahead. When she opened them, she expected to learn what the inside a tree was like. At the very least, she wanted to witness a large earthen tunnel with gnarled roots swinging to and fro overhead. But, with the pressure of a stiff breeze, she was blinking at the sky.

It was a much deeper blue here. She gasped and then inhaled again. And again—it was hard to breathe. The air was cold; it stung as it hit her lungs, and she couldn't get enough.

"It's the altitude. Just keep breathing," one of the guards murmured after he had stepped through behind her.

She nodded, still heaving. She looked up. A forest of razor straight pines in all directions, their needles weighed down with a layer of snow. But she wasn't looking at the trees.

Der had never seen mountains before, and they surrounded her now. She'd always heard them described as hills, only bigger. Now she could see that was like calling a castle only a bigger house. These mountains rose from the ground as if the fist of a god had punched them through the surface. Fresh snow had recently salted the peaks over layers of ancient snow.

She squinted. It was hard to tell if some of those distant lumps on the horizon were mountains or clouds.

Then she turned to see where she had come from. There was a towering pine in the center of a ring of smaller trees. It was twisting as it sank into the rocky soil.

"Welcome to the Riverfall Mountains!" Jacob grinned, throwing an arm wide as he approached. "We are on the edge of nowhere now."

Der finally felt as if she'd caught her breath, if only momentarily. She pointed back to the tree. "But Thistle said the chemmen knew about the tree paths, so won't they follow us?"

Jacob's smile dissolved. "Perhaps, but they can't guess where we went, and there are hundreds of tree paths on this great earth." His eyes shot to the chemmen prisoner.

Beside her, Thistle shrugged.

She frowned. "They'd know you're returning to Indelleiria; it's honestly the only place you'd go. Even I can see that."

The knight sighed. "You're not the only one who's given this some thought, kid. This is not a route they'd expect because there is no way into the kingdom from this particular path."

"This isn't Indelleiria?"

He laughed and shook his head. "This is still the Wild Lands, just on the other side. But we'll be out of here soon. And thankfully too, because Indelleiria is safer than the Wild Lands."

"Yeah, isn't that what the king and queen thought?"

His face went rigid. "I like that you speak your mind—or forcefully demonstrate it as the case may be—but shut your damned mouth."

"She's not wrong," Thistle said. "There is someone whom you cannot trust. They might've left a sign."

Amthros, riding his chestnut warhorse, approached. "Some troubles, Sir Jacob?"

"No," he called back. "Just gagging the prisoner again." But he didn't raise a hand toward Der.

The other knight chuckled. "Indeed. I bring news that the duke has decreed we camp as soon as we come to the river."

"Of course." Jacob nodded.

The next few hours oscillated between exhilaration and exhaustion as they marched, forcing their own path on the shallower slopes of the mountain. Der had never known her muscles to grow heavy so quickly or her lungs to give out so easily.

The soil crinkled and slid beneath her feet. Everything seemed to be in brighter colors here. The green on the pine forests was as crisp as the air, the blue sky was sapphire, and the clouds were so blinding it burned to stare at them too long.

Their path took them farther down. The horses slipped on the bare rocks and loose soil. Soon, they came in sight of a small clearing, littered with pines and some other trees Der didn't recognize. They were white with brown stripes, and they looked normal enough, but she'd never seen pale bark before.

A stream rushed through the open space, hurtling its way down between the mountains. It couldn't have been more than two feet at its deepest, and massive boulders squatted throughout its path. Ice lined its edges, but the water was too quick for the fingers of early winter to catch it just yet.

"The river is the only approach to the kingdom from here," Jacob whispered.

Der frowned. "I think I see the problem. The stream's too small and full of stones. Uh, maybe if we jump between the rocks..." She looked around; she couldn't be the only one who saw this.

"Don't worry about it." He smirked. "Indelleiria's borders are more protected than most. Unless you have an invitation to enter, you'd wind up boulder hopping for the rest of your life."

"Yeah, Laurel had mentioned something about that." She wondered how the chemmen broke through to murder the king and queen. Maybe this meant Thistle had to be telling the truth. Then she shuddered at the thought of herself doubting the man who had saved her and Kelin.

Jacob said, "Now, if you'll excuse me, I've got to release the horses."

She sighed. "You've got the most powerful beasts I've ever seen. It's a shame to lose them."

"Lose them? No." He shook his head. "They'll meet us where we're going. My mount knows the way, and the chemmen aren't going to bother with a pack of wild horses if they are somehow nearby."

"Is he right?" Der turned to Thistle.

The chemman shrugged. "I wouldn't."

"But what about the border, sir? How can horses find it and people can't?"

Jacob's grin slipped lower. "Der, trust me."

"But they're *horses*, and gods love 'em, but they're not the brightest animals out there."

"Trust me, Der," Jacob repeated as he walked toward the herd. He clapped his hands as he approached.

Across the field, she watched his massive black horse rear. He released a thunderous whinny and cantered around the other mounts. The sunlight glinted off his hooves and hair and shone like a thousand diamonds. He then charged and the other horses followed him, swept up in his wake.

Jacob walked away while Der observed as the herd grew smaller until they seemed to melt into the scenery as a mirage. She glanced at Thistle. "I guess we can rest for a while now. I'm aching."

"Rest is for the dead during war, child." She turned to see Amthros approaching. He gestured for her to hold out her hands. She obliged and he cut her bonds. "Come along, we've work that won't do itself."

She jogged to match pace with his stride, glancing back at Thistle and his guards. "What are we doing?"

"Building canoes."

She stopped, her feet sliding in the soft dirt. "But I don't know how to make a canoe."

"Then what a great opportunity you have to learn."

"All right, so you don't think I'm going to escape now?"

"It wasn't escape that we were concerned with." He grinned.

She followed the knight down an incline to where the sounds of axes were adding to the music of water and birds. Most of the trees up here weren't that thick, but she noticed there were quite a few larger trunks in the valley.

She saw Kelin wielding a hatchet at the base of a pine. As he swung the blade, his face didn't bear the usual resentment she had come to know since departing home.

Amthros pointed to a pile of tools. "Get an axe. Then cut off the branches from the downed trunks."

She lifted an axe. It was much lighter and thinner than what she was used to.

Amthros chuckled and pointed. "Hold your hand near the base, and don't wrap your thumb around your other fingers."

Der reddened and muttered, "This handle is just so scrawny." She knew how to swing an axe. Then she brightened. "But at least I can hit someone with this."

He laughed softly. "Derora, there are no chemmen or cultists up here."

"But can't, like, Sennha tell them where to find us or something? What if he tells them how to use the tree paths?" She had been certain that deities didn't tell people where to go and what to do, but she hadn't thought they spoke directly to people either.

He blinked. "Gods don't work that way, child."

"They might." Her shoulders slumped. "I should probably tell Sir Jacob."

Amthros frowned. "Tell him what?"

"That's the thing, I really don't want to because it didn't work out for me in Duelingar, but I *have* to know."

"Derora, if you know something, then absolutely tell us."

She waved her hand. "It's not about the storm-readers."

He relaxed. "Then is it about the cultists?"

"It's..." She exhaled.

"How about you tell me?" He tapped his chest. "I promise not to tell anyone since it's not about the chemmen, and I can advise you whether or not to inform Sir Jacob."

She stared at him. Then she licked her lips. "I think Sennha might be sending people to kill me. I mean, those cultists found us easily enough, right? It was more than just them hunting the outlaw—had to be. Right?"

"Slow down." But his expression wrinkled into worry.

"He thinks I'm one of his ancient enemies or something, when he spoke to me—"

"Stop." The knight was shaking his head. He whistled. "No, do not inform Sir Jacob. As a dragoon knight, he may be required to take further measures, even though we know you're definitely no cultist yourself."

"What does that mean?"

"It means you should probably speak to a priest of a good god, child."

She stiffened. "I tried, but he panicked. I swear, I'm—I'm just me."

"I know." The knight offered a small smile. "I'm grateful that you trusted me with this."

"Yeah." She stared down at the axe in her hand. Then she looked up. "Will you go with me when we're somewhere we can find a priest? Because last time... Uh, well, you're intimidating, and I'd appreciate that."

He laughed. "Thank you. And yes, if we all survive this, I will." He stepped back. "But for now, we each have our duties. And yours are canoes."

"Yes, sir." He left and she got to work.

Hacking away the branches wasn't a complex task. Her hands scraped and bled against the rough wood, but she didn't mind.

All around her, the elves were turning trunks into log shapes, which were then whittled down into even finer forms. They seemed master craftsmen, quickly transforming the hulks of timber into sleek canoes that were much narrower than any Der had ever seen in Riversbridge. They were also transforming some of the larger branches into short paddles.

When her arms could no longer support their own weight, she wandered down to the stream. No one stopped her as she slipped between the boulders to reach the water. She knelt and dipped her hands into the freezing current.

Its taste was music to her tongue and contained none of the dirt or other sediments she was used to in a drink from a river. It also surpassed any ale, cider, or wine she had ever tried. She blinked. This was just water. She sat back on her heels while it continued to cool and soothe.

Farther up the stream, she heard voices. They carried on as if she wasn't there. Then again, she wasn't sure if they had seen her between the rocks. A male voice pleaded, "Have you heard news of the Windgates? My sister..."

Silence. A second male voice answered, "I have." For a few moments, there was only the sound of the water rushing down the mountains, beginning its journey of thousands of miles. "You may not wish to know."

"I do, but I am afraid."

"You should be."

"But I must."

Der heard splashing upstream as the voices quieted. She popped her head up, but the boulders obscured her sight and she couldn't find the speakers.

She gasped as the water in front of her glowed golden. Stretched pictures, like small paintings, floated past her. More followed, the images elongating and disintegrating into the current.

She dipped her hand to catch the next picture as it passed and felt herself being dragged into the water. She dug her heels into the bank and heaved backward, but it was too late!

She opened her eyes to discover herself staring up at a massive pair of blue-white barred gates. They were in the shape of wings, and a white wall extended out from either side of them as far as she could see. She could see enough over the wall that thunderheads threw lightning and tornadoes howled and smashed against the gates, but they held and the breeze on this side was a passing kiss on the air.

She whirled around when she heard a scream. An elven woman, fair and slender, fell to the ground with a chemman on her heels.

Der charged the chemman, bringing up her small axe. The storm-reader didn't even look up at her, and she heaved it down into his skull...where it slid right through his head. Her hand—and the blade—had gone through him with no impact.

She scrambled to regain her balance. *What the hell?* she thought, spinning as the chemman brought his sword down through the elf's chest. The horror as she died seared itself into Der's memory. She swung the axe and again it passed through the chemman's body like a ghost.

She heaved it for another try with the same result. Meanwhile, the storm-reader turned and sprinted toward the town in front of them.

Der rubbed her eyes as she ran. The white stone of the gates constructed the settlement below. It appeared as a city in the clouds with its towers and spires. But smoke was rising all over the town.

The chemmen had overrun it. Elves bolted in all directions. None of them were in armor or had swords.

She chased the first chemman through the gate, but the heat of the flames forced her to cover her face and run deeper into the avenues. A running elf passed right through her as he fled several storm-readers.

She stepped around bloodied and broken bodies, feeling the heat from their skins. But she couldn't touch them. She ventured down an avenue, passing a tavern with a tree in its center, spreading its branches and leaves out to create a roof. It must have once been beautiful, but now, it was burning. More corpses littered the place. Half-eaten meals rested on tables.

She clenched a fist. She could do nothing but watch. By what she had heard by the stream, this had already happened. She still swung the axe through several more storm-readers. It didn't do anything, but it made her feel better.

CHAPTER TWENTY TWO

Der blinked and found that she was sitting on the stream's edge. No more golden pictures flowed by. She stuck her face into the icy water and rubbed her cheeks furiously. She yanked herself back and gasped for air, all the while trying not to notice how much her hands were shaking.

She remembered that first elf's expression, that mask of fear.

She picked up her axe and stumbled uphill to the canoes and back to work where she swung the blade against logs for as long as she could make herself.

Something inside her snapped. She threw the axe down and marched over to where Jacob was merrily swinging his own axe against a felled trunk. He wasn't using his battleaxe, she noticed, and saw it on a special sheath slung across his back that crowded next to his sword. She put her hands on her hips. "*Why* the hell are we building canoes when the river is mostly ankle deep?"

He struck his axe into the wood and stretched. "Are you even old enough to curse, Der?"

"Damn right I am." She pointed to the water. "There is no way we can pilot these things."

"'Sir,' you forgot 'sir.' This is your final warning."

"All right, sir, there is no way we can pilot these things down the river, sir. You, sir, yourself, sir, said there was no way into Indelleiria, sir."

He grinned. "We could if the river were higher. The rapids and tight turns will be a challenge, but one we can handle." He winked. "We have thought of this; don't worry. By the way, make sure your tent won't flood when it rains, because it's going to rain quite a bit."

She stared at him, but at least pondering this shut out the sights of the Windgates.

"Der, floods rise fast up here. We ride down on the flood on the river, while the water here drops down to what it was. No one can follow us."

"Right," she managed.

He sighed. "Just stay in your tent—the rain will be cold, and we don't have the right gear for it. It's hard to make it rain when it's time for snow. It's already getting into winter up here."

Der tapped the ground with her boot. "I don't think we'll need as many canoes as we've got though. I counted a score in our party, and even at two to a canoe, we have five too many."

"Do you pick up every little detail?" He cocked an eyebrow down at her.

She shrugged.

"Another party is meeting up with us." He lifted the axe again. "So tell me, where are all the sentries?"

"There's two on the path we came from," she answered and then scowled in thought. "Uh, I didn't see any more."

"Still, you got some noticing done. As for the rest..." He grinned. "They're watching over us."'

She followed his gaze up into the towering pines. "Oh."

"Now, if you don't get back to work, you'll be going without a meal."

"Yes, sir."

After a few more hours of labor, she met up with Kelin, and Jacob instructed them to put up tents for the camp.

The knight-captain came around to inspect after they'd finished. He nodded. "Good job. Now, go bathe your feet. You've got to do that every night. Your feet take care of you, so you need to care for them. After that, I order you to retire to your tent and stay there." He raised his hands. "Well, what are you waiting for?"

***

"Der! Kelin!" A voice pounced out of the darkness. Thalon came flying through the tent flap and landed between them. The soup in the wooden bowl he carried in his hands splashed as he slammed down into a seat, sending some of it soaring for freedom.

"Easy, little one," Lady Eve called. She carried a second dish. "We brought you both supper. It's leftover stew, but that's what we have out here."

"Yeah, stew a king would die for." Kelin snatched the bowl from Thalon. "You know, I think I might be too exhausted to eat."

Der accepted hers from the cook. "You, Sir Jacob, and Sir Amthros are the only people who will even speak with us."

She smiled wanly. "The others may have been more willing if you weren't so antagonistic toward the duke. Although, your speech probably saved this little one's father for now."

Thalon's head bobbed up, looking ready to cry. "I want to see him!"

"He's fine, my child." Evelyn's soft smile melted the tension. "This is a proving ground for the three of you, and though you have faced trials, this ordeal is far from over."

Der took a bite and chomped down on the spoon hard. "Ow!" She started mashing her food. "This is not what I expected from the elves—with your exception, my lady. I will say that I am not impressed."

Evelyn's smile dipped. "What you said troubled them because much of it is true—and they don't wish to admit it. Yes, we do not share in the detriments of age, but we are living creatures, and we must learn what is right and what is wrong. Wicked things tempt us. You have also met us when we are unbalanced due to tragedy. We've forgotten how to appreciate these trials that humans face every day."

Kelin sucked down a mouthful. "I can't imagine the elves making the same mistakes we do."

"Oh, we can." She nodded. "But since we're older, however, we're supposed to already know what humans are always having to learn." She sighed and the glow in her sapphire eyes faded. "To let you in on something, I married a human. But he perished, long ago."

"Old age?" Der ventured.

She shook her head. Her voice creaked, "No, he'd found a way to remain young. We wed in secret, since Indelleiria couldn't know. I met him while cooking for an army, as I am now. This wouldn't be recent to you, of course, but we were fighting the chemmen then too..." She looked back up, her eyes bright again. "However, that is past. Presently, I am entrusting Thalon's safety to you. As you know, most of the elves do not approve of his heritage."

"But—" the boy protested, pushing out his lower lip.

She smiled down at him. "You're a gods-sent gift, and now you have new friends to help you through these heartbreaks."

Kelin held up his hands. "But we're prisoners."

The lady lifted one regal eyebrow. "I cannot care for him at this time. And I know that you will fight on his behalf."

Der nodded. "Of course."

"Good." Lady Eve declared, "Then Thalon is your charge, both of yours. If there is a traitor amongst us, I know that Thalon will be safe with you."

Thalon snuggled close to Der, who nearly pushed him away in reflex.

"Do you think there is one?" Kelin asked.

The cook shrugged. "It may be a lie to sow discord and doubt in our ranks. A ruse, which if it is, you can see is working. Or perhaps a less insidious bluff to purchase another day."

Der stared. "You didn't answer the question."

The elf matched her stare without blinking, and Der felt her eyes water against those multi-faceted gems. The lady finally replied, "No, I do not think the chemman is lying, but I also do not think that he can be trusted not to lie." She left, leaving only the lingering scent of spring flowers.

Der frowned, sitting straight-backed, holding her bowl, and looking both miffed and perplexed.

Kelin sighed and tossed a pebble through the small crack in the tent flap. "So, who wants to tell a story?"

"I just want to hear the story where Mama's alive and Dad's not tied up," Thalon muttered.

"And the elves never caught us," Kelin chimed. "We ran away from the chemmen and lived out our lives in the citadel of Pallens."

"Kelin." Der swatted his shoulder.

He shrugged.

"On the whole," she pulled her knees up under her chin, "I think I like being the elves' prisoner better."

Outside the thin canvas walls, the first crash of thunder reverberated between the nearby peaks. A raindrop crashed into the roof of their tent, followed by an unending rush. Der peeked out and saw the rain leaving tiny craters in the dirt. The waning sunlight caught the fat drops, and thousands of individual rainbows glistened before they kissed the ground.

***

Two canoes slipped through the rain and darkness into the rapids, disappearing down the river.

Farther up the water's edge, and a world away through the blanketing torrent, Thistle dodged as nimbly as a dancer. The knife slammed down again, whistling through the air and rain, never finding its target. The masked attacker was tall but armed only with the knife.

The ceaseless deluge tugged their feet deeper into the mud with each step. The thunderstorm roared, only a few hundred yards above them, and the lightning was blinding.

Thistle's hands were still bound in front of him, but against a knife he had time. Time enough for his guards to arrive with their big, shiny swords. And that raised the question of why his assailant had chosen such a small blade. Would his sword have been recognizable?

He knew winning a knife fight was usually never as quick as one fatal strike. An attacker would leave himself open for counterattack if he dove for that lethal thrust with a short blade. So for now, the would-be assassin played it safely. After all, he had the only weapon.

Thistle held up his hands to block a facial slash, and the knife sliced across his forearms. He was bleeding from a dozen cuts along his arms, hands, and sides. The attacker never exposed himself for the chemman to grab him.

Thistle's eyes flickered over his assailant's shoulder. Where in the corners of hell were his guards? The thought stole over him like the icy, rising waters in the river: what if this was a guard? Several people who wished him dead had the authority to order such an action. He was certain that the attacker was not a chemman because a storm-reader would try to rescue him first.

He curled his wrists in toward his body as he felt another lick of the knife across his arms. He grunted but didn't react overtly to the new gash.

His foot connected with his attacker's knee in a satiating crack. The attacker slid in the mud, swinging with the blade. Thistle leaned back, and the knife passed above his chest.

His hands snaked out, and he snatched his assailant's wrist. He squeezed until he heard his opponent hiss. He kicked again.

The masked man jerked out of his grasp, and Thistle slipped in the mud, trying to keep his balance. The assassin limped back and dropped the knife.

Thistle reached out, but the attacker jumped away. He turned and ran, melting into the rain.

The chemman took a few steps after him but stopped.

He raised the knife and cut the cords on his wrists. He sighed and looked into the open, inviting darkness beyond the camp. Then he sat down on the cold, soaking ground and waited.

CHAPTER TWENTY THREE

Kelin poked the cloth of the tent; it wasn't the heavy canvas he was used to. Instead, it felt light and slick to the touch. Nor was it covered with a layer of wax on the outside to prevent the rains from seeping inside. He hadn't bothered studying their shelter before, having been too busy worrying about everything else. Currently, it was the most interesting thing he had.

This was better than last time, he reminded himself, because he wasn't being tortured. Now, all he did was sit in the dark and imagine terrible things.

Der had her back to him and was staring out at the endless rain on the other side of the tent. Thalon sat between them.

The cloth flap moved on its own. Kelin backed away from it. A blond elf stuck his head in and entered. He smiled, a little tiredly. "I don't know what to say, except that this is the *last* place I expected you to be."

Caleb slid inside and collapsed down to his knees. Kelin and Der stared. The elf wiped an eye and gasped, "But I'm so thankful you're here. I—"

"Caleb!" Der lunged forward and tried to tackle and hug him at the same time.

He embraced Der briefly but tightly. "I thought you were dead. Both of you."

She smirked. "We managed."

Beside her, Kelin paled and gulped. Thalon reached up and patted his shoulder.

Caleb's voice cracked, "I should have never abandoned you. It's my fa—"

"Stop," she interrupted. "We made it through."

"Did we?" Kelin growled.

Caleb dropped his chin. "I hope so."

"I was more worried about you," Der said as she glanced at Kelin in confusion.

The elf nodded, still staring at the ground. "Thank you." His gaze rose to the child. "And you must be Thalon. Well met."

The boy scooted behind Kelin and peered around him at Caleb.

The elf's voice wavered, but only a little. "I've heard much about you, and I am glad to see that you are just a child."

Thalon shook his head from near Kelin's back.

Der rounded on the prince. "Where have you been?"

His smile dipped. "Thanks to you, I escaped."

Kelin grunted. "Yeah. Thanks to us. We wouldn't have been tortured if you hadn't—if you hadn't—"

"Kelin!" Der gasped.

Caleb slouched and squeezed his hands together. "I regret what happened to you, Kelin, with all my heart." His eyes darkened as he stared into the distance. He pulled his knees to his chest. "You don't know how badly I was losing the battle to myself. And then I found you."

Kelin snorted.

"But I ran away again, convinced I'd left you to die."

Der pushed herself in front of Kelin. "What happened to you? And we didn't know you were royalty!"

"I had no idea you were nobility, Lady Saxen."

Der tensed, but Caleb shook his head and said, "I escaped in Second Acron and soon joined with others. After that, my party met with those who have kept you prisoner. We're going to Riverfall Haven, but it's treacherous to gain entrance from where we are now." He looked up, but his face remained somber. "I'm grateful to make this final push with friends."

"Are we still friends?" Kelin's voice echoed off the canvas walls. "You didn't warn us. You didn't even try to rescue us either. They crushed my teeth!"

"Kelin!" Der snapped.

Caleb pressed his lips together and bowed his head. His tone dropped, "We replaced your teeth. I have been informed about what happened with you."

Kelin folded his arms. "Now you sound like a real elf."

"So? We are still friends!" Der narrowed her gaze at him. "Or we were tortured for nothing."

He didn't back down from her glare.

"Stop it." Thalon sniffed and crawled out from behind Kelin. "We're all hurting."

They stared at him.

Caleb forced a tight smile. "He's right. We've all suffered, and it's not a contest." He looked at the child. "I lost my mother too, Thalon."

The boy looked toward the prince. "Do you cry?"

Caleb nodded. "Yes, I do. Do you?"

Thalon gazed up at him, studying the prince's face. Finally, he bobbed his head.

Kelin shivered. "I am still angry."

Caleb bowed his head. "It was *never* my intention to abandon you to such a fate. I should have held hope for your survival and done something to ensure it. For that, I am sorry."

"All right. All right. It's not you I'm angry with anyway." Kelin breathed out and loosened his shoulders, but his expression remained tensed. Caleb smiled, although it didn't reach his eyes.

Thalon hunched down and didn't look up. "My dad has something to tell you. It's important."

Caleb leaned away from the boy. "Do you know what it is?"

He shook his head. "Mama said we had to find you. She said, 'We need to find Prince Eddie'."

Der snapped her fingers. "Right, it was Ed-something."

"Edillon, Derora," the elf replied.

She shrugged.

Kelin snorted, "I don't even know what to call you. Your highness, your grace, your majesty?"

The prince reddened. "Caleb is sufficient. I am not wishing to advertise my presence. And... I haven't earned my actual name." His face brightened. "Besides, Kelin, I believe that you are the odd one here. You're the only one in this tent who doesn't have elven ancestry."

Kelin blinked. "I am the only real human here, aren't I?"

"I am human!" Der cupped her hands over her ears. "This is so little that it doesn't mean anything. It sure didn't help at our trial."

Caleb shook his head. "No, it had an impact with the judges."

"Not Farallon," Kelin muttered.

"She broke his nose, Kelin."

"But that was after the trial!" she protested. "And I'm not sure they've treated me better for it."

"It means more than I think you can appreciate. The duke thought you were a part-elf willingly helping a chemman."

"I was." She crossed her arms. "The good one."

Caleb scowled. "You don't under—"

"My dad is good!" Thalon shouted.

Caleb stiffened, but he said, "I certainly pray it is so."

Der looked up. "So, Caleb, you're going to let us go, right? No more being prisoners?"

He shook his head. "I can't. The knight-captain would have to do that."

"Oh." She deflated. "Sir Jacob probably won't."

Kelin said, "He and the cook are about the only ones who have given us a chance."

"Amthros too," Der added.

Caleb nodded. "Makes sense. I think the lady and Jacob and are the ones who have had the most contact with humans. Especially Sir Jacob—most of Silver Dawn is human these days, I believe."

"Oh, I knew that!" Der blurted. "Because they're a dragoon army. I mean, I should have known that."

After a moment, Kelin asked, "Did Thistle have a trial too?"

Caleb's face tightened. "Not exactly. He was brought before a tribunal. However, before formal proceedings could begin, he swore on Carenth and Ahtome."

"What?" Kelin burst.

Der shrugged. "Makes sense." It was common among humans too, to swear on a god the person didn't follow. The oath obliged the god to punish the person if he lied, and the god wouldn't necessarily be favorable to the person because he wasn't a follower.

Caleb whispered, "But can you understand what that means to us to hear a chemman do that?"

Kelin asked, "Isn't it the same?"

Caleb shook his head. Then he said, "Well, I suppose it is. We never expected him to know it was something he could do."

Der cocked her head. "So what information did Thistle have?"

"Only that there is an elven traitor." Caleb sighed. "The tribunal, well, you can guess the good duke's opinion. But because Thistle surrendered to Silver Dawn, they could do nothing without the knight-captain's consent. Sir Jacob spared his life, for now, but if he doesn't name someone..." He looked away.

Thalon looked up with tears shining in his eyes.

The prince's face remained stern. "We'll be on the river within the hour. These are dangerous rapids, but you're in skilled hands."

"You know," Kelin mused, "we've never been on a river before. Not like this."

The corner of Caleb's mouth inched up. "Then learn to paddle quickly."

The tent flap rustled again, and an elven guard poked his head inside. "Excuse me, your highness, you're needed by the water."

"Of course." Caleb backed toward the entrance. "You don't know how much it means to me that you survived, even though I did not have a hand in it. Farewell." And he was gone.

Thalon shivered and grabbed one of the blankets. Kelin helped him to get it around his shoulders. The temperature was barely treading above freezing.

Der listened to the rain and the sounds of the camp beyond. Snatches of conversation were audible, but she didn't understand anything over the roar of the river.

She pushed the tent flap open wider. "Let's get something to eat."

"We're not supposed to leave," Kelin said.

She shrugged. "We're allowed until someone stops us. Now come on; I'm hungry."

***

Around the camp, the rainfall passed with only a few drops trailing behind. The clouds broke apart and the moon peeked through. A small party edged close to the raging waters. Thistle stood to meet them from where he had been sitting, surrounded by guards on three sides and the river on the fourth.

"This is the end." Caleb's eyes glinted in a splinter of moonlight. "Unless you give us a name."

Thistle met the prince's gaze. Palming the recovered knife, he studied the faces of Jacob and Amthros.

Amthros snorted. "We cannot trust him. No matter what he says."

The storm-reader stared at him. The knight was less than a foot away and within easy striking distance of the hidden knife.

Thistle cleared his throat. "The chemmen would not do anything as gross as write it by hand, but from what I've deduced, it's your Duke Farallon. He betrayed your king and queen."

Amthros gasped in surprise, while Caleb and Jacob fought to keep their expressions neutral.

Thistle continued as smooth as a knife trailing through water. "He should be here, but where is he? Where is his duchess? I witnessed a small party leave on the river. I assume to advise whoever is ahead in Riverfall of your arrival. But would the duke himself need to go? His obligation is to you."

"You're lying," the prince hissed, retreating a step.

"These attacks began with the king and queen, and no enemy should have had access to them. Someone close to them aided the chemmen."

Jacob's face remained as stone. "It makes sense, I have to grant you that, but so do the best lies."

"*I* don't believe you." Caleb was shaking his head. "The duke would never— He helped my mother and father found this kingdom."

Amthros growled beneath his breath but said nothing.

Thistle swung his hand in front of himself and raised an eyebrow, keeping the knife hidden.

The prince sighed. "I will not act against one of my own on the word of my enemy."

Thistle bowed his head. "As your majesty pleases."

Caleb took another step back to take all of them into his view, including the silent guards. "This is in our confidence. Speak of it to no one." He looked straight at Thistle. "I will respect Sir Jacob's choice to spare your life. And I suspect you may be withholding something more."

"I am, but the weight of my message has already fallen into your hands." Thistle remained unmoving.

"I understand, sir prince." Jacob nodded and then frowned. The knight-captain glanced around, and his scowl darkened. "It's quiet."

"That river is anything but quiet," Amthros replied.

"Ignoring that, it's quiet."

"Is anything wrong, sir knight?" Caleb asked.

The massive elf shrugged. "I don't know. I'm going to check on the sentries. You should prepare to depart."

CHAPTER TWENTY FOUR

Kelin yawned and stretched. The thick, creamy soup had filled him to the brim, and he surprised himself to learn that he wasn't sick of soup yet. It was sweet, spicy, and above all, hot on a freezing, wet night. It even stayed warm in his stomach and spread its soothing fingers to the rest of his body.

He rubbed his belly, grinning, as he ambled around the camp. He moseyed over to Der and Thalon. "You know, I think I am feeling better."

"Good," she answered. "How are you doing, Thalon?"

The boy stared at his boots. "Fine."

"Where's Lady Eve, Kelin?" she asked. "She's usually never far from the fire."

Kelin shook his head. "I didn't see her, but there was a ladle spilled on the ground. I can't say I know her well, but I couldn't imagine her being clumsy enough to drop anything." He shrugged but frowned.

Der also shrugged and pointed toward the almost-deafening river, which had flooded much of the little valley. "Perhaps she left already. They must've launched two boats 'cause I see two of them missing."

Thalon's head snapped up. "Do you hear that?"

Kelin frowned. "No."

"I don't hear anything but the water..." Der trailed off.

It was nothing but the rapids. Kelin shifted his weight. The cold wind shook his nerves loose, and he trembled. He looked into the breeze and listened. Now he could hear something crashing through the trees, coming toward them.

Amthros ran up while drawing his sword. "Something's not right."

Caleb was behind him. He shook his head at them. "Perhaps the chemmen found us."

"But I thought Jacob said they couldn't," Der protested.

The prince glanced at her but turned back to the knight. "Sir Amthros, are we ready to launch?"

A guttural dissonance echoed throughout the camp.

Der tilted her head. "A growl?"

Kelin gulped. The crunching of foliage grew closer. Glaring moonlight spread over the area as the clouds drifted away.

Six people lurched toward them along the river, emerging from the forest between the tents and the canoes. Kelin tried to swallow again, but nothing moved in his throat.

"That's not the chemmen." Der inched in the direction of the approaching figures. "Sennha! They're followers of Sennha—I see a bracelet with his mark!" She stiffened and half-turned toward the elves, Kelin, and Thalon. "Is it me?"

"What?" Kelin barked.

"Never mind!" She clenched a fist. "They got through when the chemmen couldn't last time. D-did the storm-readers use them like hunting dogs? How did they follow us *here?*"

Kelin's nostrils flared, and he recognized the scent of blood. He staggered back and saw the dried blood caked over their wounds. No one could survive those cuts. Beside him, Der nodded to him, watching the cultists shamble toward them.

Thalon tugged on her shirt while starting to back away.

Caleb pulled Der by her shoulder. He freed his sword from his sheath, and it mirrored the moonlight around the camp. His voice was as pale as his face. "Undead."

Kelin felt his mouth dry as he stared at the cultists.

They lumbered faster toward them.

Amthros took a step in retreat. "They're between us and the canoes."

"But the chemmen—" Der started.

"They—they…" The prince shook himself and then shouted, "To the trees!" He darted to the nearest pine. "We can destroy them from above. Then we flee."

Kelin whipped to the trees standing like sentinels, tall and unyielding. He also saw that they looked slippery, dripping with rain and snow. Caleb sheathed his sword as he and the other elves scrambled up into the branches.

"I don't believe this," Kelin breathed as he followed the prince. His gaze flickered up into the dark heights. He lifted Thalon so that the boy could grasp the prince's extended hand. The lowest branches were above his head, and he was sure he couldn't jump like an elf.

He twisted toward the advancing creatures. "I don't underst—"

Caleb climbed but looked down. "They're puppets, Kelin!"

"But where are the storm-readers?"

The prince gritted his teeth as he pulled himself higher. "Not far behind." Kelin watched him clench his fingers on a branch and then raise his head, scanning for the other elves in the trees. "Archers!"

Kelin glanced around. Those with bows drew their arrows from lidded quivers tied to their legs. Perhaps there were thirty elves, and not all of them fighters.

He stared up into the pine in front of them; the branches were a network of ladders. Wet, slick ladders. The elves balanced on the thin branches easily enough, but Kelin wasn't sure about his own weight.

He and Der spun to see the undead cultists were less than ten feet away. They shambled directly at them. Looking around, he realized they were the last people on the ground.

"Here!" Amthros reached down from the next tree over. Der shoved Kelin, and they ran toward him. Kelin tossed up his hand, and with a grunt of effort, the knight of Indelleiria hauled him up into the tree. He nodded to Kelin and leaped higher into the branches. The young man lowered his arm to Der.

"Hurry!"

She hesitated, looking between him and the undead.

"Der!"

She half-turned to face the three cultists stumbling toward her. Kelin snapped his gaze at them. Now that they were closer, he could see bits of stringed flesh and fur hanging from the nearest one's fingers, and he wondered what animals hadn't been fast enough to escape.

"Don't you dare! They're undead!" he screamed.

"That's why I'm going to." The smile that split her lips scared him more than the walking dead.

She ran back toward the tents.

Above him in the trees, time was as taut as a drawn bowstring. It quivered with unreleased energy, straining against the tension. Everyone inhaled the last breath of peace.

As soon as Der had ducked between the rows of tents, the elven archers let their arrows fly. They struck the bodies of the undead in tight spreads, but the cultists stumbled forward, unabated.

Der nearly knocked down a tent as she yanked the flap open. She lunged inside, and her fingers closed around the hilt of a sword. It was light and balanced, and its edge was as sharp as the stinging cold. She whirled and jumped back outside.

She smiled as she spun toward the undead. She didn't know why. Her heart felt caged in her chest, and it would escape if it could, but she savored the rush.

Caleb kept climbing. Thalon rushed up on his heels. The prince grunted. Something wasn't right. If the chemmen were controlling these creatures, then surely he would have seen them by n—

He hollered as he came nose-to-nose with a dead elven sentry.

A snicker drifted down from above. He dragged his gaze upward to see a chemman perched in the branches above him. The storm-reader was almost invisible in the overhanging shadows, but bright orange eyes smirked down at him.

Caleb looked around and saw the same thing in every tree. The sentries were dead.

The chemmen waited above the elves, aiming their crossbows at their targets below.

The other elves hadn't seen them yet. Caleb stared back up. His mouth was dry, but he managed to bellow, "Trees! They're in the trees! In the trees!"

Unheeding, the archers let another round fly at the cultists.

The arrows struck the eyes and heads of the undead creatures at the same time the chemmen bolts struck them. Some screamed and collapsed down through the branches, grabbing at the shafts buried deep in their flesh. Others simply fell, sinking from their perches to the forest floor.

Beneath the prince, Thalon shrieked, "Dad! Dad!"

Above Caleb, the chemman's smile hadn't changed. He sniggered as Caleb's grip on the tree slackened.

***

Der charged the nearest cultist. Its stench almost tripped her up, but she let the sword lead. The blade stuck the creature through the chest and out the back. Thick blood oozed from the wound, yet the undead man continued walking at her.

It pressed its body farther onto her blade as it raised a hand at her. Cold fingertips brushed her hair, then its nails dug deep into the top of her shoulder.

Gasping, she wrenched the sword out, hopped back, and tried again. She howled in frustration and rising panic as the man didn't stop.

A dark shape shoved the creature from behind. She saw a brief flash of a blade and heard bones snap like dry branches. Then she watched the head roll away from the corpse, which veered off in a new heading.

She inched toward the figure. "Thistle?"

Then she recognized his clothing as he turned. He said, "Take as many limbs as you can. They'll stay active until they rot or the spell is canceled, but if they can't move—" He spun on his heel and leaped at the next cultist.

Der ran to the next nearest one and thrust her sword through its nose. Its hands rose and grappled at her. She wrenched the sword free and heaved at its neck. The blade got stuck about halfway through. Fingernails raked across her shoulders, but she didn't feel them.

She yanked her blade back and tried again with all the strength she could muster. This time, she decapitated it.

The head collapsed onto the mud where it continued to move its jaw and swivel its eyes. The body kept staggering forward, but with no direction, and it stumbled into a tree.

She spared a glance around the ambush. Her heart leapt into her throat when she saw so many elves dead on the ground. Then she raised her gaze to the pines, and her mouth dried at the sight.

She stiffened as she realized what the cultists were. They were just there to draw in their attention, and that made them easy targets.

Behind her, she thought she heard the snorts of an angry horse, but they had sent the horses away...

Ahead of her, Thistle attacked the next cultist, driving his knife home in its neck. Within seconds, its head dropped from its shoulders. He glanced back at Der. "Calvar!" He took off sprinting toward the trees.

"What?" she yelled.

Jacob appeared from the darkness, looming behind a cultist with his double-bladed axe in one hand. He split the undead creature in two, from crown to navel, and he barely even stopped running to do it. "He said calvar, Der. Run!"

She spun in a circle. "What's a calvar?"

From behind the knight, she froze in place as she saw several tall, beige horse-shaped beasts charge into the moonlight, screaming like banshees. Many more chemmen followed them.

***

Kelin squeezed his eyes shut for a second and thought he had missed everything when he opened them. Bodies of elves that had been alive seconds ago fell from the trees. Nearby shouting pounded against his ears, but he couldn't distinguish an order from a death scream. He tried to balance himself but found his feet sliding on the slick branches. He slipped and crashed to the ground, landing hard on his back.

Above him, he saw Amthros shoot his arm up through the sharp pine needles. The knight drove his sword into the sole of a chemman's foot and yanked. The storm-reader buckled and plunged through the limbs. The knight slashed at the falling chemman, slicing the storm-reader's neck as he passed on his way down. But he didn't see another storm-reader weaving through the branches toward him.

Kelin could do nothing but gape at the spectacle.

Amthros ducked, and the second chemman's blade smacked hard against the tree above his head. Still crouched on a single branch, the elf pivoted. He parried an attack and another before he could straighten.

Kelin wheezed as he realized this storm-reader was a woman. She also balanced on the same narrow branch as Amthros. She attacked him with a shortsword and dagger.

The knight spun out of the way, but she followed him doggedly.

Kelin wrenched himself to the side as a chemman soldier crashed down out of the tree. He gasped and stared as the fallen chemman started to pick himself up off the ground.

The human stuck out his hands and grabbed for the hilt of the storm-reader's sword. He pushed his weight forward, and his belly and chest folded over the chemman's head. Then he pried the sword free and jumped back, holding it out in front of him.

He stared at the soldier. He knew he should stab him, but he hesitated.

The chemman scrambled out of his reach, then turned and ran.

Kelin gaped at the sword in his hand. It was longer and wider than what he had practiced with in Riversbridge, but it was lighter than he expected. He licked his lips and wondered what the hell he was doing.

He wished the chemmen did not exist, so much that his throat hurt. He did not want to believe that any of this was happening. Elves were immortal—they couldn't die! Unless something killed them, he reminded himself as his gaze fell over the slaughter.

He heard footsteps behind him. He didn't want to turn, but he couldn't stop himself. As he jerked around, the point of a chemmen sword rushed at his torso. Kelin stuck his stolen blade in the way.

The chemman batted the sword to the side like a toy, and his other hand moved with an adder's swiftness toward the human's gut. Kelin caught sight of a second blade racing at him. He launched himself back, stumbling over his own feet. He swung his sword in front of him, but the storm-reader disarmed him with a deft twist of the wrist.

He tried to regrip the sword, even though there was nothing there. His hand opened and closed rapidly as he slid backward in the mud.

The chemman lunged. Kelin started to dodge sideways but then jumped forward at the last moment. Gasping, he seized his opponent's wrists. He stopped and stared. Then, as the world paused, he kicked and fled.

***

A crossbow bolt had stuck Caleb in the arm. The prince rolled away from the pine's trunk and out onto the branches. This was not happening!

A storm-reader dropped down in front of him. He thrust before the chemman could gain balance on the shifting limb. He didn't wait for his opponent's counterstrike as he swung to the branch below.

He hadn't seen what had become of Thalon. The child had disappeared.

When he had a second of respite, he ripped the bolt from his forearm. It wasn't as large as it had felt. A throbbing pain was rushing out from the wound, and he sensed a fire spreading underneath his skin.

He tried to lift his sword again, but his arm trembled. He slumped against the trunk of the tree, his body feeling distant and sluggish. He fought to open his eyes. The sword slipped from his fingers toward the ground. The elf couldn't keep his head above his shoulders. *Poison*, he thought as he tipped forward.

He squinted—he could hear the river, but he wasn't sure he could see it anymore. He crashed out of the tree and into darkness.

***

Jacob halved the last standing cultist. It had been, until recently, a portly human woman. He hit it so hard that red ooze splattered onto his armor and face.

He surveyed the fight. Half of the elves were dead, too wounded, or too scattered to do anything. The chemmen were whole and outnumbered them.

They must think they're so very clever, he snarled to himself. But how the hell did they get above the camp without the elves knowing?

How did they even know where the camp was? His gaze fell toward the escaping elves. He'd been tracking

Thistle. The most obvious answer was that he had somehow informed their position to the rest of the chemmen. But that assumption wasn't sitting well in his gut, and he found himself searching for the boy. Was it possible there was an elven traitor? However, the last time they'd trusted a chemman who had promised to be different still haunted him.

He cut wide at a chemman charging him and stormed toward the river.

CHAPTER TWENTY FIVE

Der punted one of the cultist's loose heads out of her way, but it bit hard into the leather on her boot and clung to it. She hopped for balance as she whacked at the chewing head with her sword.

She shook it off just as something sharp and heavy clipped her already bleeding shoulder. She cursed and jumped away, whirling around to face the new opponent.

She tried not to flinch as the shrieking horse-like beast reared and pointed hooves rose above her.

She thrust at the pale animal. Her sword skidded off its hairless hide, leaving only a scratch. She saw blue-green veins pulsing under its skin. She wrenched herself to the side and tried again, but her sword bounced off this time too.

The calvar struck at her with its hooves, but she jumped back. It lunged forward and chomped with its mouth. She blocked with her sword. The blade caught between its teeth, and black blood dribbled onto her steel. The beast shook its head and spat. Der thrust for the softer skin under its jaw.

She embedded the sword almost to the hilt. She grinned as the creature expired. She did it!

From the corner of her eye, she espied an approaching storm-reader. She tugged on her sword. It didn't budge. It was stuck tight. She wrenched it again—it moved an inch.

She braced and yanked on the weapon a third time. The chemman was now only a few paces away, his sword raised. She tensed to let go and jump out of the way when the storm-reader stiffened. He gasped and toppled to the ground. The figure behind him withdrew his sword.

Der blinked and stared at Kelin.

"Kelin!" She planted her foot and ripped her sword free. "You got a *chemman!*"

"Don't you dare speak to me." He pointed his bloody blade at her. "I'm so angry with you and I have a weapon."

"Why are you mad at me?"

"It's *your fault* I'm here!" She noticed how the blood glistened across his face like war paint. He stared at the dead beast. "We'll have to ask the captain what that was."

"Calvar," she replied immediately.

Kelin shot her a look. "How the hell do you know that?"

She ignored him and turned toward the rest of the combat. They stood on the outer edge. There were at least two or three chemmen for every elf she saw, and the elves were isolated and scattered.

A second calvar bounded past them and gleefully tore into the biting head of the cultist Der had kicked. Several more calvar followed and galloped up to the base of the trees. They jumped high, and to Der's surprise, punched their sharp hooves into the wood and began to climb. They used their momentum to keep their upward motion. Most fell, but they gnashed their teeth and started again. The elves above them cried in alarm, but they were already too busy with the chemmen.

She glanced at Kelin. His sword point dropped.

She gulped. "We have to find Thalon and Caleb."

***

Blood smeared the pine needles and branches around them, but Amthros and the female chemman didn't slow. He swiveled around the trunk and perched on the opposite limb. The storm-reader followed, lunging.

He waited for her to extend, then parried and flicked his blade across her arm. She grunted and hesitated. The elf grabbed a thin, green branch and shoved it in her face. The chemman caught it against her dagger and nearly sliced his hand. He forced the branch farther into her face and, with the tip of his sword, sliced her ankle.

The chemman cried aloud and stabbed down at Amthros. Her feet slid on the narrow branch they shared, and Amthros stamped hard on the base of it. The branch shuddered.

The chemman took one final thrust at him as she fell and missed by an arm's width. He turned and leaped into the next tree.

He hopped down from his perch, descending quickly to the ground. He'd seen the prince fall from another tree. Several of the elves had already clustered around him, with a ring of chemmen attacking them. He smashed into them from behind, stabbing the nearest one in the spine. The chemmen briefly scattered away from him, and he was able to slip through. On the other side of the chaos, Jacob smashed his way through the storm-readers, who danced out of reach of his weapon and then flowed back.

Peyna had materialized by the prince. The physician knelt beside Caleb and pressed a hand against the prince's forehead. "He's alive—for now. I do not know what poison they used. Is it the same as in the last war?"

Jacob shrugged. "We've got to go." The dragoon knight hoisted the unconscious prince onto his shoulder.

Amthros surveyed the fight one last time. "To the boats!"

The remaining elves converged around them, sliding into formation. The storm-readers swarmed in their unrelenting assault.

The elves pushed forward in an arrowhead formation. Jacob held Caleb in the center, with Amthros on point. Those in the rear fought the chemmen as they backed toward the rapids.

***

Thalon squeezed farther inside the overturned canoe. He felt the wood scrape against his cheek as he tried to peek without being seen. Outside, sharp hooves stabbed the ground around the watercraft. He heard sniffing sounds, and the canoe shook when something bumped against it.

In his hand, he gripped the knife he'd found. He remembered his mother's voice—she had explained to him many times that taking other people's things was wrong, and he felt bad for snatching the knife, but he really needed it!

A hoof smashed through the canoe, striking the mud below and missing him by inches. He wound himself tighter into a ball. More hoof punches followed, pounding like falling boulders.

He twisted the blade in his hands, so that the tip pointed up.

The calvar's hoof came crashing through again, and Thalon heard a deep-throated gurgle. He released his fingers from the knife's handle and pried them up from the earth. The calvar had driven the pommel far into the mud, and the blade had disappeared up into the bottom of the hoof.

The calvar screamed and reared. Through the holes in the canoe, Thalon watched the beast pounding its hoof against the ground to attempt to dislodge the knife.

The animal's head dipped forward at an odd angle. Then it stopped moving. Black blood splattered onto the canoe and boy. Someone kicked the body over. Thalon saw a shape standing there with a sword in one hand and a knife in the other. The figure bent over the boat.

Thistle lifted off the remnants of the boat and raised Thalon up in an arm.

***

The elves didn't stop as the calvar charged in front of the canoes, trapping them between the beasts on one side and the chemmen on the other.

Amthros strained to keep himself from jumping ahead and leaving formation. He cut a gash in the flank of the nearest calvar. It screamed, spun around, and kicked out with both back hooves. He dodged, but it slowed the entire rank. Another two calvar joined in. The elves marched shoulder-to-shoulder with him. He could hear the clashing of metal behind him as those in the rear defended against the chemmen. But they fought cautiously, he had to remind himself, and they'd never expose their own necks unless they were sure of victory.

"Now!" he bellowed. He and the other elves in front lunged together. The calvar screamed, bit, and kicked against the swords. Several reared, flailing with their sharpened hooves. Amthros sliced deeply into the exposed underside of the nearest hoof. That calvar roared and skittered to the side.

Behind him, Jacob held his axe up, ready to cut down anything that got through the line. The prince on his shoulder hadn't stirred at all. Next to him, Peyna pressed his fingers against the prince's neck. "Keep breathing! If you can hear me, keep breathing!"

They continued their advance toward the canoes, squeezing the calvar off to the side. Several of the screaming animals splashed backward into the river, where the current snatched them away.

CHAPTER TWENTY SIX

"Wait for us!" Der waved her sword overhead as she sprinted. Kelin tripped while running on her heels, but staggered back on balance. They charged into the calvar between them and the canoes, with the elves on the other side and the chemmen beyond them.

Der leveled her sword at a horse-beast. "Straight thrust or it bounces off!"

Kelin's blade tip barely punctured the skin on the rump of one of the animals, but it was enough of a surprise. The calvar reared.

Der stabbed at it as she sprinted ahead. "Wait for us!"

They didn't dare stop running, suddenly finding themselves lost in the middle of the thrashing herd. All around them, hooves stamped deep into the mud and teeth snapped like the jaws of starving dogs tearing at a meal. They kept poking. If she and Kelin didn't keep these monsters confused, Der realized, they would round on them. She continued to stab as they ran.

Then they were through, closing in on the elves standing over the canoes. Already, the chemmen had started to surround them as they backed up against the rapids.

The river roared so loudly that Der could not hear the splash of the boats onto the torrent. She thrust her sword at a chemman's exposed back, only to have it slide off his armor. But the chemman reeled sideways, and she and Kelin pushed past. Steps away, Jacob lowered Caleb into one of the canoes. Peyna was right behind.

The captain nodded to the physician and whirled toward the combat as the current captured the canoe. The knight smashed through several beached canoes with his axe, splitting their hulls asunder.

Most of the elves jumped aboard while the rearguard fought under increasing pressure from the chemmen. Der sensed their chances of survival dropping with the decreasing number of fighters on the bank. Soon, almost all of them had slipped away. But she felt that the storm-readers were not pressing their growing advantage as hard as they could have.

"There's Thistle!" Kelin yelled and pointed.

"Come on!" Jacob boomed, holding a canoe on the edge of the current with one foot. Carrying Thalon, Thistle dove into the craft, and then the darkness downstream swallowed them.

The knight inched backward, kicking the final intact canoe toward the river while batting aside at least three chemmen blades. Several strikes pushed through and rebounded off his armor. Still with his axe trained against the chemmen, he heaved the canoe into the water with his foot. The paddles rattled inside the craft. "Last boat out!" he hollered to Kelin and Der.

She stole a quick glance around. Everyone else was gone. Cursing, she attacked a pursuing storm-reader high while Kelin went for his knees. The chemman couldn't parry both and fell from his cut leg.

Der ran to the river. Over the few steps of distance she imagined blades at her back. The water's iciness stunned her as she hauled the canoe deeper into the current, with Jacob still anchoring it. She could feel her chilled blood traveling up her leg, and the rush of the rapids threatened to tear her foot out from under her.

She fumbled to climb into the canoe, where she struggled even more for balance as it rocked in the rapids. Her sword slipped from her hand and into the dark water. Kelin jumped in behind her.

Jacob was the last one in. They had fashioned the boats for three people, but it sat disturbingly low in the river with all of them in it. The elf raised his foot, and they jolted into speed on the open water.

A chemman, perched on a boulder over the river, took her last chance. She sprinted and jumped. She landed inside the canoe, pushing it even lower into the river. Freezing water poured into the craft. She squared her feet on both sides and swiped a small cut across Kelin's face with her sword. But she didn't have the reach. He cursed as he pressed a hand on his cheek and rolled to the bottom of the boat.

Der grabbed a paddle and slammed it into the chemman's leg as hard as she could. The chemman's ability to keep her balance amazed her, as the storm-reader then stood on only one leg in a rocking craft.

So Der hit that remaining leg with her paddle just as Jacob struck the chemman in the back with his axe. The body crumpled and splashed into the water.

Der turned around, leaning over the edge of the boat. "My sword! I dropped my sword!"

"We're not going back for it." The captain started scooping out water in cupped hands.

"I know, but it's the second sword I've lost. Including my dad's." She stared back at the way they had come. "Kelin!" She whirled. "Are you all right?"

"Yeah." The young man pressed his palm against his face. "I'm so glad you thought of me first."

"Quiet, both of you," the elf ordered.

Der sat back, trying to relax as the boat shuddered in the swirling river. White water splashed over the edges.

"Are you wounded?" Jacob asked.

"Not badly, sir."

"Then help steer."

She snatched up her paddle and stuck it in the current. She had never done this in water this fast bef—

She didn't finish the thought as a boulder loomed up out of the night. They narrowly swept to its side.

She twisted the paddle in the current and tried to feel the river but ended up mimicking what the knight was doing.

She craned her neck to see the canoe that Caleb was in, but there was nothing except darkness ahead.

She found the speed of the water comforting now, as it carried them away from the chemmen's reach.

Der tried to concentrate, but they were dodging one rock after another. She shivered—her hands were freezing from the water, and her shoulders were burning. She didn't know how long it took, but she no longer had the strength to lift the paddle. "Uh, Kelin, you need to take over."

He took the paddle from her fingers. "Are you all right?"

She nodded, slouching. "One of those cultists got me in the shoulder pretty good."

"Well, you'll have to survive for tonight," Jacob clipped.

The moonlight turned the whitewater into one giant silvery glow, but it seemed dulled to Der. She glanced ahead and studied the horizon. The tops of the canyon the river had funneled them into were brighter. "Dawn."

"Bump," the knight-captain announced.

"Wait, what—" Kelin started.

The canoe shot into the air, and Der felt lighter than ever. They were flying. The canoe seemed to hover for an endless breath, and then it smacked into the dark water several feet below.

The river erupted like a white volcano, and she was terrified the wooden boat had shattered on impact. Icy water became a globe around them before the current hurled them downstream again.

The knight scowled at the glowing horizon. "That was bad back there, but I still have the feeling it was thrown together. I fear a more organized strike soon." His jaw tightened. "If they can find us."

"They found us tonight, sir," Der pointed out.

CHAPTER TWENTY SEVEN

Vlade smirked at the chaos surrounding him. The breeze was cool against his forehead as he stood next to the town's burning buildings. They were spaced out, curving around a stream that wound throughout the settlement.

He swung the sword, smiling at the weight of it in his hand as he strolled down the avenue. Ahead of him, he saw the Pelippen River. He'd heard of it from his spies, but frankly, it looked like any other river to him.

He watched his soldiers as he stepped over a body. They had surrounded the town, invaded it, and now all he had left to do was kill any survivors. It had taken hardly any time at all.

He held up the midnight black sword and gazed at it as he walked. It was working!

He flipped it around his wrist—childish, he knew, but he just had to. When it moved, no sound existed in its vicinity.

He turned at slight movement, like a hunting cat.

A fair-haired elf burst out of a fiery house with a large rolled blanket under his arm. In the window, a wreath of blue and yellow flowers withered as it burned. He ducked to the side of the home.

Vlade jumped into his path. He raised the sword, and the elf's curse was lost in the aura of soundlessness. The bundle he held began to kick furiously.

The chemmen commander held the sword still, and the screams of battle rushed in like a thunderclap.

The elf spat at his feet and held the chemman's gaze. "I remember that blade. I watched it burn until it was nothing but a puddle." He laid a hand on the blanket. "You are not its wielder, either."

"I am now." Vlade brought the sword level and stilled it.

The elf swiveled to put himself between Vlade and the kicking bundle. A small girl's voice wailed from inside. The elf spun on his heel and started to run.

Vlade pivoted and lunged in the same moment, and the black blade bit noiselessly into the blanket. He felt the satisfying crunch of bone vibrate all the way up his arm, but there was no shriek or even a whimper.

The elf scrambled to unwrap the blanket, but jerked to a stop as blood soaked through the cloth and spread across his hands. His mouth opened in a scream as he held the dripping bundle to his chest. He folded down onto his knees. A tendril of blond hair escaped from the depths of the blanket. He clung tighter.

The chemman held the blade still again, and sound echoed back around them. "I've always wondered, what is it like to lose someone?"

The elf cradled the bundle and bowed his head.

A vicious smile split the commander's face. He brought the sword down again.

***

Der let her fingers trail in the water; it helped to keep her awake. Her legs were tense, and she didn't have room to stretch them out. The river was much wider and smoother here, and she'd lost count of how many streams had converged along the way.

She squinted; the land and water ahead looked blurry. Maybe she was just exhausted...?

Der felt the air push against her, like a strong, stationary breeze. She gasped when the sensation released her, and the river changed from glacial gray to a bright shade of blue with a sheen of sparkling diamonds.

She gripped the edge of the canoe and whipped her head back and forth gaping. They continued as the waterway skirted a majestic forest. Crimson and gold leaves carpeted the water as the craft glided downstream.

She sniffed. The river shouldn't smell like honey, she thought, but she couldn't deny her nose.

This could have been the first time she saw the world, she mused, and she had only been looking through a veil throughout her entire life.

She eased her fingers back into the water and felt satin running over her hand. The air was lighter and easier to breathe.

"Welcome to the elven lands." Jacob grinned tightly.

"It's incredible." Kelin leaned over the canoe's side.

"They are gorgeous," the knight agreed. "But they mask some of the nastiest— Ah, don't worry about it."

Der wrestled a finger against her ear—they had been constantly popping as they descended. Jacob steered the canoe until its nose kissed the mud of the bank, and then it rocked dangerously as Der clambered out of it.

"Yow!" She grabbed the back of her leg. "Cramp, cramp!" She hauled herself onto the grass using the other leg and an elbow. "Huh." She lay on the ground, realizing how solid and unyielding it felt after so much time on the water.

Kelin tiptoed out of the boat. He whistled. "Will you look at that?"

They could see the shapes of some buildings, but they blended in well with the trees. On the other side of the settlement, the world fell away over a cliff. The river curved through this hidden shelf, picked up its pace, and then plummeted into the valley below.

Ahead of them, other empty canoes waited on the edge. On the water, they'd passed by several who had stopped on the little stone shores, and Der couldn't guess at who had arrived before them.

She pushed herself off the ground and tried to dust the mud off her trousers but ended up smearing it over herself. She started toward the nearest buildings.

"Der," Jacob called. "Wait by the shore."

She turned. "Why?"

He sighed. "We will wait until we are invited."

She frowned. "Is that normal, sir?"

The knight shook his head. "No, but not one of us is a citizen of Indelleiria."

Kelin stretched, swaying a little for balance. "I can honestly say that I never want to do that again."

Der ignored him and inched toward the buildings. "Where's Caleb? Or Ed—or whatever his name actually is?"

The knight sighed louder. "Wait by the shore."

Kelin held his stomach. "I don't want to wait either, sir. It's been two days on raw fish. I'm starving."

Jacob rolled his eyes. "Fine. Go on up. Get shot full of arrows."

Der had raised her foot at the word 'fine' and was still holding it in the air when she turned. "Are you serious, sir?"

"Are you hungry enough to find out?"

"Er. No." She dropped her foot.

Another canoe glided across the water and pressed into the mud beside them. A hooded figure slipped the paddle along the inside of the boat. A much smaller figure hopped to the front of the craft. "Der! Kelin!"

Thalon grinned and waved at them. His father put a hand on his shoulder to keep the boy from jumping out. The chemman kept his own eyes downcast. He said in a voice barely above a whisper, "It is best to throw our weight behind your lot now than to wait to see if this storm passes. It won't."

Jacob's mouth hung open, and he gripped his axe. "How did you even get inside—"

Thistle tapped the elven-made boat with his foot. "Thank you for the invitation."

Thalon scrambled out of the canoe and hugged Kelin and Der in turn.

"I don't want to believe they're back," Thistle said.

"I fought to put the chemmen in Darkreign," Jacob replied.

Thistle shrugged. "I doubt we've crossed blades."

"Wait." Jacob narrowed his eyes. "You said 'they're back'."

"So?" Der asked.

"Storm-readers always say 'we'."

Thistle's face remained blank. "I have never been to Darkreign."

"Dad..." Thalon trotted back over to him.

Thistle pulled his hood lower. "My son and I have nowhere to run. They may have seen Thalon, and they will hunt him. As awful as I think Indelleiria is, I know that they won't actively kill my son."

Jacob's eyes flicked between Thistle and Thalon.

The storm-reader continued, "I notice that you haven't sounded the alarm yet. You might want to make it easier on yourselves and do just that."

The knight didn't move.

"This is not yet the worst of it. If the chemmen annihilate the elves, take your guess as to their next target. Humans or dwarves? If you, dragoon, had fought my ilk, then you know they will not be sated until only chemmen are left."

The silence that followed seemed to suck out the air around them. Der heard Jacob growl in the back of his throat. Finally, he nodded. "So be it." Then he let his gaze fall to Der, Kelin, and Thalon. "It's never fair that you kids have to carry the weight of any of this. Chemmen, torture, calvar, undead."

Kelin shivered. "Those cultists...they were dead—had been killed."

Thistle smirked. "To be so innocent."

"But we beat them," Der responded. Then she shifted her weight. "Well...we took some of each down before we ran away, at least."

Jacob shook his head. "Lucky and impressive, but remember, *you* were not their target. Would you swat a fly in battle?"

"If the fly could stab me, yes," she answered.

The knight frowned. "Why do you think they didn't kill us after the prince had left? It takes a very big reward for them to risk their own immortal hides."

She grinned and cracked her knuckles. "So it sounds like we'll get to do it again." But her smile faded as she saw Kelin paling. "What's wrong?"

The young man gulped. "They were so...so unstoppable." He gasped. "Do the chemmen do that all the time? Could it happen to us? The...undead?"

Thistle shrugged.

Jacob tightened his lips and nodded. "It's something the chemmen did quite often before they went into battle."

Thistle's face darkened. "Those cultists deserved worse."

"Dad?" Thalon asked.

"The chemmen love fodder." Jacob exhaled. "Even before their immortality, they hardly risked their lives when they had so many other bodies to use. They used to march the innocent—still alive, Kelin—in front of their armies to lay siege to cities."

Thistle nodded in agreement.

Der glanced back toward the buildings, intent on changing the topic. "Um, so, how long before we're invited?"

"I don't know." The knight set his gaze on Thistle. "And I also don't know if there is a good time to introduce your presence without an overreaction. And just to be honest, I do not trust you an inch. But I'm not worried about taking on a single storm-reader."

Thistle's expression remained impassive. He pulled up his hood.

In the thickening silence, Der tried to count the canoes laid out to dry in the grass, to see how many had made it.

Around the bend, two new canoes came into view. On a boat, someone lit a small candle and waved it in a circle.

Jacob nodded. "There is the prince, and...we'll see."

Der turned her head. People had started to melt out from the buildings. They must have been watching, even though she had seen no one peeking. In front of the silent parade, she recognized Duke Farallon.

On the river, the elves in the canoes piloted them to a small, natural looking inlet. They came to a rest in the shallow water. Amthros hopped out of one and hovered close to the other, near the physician and the prone prince. Peyna and Amthros lifted Caleb out of the craft.

The elves glided together into a smooth, rhythmic stream of people toward the edge of the water. Just their walk was like watching a well-practiced dance.

Der elbowed her way through. "Excuse me." She squeezed against the tightening pressure. "Excuse me, please?"

She pushed through the ring of people to where Caleb sat, held up by Peyna. "Are you all right?"

The physician's head snapped up. "You! Don't you owe us silence?"

She shrugged. "Not that I know of."

"How fortunate you are that you were not injured," intoned the acerbic voice of Duke Farallon.

"Poisoned, in fact." Caleb smiled weakly. Everyone else went quiet. "However, thanks to Peyna, I'm safe." He shifted forward, sitting up on his own.

She opened her mouth to say something more but hesitated. She had never realized that so many people staring could have so much weight—actual, physical weight that she could feel on her shoulders.

"Lout," Farallon murmured.

Amthros lifted an eyebrow. "At least she fought with us, while you had gone on ahead. You missed combat by only a few lucky minutes, my lord."

The duke frowned. "Yes, a few of us went. I left a message with Soheir—"

"Who was killed just after you departed," the knight of Indelleiria said calmly. His words were almost serene, but Der saw that his body had tensed.

"Killed? This is unbelievable." A tremble sneaked into Farallon's voice. He dipped his chin. "We must prepare the songs of—"

Behind them, someone cleared his throat. Jacob stepped forward. "Yes, this is a tragedy, but it is our duty to defend those still alive. We can mourn later. Please, take advice from this soldier and save your songs."

The gathered elves stared at him as if he'd spoken in another language.

"What could you mean?" asked a well-dressed elf from the assembly. "More of us have died. They are gone for as long as we shall live."

The knight persisted, "I regret very much that we've lost good people, many of whom had nothing to do with the chemmen banishment. However, time only stops for the dead."

The duke clenched his fist. "We are safe here."

"Are we?" Thistle stepped up beside the knight and pulled back his hood to reveal his face.

The elves stared. Not many of them carried weapons, but Amthros yanked out his sword. A few others nocked arrows in their bows as space widened around Thistle. Farallon moved in front of Caleb, drawing his own blade.

"Dad!" Thalon lunged, trying to run forward, but Kelin held onto his shoulders.

The storm-reader stared at Amthros. He said, in fluent Elvish, "I come to aid you."

Farallon extended his sword point. "I will accept your surrender, and then you will tell what you know about your masters' plans."

The chemman replied in a smooth tone, "I still am a prisoner of Silver Dawn, if I recall."

The duke snorted. "This is the second time you have forced your presence upon us, and the second time that you have said nothing of import."

"One elf trusted him."

Der swiveled to see Amthros speaking, "He may have invaluable information. Someone tried to kill him before he could speak; therefore, someone's afraid."

"There are many reasons why an elf would want this creature dead," Farallon retorted.

The knight of Indelleiria raised a hand. "I think that we could listen and divine for ourselves what is useful and true."

The duke's upper lip curled. "When did you change your lyrics? I believed you to be my ally in this."

"Then perhaps you thought wrongly, my lord." His gaze slid over to Thalon, and he nodded, ever so slightly, at the boy. "It's just, we...we need to care for the children. Even the ones with orange eyes. They're innocent. They always were."

Thistle moved between the knight and his son.

"This is a ruse. He has a plan." The duke kept his sword pointed toward the chemman.

Amthros scowled. "He killed chemmen in the ambush too. I saw him. I have never witnessed a chemman put a blade to another."

"Enough," a voice crystallized. Caleb winced but pushed himself to stand with the physician's aid. "He has a son, a half-elven son. I do not trust his word, but the child should not lose both parents." He turned his gaze to Thistle. His face was pale and strained, but his tone was strong, "I promise that we shall treat you fairly and not alienate you from your child."

The chemman bowed his head in assent. Kelin let go of Thalon and the boy barreled into his father's legs.

Some of the elves refused to look at Thistle as Amthros led him and Thalon away. Meanwhile, Der and Kelin stood back, watching and waiting as Peyna aided Caleb toward the settlement.

CHAPTER TWENTY EIGHT

Der frowned as she and Kelin followed Jacob. He'd called them over, and she didn't think they had a choice about whether to trail after him or not. She strained her neck back toward the far side of the settlement. She had wanted to make sure that Caleb was all right.

The knight jerked his thumb to the path along the river. "Stables are this way."

Golden and red leaves decorated the floor of the trail running astride the river before it curved into the hamlet. Der squinted, trying to count the buildings, but they were assembled with and into the forest. The woodwork was the same shade as the trees, even with the colors and shades of autumn.

She descried a bridge over a small stream running through the settlement, and it reminded her of how far away she was from home. The bridge in Riversbridge was thick and gray. This one was a quarter of the size, wooden, and carved with patterns of leaves.

The captain poked his head around the corner of a large stable with a low, shingled roof. Then he swaggered inside. "Spike!"

He threw both of his hands wide and approached the massive horse. "I thought the storm-readers would've speared you for dinner."

Der swore the horse narrowed his eyes. She asked, "How did they arrive before us? Did we really spend that long on the river?"

Jacob spun on his heel toward Der and Kelin and shrugged. "Now that we know the horses and this arrogant bully made it, how about lunch?" Behind him, Spike pawed the ground.

"What about Thistle and Thalon?" Der asked.

"You heard the prince."

"Yeah, but something still doesn't feel right about all of this." She swallowed but kept eye contact.

The knight nodded. "Lots of things don't feel right, and I will check on them when I can. But I've got to take care of you two as well. Now, come on, let's get something to chow on." He thumped Spike's shoulder and walked out of the stable.

Kelin shrugged to Der, and they trotted after him as he threaded between the slender buildings. They noticed the curling carvings and paintings were built into the design of the walls, instead of overlaid like portraits or tapestries.

Jacob seemed to know his way, or at least, he followed his nose and led them unerringly to the kitchens. Der glanced up and realized it was the only building with smoke rising from it.

Among the steaming bowls and fires, Evelyn rose from kneeling by the oven like a blossoming flower. She smiled and dipped in a half curtsey. Her ruby dress seemed too bright in the kitchen, and she moved like a leaf in the wind without so much as a dusting of crumbs on her clothing. "You two may be the first humans here." She returned to the counter to stir a bowl that sweetened the air around them. Her smile dipped. "This is Riverfall Haven, made long before the chemmen created themselves, and it's one of our dear secrets." Her face darkened. "But not, I suspect, any more."

Kelin shivered. "Then are we safe here or not?"

Jacob scowled. "It should be harder for them to get here."

"So we shouldn't risk staying?" Der guessed.

Jacob cleared his throat. "This place has too many people now. And one of them is bound to tell the chemmen."

She nodded and slipped her hands behind her to hide the goosebumps along her arms.

The knight straightened his shoulders as he turned back to the cook. "The crown prince has arrived—and alive—but... I very much suspect that you knew already."

She pursed her lips. "Indeed. I must apologize for not being there to aid at the attack."

"But you're not a fighter," Der started before petering out.

Lady Eve nodded. "That is true. I had no idea of it... Perhaps the chemmen learned from last time."

Der scratched her head. "Why? How could you have had an idea?"

Jacob and Evelyn exchanged a glance. She smiled again. "I meant that I had no idea of the attack when one is so logical in hindsight." She looked at the knight. "And you, taking humans under your tutelage as always."

He held up his hands. "I'm the only one here qualified."

"You don't seem to have time for anything else these days. It takes this horrible tragedy to even get you on our side of the mountains again."

The knight retreated a step. "We haven't crossed the Riverfall Divide yet. I'm still not on the Indelleiria side of—"

She shot him a thin-lipped expression that could freeze fire.

He backed up another step. "Er. You know, I'm going back to check on Spike and the other mounts..." He wheeled on his heel and vanished through an archway.

Lady Eve stuck her hands on her hips and exhaled sharply.

Der frowned at the archway. "Curious. He was the one who was hungry."

Kelin coughed into his hand. "Anyway, I'm hungry myself."

Evelyn shook her head. "You can't eat here. I'm creating for an event." She whipped the batter in the bowl so hard that several splatters escaped onto the floor and counter.

"Which is...?" Der prompted.

The elf gave her a stern look but said, "There is a meeting tomorrow of high-ranking elves who escaped the kingdom. That's common knowledge here in Riverfall—and not known anywhere else." She stopped stirring. "Children, forgive me, but please see one of the other cooks if you're hungry."

Kelin bowed to her and then pulled Der at the shoulder. They wandered farther into kitchens and grabbed some bread bowls filled with hearty soup that no one seemed to be minding. Then they dashed deeper into the maze of buildings.

They found a round room, open to the sky above, with a simple fountain in its center. They sat to enjoy their pilfered meal. Der felt as if she could almost make out the words of the water's song as they tickled her ears. Around them, pictures that could have been real stood against the walls.

Kelin wiped his chin. "This is the first time the elves have left us alone." He shivered. "And this place seems very weird."

Der nodded, choking down the last piece of soup-soaked bread. "You're right." She pushed herself to standing. "So let's explore."

He frowned. "Are we allowed to?"

She shrugged. "You heard Lady Eve. We may be the only humans ever to be here, so we should see all that we can." She darted out of the room, leaving Kelin to chase or be left behind.

In the next room, a fresco of the constellations and the moon glimmered with a soft radiance. Der pressed her nose against the wall and cupped her hands around her eyes. "It's glowing!" Then she spun toward to the opposite wall.

She stiffened and blurted, "Oh, we didn't see anyone. I'm sorry!"

The figures kept moving without acknowledging them. She gasped—it wasn't anyone, it was the painting. The people portrayed walked and even silently laughed. Several elves moved in a view of a valley in the mountains and continued to have an eternal, formal picnic. The life-sized figures started their endless routine again, stepping into their beginning places as seamlessly as if it were planned. Der could have sworn she saw Evelyn among them.

Kelin smiled at the moving portrait. "Is this normal for them?"

"Dunno. But if this is..." She grabbed his shoulder and pulled. "Let's see what else is here!"

"No, Der!" He tried to throw off her hand, but it was too late. They were in the next room.

She rounded into an alcove. It was much darker, but gems and lights glittered like stars. Tapestries and jewelry filled the space. A small coronet rested on a velvet pillow on top of a chest-high shelf. All the art and items boasted similar patterns with sleek, endless formations. She picked up the small crown and twirled it in her hands. An emerald was set in the center, surrounded by a thick line of blue that weaved throughout the coronet.

"What's wrong with its gems?" Kelin asked. "They're—they're not cut. It's like they were melted."

"Questing for treasure?" a voice queried from behind. They spun around and Der nearly dropped the coronet.

A pale Caleb leaned against the wall of the alcove. He shuffled forward. "You've got a good eye then, because Pallens items are not easy to come by these days."

"Caleb!" Der took two steps toward him before remembering to set the coronet back on the pillow.

"P-Pallens?" Kelin stuttered, eyeing the treasure laid out before him.

The prince offered a weak smile. "Indeed. Poor Pallens. She fought the chemmen first before Indelleiria aided her. Then she went on alone to lose to another enemy in another war." He sagged and leaned against the wall. "I will always wonder if it was because she hadn't been able to recover from fighting the storm-readers first."

Der checked the archways and corners. "Shouldn't you have guards or something?"

He smiled wanly. "They think I'm sleeping. Peyna's orders, but I couldn't."

Kelin's gaze hadn't budged. "Are these truly relics of the paladin empire?"

"Yes." Caleb pushed himself away from the wall. "Pallens' style is similar to most elvish designs—King Midan himself was elven—but there are some distinct differences." He gestured to the coronet. "We tend to prefer more wood and stone, and Pallens used more metals. However, the main dissimilarity is in the use of gems."

"We saw that there was something different," Der acknowledged.

"Very much so. We elves cut the gems so they reflect light. We even make pictures into them, but Pallens rarely used cut gems at all."

Kelin tilted his head. "What did they do with them?"

Caleb smiled. "They had a way of melting them into whatever pattern or shape they wanted, and somehow getting them to act as prisms too. It's beautiful. Even we don't know how they did it."

Der picked up the sparkling coronet again and studied it. She ran her fingers over it to find a bump or maybe an air bubble. "Damn. It's flawless." She looked up at the prince and her eyes widened. "I'm holding a remnant of the empire. I'm going to break it. I know my luck."

He offered a tired grin. "In that case, you'll have to find another relic of Pallens to replace it."

"Where do I go? Sounds like an adventure." She set the coronet back on its pillow. She found herself smiling as she glanced at the treasure and the art around the room. "This place is nothing like I ever imagined. Take that tree growing in the window over there. It's obviously meant to be there." The entire window and wall were part of a larger, intentional theme that included the tree, the plants, and the ivy, both real and painted.

Kelin said, "All the, well, I don't want to use the word 'streets'—that's too mundane—but all the avenues and walkways are so wide!"

The prince leaned against the wall and exhaled. "I'm glad that you find our little haven exciting."

"Yeah," Kelin agreed. "I don't think Der's feet have touched the ground yet."

She raised an eyebrow. "I've *never* had my feet on the ground."

"I know how you feel," Caleb agreed. "We'll find ground though, and hit it running."

She grinned. "And kicking."

He turned at a noise behind them to see a patrol making its rounds throughout the city. He shook his head and moved to hide his face. "Patrols in an elven home. I'll never get used to it."

Der looked over his shoulders at the elves—they looked like soldiers to her. They walked in step, and even their solemn faces matched each other's exactly. Every one of them carried a sword, a bow, and a quiver. Most of them were men, but a few women marched with them.

Caleb muttered something in Elvish under his breath.

Der blinked. "Well, that was rather rude."

The prince stared at her. "How in the corners of hell did you understand that?"

She blushed. "Oh, uh, the physician gave me the language when he healed me. I didn't ask for it. And Kelin too."

"Oh." He dropped his shoulders. "If I...you wouldn't have been in that position if I—"

"We're here now." Der looked at Caleb. "And we're fine."

Kelin shivered. "Some of us aren't made of steel, Der."

"I wish we were," Caleb whispered. "We elves do not have a standing army. Yes, we have guards and some knights, but even they have other lives."

"Makes sense, I suppose, especially with all the magic you have guarding your kingdom," Kelin mused.

Caleb grunted. "Which has its flaws. As we know now."

Der glanced away, and her gaze wandered back to the artifacts from the paladin empire. The palm of her hand rested on the velvet pillow. "I didn't realize how different we are. You knew all along."

The prince met her gaze. "I wasn't aware of how similar we are until I came to know you and Kelin."

"Thank you," Kelin said.

Der shook her head. "But you live so much better. It's not fair. Your camp was normal enough, but this place is beautiful. I mean, you have things from

Pallens. Why can't humans live like this? Just a spoonful of this could do us wonders."

"It's not medicine, Der." Caleb dropped his gaze. "And I doubt everyone would share your enthusiasm. The other humans I met, ah, weren't so accommodating."

Kelin nudged her arm. "They can't force it on us, Der. That's how enemies are made. And these things can't be easy for even the elves to make, let alone enough for all of humanity."

"But..." She let her arms hang limply.

"Forcing is exactly what the chemmen do," Caleb whispered. "They are a force. On people. On the land. And I don't think we can stop them."

She shifted her weight in the ensuing silence.

Kelin recalled, "When we would gather firewood, my mother also used to tell me that nature was about balance. So wouldn't the chemmen be the natural balance to the elves?"

Both Der and Caleb stared. The prince finally shook his head. "No. There are so many differences that don't balance out. The chemmen created themselves, while we elves were always this way. And besides, the chemmen outnumber us. Offspring are a resource to them, not a family."

Der shook her head. "Thistle cares about his son."

Caleb wrung his hands together. "Thistle seems different. I wish I could believe he is. True storm-readers would never have a child such as Thalon. They can't share being storm-readers. Is this all a plot?"

Der shrugged, looking uneasy.

"I don't know what to think." The prince's shoulders slouched. "And now...to me, not all life is sacred anymore. That belief has simply died." He pressed a hand against his chest.

Der sucked in her breath. Beside her, Kelin's eyes widened.

Caleb plunged on. "You don't know how much effort it took me to say that aloud, and I never could to anyone else here." He gasped. "It's so hard to *say*, but it's something so easy to *think* over and over. And now, I want to kill the storm-readers just because they are storm-readers." He hung his head. "I'm horrible."

"I don't think you do," Der whispered. "You've spared Thistle."

"Is that a mistake though?" Caleb hung his head. "I'm not so sure we have learned from our own past." The prince's eyes burned. "But for what the storm-readers did—we can't forget that. They murdered so many to achieve immortality."

Kelin shook his head. "I still can't comprehend that."

"The Centum Wars killed more people than are alive today."

Der saw that Kelin couldn't meet the elf's eyes. He swallowed. "Why didn't you stop it before they were immortal? When they were killing...?"

Caleb paled, and his voice was smaller, "We didn't know." He held up his hands. "Perhaps we should have, but we didn't until it was too late. That's what my father taught me. But when they turned on the elves, we banished them to Darkreign."

"Darkreign?" Kelin repeated. "We've heard the name, but..." He trailed off and shook his head.

"That's how it translates into Common. But that's not what they call it," Caleb's voice lowered. "They call it home." He sighed. "But no one is supposed to leave. That's the lore." He held out his hands, palms up. "It may have been the wrong decision, but I don't think there was a right one, not then, and probably not even now."

He wheezed and stared ahead at nothing. Der reached out and patted his shoulder.

Kelin raised his hand. "Um, if it's a magically sealed realm or whatever, how were they banished there?"

Caleb flattened his lips. "The Baroness of Elloan. She did it at my father's command. I can only assume that they must still fear her."

Der shrugged. "Well, if she's still around, then why can't she do it again?"

Caleb shrugged and sighed. "Pallens isn't here to help this time." He turned and walked away, and they followed.

They passed through corridors of trees, arched over the street like interlocked fingers. Sunlight trickled through the branches and set the autumn colors alight. The small stream that wound through the haven meandered by them, and they crossed a wooden bridge with four strong, living trees as posts. Once on the other side, a mural that overlooked the heart of the vista drew Der's eyes.

She drifted in front of the painting. "This is your family..." She gazed at the four still figures; they were so lifelike that she swore they could've stepped right off the wall. Caleb was younger, and she couldn't ever recall seeing her friend smiling that happily in life.

"Yes." The prince pressed a hand against his brother's face.

Her eyes lingered on King Valladen. He seemed to be an older Caleb. The crown on his head was sleek and bright, rising to sharp points. Cut gems flowed around it like braided streams. In the center was a jewel, but it appeared gold.

Kelin hovered his fingers over the art. "I think I could walk into this painting."

Der's eyes studied the face of the late king. Then she turned to Caleb. "This is truly you, then. The crown prince, soon to be the king of the elves."

He leaned against the wall, clutching his arms to his chest. "It was never meant to be. My father was supposed to outlive his kingdom." He started to lift his gaze to the images, but then dropped away.

"It seems your destiny has arrived instead." She stepped back from the mural.

Caleb's lip trembled. "I don't want it. I want my mother and father." He rubbed his face. "I can't be a child ruler to a race of immortals!" He clutched his arms to his chest. "They have said nothing, but I see the way they watch me."

"You worried about your back?" Der's nose wrinkled.

Caleb shook his head but then paused and nodded. "What if there is a traitor? Why? What does he want? Does he not realize what floodgates he's opened?"

She shrugged. "You're always free to run away with us."

Kelin's eyes bulged. "Excuse me?"

Caleb stared. Then a ghost of a smile graced his face. "Thank you. But..."

She chuckled. "If it's any consolation, we're also completely unsure of where we're gonna go, and what to do."

"Hey." Kelin crossed his arms, and Der saw him trying not to grin. "I'm a blacksmith, Der. You're the soldier with no training, army, or allegiance."

"Yeah. But." She kicked her toe against the ground. "I have friends."

Caleb seemed to freeze, but then he nodded and smiled. "And so do I. But first, I need to know my brother is safe, at least. He could never survive in human lands."

"You did," Der pointed out.

"I am not my brother."

She grinned. "Yeah, he's not the one taking advice from a mortal, penniless warrior."

"You're hardly penniless, Der."

"No, I am." She patted her trousers. "I have absolutely no money on me."

Kelin sighed. "But you have the future king of the elves as a friend."

Caleb's expression mellowed. "If we don't die horribly. And I will not be the king of *all* elves."

Kelin rolled his eyes and tried to hide a small smile. "I'm sorry, king of the elven kingdom. You'll be the most powerful man alive."

Caleb frowned. "That will not be accurate." After a moment of silence, Der watched him gaze at his family. He traced his fingers over his father's face. "We lost his crown." He gulped and looked away. "I'm sure it's destroyed by now." He shook his head. "But the lives of everyone are more important than some jewelry I never wanted."

"I am so very sorry for you," she said.

"Thank you." Caleb closed his eyes. "But it's nothing. I have to *stay* this time."

Der shook her head. "It's not nothing. It was your father's crown. It's what you would have had that's left of him."

He kept his eyes shut. "I wish the chemmen had stayed gone, because then we wouldn't have to do something so horrible as take lives—or lose ours." He looked back up at them, his eyes watering with unshed tears. "I fear that if—I fear that to survive, we'll have to commit another tragedy, and I'm terrified that part of me wants to."

Kelin and Der exchanged an uneasy glance. He shrugged at her and she held up her empty hands, unsure of what to say.

Caleb turned to face them, putting his back to the mural. "They're gone. And so are those on the river." He exhaled and raised a hand toward the center of the haven. "So, please, enjoy what luxuries we have while we still draw breath ourselves."

"Caleb..." Der started.

He sniffed. "And maybe even get a bath."

Kelin snorted and smirked. "Well, I don't think you're wrong on that."

He dipped his head. "The absolute worst part is that I not only have to show bravery when I don't feel it, but that I actually have to be brave."

Der grinned. "And you have been. Ain't nothin' to it after you fall a couple of times."

Kelin rolled his eyes.

Caleb looked at Der with a mix of confusion and exasperation. "Well, anyway, I've got a meeting to attend, but you," he smiled, "you get to relax. I'm envious."

CHAPTER TWENTY NINE

Nothing allowed for a better cleansing of his mind than candles, a warm fire, wine, bath salts, and plenty of steamy mountain water. Only Kelin's nose and toes poked through the bath's surface.

On the ceiling above him, the water's reflection danced like children at play. He wiggled his toes. He'd never had a bath where someone else hadn't used it first. It almost made the ordeals so far worthwhile. Almost. It certainly helped to drown the memories.

He'd never had wine like this before, but it was filling, both sweet and smooth at the same time. He savored each taste. They said that it was only a thimbleful of alcohol in the glass and the rest was water, but his head was still spinning. He settled for occasional sips as he relaxed into the warming hum it brought throughout his entire body.

Someone had laid out new clothes, including shoes, for him. He didn't ask where they'd taken his old clothes. With any luck, to burn them.

But right now, he was free and floating. The chemmen were still an ancient myth. He'd have to go back to the forge come sunrise. For now, he was safe.

***

In a narrow, oval room, the elves seated themselves along mahogany benches. Daylight warmed the chamber through windows, and the surrounding stone walls were inlaid with glowing star patterns that led up to a dome overhead. Ivy covered the false lattice supports behind the benches, creating an illusion of summer. Off to the side, there was a table laden with an abundance of small foods; nothing as large as a supper, but enough to sustain people for a long discussion.

Sir Amthros, Knight-Captain Jacob, Duke Farallon, Duchess Sabielle, several other elves, and Evelyn sat upright on the benches. Between them, an illusory map rose above the stone floor. The entire kingdom was detailed. The rivers flowed, and the mountains soared with clouds and snow on their peaks.

Caleb slouched in a high-backed chair at the head of the benches. Above him, a picture of a tree weathering through the four seasons adorned the chair. He eyed the food and his stomach rumbled in response, but he didn't want to eat.

Farallon approached carrying a small, full plate over to him. He held it out and smiled. The prince frowned—the other elf's expression appeared genuine.

The duke said, "The lady and I have our disagreements, but no one cannot enjoy her dishes."

"I'm grateful, my lord duke, but I can't seem to make myself hungry at the moment."

"Very well." He retracted the plate. "Please let me know when you are."

"I will, thank you." He offered his own stiff smile. "It is good to see your nose healed."

The duke fought back a scowl as he rubbed it. "Yes. Master Peyna had wasted his supplies on that girl. Thankfully, there were more supplies here." He set the plate down on the bench behind him.

The prince nodded. "Of course."

Jacob rose. He walked over and bent low, so that only he, Caleb, and the duke could hear. "The chemmen prisoner has requested an audience. He also says he will say nothing but to the three of us."

"Absolutely not!" Farallon bellowed. Caleb glanced back toward the benches; everyone was staring.

The knight pursed his lips and whispered, "You must consider the possibility that he is a chemmen renegade."

The duke rolled his eyes. "And he claimed to be married to an elf who died *just before* he stepped into our lives? We remember the last time a chemman promised to be different. The one who wielded that silent weapon."

Jacob shrugged. "Or, my lord duke, we're so blinded by our previous knowledge of the chemmen that we cannot see the truth. After all, the humans told us the truth in their trial."

"They told us *their* truth, captain. It does not make the prisoner credible. And he says he escaped the banishment, which is absolutely is a lie."

Caleb frowned. "Perhaps we should hear what he has to say and decipher *our* truth from it."

Farallon inhaled to speak, but the doors at the end of the hall cracked open, and several hooded figures slipped into the room.

Caleb half rose out of his seat. "Who?" he mouthed.

The shortest of the newcomers tossed back his hood. Tousled auburn hair adorned a young face marked with nervous, golden eyes.

"Alsalon," the crown prince breathed. He threw himself away from his chair and caught the younger elf in an embrace. Alsalon hugged him so hard that Caleb wheezed to inhale.

Caleb pushed the boy back and held him by the shoulders. "You made it." He choked down the emotions in his voice, but he could feel them drowning him from the inside. None of the other members of the council had even raised their eyebrows at this display. He gasped for breath. "You must tell me of your escape."

Alsalon nodded. "Of course." He blinked back tears. "I missed you. I so feared that you—that..." He broke off with a sob in his voice.

"And I as well." Caleb embraced his brother again. "I'm so grateful you're safe."

"Are we?" Jacob whispered.

The younger prince took a seat on a bench, and Caleb returned to his chair. He looked into the eyes of everyone present. Each was vital to their survival as a kingdom, he told himself. He tried not to flinch at the thought of one of them being a traitor. His gaze wandered over to the duke. But he'd always been a loyal friend of his father's. He'd fought the chemmen to their banishment. It couldn't be possible.

Caleb cleared his throat. He caught Alsalon's eye and gulped back another sob of relief. Then he raised his gaze to the others. "The chemmen want our people slain because their hate demands it, and nothing less." He swallowed. "We are here in Riverfall because Long Range Palace has been abandoned for the first time in history. The elven court has never been forced to seek sanctuary before now." He lifted his chin higher. "However, that changes nothing."

Gasps raced around the room.

The prince's gaze focused on the map. "It changes nothing. We are still the same people. We are willing to fight. We shall not continue to run while the storm-readers nip at our heels."

"But we don't even know—" Amthros began.

"Where shall we begin, my prince?" Evelyn interrupted, sitting straight with her hands in her lap.

Caleb rubbed his forehead but nodded his thanks to her. "Saving our people." He spread an opening hand toward the map. "Their attacks have been chaotic at best, and far apart." Fires of burned cities and towns glowed. "So they can't simply be marching across our lands." He sank back into his chair.

Alsalon gulped and said, "Brother, we have to go home. Once we're there, we can access the whole of the kingdom." The features of the map lost their brilliant colors and fell into the floor. Immediately, another meticulous, perfect image of the elven palace and its hinterlands rose. A fire sprouted into life above the royal residence.

The crown prince's eyes reflected the magic flames. "Not yet. First, we must determine what to do about this supposed elf spy for the chemmen, or we waste any plans we make here."

"There's a spy?" exploded one of the ladies as her face flushed. She smoothed her ivory dress. Caleb remembered that she was the mayor of Riverfall, and he was certain he'd met her before, but he did not recall her name.

Nearly everyone in the room edged to the lip of their seats.

The prince held up his hands. "Perhaps, and it may be someone of rank, but I do not want to believe that there is indeed a traitor amongst us." He licked his lips and tried to keep from looking at Farallon. "I wholeheartedly wish that it is just an attempt to sow discord at a time when we need trust the most."

And our chemmen prisoner could so easily be lying, he thought. *They assume we have a weakness for children and won't kill Thalon.* Which wasn't wrong, he admitted.

But what could an elven traitor, if there was one, hope to gain against the chemmen? There was no compromise. They'd proven that during the last war. He rubbed his forehead again. He couldn't just excuse the duke from this council. If he did, he doubted Farallon would even leave, and then how much less authority would he have?

"Prince Edillon—" the mayor eased.

He flinched. He didn't want to hear that name.

Jacob cleared his throat and attention shifted over to him. "However, the possibility of a spy is not prudent to ignore. They trapped us on the river when they should have never known we were there."

"What could ever possess an elf to turn on this kingdom?" demanded the mayor.

Jacob grunted. "Perhaps someone wants to improve his or her own rank."

Caleb stiffened and watched as the thought settled across their faces.

Farallon shot out of his seat and stormed into the illusion of the map. "Such a suggestion is insulting, dragoon. But you cannot understand since you're not of Indelleiria."

Jacob's face didn't move a muscle.

Caleb tensed as Farallon spun toward him. The duke spat, "This is outrageous. What you have not said is that the source of this information about a spy is a chemman, *and there are no chemmen traitors.* How do you think they found us on the river? He told them! There is no disloyal elf—it's all that chemman!"

Caleb caught Jacob and Amthros watching the duke coolly. He tried to match their expressions.

Alsalon spun toward him. "If a chemman told you this, why would you ever believe it, brother?"

"The young prince is wise," the mayor of Riverfall affirmed.

Farallon coughed, and the elves who had been on the river did not meet each other's eyes.

Caleb sighed. "Because this chemman has a son."

The mayor of Riverfall shook her head. "The chemmen have many children."

"No." Caleb struggled to push the air out of his lungs. "The child is half elven."

The following silence fell as thick as a blanket smothering a fire.

"We'd heard rumors since you've arrived," the mayor whispered. "But how could one of us...?"

Farallon muttered, "Maybe our prisoner killed the elf in the Wild Lands before we discovered their camp. Hidden with a bow in the night so the humans just blamed it on the cultists."

The mayor protested, "None of this makes sense. The chemmen were banished, how would that have been possible?"

Lady Sabielle lifted her chin. "How did they escape? How did any of this happen?"

"Perhaps they've been back long before they assaulted us." Evelyn looked down at the map. "They're resourceful. We weren't watching. They must have been plotting this since the day they were thrown off this world, and they are likely the very same enemies we fought before."

"Dis and Vlade." Farallon coughed into his hand. "Those are memories— Remember, children born to immortal parents are immortal. They all had to be killed or banished, every single one of them. We can't even spare their children. We made that mistake before." He hesitated. "That's why King Valladen chose to banish them."

Amthros stared down at his hands. He curled his fingers toward his body. "I don't think I could defend my life again."

"Even bringing those memories alive is a tragedy," Lady Sabielle snapped.

Evelyn shook her head at the duke. "Life is sacred, my lord. It is our duty as immortals not to forget that as they have."

"They're still human," he snapped back. "They just didn't die when they were supposed to."

Evelyn kept her gaze steady. "Would you also impose blanket death on regular humans too, my lord?"

Farallon scowled at her. Caleb pressed his lips together, keeping himself from speaking.

Amthros ran his hands over his face. "The world needs it to be this way, doesn't it? Slaughter in exchange for slaughter." He cracked his knuckles, and the elves flinched as he did so. He sighed. "We have no way to end this war quickly. This could persist for centuries if we don't act now. Draw them out; we need a battle."

Caleb sat back as he watched as one of the other elves shook his head. He didn't recognize the speaker. The unfamiliar elf said, "A fool's errand, Sir Amthros. Such rash action will only get us exposed and killed."

"I believe it to be our best choice. To end this now."

Lady Eve frowned. "No, sir knight, patience may be our ally, even throughout the horrors we endure. We don't know how they're back, so how could we defend against that?"

"Surely, you know something." Lady Sabielle stared at Evelyn.

"What I suspect is irrelevant," Lady Eve replied.

Surely more than 'suspect,' Caleb thought, but he held his tongue.

The mayor held Evelyn's gaze. "And why would you say that?"

The cook presented a winsome smile. "Unfortunately, I have said all that I can offer."

Amthros persisted, "No, we should draw out their army. We must lead them away from destroying more hapless towns and people. We need them to come to us."

"We don't have the soldiers to field against them," Lady Sabielle protested. She glanced at Jacob. "And Silver Dawn is..."

"—is smaller than most people think," the knight-captain finished. "We're not enough to cover Indelleiria's countryside, and that's if you allow our mixed-race soldiers into the kingdom. And even with the tree paths, gathering and marching is not instant. And frankly, I am not comfortable discussing battle strategy with all ears open right now."

The elves shifted their weights and looked away.

Caleb took in a deep breath before speaking, waiting for the others to be silent. "Our captive chemman must have lied to us. I trust everyone in this room." He put both his arms on their armrests. "So speak freely."

He knew he was contradicting what he had said earlier, but he couldn't make himself believe that Farallon could be a traitor. The duke had been part of his family all his life.

His gaze drifted over to his brother as he realized Farallon was speaking. "We don't know where they are, or how many of them there are. We can't guess where they will strike next. We know they want the princes. So perhaps here is their next target."

"They should not be able to strike here, even if the spy told them," the mayor replied. "But other places were more magically guarded than this..." She cast her gaze down at the palace on the map.

Lady Eve looked at Caleb. "It's obvious the seals on Darkreign were not enough. Perhaps we should do more to encourage those locks and banish them again."

Amthros growled, "We can't go through this a third time. Destroy them all. Except the children. We can teach them better this time since we know what to expect."

Jacob shook his head at Caleb. The prince tried to keep a straight expression.

"What can we do?" Alsalon asked. "Return to Long Range?"

"No." The dragoon knight didn't raise his eyes from the map as it changed back to show the whole kingdom, and the palace became a small, burning spot. "Stop fleeing. Gather your people from across the kingdom and move away from the cities since those seem to be targets."

"And how would we do that?" Amthros queried. "Rescuing people, while honorable, does not save us from the threat."

Jacob frowned. "It saves *them*. And for now, we must have a goal we can attain. Got to climb a mountain one stone at a time."

Farallon waved a hand at the map. "They expect us to attack Long Range. They *want* us to attack our own sacred ground."

"Do they still have a force there?" the dragoon asked. "Or did they just piss on it and chase after the rest of us?"

"Mind your tongue, sir!" yipped Lady Sabielle.

He shrugged, and Caleb watched him turn his attention back to the miniature palace on the map. The captain continued, "Long Range would be a fool's errand. It's empty of your people. We would only damage it and the lands around it, losing more lives in the process."

"They want that," the duke snarled as he folded his arms.

Caleb pursed his lips and nodded. The glowing ghost of a palace in the mountains absorbed his gaze. Home. "Then that is a fight we shall avoid. It must be freed by victory elsewhere."

"Well, where could we strike with victory assured?" Alsalon asked.

"I'm not sure there *is* such a place," Jacob answered.

Caleb cocked his head, staring at the map. His gaze drifted to the walls.

"Is something wrong, my prince?" the duke asked.

Caleb peered at the ivy-enshrouded wall. Finally, he shook his head. "No. I thought I heard something."

"There have also been attacks along the Pelippen River." Caleb looked at the elf who had spoken, and the prince sought for his name in his memory. He'd seen him before in his father's court. The elf continued to speak as more illusory fires began to glow over destroyed towns, "I doubt they will remain there though." On the map, the river flowed down through a canyon between the encircling mountains and toward the lands to the south of the kingdom.

Lady Eve closed her sapphire eyes. "I heard a silence on the wind blowing up the river. The rumor may be true. They may have that sword again."

"It was destroyed," said the elf whose name Caleb was still fighting to remember. "We watched it melt."

No one spoke for a moment, each dwelling on the memories and stories of that noiseless blade and the warrior who wielded it.

The crown prince frowned. "I was not there, but I know the tales, and they frighten me. The silent sword." His eyes drifted over to Amthros. "And its wielder." He dropped his gaze back to the map.

Amthros waved at the map. "We need to find them before we can truly plan against them." He scanned the whole of the kingdom with its many fires. "And we must act soon."

"You have no army," Jacob stated. "You're scattered. The dragoons are on their way, but I fear they may not make it in time."

"We need to act now," Farallon growled. Caleb watched him narrow his eyes at the map. He followed his gaze to the duke's domain in the north and the fires raging over it. Farallon's voice burned, "Lest they continue to snap at our heels until we've no feet left with which to run."

There was a loud crack and muffled cursing behind the wall of ivy. The elves turned with widening eyes. Jacob rose from his seat, balling a fist. Caleb swallowed his rising bile, but something about the imprecations didn't sound chemmen in nature.

"Damn!" a voice called from the top of the wall. The owner of the voice's foot slipped on a vine and lost balance entirely.

Der hung upside down for an instant before the vine trapping her ankle snapped and she plummeted to the floor.

CHAPTER THIRTY

She lay splayed and dazed before pushing herself to her feet. Der brushed herself off and pulled a few leaves from her hair. She limped toward the nearest bench, ignoring the stares of the council of elves and Caleb.

She smiled to everyone. "Sorry I'm late, but the door into this room is missing from the outside, so I had to find another way in. You might want to look into the spell that's messing with it." She took a seat next to Amthros.

"What have I missed?" She glanced around the conference and met a range of expressions. Jacob's face was twisted between being stunned and laughing. Farallon was livid. Lady Eve hid a smirk behind a hand. Everyone else stared with slack jaws.

Caleb ran a palm over an eye and looked at her from between his fingers. "Der, what are you doing here?"

Her smile fled, replaced by steel. "I'm not being left out of this."

Farallon's face burned red. "You have a remarkable talent for being in places you should not be. Unless Carenth Himself granted you special orders to be here, I want you gone. Now. You're a chemmen agent."

She shook her head.

"And how would you know that with such certainty, my lord?" Amthros's voice remained smooth and calm, but his brow had narrowed.

The duke gasped and froze. Then he blasted out, "It is the only logical assumption!"

"I'm just trying to help." Der kicked her foot out over the map, as if to point at it. "That's amazing. Look at it." She then leaned toward the duke and met his gaze.

Farallon gripped the bench so hard that splinters broke off under his hand. "Let me explain this to you, child—we're elves, and you're only one sixteenth. We are immortal royalty, nobility, or highly ranked military officers with much battle experience. Don't think you can play with us."

Der shrugged, and seemingly as an afterthought, straightened her shoulders. "You think this is a game?"

Farallon crashed his fist into his thigh and pointed with his other hand. "Get out of here!"

The crown prince clapped his hands together. "Enough."

Der spun toward him. "Oh come on, Caleb, I'm trying to help."

The duke gasped so forcefully that he hit a higher octave.

Caleb raised a hand. "My lord duke! When I had met Derora and Kelin, I kept my identity disguised, so they came into the habit of referring to me by a casual name. It is no dishonor."

Farallon sneered. "This mortal has no respect."

The prince shifted in his seat. "I enjoy my false name. It doesn't have the weight of my true one." He let his gaze glide over to Der. "In this war, we may need more of such an attitude."

"My prince, it's not an attitude; it's insanity."

"Hey!" Der interjected. "I can understand you this time."

"Good!"

"This isn't a trial, Der." Jacob frowned at her. "So don't make it into one."

Caleb set his hands on his armrests, eyeing both the duke and Der. "She and Kelin have been tortured at the hand of our enemy, which is more than I can say for either of us."

Der rubbed her face. The torture now seemed to be only a dazzling splinter in her memory, but it was enough to sidetrack her. She had been doing so well with *not* thinking of it too.

"Giving the duke refuge for his words," the mayor of Riverfall interceded, "Derora Saxen, we captured you in condemning circumstances. You should not be here."

Der stared at the mayor. "Who are you, my lady, and how did you know that?"

The elf straightened her dress over her knees. "Your story is known, child."

"Guards!" the duke roared. Two armored warriors appeared from out of the shadows. "Get her out of this place!"

Der dodged one questing pair of hands and landed right into another. She twisted and struggled, but to no avail.

Jacob coughed and clamped a hand over his mouth, but his shoulders were shaking.

"Wait! Wait!" She let her feet slide, forcing the guards to drag her. "I've figured out how you can defeat the chemmen! I have a plan!"

Caleb shook his head to her.

"Hold!" Lady Eve's curls slipped and rolled like silk as she stood. A frown creased her face. "Do you believe that, Derora?"

Farallon exhaled. "It doesn't matter what she believes."

The guards didn't release their grip on Der, but they had stopped dragging her away. She pulled against them anyway and met with Evelyn's gaze. "Invade Darkreign! Look, we're running with our tail between our legs. We're scared of them, but they need to be scared of us too! So we need to attack them."

Farallon was still shaking his head. "Get her gone. I do to need to entertain this idiot."

"Fine." Der sniffed. "I'll go. *You* don't have to."

Lady Sabielle pressed against her husband's arm just as he tensed to jump forward.

"I'll go," Der repeated.

Jacob snickered. Then he grinned and shook his head. "I like the spirit, Der, I do, but no."

Farallon snapped his fingers at the guards and pointed to the door. The soldiers began to drag her away.

Der went limp in their grasp again. "Then make them *think* you have enough men. If nothing else, it buys you time!"

Lady Eve nodded to Caleb. He waved at the guards, who let go of Der.

Across the room, Farallon glared at Evelyn, but the lady's gaze moved back to the map.

Evelyn raised a hand to Der. "She has a point. An elf or human in their territory would steal their attention."

"Yeah!" Der bounced on her feet. "Thistle could get us in..." she petered out against the weight of the stares. She sighed.

"Can't." Caleb shook his head. "Uh."

She cast her gaze on him. "Just a small party. Enough to make some noise."

The prince stared at her, slack-jawed.

She jumped up to stand on a bench. "Finally, I'm taller than everyone. All right, listen. The chemmen are

331

running all over the surface of the world, raiding your towns, killing your people, watching us duck and hide every time we think one of them is nearby. Do you think they're watching their own lands that much?"

"Sit down, girl!" She felt Farallon's glare, sharp as a knife's edge.

Der shifted her attention to Caleb. "I'm probably seeing things in a simplistic manner, but at least I'm not making this too complicated. You need a method to draw the chemmen's attention, and here it is. If you want to live, shove this fight down their throats."

"We can't possibly do this." The mayor wrung her fingers together while continuing to stare down at the map.

"No!" Farallon slapped his thigh. "That wasn't even attempted during the Centum Wars. No one in the history of the entire world has ever been so foolish."

"Surprise!" Der hollered. "They won't expect it." A smile forced itself upon her lips and she did her best to bite it back. She couldn't think of why she would smile now, but she was. She took a deep breath, giving her mind time to catch up with her mouth. "They started this war, and you're just sitting here letting them finish it!"

The elves sat on their mahogany benches as if turned to stone.

Jacob drummed his hands on his thighs. "Well... I doubt the chemmen would see it coming."

"The most reward is from the greatest risk." Gasps echoed around the room as Der studied the youngest elf in the room's sad but determined face. She nodded to him while many of the council looked at him in surprise.

"Yeah," she added. "It's enough to make it look like we've attacked their stronghold in Darkreign. Just enough to hold their focus while you get your army together."

"Well, you may be a tactical genius, or an idiot." The knight-captain leaned back, and she heard him clicking his tongue. "Of course, the raiding party would have to have a load of guts between the lot of them."

"And wouldn't mind losing them," Amthros breathed through a glassy stare.

"We know nothing of Darkreign itself!" Lady Sabielle exclaimed. "Nothing—it's just where ancient criminals were banished to."

Farallon shook himself free. "You wouldn't be able to leave, not that we'd miss you. That was always the lore: no one leaves Darkreign."

"And we still don't know how the chemmen escaped." Der folded her arms. "I guess we could figure it out as we go. Or make one of them tell us."

Confusion marred Farallon's features. "You can't be a spy for them because this is too stupid."

She blinked. "Thank you...?"

Amthros scowled. "I'm hesitant to even say this, but this raid would be enough of a distraction for us to gather our strength—if they believe it."

"Of course..." Jacob trailed off. "We don't know any path *into* Darkreign."

Evelyn offered, "With the prisoner's help, I may—"

Jacob shook his head at her.

"Better than doing nothing." Amthros's voice was hollow. "Or we can wait for them to mark us like they did our king and queen. One by one."

"How can you say such things?" Lady Sabielle snapped. "And so tactlessly in front of grieving children?" She nodded at the princes.

Jacob replied, "We're here to save lives, my lady, which isn't always the polite thing to do."

Evelyn suggested, "We could attempt a different, or perhaps simultaneous, distraction. The chemmen have three priority targets remaining. The two princes and myself."

Jacob shook his head, his face reddening. "Eve!" He cleared his throat. "My lady, no. Invading Darkreign is a less dangerous choice."

"I don't know about that." She smiled softly. "If they learn of my whereabouts, they will come running."

Der stepped down off the bench and took a seat. "You're not just a cook, are you?"

The lady shook her head. "Cooking is my passion, but no, I am not. The name that everyone knows to call me now is Evelyn of Elloan, but it wasn't my name when I first encountered the storm-readers."

Der frowned. "I was wondering why you had a human name."

"That is a story for another day. I am the Baroness of Elloan, and it was I who banished the chemmen into Darkreign at King Valladen's orders." She sat upright on the bench and swiveled toward Jacob. "It's misdirection, sir knight."

Caleb scowled. "I will not leave you to such a fate, my lady."

"That's right," Jacob seconded.

"I should go," the prince continued, still watching the lady, "You're more valuable than I am."

"Absolutely not!" Farallon bellowed.

Der cocked her head at the baroness. "But, if you're a magic user, why can't you just tell us what the chemmen are planning? Or who this traitor is?"

Evelyn's smile saddened. "I would like to, but all I can see are potentials flowing like water, and sometimes, the river gets dammed. So we must make our choices with the information we have."

The duke waved his hand over the map. "My lady, I also must protest. You may be the only one who can damn them back into Darkreign."

Lady Eve looked to Der. "If we do nothing to argue our fate, then it will speak for us, and waiting for fate is always a weak position."

Caleb jerked his head from side to side. "My lady, I cannot leave you to do this... I prefer the raid idea."

"One often needs the enemy to believe something other than the truth." The baroness's smile spread. "They said the tactic of the Battle of the Bridge wouldn't work either." Echoes of horror and gasps bounced around the chamber. "Misdirection worked then, and it can work now."

"It nearly didn't," Jacob's voice rang hollowly, and Der watched a little piece of hell burning in his eyes. "But it had to be done."

"Sounds like you know the legend well," she observed.

"That happens when you see it for yourself."

Der leaned back and shook her head in surprise. "But that's ancient history!"

Farallon snapped, "About time you realized with whom you're dealing, child." He waved his hand. "And this stupid, outrageous idea of a raid on Darkreign was thought of by a fool who's never been in a war before. She doesn't know what she's talking about."

Der grinned. "But at least we can all agree that we need to defeat the chemmen. You're scattered with no army, and defenseless people are being slain. The only thing you can do is cause a distraction, and fast. It's all common sense, really. But they're your enemy, not mine."

"They're the enemy of every sentient being, child," the mayor barked. "In fact, I'm surprised that the chemmen didn't attack the dwarves first."

Caleb stared ahead as he shook his head. "Of course they're enemies too, but not as much as we are."

Der shrugged. "They're still enemies." She watched her friend's expression; he was pale and looked defeated.

Jacob cleared his throat. "I think this is crazy, but I can't dismiss it outright. Not when we are this desperate."

Der straightened in her seat.

The duke pointed to the map. "No. Draw them out into the open surface, our territory, where we will be superior."

"Will be," Jacob echoed. "But we are not now."

Farallon snapped, "I thought the dragoon orders were the greatest armies in the world."

"In our world." Jacob stared at the map. "There is no goal to be achieved but slaughter with an open battle. You know better than that, certainly."

"I can't believe we're discussing this preposterous idea of raiding the chemmen!" the duchess interjected.

The captain eyed Lady Eve, but then blew out a sigh. "If we're going to be this reckless, if we go ahead on this fool's errand, we must twist a knife into their paranoia. I don't think they would believe that this is a ruse if we make it seem like a forward scout for an invasion. It's too much of a chance for them to take. If it works, we will get you the time to get our army here. If it doesn't, not much is lost."

"How many soldiers' lives are 'not much'?" Amthros whispered. "But at least they would be soldiers..."

"A fool's errand indeed." The duke stamped his boot over the surface of the map. The images once again melted into the floor, and none replaced them.

Caleb sighed. "Volunteers."

The mayor shook her head. Her face twisted. "My prince, you're willing to allow this errand?"

He nodded. "Yes. If successful, we will earn an advantage."

"Not like this." Farallon looked at Der in disgust. "Not on the advice of a human. The chemmen are human, for gods' sakes!"

"They haven't been for some time now." The prince's voice remained calm. "Perhaps on the advice of a human. Now is the time we should seek out the other races again. As a people, we have been quite reactionary since the end of the Centum Wars. We barely associate with the younger races. I've learned much in the short time with Derora and Kelin." He stared back at the floor. "If we were alone in the world and superior, we would not be losing this war."

"That's as may be, my prince," Farallon said, "but you cannot be serious about this."

Der stuck up a hand. "I am serious." But then she hunched her shoulders and glanced back at Caleb. "But if there is a spy here, the chemmen will know."

"When are you going to tell them?" Farallon snorted.

"We will keep our plans to ourselves, girl," the mayor growled.

"And if the spy is in this room?" Jacob asked in a low voice.

Der saw that he kept his eyes fixed on Caleb, but she also caught Amthros's gaze jerking to Farallon.

"Then we may already have lost," Caleb muttered. She watched him slouch back in his chair and look at the younger elf next to him. He sighed again. "If they're successful, this war can be over within weeks." He looked between Jacob and Der. "If there are those willing, we shouldn't deny them."

Farallon straightened his shirt. "We won't deny them being tortured to death."

Der flinched.

CHAPTER THIRTY ONE

Kelin charged. *"Der!"* He grabbed her arm and yanked her around. "I don't know what you said or when you said it, but this outrageous foray has your scent all over it!"

"How...? It's a secret. Was it Farallon?" She tried to jerk away, but his grip was iron. They were in a long hallway, which was open on one side to the majesty of the mountains.

"Why did they listen to you? Why?"

"Because we could end this war." She offered a weak smile.

"You want to go *back* to them? Have you forgotten what they did?" He slapped his leg, hard. He had to hit *something*. "This plan will fail worse than your last one, *and you know what happened to us.*" He strangled the air with his hands. "Do you need a perspective on this? You're walking up to the dragon's snout and telling it that it's ugly and needs to bathe!"

She plugged her nose. "It's not the only one."

"Stop joking! Just stop it!" He waved his finger at her. "I'll tell you exactly what you're doing. You're taking the scariest myth we have and poking it *on their home ground* that is not even part of this world." His knees quaked, threatening to give out. He couldn't catch his breath. "I can't go through that again. Please..."

She sighed, but nodded.

"You're human, Der, despite what little elvish blood you have, you were raised human and you will die as one. So what did you know that they don't?"

She straightened her sleeves. "How to try something new."

His tone melted away from anger and dropped into pleading, "This will be worse, and I can't imagine worse."

"Can't you?" she whispered. "I can, and I'm terrified of what will happen if we don't do this."

Kelin growled deep in his throat. "Now you're sounding like an elf!"

"What's wrong with that?"

They spun. Jacob leaned against the wall, arms crossed and an eyebrow raised.

Sir Amthros stood behind the dragoon, breathing slightly harder than the other knight. "We heard shouting." He glanced at the other's repose. "He was closer."

Kelin folded his arms and narrowed his eyes at his friend. "Only Der's stupid idea. And you elves are just as bad for going along with it."

Jacob kept his gaze steady. "Well, she's not going."

"Why not?" Der stormed toward him. "It's my plan!"

The captain laughed. "I'm sorry, kid. You got the spirit, but you don't have the experience or the training. Also, we've spoken to Thistle. Things may have changed."

"What?" Amthros straightened.

Jacob glanced at the other knight. "Farallon was in that council."

Kelin asked, "What's wrong with the duke being in the council?"

"Why wasn't I told?" Amthros frowned.

Jacob shrugged. "It isn't my place to keep you informed, sir."

Der scowled. "So what about us?"

Amthros spoke while still watching the other knight, "You children will be kept safe. There's nowhere safer than here. For right now, at least. The chemmen may have tortured you, but—"

"Yeah," Der interrupted. "That's why I want to fight them—so they can't do that again."

"Perhaps you're missing my point. You survived. You can flee this. We cannot."

Kelin forced a hopeful smile. "Der, c'mon, they won't bother us."

The captain shrugged again. "They wouldn't put too much effort into chasing two mortals."

"I'm not running." Der tightened her jaw.

Amthros bowed his head. "It might be best for you."

"I'm not running!"

Jacob sighed. "No, you're not, kid. But you're not fighting either."

Kelin sucked in a deep breath. "This isn't the meadow, on a plow pony, dreaming of knighthood. This is real, and there's nothing we can do that the elves can't do better."

Her face tightened even more. "Caleb is our friend, and friends don't run away."

"If we leave, he won't have to worry about some clumsy humans stumbling in the way."

"No, he'll just have to worry about us on our own."

Jacob said, "I'm sure the prince can arrange something safe for you."

"Then he can arrange something safe for himself." She crossed her arms.

The knight's mouth opened and then clicked shut. "I want to impress on you the difference between your situation and his."

"We'll stay here, thank you very much."

Amthros sighed. "I wish you understood the chemmen better. No one is safe, especially around Thistle, despite what you may think of him." He cracked his knuckles.

"What about Thalon then?" Der asked.

The knight of Indelleiria shook his head. "He's a child. Children are...different."

"As for Thalon," Jacob said softly, "we'll hope his elven side shines through for now."

"What does that mean?" Kelin asked.

The captain looked at the other knight. "I wasn't there, unlike some." Amthros dropped his gaze. Jacob continued, "But it was what led the elf king to banish the chemmen from the earth. There was a battle over a chemmen town called Darii, and the elves did not keep any chemmen alive. The war had grown desperate enough that neither side was taking prisoners."

"Except for the children." Amthros gripped a fist at his side. "We spared the children. We kept them in a prison but treated them well. They looked and acted like they were frightened, and we thought there was hope for them."

"What happened?" Der asked.

Amthros shuddered. "They, the chemmen children, thought they were doing the right thing. They broke free and attacked us in the middle of the night, killing some of my dear friends. And we..." He stopped and his eyes didn't focus on anything present.

Jacob finished, "In order to survive, the elves were forced to defend themselves."

Amthros stared at the floor. "I wish it never happened. I wish we never had to."

Der shifted her weight from foot to foot.

Jacob cleared his throat. "Well, since we've all got our long faces on, then it is time we should head to the vanishing ceremony."

"What's that?" Der asked.

Amthros frowned. "What do they call it more colloquially in Common? I'm not sure if I know the word."

"A funeral," Jacob answered.

CHAPTER THIRTY TWO

Colors seemed to carry no glow in the circular hall, and the air was thick, heavy, and ultimately still.

Kelin and Der blinked, but their vision did not adjust. They shuffled to the back while Amthros marched to the front of the hall. It didn't look like the temple in Duelingar, Der thought, but it had a chapel feel to it with the vaulted ceiling and large windows.

They must have been the last to arrive. Jacob nodded a silent farewell and ducked outside the door, closing it behind him.

Caleb stood in the center of the dais. Prince Alsalon, Evelyn of Elloan, the mayor of Riverfall, and Duke Farallon surrounded him. Amthros moved to stand in front of them and kept his hand near his sword.

The room dimmed even more. Der glanced back at the shut door and felt her shoulders squeeze together in this tight place.

Unified voices lifted a song into the chapel. The slow melody was a rising river, and Der's heart beat swiftly as its current washed over her.

The song swept faster around them and it entered her mind. It scoured those cold and cobwebbed corners, weaving into her thoughts, and bringing back forgotten memories.

Its magic took her far away from the elvish haven. She forgot she was even in a room when her parents flitted across her vision, and a worn memory surged upward.

When the river had flash flooded, Der and her father had rushed into town. They had helped people from their homes onto logs and barrels, tied with ropes leading all the way back to shore. She remembered the hot dinner Rhoesia and Chera had prepared them when they arrived home, soaking and cold. Half the village had slept on their floor and in the barn that night. But what she most remembered was her family eating together while watching the water. She pressed a hand over her heart and realized how far away they were—and how much she missed them.

A final, glorious note saturated the air for a moment of bittersweet ecstasy. The song cut off, ending suddenly.

Silence swept across the hall. Der leaned against the door for balance, gasping.

On the dais, Prince Alsalon flashed a glance to his older brother, who nodded. The younger prince inhaled deeply. "We must never forget those whose grace has been stolen by the hand of our enemy." He knotted his fingers together. "They killed our king and queen, my father and mother, in our own sacred garden. That horror defines me now. We were there that day, and we did not want to leave them. Our parents implored us to run while they remained. They were marked for death. Marked by..." Tears on his face fell like rain. He turned toward his brother. "I can't..."

"It's all right," Caleb whispered. He stepped forward to stand next to Alsalon and spoke, "Marked by a traitor who also allowed our enemy into the palace." He swallowed and pressed on, "And so many others know my pain here today. So let us remember everyone who has been taken from us." He dipped his chin but then raised his face as his lips parted, and a new song brightened the chapel. More voices joined, and the melody bounced off the walls in harmony.

Kelin grabbed his head and gasped. In his mind, he saw and suddenly came to know the individuals who had died at the hands of the chemmen. He recognized some of their faces from the river, but now he knew their names, where they were from, and what they enjoyed doing in life. A mental picture of each of the slain materialized, not at their point of death, but in a smiling moment. Kelin wished he didn't know. It would have hurt so much less.

He'd thought the past weeks had numbed him, but this left him dizzy and sobbing. He couldn't contain the searing pressure building in his chest. He was boiling from the inside. He stumbled back into the wall. Why did the elves do this to themselves?

Death hurts them more, he thought. But he hoped they could also learn the same lesson he did when his grandmother passed, to appreciate life a thousand times more. They didn't have to in the way everyday humans did. But how could he communicate something so alien as that to them?

The song continued. The elven king and queen crystallized in his mind, and their dulcet laughter coursed through his body. The king propped a small Alsalon on his shoulders, while a young Caleb trotted at his side, gazing up at his father. The queen smiled and waved to her youngest, pretending he was sitting on something as high as a mountain.

The canticle faded. Kelin found himself clawing at the air in front of him. The song had been anguishing, but he craved it back. Now there was just a void, with no music or life in it.

"My parents were my heart." Caleb stepped to the edge of the dais, and his hands hung at his sides. His voice fell over the room as softly as a whisper of rain. "And it died with them. No matter how much earth we shovel into a grave, it will never be enough to fill these holes we feel. No one will share in their beauty and laughter again, and I miss a future with them as much as I miss them now." He gulped. "I want no one else to have to know this pain. We've all lost someone." He raised his head and clenched a fist and then stared out at the assembly with burning eyes. "So we will take action. This is not the end. Not for us, not for our enemy. Only those who have died are free of this fight. And we shall not wait for the enemy to kill another elf. We shall stab their heart this time, in their own city. A raiding party has volunteered. They will risk their lives for all our sakes."

Kelin wheeled toward Der, but she wasn't there. The door behind him was cracked open. He swayed for balance as a new song split the air. It was a chant for the warriors, a blessing and a warning mixed in the lyrics. The tune was sharper, like the edge of a sword, and much faster paced. He glanced around. He didn't think he had any tears left, and his heart was pumping in anger.

He growled underneath his breath. How could she leave? He tiptoed through the door.

The sunset's orange glow made him squint in the exterior walkway. He shaded his eyes while looking up and down the open corridor. He fired a glimpse at the sun. Had he been in that room for most of the day? It felt like a quarter of an hour, at most.

He found Der resting beside an opening that boasted a view of the mountains. She scratched hard at the tears on her cheek. "I don't understand what's so impossible to accept about what happened. Yeah, it's terrible and horrifying, but life goes on."

He sighed and approached. "I don't know. Maybe if no one died around us, we'd see it differently too."

"And I guess that's why they're so hesitant to fight. I mean, all they've done so far is run away."

"Elves usually avoid battles because it's not worth the sacrifice." Jacob shrugged. They spun toward him. He must have been standing there the whole time. He continued, "You don't understand what it takes for them to go to war. They don't want to now, and they're *already* at war."

"Yes," Der said. "But you're the one who's going on this raid. Isn't it too dangerous for you then?"

He chuckled. "Jacob isn't an elvish name."

"I figured—like Lady Evelyn, right?"

He shook his head. "Not quite. She did it because she chose to." He sighed. "You know, I've been thinking today. You wouldn't be risking as much as an elf."

"What are you saying, sir?" Kelin narrowed his eyes.

"I'm commanding this raid." He raised his finger, and Der went cross-eyed fixating on it. He intoned, "So you'd better learn to take my orders without question."

Kelin's jaw fell open. "You're going to allow her?"

Next to him, Der gasped and grabbed the railing to keep her balance. She couldn't fight off a grin.

Jacob shrugged. "She's not useless with a sword, and she's already held her own against the chemmen. Also, it's not as though other volunteers are coming forth." He glanced up and down the corridor. "And maybe another little wrinkle best spoken in private." He looked at Der. "Well, it's your idea. I trust you can do this. Do you accept?"

She bounced on the balls of her feet. "Yes, sir!" She tapped her chest with a fist in salute.

He didn't grin back. "If it's too much for you, tell me before it's too late." He turned to Kelin. "And you?"

Kelin narrowed his gaze at the knight and then whipped it onto Der. Birds would have fallen out of the sky for that glare. She didn't flinch. He dusted his hands. "You're both lunatics."

"It'll work." She folded her arms and raised an eyebrow.

Jacob waved a hand. "Kelin, hear us out first. This raid is not as shallow as it looks to be."

"It isn't?" Kelin sneered.

The knight smiled weakly. "Actually, you being human and, sadly, previously tortured by the chemmen, will only grease the wheels. We are not going to attack the chemmen head-on, we're just going to give a little distraction to buy time for Silver Dawn to arrive."

"Please, Kelin," Der whispered. "Think of all the good we can do."

He scowled at the floor and crossed his arms. "Dying's all we've got to look forward to anyway. Damn my own stupidity, and damn you too. I'll go."

"Good." The knight nodded and grabbed a shoulder from each of them in his massive hands. "Now, try to chase some sleep tonight, if you can."

Der waved a hand back at toward the chapel. "But what about that?"

Jacob shrugged. "I expect they'll be done before dawn. But understand that these are very truncated obsequies."

He pushed them down the hall. Behind them, the songs continued until the moon itself had gone to sleep.

CHAPTER THIRTY THREE

"He killed chemmen, Dis!" Vlade roared. Dis raised a hand to protect himself from the commander's spittle as his voice echoed around the cave. They'd been forced to hide here since the elves had raided their Altice Domain outpost. "Your precious spy wounded and slew our own!" Saliva frothed in the corners of his mouth. He looked at the mirror that the king had angled to fit against the cave's wall.

Dis fought to remain calm in his seat. The king rubbed the scars on his forearms and wondered where he'd picked up the cuts. He sighed and glanced back at the obsidian mirror.

Vlade held his eyes closed with his fingertips. "We should have returned to Darkreign, and if I knew you were going to do so little here, I would have *suggested* that I direct the war from there. In fact, I am returning after I'm done with you." He let his hands fall and drew out a sigh. "And there's worse. Our troops tell us that they saw a young boy with eyes such as our own."

"We have no children authorized to fight." Dis frowned. "The elves would surely slay him."

"We have not located him, so he may be lost. I wondered about it through my next campaign."

"That town wasn't in our plan."

The commander snarled, "I needed to show them that the sword is back."

"And yet you let the princeling escape on the river."

"I wasn't there for that attack. I was too far from a tree path, but you know my soldiers are well trained."

"You were too far away because you were busy with your toy sword."

"It worked!" Vlade snapped. Dis watched his feet dancing beneath him before he could rope them back under his control. "I saw their faces. I witnessed the fear reborn."

"You still failed the chemmen cause. You failed me. The prince is—"

"You failed *us*, Dis." Vlade drew the silent sword, letting his fingers slide down the length of it. He held it still. "And I wasn't aware I was acting on your behalf."

"You are because I am your king."

Vlade snorted. "If you must remind me, then I'm not so sure you are. My plan, my vengeance, my army."

"I am and always have been. I was the one who saved us, and I am the one who will bring us revenge!"

"This is my war!" Vlade struck the end of Dis's obsidian armrest with his sword. Pieces of surgically sharp glass shot across the room.

The king lowered his unharmed hand. Then he exploded off the throne and shoved his arm out toward Vlade. "This is your fault!" Dis ripped back his sleeve, and the straight laceration glistened on his forearm. He dug his fingernails into it.

Vlade grabbed his own arm. An identical wound bloodied his skin. The two of them had shared wounds since right before the banishment.

The king stalked closer, briefly glancing back at the mirror. "When I find the magic that binds us, I will break it and you. Though you may be my brother, I loathe you, and I will raise my hand against you."

"If your plan is to talk me to death." Vlade straightened and slammed his sword into its sheath. He gripped his hilt hard enough to choke a person. "You and I share the same pains."

Dis tapped his chin, smiling as he watched his counterpart's intensity. He was envious of it, in fact. Vlade had always craved war, had always wanted to show off how much better he was than everyone else. *Including me,* the king acknowledged. He had clawed his way up the ranks—he had battle victories even as a child. He was a self-made hero. And throughout his long life, he ignored how that made him different.

But Dis had let him. The king always had to do something with his anger, so he'd allowed Vlade to make their plans. But Vlade's conquests never filled that void inside.

All because he had known who his father was. He wouldn't have had this hollow in his chest if he'd been raised together with the other children. He knew that he had to have siblings somewhere in his ranks, and those unknown brothers and sisters had no idea what a sibling was. How he wished for that.

At least he'd been made king because of who his father had been, but killing that old bastard hadn't filled that hole either. Conquering those kingdoms hadn't. Everlasting life hadn't. Failing to fell Pallens had not, *especially* after that thief had double-crossed them first, despite his promise to let them into the empire unseen. Making a home in Darkreign had failed him.

But if they got their vengeance against Indelleiria, maybe then he could finally rest.

He sighed and bowed his head. "We must return to our goals. We must kill the princes and that damned baroness. Then, without them or their witch, the others will fall to our swords with ease."

The tension visibly left Vlade's shoulders. A smile slithered across his face, and he nodded.

***

"Good morning, recruits!"

Der squinted—a red blur obscured the world. She blinked. "Sir, it's not morning. There's no sun."

Jacob craned his head toward the window. "Yes, there is. Almost. Anyway, get out of bed."

"Wha..." Across the room, the shape under Kelin's covers wriggled.

The captain reached out and yanked the blankets off the young man. "Get up! You've got a quarter hour to get dressed, down to the kitchen, and fed."

Der sat up on her bedroll. "That's not much time, sir."

"So get moving."

"What's going on?" Kelin rubbed his eyes and yawned.

Jacob chuckled. "You'll see."

"This is going to hurt, isn't it?" The human stretched his legs and feet.

The knight kept grinning. "Would I harm my newest recruits?"

"Yes."

"It's for your own good." He shrugged. "Now step up!" He left them blinking in the pre-dawn light. Der rolled to the side and pushed herself up.

When they collapsed into the chairs in the kitchen, Lady Eve—who by now they took for granted did not require sleep and always had food prepared—already had two bowls waiting for them.

Her smile lit her multi-faceted eyes. "It's cold vegetables and boiled ham. The captain insisted. You're fortunate he didn't try to make it himself." With a sympathetic nod, she turned and disappeared through an arched doorway.

Jacob entered from the other archway and took his place at the opposite side of the table. He sipped from a large mug in his hand. "Eat up; two minutes left."

"What's after breakfast?" Kelin narrowed his eyes at the knight.

"Training." The captain took another drink.

"What about the raid?" Der inquired. "Do we even have time for training?"

"Yes. You won't be going without it. Now, finish up."

***

The impromptu arena was a large open courtyard enclosed by trees, like many of the spaces in Riverfall, but this one had a small, waist-high stone wall encircling it. The ground was even and swept clean of any leaves.

"Your mail and weapons are over there." The captain raised a hand over to the wall.

Kelin gasped and raced over. "My sword!"

Der trotted after him. She looked the slightly curved sword up and down before shaking her head. "No, it's not. Look." It was differently colored and the blade was longer, but it was similar. There were a few other blades and pieces of equipment next to it along with a trunk.

He breathed out a smile as his fingers closed around it. "I feel...a bit of home anyway though."

Jacob pointed with his foot to the items beside the swords. "See if that armor fits you."

Kelin lifted a chainmail shirt. He pushed it up and down in his hands. "I wouldn't have thought elvish armor would weigh so much." Rust speckled parts of it. "Or look ready to fall apart."

"Oh, this isn't elvish. Don't think you get to be so lucky. No, you'll start with these old patches of iron." He clapped once. "First lesson, taking care of your equipment."

"Aren't we going to learn how to fight, sir?" Der fiddled with a rusted pot helm. "Why do you even have this stuff here?"

"Riverfall is an outpost, so maybe somebody found it and brought it home." He shrugged. "And yes, Der, you will learn how to fight, but you can't use a sword if you don't take care of it. Not for long, anyway."

"Elvish swords and mail rust?"

"They can if you don't care for them." He indicated with a finger. "You'll need to oil any leather: boots, belts, sheaths, and so on. I would have you do that now, but since we're rushed today, I'm ordering you to do that on your own. All right, next." His eyebrows narrowed. "Well, you've already fought some of the worst things humans can fight, and you didn't run away. Did well, in fact, for being untrained. Um." He blinked several times. "Aside from chemmen, undead, and calvar, there's not too much else that's scarier."

"What about dragons, sir?" Der grinned.

He held up his index finger. "Don't get me started on dragons. I've seen enough dragons."

"'Cause you're a dragoon knight."

"Right." He nodded. He shrugged off his baldric, drew his sword, inspected it quickly, and sheathed it. His huge, double-bladed axe leaned against the wall, and he plucked up its shortened handle. In his other hand, he hefted a massive shield that complemented his armor in color.

Der tilted her head. "You have a kite shield and full platemail. You don't need both. And what's with the axe *and* the sword?"

Kelin stepped up beside her. "I was wondering about that too."

Jacob took one deep breath. "Because after the shield, it's the armor, after the armor, it's my skin. The more heavy metal between my enemy and me, the better. With the axe and the sword, same principle."

"Elves don't use axes." Kelin stared at it. "So I always thought."

The knight laughed. "Swords are merely old; axes are ancient."

Der wrinkled her nose. "Fine. But how much does it all weigh?"

"More than you." Jacob winked.

Kelin leaned toward Der. "That means don't try to arm wrestle him."

Jacob chuckled. "Sound advice. All right, you two fight each other. I want to see how well you can handle your weapons first." He pointed at a medium-length sword. "Der, you take that one."

She swiped up the sword and grinned. Kelin brought his up on guard.

She ran him into the wall instantly. He wasn't fast enough to escape her blade, especially once she found she could move this blade easier than her father's. In fact, she overcorrected herself several times, but it didn't matter because Kelin still backed away as quickly as he could.

She stepped back and let him return to his ready stance. They fought again. Der struck him two or three hits for every touch he landed on her. He was stronger, but she was faster and knew swordplay better. She also never stopped. They danced across the courtyard, their feet trampling over their own dusty footprints as they circled around and around.

The captain clapped his hands. "Stop." He stepped forward as the pair lowered their weapons. "Kelin, you keep shifting your grip. Don't. Der, you need to retreat, just half a step or so when you parry. Right now, you don't back up at all. If you do, it gives you more space to execute your moves, and you don't get too close to your enemy. Both of you follow?"

They nodded.

Jacob grinned. "Good. All right, Der, let's go." He drew his sword.

For the first time, she hunched her shoulders. "Um."

His grin spread. "You wanted to be a warrior; now's your moment."

She nodded and lifted the point of her blade. Her forward stance and style didn't change and she was entirely overwhelmed, but still didn't take a step backward.

"Retreat!"

She tried—but concentrated on the step back so much that she fumbled her parry. She barked a curse.

She shouldn't have wasted her breath swearing as Jacob forced her back even more.

This wasn't working for her at all, she decided, and she didn't try to retreat again. She attacked awkwardly, and he laughed as he blocked anything she tried.

The knight stopped his assault. He grinned. "You don't know when to be intimidated."

Der shook her head, panting for air.

Jacob pointed at her with his sword. "So. Are you going to retreat or die?"

She tried not to shift her weight. "Neither?"

He sighed and set down his sword before picking up the massive axe. Kelin took two steps back, but Der stood there, eyes wide.

The knight attacked with a sudden move. She ducked the blow, stuck her sword out, and skittered to the side.

"Oh, now you want to run!" He closed ground with enormous strides and was upon her before she was ready. He forced her to run away several more times before she settled into a pattern where she could at least launch a few counter-attacks. And she knew it was because he allowed them. As they fought, she kept waiting for his arm to sag. How could anyone hold that huge axe one-handed for so long and still be so fast? Her sword already weighed her down.

"Halt!" Jacob held up his left hand. "That's enough for now. You're getting the idea. In formation, you obviously can't give ground like that since you don't have the freedom of movement you do in one-on-one." He leveled the axe at Kelin. "Your turn."

"But your sword's still over there, sir." Kelin pointed while already backing away.

"Der got the axe, so it's only fair you do too."

"Yes, sir." He dropped his gaze and raised his sword.

But it wasn't the same whirlwind of attacks Der had provoked. The knight was slower and more calculated. Jacob instructed, "Keep your moves as small and tight as possible." Their weapons clashed together again. "That's too small. Keep them useful!"

Through the rest of the morning, he directed them in standard drills on footwork, bladework, and everything else they could imagine. Der swore her body should have given up long ago, but it kept moving and she couldn't explain how.

Finally, Jacob allowed them a respite. "Drink up." He tossed a waterskin in Kelin's direction.

As they took turns sipping, the knight walked back and forth in front of them. "Always attack when you have an opening. Der, I don't believe you have a problem with this, but sometimes you attack when you don't have an opening."

"Yes, sir." She wiped the sweat from her face.

He leaned against an oak that extended over the wall. "This is enough for now. You need to rest." He grimaced. "Well, no, it isn't enough, but it's what we've got." He glanced back at them. "You've both had training before though."

Der nodded. "My father."

"Good. But I bet he didn't teach you to be arrogant when you fight. Watch out for that."

She frowned. "But you fight like that."

He grinned. "I'm just confident."

"What's the difference?"

"Experience."

Kelin leaned over and whispered loudly, "Which means he's made a lot more mistakes than you."

Der laughed before she got her hand up to her mouth. Kelin stepped behind her, but the captain chuckled too. "There *might* be truth in that."

"Are you training or joking around?" Caleb stood in the entrance to the courtyard, along with Amthros and two other elven warriors. Der was sure the sun glowed a little brighter as he stepped into the arena. The prince continued, "Because I very much loathe missing a good joke."

Jacob bowed his head. "Sir prince."

Der waved her hand. "Good to see you again, Caleb!"

Kelin kicked her in the ankle, but the prince smiled and held up his hand to the two elven fighters. "These are your other volunteers."

"Two more than I expected," Jacob murmured.

A dark-haired elf with flashing silver eyes bowed stiffly. "I am Fienan of the Aeolian Plateau, and I used to make my home at the Windgates. Well met."

"Well met," Der and Kelin echoed.

The other elf, who was fair-haired, also bowed. "And I am Salinienn of Elloan, and I am here at my lady's request."

"I thought this mission was for volunteers," Der remarked.

He smiled. "She was the one who informed me that there was a dangerous mission, but this is my choice."

The prince's face darkened. "Just five volunteers. I can't believe that this war may depend on so few souls."

"Five volunteers, yes," Jacob said. "Six on the mission."

"What?" Fienan asked. "Conscription is against our law."

"The chemman prisoner is joining you." Caleb kept his chin high, but his voice was low.

Salinienn thrust up his hands and shook his head. "I will not travel with a chemman!"

Fienan made a disgusted face. "I also must protest, my prince. We cannot trust a storm-reader."

Caleb raised his eyebrows as he turned to them. "He can give and gain insights we cannot, even if he has never been to Darkreign as he claims. I believe he's fighting this war for the sake of his son."

"Yes, but he's *chemmen*," Salinienn hissed.

Jacob shook his head. "Doesn't matter. I say he goes, and I'm in command here—begging your highness's pardon. If you don't want to volunteer, you don't have to."

Fienan glared. "This raid could end the war. I will go." He exchanged a glance with Salinienn, whose shoulders slipped forward before he nodded.

"Wait, wait. If Thistle goes, what about Thalon?" Kelin asked.

Amthros dipped his chin. "Since I am staying with the princes, I could care for him."

"No!" Jacob barked. "You're a knight. You have other duties."

"I thought you'd come with us, Sir Amthros." Der tilted her head at him. "You've been with us through everything so far."

The knight of Indelleiria frowned. "I'm sorry, but my duty is to protect the children, especially those of the king and queen."

"I am not a child," Caleb snapped.

"Of course not, my prince. I only meant to protect you." He shifted his weight. "I was hoping that we could also take the boy with Lady Evelyn to Elloan."

Caleb exhaled and rubbed his forehead. "Sir Amthros. Perhaps it is best if we keep *some* secrets in case their mission isn't flawless. You know how possible it is that they may be captured."

Salinienn grimaced. "It is known that prisoners of the chemmen are tortured for whatever knowledge they may possess."

"Ah." Der tried not to shudder at her memories. "So that's common then, is it?"

Fienan nodded. "They seem to have kept to their old habits."

Amthros lowered his voice, "It is imperative that no one speaks to Duke Farallon of this. It's dangerous enough that he knows of the raid. But we're watching him. It's a risk, I know, but so is—" his eyes slid over to Jacob "—oh, I don't know, invading the chemmen."

Caleb closed his eyes and exhaled. "These are dark times indeed. We do not know whom we can trust, and yet, we must risk our lives upon such information." He looked up. "Derora, Kelin, this is not your war."

"It has been ever since Duelingar," she countered. "And this is my plan." She shot a look at Jacob, who shrugged but nodded.

The prince looked out between the trees. Der's gaze followed. She saw what she had seen when they'd first arrived, the landscape dropping off a cliff outside Riverfall. It felt as if the settlement were flying.

The prince's voice danced into her thoughts. "I remember the lesson of a poem that my father wrote long ago. In times of disaster and grave need, heroes will always come forth because nature is about balance. But even when the disaster doesn't claim complete destruction, there are always scars."

Der scrunched up her face. "Uh, did he write a poem about victory or something? I'd rather hear that instead."

CHAPTER THIRTY FOUR

Underneath the yellow and red falling leaves of the deciduous trees, Lady Eve waited beside Thalon while Thistle stood back with a straight face. But the boy pushed himself away from the baroness and threw himself into his father's knees.

"Dad, this isn't fair!" He smacked his fist against Thistle's thigh. "Don't leave me behind!"

Thistle knelt to be level with him. "This has to be done. The lady will care for you."

Thalon shoved against his shoulder as hard as he could. "You said I wasn't to trust anyone except you and Mama. *Anyone.* You don't know her!" He jerked his hand at the baroness.

His father's orange eyes didn't flicker. "Thalon. After this, we'll go wherever you want, to whatever mountains or oceans you want to see. I promise."

The boy sniffed back his tears. "Why can't I go with you now?"

"Because I am going somewhere dangerous."

Thalon inhaled again. "More dangerous than the river?" He puffed up his chest. "I wasn't scared!"

Thistle held his gaze evenly. "And I am proud of you. You're getting big now, so you're ready for the truth." He paused but didn't look away. "We're going to Darkreign."

Thalon's eyes exploded wide. He grabbed his father's shirt. "But you said we were never to go there, never ever!"

The chemman grimaced. "I know. But after this, we'll be free. No more chemmen or elves. Just you and me." He rose and spun the boy on his heel. "Now, you see this lady?"

Evelyn smiled and curtsied.

His father pointed over his shoulder. "I need you to watch over her and keep her safe."

Thalon whirled back around. "No! Why can't I go with you? I can fight!"

The elf chuckled, and the sound drifted over them like leaves playing on the wind. "He's been listening to Derora Saxen again."

"That's right!" Thalon exclaimed. "Der's going! It's not too dangerous for her!"

"Der isn't six years old." Evelyn took the boy's hand. "Come along, Thalon, we can watch them leave after you have a proper meal." He tugged, but her grip was strong. She pulled him down the open corridor.

"Dad, don't leave me! Dad!" he screamed.

Thistle hung his head and waited until the sounds of yelling and footsteps faded. He spun on his heel and raised his fist to pound the wall when he saw the sentries watching him. They had been silent and in the shadows all along.

But they said nothing as they followed him. He marched toward the courtyard that Jacob told him was being used for training. As he came around the final bend, he heard, "Close your eyes."

***

"What?" Der backed away and swung her sword between herself and Fienan.

"I said, 'close your eyes.'" Jacob grinned, shoulder resting against a tree. "You're watching him more than you're relying on your instincts."

Behind him, she heard Salinienn chuckle. Ahead of her, Fienan remained stern and on guard.

She fought herself as she dropped her eyelids. She felt her entire body tense. Her arm shivered as she pushed her blade out blindly in front of her. She hit nothing. Her eyes shot wide open.

Fienan hadn't moved at all.

The elf looked at her impassively. She forced herself to shut her eyes again. What was he doing? She stood unmoving, until she realized how stupid that was. But how could she fight without seeing anything?

She waited, but nothing happened. Then she saw the near complete blackness of that chemmen cell underneath the old castle as her memories surged up. She gasped and shuddered, trying to block it all out.

Focus! she told herself.

What would an opponent facing a blind person do? Thrust, probably straight. Ergo, she should parry. Her blade met his with a jarring crash. She almost opened her eyes. His sword must have been waiting for hers. After a parry, a swordsman should riposte. She brought her blade toward him. He parried, and she was ready to counter his immediate riposte.

She thought she was getting the rhythm after a few minutes of sparring. Then she disengaged her sword from his and stabbed low. Fienan's blade countered hers easily, but she took satisfaction in that she tried. Her stance was awkward, she was too slow, and she was barely shifting her feet.

As they trained, she often missed his blade or caught a bad angle on a parry. The awkwardness and strain continued to increase, until she had to start moving her feet more. Then her bladework fell apart as she concentrated on her footing on unknown terrain. But the lesson didn't stop, and she kept her eyes mashed shut. Her body felt about to drop, but her mind was more alert than it had been. She learned to sense the pressure on the blade and how it betrayed the opponent's next move.

The swordplay stopped. Der remained ready, just in case. Something smashed into her chest, and she caught it with her left arm. Wetness was growing across her shirt. Her eyes shot open. When she looked down she saw she was holding a waterskin.

"Not a *bad* catch," Jacob commented. "But always be on guard. And drink up."

She tried to focus on him, but her gaze slid to the figure standing back by the trees. She stuttered, "Th-Thistle? How long have you been here?"

"Long enough."

She glanced at Fienan and Salinienn. Both had stiffened and were holding their swords almost on guard.

"As promised." Jacob raised a hand toward the row of weapons. "Thistle, if you would."

The chemman nodded and walked over.

Jacob looked up to the two trailing guards. "And you're dismissed. If we can't trust him now, we certainly can't trust him below."

"But, sir—" a guard started.

"Silver Dawn business." Jacob grinned as he raised a hand.

The guard scowled. "But we are in Indelleiria's territory."

"In that case, please go ask the prince to clarify your orders if you're unsure."

"We will remain here, sir."

Jacob's smile froze behind a slight grimace. But then he turned back toward the raiding party and let his gaze settle on Kelin. "Your turn." He rolled his face toward Thistle. "And yours."

Kelin's eyes flickered between the storm-reader and Jacob, but he sighed and picked up his sword. He stepped near the center of the courtyard. "You're not going to make me fight him blind, are you?"

Jacob shrugged. "You can if you want to, but I wouldn't recommend it."

Der watched the chemman drill her friend into the dirt by advancing, retreating, and circling. The young man stumbled around, panting heavily. Thistle was quick, zipping about him like a hummingbird.

Kelin had paled underneath a sheen of sweat. He tripped but still managed to keep his sword between himself and his opponent. He staggered, only to have Thistle kick out his ankle and then tap his collarbone with the blade. Kelin coughed but nodded and stood back up. As they drilled, Der tried to keep track of how many times he'd taken the flat of the blade, but she lost count.

"Enough." Jacob clapped his hands.

The chemman withdrew and sheathed his weapon. Der tossed Kelin the waterskin and offered a conciliatory smile.

Thistle stepped back. "There's a simple counter to that sliding thrust."

Kelin raised an eyebrow but crouched his shoulders.

"Just shuffle both your feet back when you parry."

Salinienn folded his arms. "I did not expect that a chemman would train a human to kill his own ilk."

Thistle's hand remained planted on his sword but he said nothing.

"None of that." Jacob turned to Kelin. "You have improved, at least since this morning. But we need to do so much more, and there isn't enough time."

Fienan remained stiff. "Of course, if all goes as planned, we won't have to fight."

Salinienn kept his eyes trained on Thistle. "Very doubtful, I fear."

"I am aware," Fienan replied. "And they have that quiet sword, damn them."

Salinienn made a face. "We melted it. I was there at the ceremony. So many of us were."

Der inched forward. "If the chemmen made this silent sword you've been discussing—and you destroyed it—why couldn't they make another one?" She raised her hands against their stunned expressions, and she found herself feeling a little homesick. They reminded her of the looks she earned all the time in Riversbridge just after she'd say something.

Salinienn blinked. "But then, it's not the thing to be feared."

Even Jacob shook his head. "It's not the same thing, Der; it didn't commit all those atrocities."

"Still," she pressed, "if you can't tell any difference, is there any?"

Once again, stillness surrounded the courtyard. Thistle's mouth twisted into something akin to a smile, and he nodded to her.

"We had not thought like that." Salinienn bowed his head.

Der slapped her hands on her hips. "And you immortals are supposed to be smarter." She immediately earned glares that soon cracked into smiles.

A laugh tickled a throat. Then another. The elves chuckled but looked away. Thistle's mouth twitched, which probably counted. Suddenly, an awkward silence snatched the training circle as they realized they were laughing together. Thistle backed up, and so did the elves.

Kelin stepped back too, bewilderment splattered across his face. "Just like in the meadow. Convincing everyone to joust on plow ponies."

She grinned.

Fienan's smile began to fade. "Well, I hope you keep such wit about you in the coming days."

Kelin's expression froze. "Der, I don't want to do this. I think I'm a coward after all..."

Jacob's shovel of a hand landed on his shoulder. "You're not, Kelin. I've been a soldier for a long time now, and being fearful doesn't make you a coward. You survived, with your wits intact, that which would make most men spoil their trousers at the color orange."

Der opened her mouth, but the knight waved to shush her and then looked back to Kelin. "I've seen bravery and cowardice. I know who will be a coward. It's someone who runs away from something he can overcome. Now, for this raid, we don't know if we can climb this mountain. Being afraid but still willing to go doesn't make you a coward, Kelin, it makes you brave."

The young man dropped his eyes. "It's easier to sound brave when we're in this place. But there..."

Thistle approached. "The chemmen are taught that fear is a weakness and pride can only be a strength. Both are untrue. Fear can be a weakness, but you can also train it to become a strength. Just something to keep you alert, keep you ready."

Kelin nodded. "Thanks..."

"You'll need your fear to survive Darkreign."

"What's it like?" Fienan inquired. He didn't keep eye contact with Thistle.

"Don't know."

Jacob watched Thistle. "I've been wondering how. In the banishment, it didn't matter where a storm-reader was."

Thistle shook his head. "It may be a trick I need again."

Jacob frowned but didn't say anything more. Beside him, Kelin shook his head ever so slightly toward Der.

"Ha," Salinienn wheezed. "Since this one claims to know nothing of this realm, we are blind."

Thistle remained impassive. "From what I've learned in my spying at the outpost is that the chemmen spent centuries conquering Darkreign and slaying its other inhabitants. They built their own kingdom, well, rebuilt their kingdom, including their cities, Zazocorma and Darii."

"And Zazocorma was the capital, I remember," Jacob murmured.

Thistle nodded. "And the streets may be the very same."

"Gods and lords," Fienan whispered. "It will be like we've walked back through time."

Jacob shifted his weight. "Let's hope not."

Der coughed into her hand and looked around at everyone. "This distraction..." She ran her foot over the ground. "Is this honorable? It's not like we're facing them on the battlefield."

Jacob inhaled deeply and then blew it all out. "You humans are certainly getting philosophical today."

Fienan chuckled. "Oh yes, like Pallens, when you couldn't walk down the street without hearing an argument about truth or the divine nature of the world."

"You didn't answer my question, sir." Der looked straight at Jacob.

He sighed again. "Fine. Der, I won't try to sweeten war—not after what you've already seen. But on the battlefield, we're in it for survival. And while our enemy may take prisoners, as you know, it's not for any honorable reasons."

Her expression betrayed her disappointment.

He raised an index finger. "Honor is defined by what do you after combat, 'cause in the fight, everyone's a bastard. If you aren't, you die."

Pain crossed Der's face. "I just want to hear 'yes' or 'no'." She bit her lip. "But it's not that simple, is it?"

He shook his head. "No, it's not. Don't dwell on it though. I'm the commanding officer, so it's my responsibility, all right?"

"Yes, sir." She kicked a foot against the ground.

"Do not worry about it. That's an order." He ran a hand over his face. "There is honor in war, Der. It helps to separate the good from the rot. But there are only rules when *everyone* obeys them."

"That's confusing, sir."

He offered a weak smile. "You'll learn. I know you will 'cause you're too stubborn to do wrong." The knight nodded. "Right. Now, let's get you some proper armor."

Salinienn opened a footlocker beside the racks of swords to reveal two lightweight shirts of elven mail. They glistened in the sunlight like fresh waves over water.

Jacob handed Der a thin, red-brown sword belt with a blade in it. An intricate pattern was imprinted on the leather. She drew the sword. The blade was without a single nick, and it shone brighter than the practice weapon she'd been using. She looked between the sheath and sword, remembering what she had left home with—her father's sword and a sword belt with length cut out of the back to make it fit.

He hinted at a cold smile. "You wanted to be a warrior, so here is a warrior's sword."

The sun could've been behind Der's head for the way she glowed, all fears and concerns tossed over her shoulder for now. "Yes, sir!"

CHAPTER THIRTY FIVE

Evelyn led Thalon through the interior hall. Its walls were wooden and arched, and it reminded him of a tunnel. He tightened his grip on her hand. He had just dried another round of tears and allowed himself to be pulled along by the lady.

She guided him down wide, low-cut stairs that spiraled around a two-story statue of a stag charging up a cliff. He ducked his chin to his chest and did his best not to look at the beauty of the haven. It was too easy to be distracted if he did.

They came to an ivy-enshrouded wall at the bottom of the steps. A dead end. He twisted his gaze up to the lady because she wasn't slowing.

As he watched, the stones and the greenery vanished before his eyes. The corridor continued. Evelyn kept walking without hesitation, but this time, Thalon dragged his feet because he was staring.

The hall led to a wide, open balcony with a grand vista of the mountains. Several elves stood watching the crown prince, who was gripping the railing with both hands. Thalon recognized Sir Amthros, the duke, and the duchess, but he didn't know the youngest elf with golden eyes.

He overheard Farallon as they swept closer, "They've already assumed victory over us."

"Then let's hope they're wrong." Caleb turned to face Thalon and the lady. "Lady Evelyn, Thalon."

The baroness curtsied, and Thalon managed a quick bow. He remembered his mother saying something about it being rude not to drop one's eyes. It meant a lack of trust. He kept his gaze straight up at the prince.

Amthros shook his head. "It won't be a fortnight before the chemmen attack the humans outright. Probably Thealith first."

Lady Eve bowed her head. "I wish to protest his highness's decision to accompany us to Elloan. There may be other places where you can hide through this dark trial."

Amthros knelt beside the prince. "Please. This will end in death. Let it not be yours. You are innocent of this war. Do not join the lady in Elloan."

Caleb stared off at the horizon. "I can almost see the fires of our cities from here." He gripped the railing tighter. "Our fate may come down to an ill-conceived plan with a hair's width chance of success. And it was our people's prior decisions, both wise and otherwise, that have led us to this precipice."

"Yes, my prince." Farallon rolled his eyes. "However, *our* duty is to keep you safe, you and Prince Alsalon."

The younger elf nodded, keeping his gaze anywhere but on the duke.

Caleb shook his head. "I must see this through."

"My prince." Farallon bowed. "I cannot, in good faith, accept this of you."

"Your lives and experience are worth more than mine."

"Prince Edillon, I remember when you were just a child, and—"

"This is my decision," he interrupted.

Farallon pursed his lips, reddening. "I disagree."

The prince shrugged.

Thalon shuffled away from Lady Eve. He glanced at the open archway behind him and took a few more steps back.

Lady Sabielle clasped her hands together. "Please, heed our advice, my young prince. It would further devastate us to lose you as well. My husband is right—"

Caleb turned away. "I have spoken, my lady."

She gasped as if he had slapped her.

"You and your brother are your parents' legacy," Amthros pressed. "We must preserve that. You cannot—"

Caleb growled, deep in his throat. He pushed himself off from the railing and marched away.

***

"Brother, wait." Alsalon jogged up the slope. He caught up with Caleb just as the older elf had started on a trail weaving up the mountainside. The cold winds chased after them and snow drifted on the air now that they were outside the haven.

"I'm leaving my friends to their fate. Again." He stormed up the path. "And again, Farallon and the others beg me to run away. It's not as if I'm anything special!"

Alsalon scrambled after him, slipping on his feet in an effort to keep up. "The humans survived last time."

"Ha. Last time." He stopped and pressed a hand against his chest. "I pray you never know how this feels. Mortals and immortals are willing to die on my behalf! On my word! I feel as though I am the one who has lost my sanity, but clearly it isn't *me.*"

Alsalon shook his head and tears welled up in his eyes. "I don't know how Mother and Father did this at all—what they would say."

"I don't either," Caleb snapped. He held his breath before finally exhaling. "And yet, what I fear most, Alsalon, is not dying." His voice retreated to a whisper, "It is losing someone else, especially you."

Alsalon dashed forward and hugged him. "I miss Mother and Father." He squeezed tighter.

"I miss them too—with every breath. We're too young for this. Everyone else has thousands more years of living, so why do they all seem to stupid?"

"I believe in you." Alsalon nodded and gazed at him with steel shining in his golden eyes. "So I won't leave you like everyone left us, I want to go with you to Elloan."

Caleb stiffened. "Absolutely not."

"We're the only family we have left. I demand it. If we lose, we are lost. And I will be lost with you."

CHAPTER THIRTY SIX

"This is not a way to start a quest." Der rubbed her eyes and tried not to yawn. She rolled her shoulders, unused to the weight of the backpack.

"You can sleep tonight, kid." Jacob chuckled. "Now keep a straight face."

She, Jacob, Kelin, Thistle, Fienan, and Salinienn crossed under an archway and into an open grass corridor surrounded by trees on one side and a stream on the other. The cold wind threw a few gold and red leaves at their feet.

Der's gaze followed a leaf as it spun to the ground. There were far fewer of them to fall off their branches than a few days ago. The party was silent as they passed down into curving stone stairs that reminded her of a well. As they descended, the artwork faded, and the stairs became narrow and steep. The stonework looked ancient and smelled of moss.

"It gets slick ahead," the captain murmured. "Watch your footing."

"Why?" Der asked.

He pointed down. She bent at the knees to peer around the turn and realized that the encasing walls ended but the stairwell continued.

She felt the blood rush away from her head on her next step down, and she pressed against the central pillar holding the stairs together. Below them, she could see the sliver of a river, all the way down. She could hardly fathom that it was the same waterway they'd rode in on. She couldn't descry the waterfall from here, but she imagined how far it must plummet. The stairwell continued to descend over air.

The wind whipped up around her, tearing at her hair and clothes with its icy fingers. Below, clouds crawled up toward the bottom of the mountains. It wasn't quite the abyss, Der reasoned, but certainly a cousin.

She gritted her teeth and forced a toe out onto the next step. "I thought you elves, you know, being immortal and all, having to risk a little more life than we mere humans, *would make this safer!*"

Jacob, with both hands gripping the central spire, didn't look back. "Well, they don't use this exit. From what they've told me, it existed before the haven."

"How can you have a magical exit and not use it?"

"Tree paths are safer, so we're using this because I doubt our alleged spy would consider it."

Above her, the wind stole the surprised curses of Thistle and Kelin. It didn't matter, she knew what Kelin had meant to say, and she felt the absence of him right behind her. She didn't dare turn her head to see how far he was hanging back. Ahead, she saw the knight vanish around the next bend. Swearing every half-inch, she followed.

Jacob stooped in front of a small stone arch that marked a definite end to the stairwell. It looked hauntingly familiar, and she realized it was like the entrances to the graves of nobility she'd seen when she was young. Those squat mounds of rocks with that arch that was only large enough to slide a casket through.

The knight was grinning. Before she had time to shake her head, he grabbed her arm and pulled. She bit off a yell and slammed her eyes closed as she stumbled forward. Jacob released his grip, but it was too late; she was already moving through the arch.

She crashed down onto something loose but solid enough. Her face slammed into the powdery and coarse ground.

Salty scents washed over her, and she felt warmth tingling the back of her head. She raised one eyelid against the blinding light, and someone landed on her from behind.

"What the hell was that?" Kelin yelped. He rolled off her back.

Once she realized she could breathe, she tried to cough out all this bone-white stuff she had accidentally inhaled. She spat and spat. Then she sat up in wide-eyed wonder.

"Is this sand?" Kelin asked, running his fingers through the fine grains. "I've never seen sand like this. It's so light!"

Thistle, Fienan, Jacob, and Salinienn followed, and neither Der nor Kelin could mask their expressions of surprise as the others emerged from nothing but air.

She stared back down at the sand upon which she sat. She hadn't ever imagined any place like this could exist. They were on a beach with trees boasting broad, green leaves. Many smaller bushes and other green growth choked the areas where they had taken hold. The sand could have not been more than one hundred paces across, surrounded by water. She had never seen truly blue water before. She'd always heard the sea was blue, but not like this. It boasted shifting shades of royal blue and living green.

She giggled at Kelin's dumbfounded expression as his gaze moved with the waves that were licking the beach. Then she tugged at her collar, realizing how much she was sweating, and how her coat was already heating beyond comfort.

She didn't see any animals other than birds and bugs. She glanced around—there was something she'd seen before, there in the center of this new world: a circle of trees surrounding an older, larger tree. In this case, a palm tree.

She pointed at it and glared at Jacob. "Tree path? But you said we could go anywhere."

"I did," he replied. "Between Thistle and the spy, I wanted a few extra steps between us and where we're actually going."

"I am not dropping any notes," Thistle whispered.

"Oh, I never suggested that you and the spy were colluding," the knight chuckled. "Despite what some, all right, everyone in Riverfall was. I'm just being careful."

"Where *are* we going, sir?" Der asked.

He rolled his eyes. "Nowhere special. A little place that Lady Eve divined."

"That's not an answer, sir."

"That's what you get."

She wiped her forehead with her glove and sat, heating up in the sand. She found herself even more awestruck by this sandbar than she had been by the majesty of Riverfall.

The knight-captain clapped. "I wish we could stay, but alas, we've got to get our asses back into the cold."

They lined up before the palm. While Jacob knelt in front of the tree, Der swept her hands across her trousers and realized the sand was getting everywhere.

Thistle whirled around, reaching for his sword. Salinienn moved beside him, hand on his own weapon, but his eyes focused on the chemman. "What is it?"

The storm-reader snorted. "I thought I heard something."

Salinienn shrugged. "A bird, perhaps?"

"We're moving now," Jacob called.

They each knelt and entered the tree. Once again, they pushed through what felt like a fog curtain, and the cold on the other side sapped all the warmth Der had just earned. Her sweat turned bitingly icy in a heartbeat.

She hopped in place to try to regain some heat. Looking around, this terrain appeared much more like home with its tree-lined rolling hills sprinkled with an early snow. The clouds hung low, and she had to blink several times to focus.

Jacob sighed and watched his breath turn into fog. "Come on." He trudged over the leaf-strewn, muddy soil. With wistful glances back at the tree, Der fell in line with the party.

Fienan began a song, making it up as they walked. The others picked up its simple, three-lined chorus. Salinienn took the reins of the next verse; he sang about a tavern, the girl he met there, and the troubles that ensued when he encountered her other suitors. They sang the following chorus through their laughter. Thistle was the only one who remained taciturn.

Der cringed as she listened to Kelin try his voice, singing about when they would return home. Jacob took the verse after that. The song, with mismatched verses and horrible rhymes, continued and eased their march.

As they walked, the hills grew tighter together and steeper while the trees became fewer and shorter. Jacob called for quiet when they passed a marker of three rocks set up in a triangle.

They treaded ahead in silence. Eventually, Der trotted faster until she was even with the captain. "Will we be out this way for days, sir, or are we close?"

"Close."

She nodded, glancing at the hills as they squeezed the party into nearly single-file.

Jacob said, "Hey. Sometimes, you have to take that deep breath and go for it. It's a gamble, but we've stacked our deck enough."

"Would you wager on that, sir?"

He laughed. "No, probably not. War doesn't determine who is right; war determines who is left."

Der's mouth hung open and she blinked. She looked at her right hand and then her left. "That wasn't funny, sir."

He smirked. "Got to make jokes when you can." He grunted under the weight of his pack, armor, and weapons as they began to push their way uphill again.

He didn't say anything about the skeleton he had to step over. Der stopped and stared, which caused the rest of the party to huddle around it. The bones were yellowed and falling away from each other, but it was still recognizably humanoid.

She swallowed and burst into speed after the knight. The others followed without comment.

"Where are we, sir?" She kept glancing over her shoulder at the long-rotted corpse.

She watched Jacob look at her and then at the others. "Far away."

"*How* far away, sir?"

He grinned. "Oh, about ogre country far away."

She gasped.

He sliced his hand across his throat, motioning for silence. "Don't. Also, don't speak loudly, no songs, no fires, and we won't be here long enough for it to matter."

"No worries," Der drawled.

They reached the crest of the hill. Below them, a wide, braided, and brown river curved in from the horizon and disappeared.

The swallow hole wasn't much. The ground dipped down, and water flowed into it. Then in a large muddy ring, it vanished.

Kelin's brow bunched up. "How does it happen?"

Jacob grinned. "Not much to it, really. See, there's not so much water in this region except for the river, of course. We're on limestone here, which cracks horizontally and vertically in what we call joints. This type of rock is permeable, so water creeps into it. The river falls into an enlarged joint and keeps going underground."

Der and Kelin both tilted their heads. "What?"

Fienan rolled his eyes. "He means there's a big crack in the ground, and the water falls in."

"How do you know that, sir?" Der asked.

Jacob stiffened but then sighed. "I had a friend who liked rocks. I try to remember for the sake of his memory. It's not a passion of mine."

"Huh." Kelin tapped his chin. "How do we get to Darkreign from here?"

Der glanced over her shoulder at the desolate landscape. "If we're not there already...?"

"No," the knight replied. "We're still in our world."

Salinienn cleared his throat. "Lady Evelyn instructed myself and Fienan after her divination. The swallow hole is a thin place between worlds where crossing into Darkreign is possible. There are several around the world, and we never knew to look for them before this disaster. But she was able to see them in her trance." The elf's expression darkened and he shivered.

Fienan continued, "They result from too many people making mistakes with too many spells—especially with transportation magic. The spoils had to dump somewhere, and it thins the walls of our reality." He sighed. "I imagine this is how the chemmen escaped." He glanced sideways at Thistle.

The storm-reader shrugged.

The noisome air grew loud in their noses as they approached the swallow hole. Salinienn pinched his nostrils closed. The ground squished more with every step.

Jacob stopped. "Time for lunch."

"Out here?" Der swung her head back and forth, searching for any signs of ogres.

"Out here, we know the dangers. Once we get into Darkreign, only gods and chemmen know what's there."

They slung off their packs, and Der pulled out a brown package. It rattled when she shook it. "What the hell is this?"

Fienan chuckled. "That would be one of the many luxurious meals prepared for us."

Kelin shook his own package. "Bread crumbs?"

Salinienn half-smiled. "Of course not. Perhaps a little. No, these are dried meals. All we need to do is add water."

The humans stared at him.

He held up his package and cut the wax that had kept it sealed. He poured in water from one of his skins. "I admit that I prefer these with hot water, but cool water is still fine."

"What?" Der's forehead wrinkled.

Thistle rolled his eyes. "Like this." He poured from his waterskin into the bag. "And now we wait."

Fienan asked, "How are you familiar with this?"

Thistle met his gaze. "My wife."

Kelin and Der exchanged a glance.

Fienan forced a smile at them. "These are much lighter to carry."

They used their waterskins to fill their pouches. The river water could only taste worse than it smelled. Soon, the dried food began to soak up the water and became moist, and looking like stew. As the party waited, they looked around at their surroundings.

Der murmured, "I see something back there."

Jacob replied, "I hope that you're just on edge. But..."

She watched. She was fairly certain she saw shadows moving against the wind, behind the trees, behind that rock.

"That's good."

She startled out of her concentration to see Fienan sitting next to her, also watching, and she realized it was he who had spoken.

"Take a good look around. It might be the last time." He waved his hand at the blanket of clouds. The light was leaking from the horizon—it was fast becoming night, and the world washed out to gray.

Salinienn stepped up beside them. "The storm-reader's light. It's often said that this is when chemmen eyes are the most acute."

Thistle shrugged. Then he popped up from the ground, hand going for his sword. "Movement."

The brush under the trees trembled, and a small figure burst from it, running as fast as his legs could carry him.

"Thalon!" Kelin yelled.

The boy stumbled as he closed the distance. "They're out there! They're coming!" He stopped short of diving in between his father's legs.

"What's coming?" Fienan whispered sharply.

"Big things. Teeth. Smell like puke!" Der watched him stare up at his father in horror. "I'm sorry!" he squeaked.

"Ogres." Jacob removed the sheath from his axe.

Thistle grabbed his son by the ear and yanked. He growled something in a language Der did not know, and the boy's face paled even more.

"Lunch is over." The knight crept forward with a grip on his axe. "We're going, now."

"But the boy!" Salinienn protested, wide-eyed. "We can't take him with us."

"We can't leave him here," Fienan retorted.

Thalon banged on his father's leg with a fist. "Dad, you can't leave me behind, not again!"

"Be silent!" Jacob hissed. But it was too late; they already heard the rustling in the bushes and grass surrounding them. "Go!"

A few crude, ugly logs of arrows thudded down short of their feet. They flew without precision but stuck deep in the soft soil.

The party sprinted toward the center of the muddy ring, sinking farther into the ground with every step. Der feared losing a boot as she slowed and descended to her knees in the mud.

"We won't be able to breathe!" Kelin yelled.

"It's a break between worlds," Fienan hollered. "Hold your breath and you'll come out the other side!"

Jacob waded toward the center and threw mud back with his hands. He sucked in a large breath and plunged face first into the muck. He vanished into the earth.

Thalon, riding on Thistle's shoulders, beat on his father's head. "Go! Go! Der, come on!"

More arrows spiked down around them, much closer this time.

Der pressed a hand against her drumming heart, fighting for every step forward. *This would be the worst place to get stuck,* she told herself, *and also the most likely.*

She looked over her shoulder and saw the ogres. They were gray and bigger than she expected, and she had expected big. She had imagined they wielded spiked clubs, but these raised swords and maces as they charged—maces that were larger than her entire head, she realized. Two of them were shooting their bows.

She whirled back around at the slurping mud. Ahead of her, she saw the ground swallow Thistle and Thalon. Fienan and Salinienn vanished next. Only she and Kelin remained. He threw out a hand.

"Last boat out?" she asked as she grabbed his wrist. With all his blacksmith strength, he tugged her into the sucking river. Then the earth ate him too.

She hovered at the edge of the hole, taking rapid breaths. Even with the arrows and charging ogres, she hesitated. She heard the ground gulping down the water and felt it rushing around her, pulling her down. She inhaled one last time and held her breath. She took a step forward and let the world disappear beneath her feet.

In the next instant, she was stuck with no way up or down. Water and mud slithered past her while the earth tightened its stranglehold on her body. She tried to kick and flail, but there was no space to move in.

Suddenly, she slipped down and hit a rock with her feet, jarring every bone. As she continued to slide, the rock scraped up her legs and back. Icy water closed over her. It pulled her down faster, freezing her, and felt like thousands of tiny blades cutting into her skin.

Is this it?

She tried to push herself lower, but she was just floating. Her lungs were burning.

Is this really it?

Something gripped her ankle and yanked. Her shoulder slammed into a stone. She exhaled in shock, and her mouth filled with mud. Then someone plucked her out of the water by her ankle as if she was a small branch.

A massive hand slapped her on the back. She coughed, spitting out heaps of mud.

As soon as she could breathe, she was set down on a rough rock floor. She dimly recognized the captain's voice.

"Der? You're all right. Say something."

She nodded and coughed again. "I'm...here." Silty water dripped off of her hair, face, and clothes. She turned toward the hole in the ceiling. It was churning and water trickled down from it, but it wasn't the flood she had expected. Then again, it was nearly too dark to see anything. Only a splinter of light pierced its way into the room.

He grinned. "That may not be a good thing." He glanced around. "That's all of us."

"Yeah," Kelin squeezed his arms together. He looked like a mud monster; they all did.

Der squinted. It was hard to see clearly here, but the thought passed as she tried to focus on recovering her breath. She rubbed the mud against her clothing, trying to scrape off chunks. "So this is another world, yeah? Doesn't feel any different."

Salinienn pointed toward the light.

She raised her gaze. It looked like they were in some sort of cave.

"Are the ogres following us?" Thalon gripped his father's trousers and turned his face up to the muddy, swirling ceiling.

Jacob shook his head. "I doubt it. If so, we definitely have an adventure."

"We left our packs behind," Fienan remarked. "Damn."

The knight-captain snorted. "Oh well."

Thistle glared at his son, who paled and looked ready to cry.

Der continued to blink, attempting to force her eyes to adjust. She pushed her wet hair back from her face, while her other hand rubbed the scratches she could reach on her legs. "It'll be impossible to get out against the current and mud."

"I disagree," Salinienn said. "It can be done, but not without effort."

She shivered. She didn't want to try. Then she shivered again. The memories of the last time she was in a chemmen-controlled area chilled her mind as much as the water dripping off her clothing. This would be better, she told herself. She had resources, allies, and a plan.

They tiptoed toward the mouth of the cave, squelching with every step.

They slithered out into a forest. It appeared as any other forest in spring, although with few budding flowers among the scrawny trees. A crowd of bugs buzzed around them instantly. But they hardly noticed—they were all already staring in astonishment.

They turned to Thistle, whose eyes were gray here, just like all of theirs.

There was no color. Everything was a depth of gray, black, or white.

Kelin clutched his arms against his chest. "If I had any hope of survival before, I don't now."

"This is unexpected," Fienan whispered.

Thalon bumped against his father's leg. "Where are we?"

"You weren't supposed to be here." Thistle reached down and grabbed his son's shoulder. "We shall have words." He pulled the child back toward the cave. "Go deep, hide." Then he turned to the others. "I will scout a path."

Jacob hesitated but nodded.

The chemman melted ahead into the storm-readers' light. This was a whole realm of it.

Salinienn snorted. "This is a wicked place."

Der sat down.

"Can we rest, sir?" Kelin asked through his panting.

Jacob held up a hand. "I don't think that's a good idea."

The buzzing of insects grew louder as the flies descended on them. Der swatted at a few of them as they picked at the drying mud on her skin. No matter where her gaze roamed, the trees seemed brittle, with scrawny leaves clutching drooping branches. Then she gave up while they waited for Thistle.

Fienan threw his hand toward his sword. "I hear something."

Der hopped to her feet and tried to imagine what beast might be coming for them. But she couldn't picture anything but those attacking ogres as they watched.

Fienan shook his head. "I'm sorry, everyone, I suppose I was overeager."

Der shrugged. Then she froze, listening. She was certain she'd heard...

"No!" She stamped her foot, but a resounding echo didn't ring.

Thistle stepped out from the forest. Around him, at least a dozen other chemmen appeared from behind the trees.

"You bastard," Jacob breathed. He pulled his axe free.

Thistle said nothing. None of the other storm-readers even glanced at him.

Jacob raised the axe. Der stared at him, hand on her sword and ready to draw. She was afraid to blink, afraid she'd miss the signal.

He raised his other hand and held the axe out away from his body.

Der's eyes widened and she shook her head. Beside her, Kelin collapsed to his knees. "Not again. Not again."

Salinienn released his sword. It landed on the soil next to his feet.

Not like this! she raged. *Not without a fight!* She ripped her gaze toward Thistle. *How could you...?*

But that doubt had been there all along, she realized.

Salinienn turned. He had paled and his eyes had almost rolled up in his head.

He ducked under a chemman blade and shoved his way past, scrambling for the cave at a full sprint.

But she couldn't spare him attention as she felt the wind of a blade on her face. She lurched sideways from the attack. She crouched underneath a beheading swipe and sliced upward at her assailant's body as she drew her sword. It was a lucky slash, and the chemman hopped back. She didn't have time to try to finish him though; she was already parrying another storm-reader.

But the lack of color was too disorienting, and she overcorrected her sword, swinging her entire body off balance.

"Der, *stop!*"

She froze at the thunder in Jacob's command. The sword she hadn't even seen coming halted at her neck.

She struggled for a breath, eyeing the blade.

"Drop it," Jacob ordered.

She heard the dull thump of his axe landing on the ground, followed by his sword and shield. From the corner of her vision, she saw Kelin, on his knees, staring ahead in horror. Fienan tossed down his blade and stepped back while raising his hands.

"No," she wheezed. But her traitor fingers unwrapped themselves from her sword. It fell.

CHAPTER THIRTY SEVEN

Salinienn stumbled and crashed into the gladioli covering the field. He cursed the late blooming flowers for hiding holes. The mud from the river was still damp on his skin. He'd outrun the ogres to the tree path to get here. He hadn't stopped running except to kneel before the holy tree.

He wiped petals off his mouth. Winter hadn't yet curled its tendrils into this pocket of the elven kingdom. The season was always late in Elloan, and spring was always early. He picked himself back up and charged the castle at the top of the hill. Unlike the elegance of Riverfall, or the glorious spires of Long Range Palace, this castle looked squat and heavy. But they could defend this castle with its archery loops and murder holes. Moonrise Castle was built for war.

He stared at the gladiolus stems passing under his feet. The yellow, purple, pink, red, and white flowers grew up all the way to the castle walls. As he ran, he remembered the flower's name meant "sword-flag," and hundreds of the bright banners rustled in the wind on the fields.

***

"Good, I think it is for the best," Farallon said. Caleb watched him in the mirror; he hadn't been listening. They were in a guest chamber, and it was a simple room with a single, narrow window.

His peripheral vision caught the fluttering of blue clothing. He spun. The duke, noticing his movement, also turned. Amthros stepped out of the corner where he had been standing guard.

"Highness!" the messenger went from running to a curtsy without stopping in between. Her expression twisted with apprehension.

Caleb gulped. "Arise."

She hesitated kept her face cast at his feet. "Your grace, Salinienn, from the raiding party, has arrived. He is not well."

"But they left when we did!"

"He says..." She faltered as his expression became agonized. "He reports that the storm-readers immediately ambushed the raiding party. He was the only one to escape."

"Ambushed?" Caleb whispered. He felt as if he were treading on a fault and the earth had shifted.

"Yes, my prince, ambushed. He claims the chemmen prisoner betrayed them."

He staggered back. Farallon stepped between them. The duke's voice was clipped. "You may go." The messenger hastened away.

Caleb whirled to face the mirror again. He swallowed, staring at himself. "I knew this would happen..." But hearing it, confirming it, fell like a hammer's blow.

Amthros hung his head. "I wish I could be surprised."

The prince dropped to his knees. Hot sweat mixed with cold tears on his cheeks. "I left them to die. All over again."

Amthros offered a weak smile. "But you live."

The duke stood behind him. "This foolhardy escapade was their idea and decision, my prince."

Caleb held himself up on one trembling hand. "I let them do it. I wanted to be there too—I didn't want to send them on behalf of me!"

"Never." Amthros shook his head. "You *are* our king."

"I am not king now."

"You will be," the duke asseverated.

The prince hissed. "I am not my father."

"No, you are not," Farallon whispered.

Caleb felt an abyss opening right underneath him. "He would know what to do."

"I would never ask you to be him." The duke's dark eyes flickered toward the mirror. "Nor ask you to be his reflection. You have your own wisdom and courage." He put a gentle hand on Caleb's shoulder.

"That doesn't answer any of my challenges, my lord duke. Why do the people I care about keep dying?"

Amthros folded his hands together. "Because our enemy is cruel." He glanced up at Farallon. "Especially when there is one we cannot trust."

Caleb gazed into the mirror. He stared so long without blinking that his vision blurred and colored. The elves on the raid had volunteered when he announced the idea. Elves died. His friends—the only two he'd ever been able to be honest with—gone.

He grabbed his head. He allowed this, he allowed it! Immortals had died for him, and he had sent them to their deaths! His friends died for him!

So did his parents.

He felt his body sinking into the floor, but he couldn't sink low enough. He didn't know what his father would do, and he had no idea what *he* should do.

He gulped and told himself that Der, Kelin, Jacob, and Fienan were still alive. It didn't matter what he'd just thought! That was just panic. The chemmen took prisoners alive when there was information to gain. It was their pattern. But knowing he'd let his friends walk straight to the torturer's rack made his stomach twist. They knew the risks, and they'd volunteered.

Would he ever see them again? Perhaps... The memories of the undead from the Riverfall Mountains danced in his mind's eye. He cursed his imagination, and then he cursed chemmen imagination creating such evils.

He stood and straightened his shirt and his hair in his reflection. But he didn't dry his tears. *Wishing never accomplishes deeds*, he thought as he glanced back at his own face one more time. For an instant, he thought he saw his father.

He turned toward the door. "Don't follow me."

He stalked down the empty corridor, allowing his eyes to drift over the stone walls. Usually, he walked softly, but this time he let his footsteps echo. At least he could hear himself coming while he wondered if his friends had heard the chemmen coming.

"I wish we didn't know who told the chemmen of the raid." Alsalon appeared around a corner like a ghost, carrying a gladiolus in his hand. He fell in step. "I will meet Salinienn with you."

Caleb didn't reply.

"This means that our fate is foretold. The chemmen will come here." The younger prince had to jog to keep stride. "Lady Evelyn says that Thalon has disappeared."

"Suspicious timing." Caleb scowled. "And you're right, they'll be coming here. Silver Dawn has not yet arrived, and our knights and soldiers are few." His jaw tightened. "I suppose soon enough we'll find out which one of these immortal races, chemmen or elf, is king."

CHAPTER THIRTY EIGHT

Even in the colorless gray, the knives and whatever the hell those prong-things were reflected in the white candlelight. Kelin never imagined that light could still reflect here, or that it could make those blades look so very sharp.

Not again.

His head rolled around on the back of the steel table to which they had tied him. He didn't know how long he'd been there—time was impossible to guess in this constant gloaming.

The room was small, plain with gray walls and a high window with blinding light coming through it.

He closed his eyes. Can't be tortured again. Can't be tortured again. This isn't real. This cannot be real. *The chemmen aren't real!* This was all Der's fault.

Not again.

A whimper squeezed through his lips as the door creaked open. He prayed, wished, hoped that the chemman who entered was Thistle. He'd saved them before. It didn't matter if he'd told the other chemmen they'd come to Darkreign. He'd saved them before.

"I remember you," the storm-reader chuckled. "You and your friend are still alive. How unexpected."

"Who are you?" Kelin tried not to shiver.

"Don't you know your history? I am Vlade."

Kelin closed his eyes. He had recently learned the name, but a name from over two thousand years ago seemed so removed.

"But what are you doing here?" Vlade continued in an almost singsong voice. He brushed his fingers over some of the blades on the table beside Kelin. "I was told you made it through a whole minute last time, but that may have only been because there was so much meat to cut through." The human watched the chemman pick up a scalpel. "Will it be more or less this time?"

Kelin stared hard at the ceiling, avoiding the chemman's gaze.

Vlade snickered. "Of course, now you must pay for your crime of spilling chemmen blood. We'll take our time getting to that though. There's no rush *here.*"

Kelin gulped.

The chemman paused, and then a wide, vicious smile anchored his features. He twirled the scalpel between his fingers. "Let us begin."

Kelin kicked against his bindings and squirmed as far away as he could.

Even his lung twinged at the memory of last time. He didn't want to scream, to break down, but he heard his body yelling on its own. Tears squeezed from the corners of his eyes. "Thistle sold us out!" A sob broke through his voice. "I thought he was on our side, but he wasn't! He was—he is—!"

The blade hung between Vlade's fingers, and Kelin stared at it hovering over his eye. The storm-reader leaned in. "He is what?"

"*He is chemmen!*" Kelin screamed as a sob erupted from deep in his chest.

"Good." Vlade's breath hammered against his ear. "More."

He heaved against his bindings. They shouldn't have been caught—not like this!

He inhaled, but suddenly found himself calm. He was riding the storm. He could see his fear as lightning, his memories of last time as electric clouds that were lashing out inside the tempest, but he was at peace in the center.

He heard himself yelling, but it was as if someone else were doing it. "He's the chemman who helped us! I thought we could trust him! But he's a chemman!"

Vlade closed his eyes and inhaled with a small smile. He pressed the knife against the young man's skin and ripped.

Kelin yelped, even though he felt no pain at first. Then the laceration began to burn. In that white-hot instant, he remembered every gruesome detail of the last time—every horrible, heart-pounding, agony-laden moment. And it simply passed him by.

"Do they have an army?" The chemman smiled as he dipped the knife below Kelin's skin again.

The knife hurt, and he felt it, but he found himself laughing at such a little cut. He knew he'd have lines to say, a part to play if he wanted to escape. He gasped, "No! Yes! Silver Dawn is on the way, but they're not there yet. And they're—they're gathering the elves who will fight, but no, they don't! Just a handful of soldiers!"

"Where is the princeling?" The tip of the blade rested against Kelin's arm. "I think there's a nerve here." He pressed it down but didn't break the skin.

Kelin licked his lips so he could speak. "El-oh..." He squeezed the air past his throat. "Elloan. Some place called Moonrise Castle with the baroness and both princes!"

Kelin watched as Vlade's eyes glow. "Both princes, and the elven witch." He chuckled and withdrew the scalpel. Smiling, he dropped the blade and snapped his fingers. Another chemman materialized.

She was the first female chemman Kelin had ever seen outside of combat, but he didn't bother with the fact. She had the same haircut and the same clothes, but a more aquiline face. He was sure she had the same eyes, although they looked gray here. Vlade grinned at her. "Send him back to his cell since he's been such a good dog."

***

Der paced in tight circles Their square prison had three stone sides and a wall of bars. Beyond them

412

seemed to be a corridor, but she had no idea where it went. They'd had their heads covered with hoods when they'd arrived.

She scowled. "Why was Kelin taken? It should have been me. He hadn't wanted to come! And *why* is everything gray here?" She blinked her eyes almost constantly, hoping to suddenly see color instead of this aberrant grayness. She could not get used to it.

"We knew the danger." Jacob folded his arms and remained in his corner. He didn't look any smaller without his armor, but its loss had shattered his illusion of invincibility.

Der slammed a boot against the bars. "Argh!" She stomped to the back of the cell, spun on her heel, and returned. "Where's Thistle?"

Fienan rolled his eyes. "Oh, please, human. He's one of them. I cannot believe he convinced us, and that we listened." He rested his forehead on the bars. "We made the same mistake again, even though he doesn't have that sword."

"But what if he did it for Thalon's sake?" she whispered.

"Then he has killed all of us for the boy!"

Jacob raised his hands. "All right, that's enough, both of you."

Der shook her head at Fienan. "But Thistle saved our lives."

"Not this time, girl," he hissed. "Don't you understand? There are no chemmen traitors."

The knight called, "I heard myself give an order."

Fienan clicked his mouth closed.

She hunched her shoulders. "Yes, sir."

Footsteps crunched down the corridor. Der hopped up and craned her neck but still could see nothing.

Kelin came into focus. A chemman soldier pushed him forward. Despite the blood on his arm, he held his head high. She sighed with relief. The guard stopped in front of the door, and she pointed to the back of the cell. The prisoners shuffled to the far wall. The chemman shoved Kelin past the bars and relocked the door. The human collapsed.

Der slipped forward. "How bad?"

He raised his arm. "Worst of it." He turned his face away. "I'm so sorry," he gasped. "I told them where the princes were."

Der paused but didn't speak. She glanced at Jacob, who shrugged.

Fienan, shaking his head, stepped up to the door and ran his fingers over it. "Can't pick this lock without tools."

"You know how to pick locks?" Der blurted.

The elf nodded. "I wasn't always the good soldier."

She strained to see into the corridor. "Well, at least there aren't guards just standing here."

Jacob rolled his eyes. "The chemmen aren't that obvious. You can wager they're spying on us somehow." He looked past the bars and through a thin window at the base of the ceiling. "It'll be nightfall soon."

CHAPTER THIRTY NINE

Der glared through the blackness. Every hour or so, she'd taken to closing her eyes and rubbing them to see the patterns that emerged. Those were still in color at least.

She leaned her head against the bars. She couldn't sleep, so she waited until the darkness faded into the dull grayness of morning.

She snorted when she heard footsteps, realizing she'd drifted off. Then she listened. These were much quicker and lighter than what she had expected. She watched.

A small figured hugged the wall and then sprinted toward them.

"Thalon!" She bit her tongue to avoid from yelling.

The boy reached up with a ring of keys. He was grinning. "They keep everything in an office down the hall."

Jacob moved like lightning to the front of the cell and glared at the child. "Boy, what the hell are you doing?" He snatched the keys.

Thalon appeared wounded. He pointed. "There's only one guard. And there's another bunch of prisoners down the hall too. But I think most everyone's gone from here—it's like this ghost town Mama and I—"

The knight tried several keys in the lock. "Yes, Thalon, I understand. How did you even get here? How did you escape capture?"

The boy shrugged. "I hid, like Dad said. But I still could hear...so I followed you. They didn't even look for me."

"Because you're not supposed to be here." The knight finally found a key that clicked. "No one's come running. That's something I suppose."

Kelin hauled himself to his feet, supported by Der. "So can we just go?"

The door swung free to the knight's touch. "Well, let's take care of that guard and see what other poor bastards the chemmen have brought down here."

"How are your eyes, Thalon?" Der asked.

The boy looked up at her with gray orbs. "Everything's a little clearer here. Different, but not weird." He cocked his head. "Are yours all right, Der?"

She nodded. "Uh, yeah."

Jacob peered down the empty corridor. "I will find that guard. Fienan, you're with me." He tossed the keys at Der. "You, Kelin, Thalon, go find the other prisoners, and if they're useful, let them out."

"If they're useful?" Kelin repeated.

"See if they're friendly. Or you can pat them on the back and send them to cover our escape. Useful. Now go!" He pointed, and then he and Fienan vanished down the hall.

The corridor was plain and that same dull, lackluster, patternless gray. Der frowned, finding it difficult to fear a clean hallway. She had always imagined in those brief moments when they'd made up stories about the chemmen that they lived in dark palaces full of bloody skeletons. The outpost in the Wild Lands had fit that story. But here, in their home, she hadn't expected well-organized and well-swept buildings. This was almost boring.

She glanced down the hall; the other barred door seemed to come out of a mirage. She looked back— their cell already appeared a long way off. As they inched closer, she wondered who else the storm-readers had locked away down here. They could be spies who had failed the chemmen like the cultists they had made into undead.

Thalon gripped the back of her leg. He looked up. At least here his eyes were gray, and that would avoid an awkward explanation if the other prisoners were human or elves. He offered a grin. "You go first."

Kelin nodded. "Yeah, Der, you go first."

She stopped walking. "I'd feel a lot better if I had a sword."

The others shrugged and waved her ahead while they stayed put.

She swallowed and stepped forward. Her gaze slipped through the bars, and she sighed with relief. She looked over her shoulder at Kelin and Thalon. "Dwarves."

She offered a small smile to the other prisoners. "Well met. We're, uh, here to rescue you...?"

Three dwarves clustered together. They looked like fallen warriors, sitting in squalor on the floor. Their hair and magnificent beards were matted and frazzled. One of them opened an eye, and he stared.

Der scrambled to find the correct key and cursed as every key so far fit but didn't turn. Kelin and Thalon sneaked up behind her.

A dwarf pushed himself to his feet and tottered forward. When he arrived at the bars, he squinted and leaned toward her. Then he reached into his pocket and pulled out a pair of thick spectacles. He slipped them over his eyes.

"Humans?" he said in Common. He took a turn staring at each of them. He removed his spectacles, buffed them on his torn sleeve, and put them back on.

Der smiled as a key turned. "We, uh, just escaped from down the hall." She heaved the door open.

The dwarf spoke quickly to the others in a guttural language. He whirled back. "How were you captured and brought to this hell?"

Her grin widened. "Oh, we were caught trying to raid this place. How about you?"

Behind her, Kelin covered his eyes with his hand.

None of the dwarves moved toward the door.

"Is something wrong?" she asked.

The dwarf shook his head, sending his beard swaying. "Aside from being in Darkreign itself, prisoners of the accursed chemmen, and being rescued by mad children, no...?"

She grinned. "Oh, we have a plan. Er, we don't exactly have a plan to escape since we didn't know what to expect in Darkreign, but we'll figure it out. Not to worry."

Behind him, one of the other dwarves muttered something that sounded like rocks being kicked around. The speaker then looked to Der. "He wants to know if you're daft."

"Yes," Kelin stated. "However, we would like to get the hell out of here with our hides intact. You're welcome to come." He darted into the cell. "Can you all stand and walk? My name's Kelin Miller of Riversbridge."

The bespectacled dwarf nodded. "Yes, we are able." Once more, he took his time to study all three of them. "I am Carak. It's best to say short names for now. These are Boison and Striggal. We are of Clan Heavyaxe."

Der grinned. "I know that name."

Kelin offered his hand to one of the reclining dwarves and seemed to strain as he helped the dwarf to stand. "Duelingar, right?"

"Yeah," she replied. "Seems like a year ago."

Thalon, standing guard in the hall, peered around anxiously. "Can we go already?"

Carak pointed at Thalon. "That boy a half-elf?"

Der and Kelin froze under that gaze, but Kelin eventually nodded. "Uh, yes." He swiveled his head. "Here come the captain and Fienan. Oh, they don't look happy."

Jacob, wearing his recovered armor and weapons, carried two backpacks in one hand.

Carak stared up and down at him. "Dragoon?"

"Silver Dawn," the knight answered.

"You with them? How did you land here truly?"

"We were betrayed."

Fienan bunched a fist at his side, but his gaze fell to Thalon. He sighed as he looked away. "Let's just leave." He pulled at a backpack and retrieved his mail shirt. He tossed Der's to her.

She struggled to pull the armor over her shoulders. "Right." She glanced up the quiet corridor and turned to Jacob. "Our swords?"

He pointed down at the backpack. Three dwarven axes—with a pickaxe on side and a fighting axe on the other—and two short swords poked their handles out of one, but they weren't the swords they had brought. Fienan and Kelin snatched up the swords before she could. She huffed as she scooped up a small knife and stuck it into her belt.

"We can't leave without my dad," Thalon piped up. "I thought he'd be with you."

"Er." Kelin bent down to Thalon's level. "Your dad's got the best chance for surviving down here, so I'm sure he's fine. Which way is out?"

Thalon pointed down the hall.

"I've oft wondered what this building is," Carak rumbled as they began to walk. "It's too neat to be a proper prison."

"The cells are real enough," Der muttered.

"I don't think that it is, sir dwarf," Fienan responded quietly.

"Ghost town," Thalon whispered.

"It reminds me..." Fienan hummed a little to himself. "It reminds me of those town halls in the empire."

"What halls?" Der asked.

"Walk." Jacob waved them toward a corner, and they fell in line behind him.

They passed into a new, identical corridor. The doors here weren't barred but instead crafted of solid wood.

Der nudged Fienan. "What were you going to say?"

The elf ducked his head and whispered, "Just that every city, even the small towns, had them. They had quite a lot in them: government, the medicinal hub, the local jail, libraries—"

"And schools," Jacob finished. He pointed into one of the rooms they were sneaking past. In the back of the room were bunks, stacked all the way from the floor to the ceiling. In the center were wooden desks, arranged into rows and facing the front. There were also a couple of windows high on the exterior wall.

"This room's the same," Der called from across the corridor.

"I guess this is where they send the chemmen children," Carak mused. "Those desks are too small for anything other than little ones."

"Why are they empty?" Thalon asked.

Jacob shook his head and shrugged. "They're off to war."

"What, like fighting?" Der narrowed her eyes.

"Probably cooking, cleaning, those things. They're not *meant* to fight."

"This way." Thalon pointed. Then he stared at the dwarves. "Why're you here?"

"There was a man with a young girl," Carak whispered as they tiptoed down the hall. "We thought he was human, but it was the girl I didn't trust. She sat there, didn't ask questions, and didn't look around. I've never seen a human child not at least nervous to be in a dwarf hall." He shrugged. "It was too dark, and the man had his face hidden by a hood, so we didn't see the color of their eyes until it was too late." He gestured to Boison and Striggal. "We were the only ones in our outpost who survived, and that was eight years ago."

"You've been down here for eight *years?*" Der barked.

"Did you think the chemmen were rushing headlong into whatever they're doing?"

She hesitated. "I hope they are now."

The dwarf hung his head. "We remember the horror of the storm-reader tales. But we too fooled ourselves into thinking that they had perished. I was sure we they were going to use us when they set out on our cities."

Der snorted. "Is it only humans that don't know that the chemmen existed then?"

Fienan shrugged. "Dwarven history isn't as fragmented as human history is—especially after Pallens died."

She felt her face flush. "We're learning now."

Jacob asked, "Ah, Sir Carak, do your companions speak Common as well?"

Boison nodded. "Small. Speak small."

"Ah, that's good. You can understand us."

Boison and Striggal nodded. "Yes," they said.

The party rounded another corner and started down a new corridor. Jacob glanced around. "I hope we haven't been this way before."

Der fought against folding her arms. "Looks like it."

Thalon pointed. "There's the door. It's the same one I came through. I think."

The knight raised his hand. "All right, spread out, poke your noses up against the glass, and watch for activity. We're not stepping a foot outside only to be shown right back in."

Der, Kelin, and Thalon tiptoed into a classroom. It looked like the previous one, with the bunks and desks all in order. They pushed a desk over to the wall, but it was too short.

"Let's try with both." Der dragged a second desk across the floor. Stacked together, she still had to stretch to gaze over the lip of the window. She held her breath and watched. To her surprise, the sun's white light briefly blinded her. She covered her eyes and squinted. All she could make out were some white, square buildings and forest. Gray trees, hiding in black shadows, slouched in the gray light. "Um..."

"Do you see any chemmen?" Kelin asked from below as he steadied the desks.

She refocused her gaze. "No, but..." She tried to look harder. "No, I don't. This is unlike anything I've ever seen though."

Fienan materialized in the doorway. "Any luck?"

Kelin nodded. "No chemmen."

The elf smiled grimly. "All right then, let's meet at the door."

Der climbed down and they followed him away from the classroom. She tossed a glance over her shoulder, smirking at the two desks now completely out of place. She darted back inside the room and kicked over a third desk. Then she trotted after the others to the exit.

She crowded up next to the door with everyone.

Jacob bent low. "The plan is that we run out in twos. No one stops until they get beyond the tree line. Close the door *most* of the way, then wait to the count of one hundred before you follow. I'm going first with

Fienan. Then Boison and Striggal. Kelin and Thalon. Der and Carak. Understood?"

"Yes, sir," Kelin and Der whispered. The others nodded.

He heaved the door open, and after a quick sweep of his eyes, he and Fienan dashed out of the building.

One. Two. Three…

A hundred count later, Boison and Striggal vanished into the gray forest. The count started over, and then Kelin and Thalon were gone.

Suddenly, one hundred passed. Carak nudged Der. "Fly, fly." She and the dwarf pushed their heads through the door and took the plunge.

She sprinted, eyes nailed ahead in the trees, expecting arrows in her back any second.

Then she noticed that the dwarf wasn't beside her anymore. She glanced behind to see him in a tottering run, but she didn't dare stop.

Once into the trees, she nearly collapsed on top of the others. Fienan nodded. "Breathe."

Carak careened into a tree and latched onto it. He wheezed, glaring at Der. "We've been locked up for eight years, long legs!"

She held up her hands. "I didn't say anything." She caught Jacob's glance, and he shook his head. She turned back toward the building, trying to remember if she had closed the door behind them.

The knight snapped a twig off the nearest branch. "Trees aren't healthy."

Der looked down. The needles under their feet were dry and small. She craned her neck high and saw bare twigs poking out from thin branches.

The dwarves shrugged.

"Everyone all right?" Jacob asked. "Let's march."

CHAPTER FORTY

Der counted ten chemmen guarding the cave as she crouched low in the grasses and trees. She and Fienan crawled back to the party on their hands and knees. The elf said, "Didn't even see ten of them in the building. Something's strange."

Jacob grimaced. "Were they on guard?"

"They looked bored, but I'll say that they were."

Der gulped. "Can we win?"

The knight shrugged. "Now would be a good time to have a bow." He sighed. "I guess we'll have to use tactics instead."

Thalon shook his head. "No, not without Dad. Not without Dad!"

Jacob tightened his face. "It's your safety I'm fearing for. Your dad can take care of himself."

The child started to whimper and it blossomed into tears.

"Keep crying, boy. My decision's been made."

Carak tapped on Kelin's wrist. "Has his father died? Does the boy not know?"

"We don't know," he answered with complete honesty.

"We may all die soon enough." The dwarf's face twisted into disgust as he turned away.

Boison raised a finger. "He not like fight. He reader." He offered a yellow-toothed grin through his scraggly beard and pantomimed writing.

"Oh." Kelin blinked. Then he chucked, "Of course, of course. I'd just assumed—"

Jacob leaned forward. "Everyone's going to have to carry their own weight on this one. Boison, Striggal, Fienan, and I are going straight in. However, before we get there, Der, Kelin, Carak, you're going to sneak around behind them. As soon as they get to us, you attack them from behind. That surprise is our only advantage. We beat them back and run into the cave. Thalon, you stay down and hide. Be ready to run."

"But Dad!" the boy sobbed.

"But he—" Der bit her tongue. She patted the child's shoulder. "I'm sure he's fine. And you know he's coming for you."

"Let's hope he's not coming for the rest of us," Fienan murmured.

"Quiet," Jacob commanded. "You in the flank, count to five hundred. And be silent. They *cannot* know that you're behind them, understand?"

"Yes, sir," Der whispered.

"All right. Get going."

She nodded. The decaying pine needles made it easier than expected to mask their sounds. She tried to keep count but gave up after she walked into a tree. She couldn't focus on counting, hiding, and moving at the same time—not with how quickly her heart was racing.

She watched Kelin mouthing a prayer beneath his breath. She glanced at the dwarf, but couldn't read his expression. Kelin and Carak stopped and lay on the ground. They drew their weapons and began to crawl.

Der remained crouched by a tree and looked up. Well, she didn't think the chemmen would expect that.

***

"You're my height." Thalon looked critically at Boison. "How can you weigh so much?"

The dwarf grunted and kicked, trying to scramble up the rock face. It may have only been six feet, but it was an effective stop for the dwarves and the child.

"Is it the beard?" the boy persisted.

Boison growled, and with his free hand drove the pickaxe side of his axe into the stone. He heaved his weight up and over the edge.

The boy hopped and grabbed onto a thin overhanging stick, then pulled himself up with minimal effort. They tiptoed forward and nearly tripped over Jacob. How an elf as large as he could hide so easily was still a mystery. At least here, his armor was gray and blended in better.

Hidden low in the brush, the knight eyed the chemmen guards. He scowled. "We'll be seen," he whispered. "No help for it. Ready?"

He waited for each individual person to nod and spared a long look for Thalon. The boy hunkered down against the ground.

The knight pulled out his axe in front of him. The others readied their stolen or recovered weapons.

Jacob let loose a bull-throated roar and they ran.

Hammering seconds passed as they closed on the storm-readers. Two chemmen broke from the line, leaving eight to face the attackers. They turned to run into the forest and met Kelin and Carak rising from the trees.

One of them immediately folded over the dwarf's axe, and Kelin thrust his sword straight at the other. That chemman skittered to the side, wild-eyed, and took a swipe at the young man. Kelin parried, but the chemman was already sprinting away. He followed for a couple steps, but couldn't match his target's speed. He whirled around and ran toward the line of combat.

The remaining storm-readers met their opponents' weapons with their swords. Jacob had felled his second. The rest held their ground in front of the cave. The dwarves leveled their axes at chemmen thighs and let their own momentum carry them forward while Fienan batted aside the storm-reader swords over their heads. Kelin and Carak ran up to join their comrades.

Der launched from over the lip of the cave, blocking out the white sun as she flew through the air. Her knife bit deep into a chemman's neck. He dropped like a sack of flour.

Her feet smacked against the ground as she fell on top of the body. She yanked the knife free and struggled to stand. Another chemman hopped back from the line, his sword striking for her. She managed a slim parry, driving his point into the soil, but it also left her no angle of attack. Her knife was far too stubby against a sword.

She backpedaled toward the cave but the chemman forced her sideways before she could get there. She crouched and retreated under an overhanging rock wall near the entrance and couldn't move any farther.

The chemman followed, thrusting. His sword pricked the back of her knee as he lunged after her and she rolled to the side. On the next thrust, she caught his sword against the rock with her foot. She held it there long enough for her to squirm forward and stab him in the face with her knife.

He went limp. She crawled out and jumped to rejoin the fracas. She stumbled in line beside Kelin. "So hard without color!"

"I know!" he shouted back.

Jacob brought his axe down one more time, and it was over. He pointed at the cave. "Cuts and bruises will have to wait!" the knight bellowed. "Thalon!"

The boy was looking over his shoulder as he shuffled forward.

"One got away! One got away!" Kelin waved toward the trees.

"Doesn't matter, go!" Jacob roared.

"I'm not leaving Dad!" Thalon screamed.

"Yes, you are." Jacob pushed him toward the cave.

Thalon glared but ran into the cave. "Dad? Please be here!" He rebounded off something and squeaked in alarm.

"What the hell?" Kelin shoved his way forward. His forehead smacked into some invisible force.

"Barrier!" Fienan kicked it, striking his foot. "They sealed it!"

"Back to the forest! Back to the forest!" Carak pulled on Der's arm.

"They'll set another trap!" Kelin wailed. "We'll be caught."

Carak grunted. "They don't need a trap; we're *already* trapped."

CHAPTER FORTY ONE

Vlade stalked down the corridor with a spring in his step. A chuckle danced on his lips. His plan, teetering on a precipice, was finally solidifying. With the three known—no—four known thin spots now, thanks to the intruders, it was only an hour to his targets. And his sorcerers had learned to direct them to other destinations on earth; they could go where they pleased, and because of the elf they were using, Indelleiria's magical defenses were no challenge.

At least here, everything was in its normal color, so far as he defined the concept for himself. He didn't strain his eyes, and it was hard to recall a time when those harsh hues of earth had been considered natural.

He pushed open a door into an austere room with a single chair in its center. The space was lit by a magical lantern high in a corner. In the chair sat a chemman wearing an elven-style shirt and trousers.

The soldier looked up expectantly. "Yes, my lord commander?" he asked in the chemmen language. He held his hands at his sides.

Vlade opened his mouth but then frowned.

Thistle spoke first, "Has my mission been successful, my lord?"

"Your mission?" the commander repeated.

"Did King Dis not inform you?" Thistle inquired. "This mission has been a long time in process. To earn our enemies' trust."

"Perhaps," Vlade managed, staring at the other chemman.

"I have confirmation that the princes and the wicked baroness are in Elloan." Thistle folded his hands together. "I don't know how long they'll remain there, however."

"Yes, yes, excellent." He lifted onto the balls of his feet. "All three targets are in the same place, so you tell me as well."

"Yes, my lord," Thistle replied.

"This mission..." He looked Thistle up and down. "How did you accomplish such a feat? They knew your face, your eyes, and yet they still followed you?"

Thistle stared ahead. "I pretended to have escaped the banishment, my lord. That I had been on my own since the old war, and thus, had learned different customs."

"Ah." Vlade nodded. "And they believed you?"

Thistle nodded. "Of course, my lord."

A grin crawled across the chemmen commander's countenance. It was all coming together! Three distinct, individual sources had told him that his targets were there: the human prisoner, their spy, and now this chemman.

A thought brought the commander's heels back down to the ground like a falling boulder. "What about the child? The half-breed bastard?"

Thistle's face remained blank. "Per the king's orders, the child was an experiment: to see if we could gain elvish healing ability."

Vlade blinked. "Impressive." His frown deepened. "Did it work?"

Thistle shrugged. "We were waiting for him to mature further."

"How was this child...made?"

"What do you mean, my lord?"

Vlade licked his lips. "You did not...mate?"

Thistle sneered. "Couldn't stomach it, so I used alternative methods."

The commander bit off a chuckle rattling in his throat. "Good, good. Present the boy for dissection and study, wherever you stashed him."

Thistle bowed his head. "At once, my lord." He tensed as if to rise but remained seated. "I am unworthy of this request, my lord. But I would like a bath and a change of clothes. I wish not to smell like this anymore."

Vlade nodded. "Naturally. I am sure you will want to join us for the final battle."

"Wouldn't miss it, my lord." Thistle looked at the sword on the commander's hip. "It's good to see it again. I remember the first one and its wielder well."

Vlade placed his hand on the pommel. "I am the wielder now." Then a grin slinked across his lips. "We are in reach of victory. After so long. We are in reach!"

Thistle nodded, still eyeing the sword. "Yes, in reach."

"I have duties to attend." Vlade spun on his heel toward the door. When he was in the doorframe, he paused, dropped his head, and turned back around.

Thistle maintained a helpful expression. "Is there something more, commander?"

The other chemman startled. "What? Commander?" He swept into the room. "It is I, Dis, your king!"

Thistle's jaw fell open. He ducked his face, staring hard at the floor. "Yes, my king."

"Why would you— How could you confuse your king?"

He blinked rapidly. "I am sorry. You have the commander's sword."

Dis looked down. "Oh." Bewilderment swirled across his features. "Why—" He shook his head. "Stupid replica anyway. I didn't notice. I never draw my own sword. Don't have to."

Thistle kept staring. "Yes, my king."

Dis pulled it out and swung it around; the sound vanished from the room. The king stopped moving the weapon. "Damned annoying thing, really. I wonder why he gave it to me. He's always drooling over it."

Thistle pushed himself off the chair and dropped to one knee. "I shall return it if you like. That way my king need not bother with it."

"Who are you anyway, toady?" Dis frowned. "And why are you dressed like an elf?"

"I was a spy, my king. I brought you the prisoners."

"Ah. Yes. Of course. Now, I must return to earth for our hour of victory." Dis unbuckled and removed the belt, sheathed the sword, and tossed it to Thistle. "Get that back to your commander, and go and change your clothes."

***

Dis gazed into the obsidian mirror. He'd brought it back with him to his personal apartments so it could be surrounded by his fountains, couches, and beds. The mirror had been a gift. It had been a gift from... He frowned into his reflection. ...From whom? It had always been his, as long as he could recall, but he also knew that it had been a gift.

He turned around, but it was Vlade who gazed at the room. His smile spread. Their army, though scattered across the elven kingdom, had begun pooling together, and like a flood, they would wash away the last leadership of the elves. Their vengeance was almost in his hand.

Dis suddenly whispered over his shoulder, "What's got you so teary-eyed, brother?"

Vlade whirled around and glared at the king in the mirror. "Victory, Dis."

"Yes... After this, after we've won, I will finally find peace."

Vlade snorted but then swallowed a chuckle. "With this sword—"

Dis's reflection pointed. "What sword?"

Vlade's hand dropped to his hip and he bit his tongue. "Where is it?" He pawed at his clothes. *"Where is it?"*

The king shrugged. "I don't know."

"Who would dare?"

This time, it was Dis who chuckled. "Perhaps that bull-headed girl locked away in the prison with the others."

"This isn't a time to jest, Dis!" Vlade stomped in a tight circle. "That sword was part of my plan."

"It was stupid! It wasn't even the real blade." The chemmen king grinned. "Oh, and I'd lied. One of your spies has it. Giving it to him was essential to gain information about you, and us."

Vlade gasped so hard he choked. He leaned forward, spewing coughs.

Dis recovered from his coughing as well.

"I can't believe you!" the commander screamed. "It is my sword. I made it. They remembered the horror. It was *mine*, Dis!" He slapped his fist against the mirror and the king reeled. Vlade didn't see himself also reeling.

The commander smashed his fist against the wall.

Dis hissed, holding his bleeding knuckles in front of him. "I do not care about the pains you inflict upon yourself, but not on me!"

"The same pains," Vlade sneered. He remembered holding in his guts and heaving in the closing battle of the last war. He'd rolled over to see Dis face down in the mud beside him. But then, when he'd woken up, his soldiers had informed him that the other chemmen had linked their lives because their bodies had been failing and the chemmen couldn't lose their leaders. They'd been told they shared the same water of life— but nothing about sharing the same body.

Dis had never been far from that day on.

Vlade bit his tongue until the metallic taste of blood filled his mouth. He whirled and spat at the king's feet in the mirror.

Dis raised his hand to his own bloody teeth. "How *dare* you harm your king!"

Vlade stopped and stared at the king.

A knock thundered at the entry to the chamber.

"What?" Dis snapped, loud enough to be heard through the door.

"The prisoners have escaped, my king, my commander!"

Vlade snarled, "Enemies loose in *our* city?"

But Dis smiled and spoke with soothing poison on his lips, "They will not survive. This is our world. Your epic still has a pulse, Vlade. Pull our army to Moonrise Castle. You can witness their agony in the glory of color. It has been too long since I have seen men die in red blood. If there are outsiders in our city, do not fret; let our world eat them."

CHAPTER FORTY TWO

"You see much?" Boison whispered up from below.

Kelin looked down. "I see a lot. Nothing of Der, Jacob, or Carak though." He leaned against the metal support halfway up the windmill. Where could they be? He still couldn't believe that he hadn't noticed when they'd gotten separated in their mad dash away from the cave. Just suddenly, he had been running with only Fienan, Boison, Striggal, and Thalon. He tore through his memories but had no idea when they'd broken up as a unit. Was it when they'd fallen into the ravine?

Overhead, the giant blades of the windmill hung unmoving. It was much bigger than any mill he'd ever seen. His father's back in Riversbridge was water-powered and used to grind flour. This one had massive chains disappearing into the ground below. He guessed it was probably a type of well, but he had no idea how deep the water would have to be to demand this construction.

Around him, he could see the forest, the city, and the endless patchwork of farmlands. Dry ditches led away from the mill and into the fields, where other massive mills dotted the landscape. A perfect square of irrigation channels divided each field.

But none of the windmills were turning, and Kelin couldn't find any plants higher than his knees. He wasn't sure if they were green or not, but he doubted it. They looked too dry. He thought of the forest, where the leaves had hardly grown, and the trees were withering.

He gripped the steel frame so hard that several of his fingernails bent back.

No one could last here. Not for much longer anyway. Darkreign was rotting underneath the chemmen's identical boots.

They had killed their world.

He swung his head toward the city, and Zazocorma opened up like a split belly. The capital was constructed of squares. The streets marched in straight lines, like these fields, intersecting at every corner. Kelin's eyes watered. He had never seen anything like that. He was used to winding, curling streets that followed the paths of cows long gone. The villages and towns had grown up around them. He'd never imagined a city that had been planned.

The rectangular buildings were anything but frightening. It didn't ring true with the ancient horrors of the chemmen. And that made it worse because he knew exactly what the chemmen would do to a prisoner.

He tightened his jaw. He had seen and felt their horrors, and now he had seen they'd killed their world.

He let his gaze drift over to the fields. If they concentrated on farming as much as they did on war, they could probably coax their world back into growth. But they'd built swords instead of plows.

Shuddering, he found himself thankful the chemmen had given up their humanity. This way, he didn't have to call them cousins.

His foot felt down the metal until it reached a hold, and he eased himself toward the ground.

"See things? Good," Boison said encouragingly. Beside him, Striggal nodded. Behind them, Thalon was playing with some twigs in the soil.

"Yeah, I saw a lot of things." He turned to Fienan. "I saw that you should have killed every last one back in the old war." He dove right through the elf's gasp. "But you couldn't do it, could you?"

The dwarves shrugged, but they likely hadn't been able to keep up with Kelin's burst of speed.

Fienan clapped a hand over his open mouth. "You don't understand. Life is sacred. Sending them here was giving ourselves *and them* a chance."

"And look at what they did with it!" Kelin stalked forward, pointing toward the direction of the city.

"Shh, shh." Boison waved his hands down.

The young man continued staring at the elf. "Your life isn't sacred to them. Not yours, not mine, not even little Thalon's. That's why they're back, because you played by your code of honor when the chemmen had no such thing. Look at what they did to their world. Look at it!"

The elf raised his hand as if to slap him. Instead, he growled and jerked to the side. He exhaled and unclenched his hands. "I have no answer. Every solution that would provide us with peace breaks my beliefs."

Kelin watched as the elf let his gaze settle to the distance. The human cleared his throat and said, "There's no water here. No signs of Der, Jacob, or Carak either."

"No here, no here." Striggal motioned pushing something away. "Move."

Fienan tilted his head to the side and nodded. "Yes, master dwarf. We should move." He started walking through one of the irrigation ditches. Kelin and the dwarves followed, but the human turned around when he realized Thalon hadn't moved.

The boy remained sitting. "Is Dad back yet?"

Kelin shook his head. "No. And we don't know how to find him or the others." He offered down his hand and helped the child to stand.

"Go," Boison pointed away from where they were standing.

Fienan bowed his head. "I agree. We need to escape. The others are on their own."

"No!" Thalon exploded. "We have to find Dad!"

Fienan knelt in front of the boy. "Sir Jacob was right. It is your safety that we fear for, my child. That's why we must flee. Your father is the most likely to survive, but he can't do it with us surrounding him. Do you understand?"

"No." Thalon quivered. "Are you mad at him?"

The elf stood and sighed.

"Out?" Striggal asked.

Fienan nodded. "There are other thin spots; we just have to find one."

"Won't the chemmen guard the others?" Thalon inquired.

"Probably."

Kelin said, "We can hope that the guard isn't heavy, but they know we're here."

The elf snipped off a developing smile. "Well, I must say that you've certainly taken up the sword since your friend has gone missing."

He shrugged. "Someone has to do it."

Fienan nodded. "We ought to find a road that seems to be well traveled, and watch. The chemmen must be going to earth routinely this far into their assault, so we should be able to locate at least one thin spot they're using. We can only hope it's by a tree path or near allies."

"That's more cautious than I'm used to." Kelin paused. "I like it." As they crouched and walked through the ditches, he realized that he wasn't noticing how the grass and the dirt weren't brown. He had finally adapted to an environment without color.

He recalled something Donley's father, the village forester, had told him back in Riversbridge: a man could not be self-aware while sneaking or hiding. No thoughts, no breath, a man was not a conscious thing; it was best to think of yourself as a rock or a tree. He'd meant it for hunting though, not for tiptoeing through enemy territory.

He felt himself shiver at the thought. He missed home. The people back in the village didn't believe in the existence of the chemmen, and here he was, in their domain, trying to end a war.

He slithered around one of the sharp corners where two ditches met and nearly toppled over a storm-reader. His head snapped up. It looked to be a patrol of five or six soldiers.

Both parties stared in amazement at each other.

Fienan snatched Thalon up in his arms as he whirled to run. The dwarves kept up, their shorter legs pumping twice as fast. Kelin was the last to wheel around and sprint away. He was sure he felt blades licking his back. He urged his feet to fly, his knees to keep up, and his head to outrun them all.

CHAPTER FORTY THREE

"Where are we, sir?"

Jacob rolled his eyes. "Somewhere in Darkreign, Der."

"More specifically?"

"How about lost?" Carak waved their lone makeshift torch in front of him. It lit up another sterile stone corridor.

"Yeah, but how many other chemmen buildings have we seen that are built underground?"

"Well, this one so far," Jacob answered. "Because this is first building we hid in."

"Right, right," she replied, poking around the next corner. "This was definitely not part of the plan." She slowed. "And maybe that's all right. It's about the goal, and that can still happen." She frowned. "Right?"

Jacob wagged a finger at her. "We're supposed to be silent."

"Yes, sir." However, on her next step, she opened her mouth. The knight reached out with one shovel-sized hand and pushed her. She coughed and rebounded against the wall.

The wall swung open, revealing more darkness beyond.

Large, hidden hinges mounted the door flush with the stone. Carak poked his head toward the new passage. "Old trick. Done well though."

"Why would they have a secret lair?" Der scratched her head. "There are no chemmen traitors and all."

"I guess those human habits never quite faded," Jacob mused. He frowned. "I doubt every chemman knows about this."

The dwarf glanced over his shoulder. "Probably not. Maybe. Good of a place as any to hide."

Der stuck her knife through the opening, but nothing tried to crush it from the inside.

"Good try," the knight chuckled. "Chemmen traps are usually more subtle."

"There is light." Carak stepped ahead and into a pale, gray glow that seemed to have no origin.

They had taken no more than three steps beyond the door when it swung shut behind them.

Jacob darted back to it, but the surface was smooth, and the crack was a fingernail's width. "Find the switch!"

Carak's fingers combed over the walls. "Nothing, nothing."

"I guess they didn't forget how to lock intruders inside either," Der drawled.

Ten more minutes of scouring the stones produced no results. The wall remained a wall and not a door.

Der pointed into the hall. "Maybe it's farther inside?"

"Fine," Jacob growled. He swung his axe up on his shoulder.

They ventured into a chamber with a slick black floor and dozens of chest-high hanging glassy ovals of varying sizes. Each translucent bulb boasted something sealed inside.

"What is this place?" Der whispered.

Jacob shrugged.

Carak trotted over to the nearest one and rose on his toes. "Eh, elf, can you read Chemmen? They've labeled it." He tapped a finger against the oval. "It's crystal."

Der peered over his head. Through the bulb, she saw what appeared to be a wide-chained necklace. She couldn't tell if it was silver, gold, or something else in the grayness. Someone had affixed a tiny plaque to the base of the oval.

"That's Palls." Jacob looked up, perplexity dancing across his features. "A trophy room?"

The dwarf coughed. "What?"

He pointed at the plaque. "*Monile lapideum*. A necklace of stone." He thumped a hand against his helmet. "Huh. Really makes you wonder who they didn't want reading this. Or are they truly fancying themselves scholars?"

"It's not stone." Der pushed her nose against the clear crystal. "It's metal." She looked at the plaque and saw that she could read the letters, but they were arranged in a gibberish order to her.

"Der, I have no idea," the knight sighed.

Carak wandered deeper into the trophies. "Now this is what I would expect of the storm-readers." The bulb he pointed at bore a beautiful, ornate silver bowl containing a half-rotted head staring in sightless horror.

"What's it say?"

Jacob bent down to read the inscription. "A leader should serve his people." His lip curled in disgust. "Ugh, you're right. This is what I would expect." He moved on. "Golden chalice of golden wine. The emerald of faith. A singer of dead beads."

He paused at a bulb with a crack open in its side. "Crystal in crystal," he read.

Der lifted up onto her toes to see into the bulb. She poked her finger through the hole. "A thief, here?" The two translucent shelves inside were empty.

Jacob shrugged. "Looks like they missed a few."

As she peered at the broken crystal's base, she saw a few fragmented splinters. "But they look like bones."

The knight shrugged again and kept walking. "Summer's winter—looks like a pinecone to me. The cloak of breeze. My boot up this title maker's ass."

"Which one is that?" Der asked.

The knight snickered. "Come here. I'll *show* you."

"Hey, elf, what's this?" Carak called from across the shadows. He pointed to a banner nailed to the wall.

Jacob frowned, but the light wasn't strong enough from their position. He walked closer, then stopped and cursed.

Der flinched as the flag came into focus.

The banner was ebony with two opposite-facing parallel swords lying horizontal across it. Curling around the swords was a serpent with a vicious striking head on each end.

All four of the serpent's eyes had been burned out.

Bile slid into the back of Der's throat. She'd never seen the flag before, but she wished she didn't know that snake.

And apparently, it knew her. She hadn't even heard of Sennha before she left home!

She licked her lips. "Do you think he could have mistaken me for someone else, like someone who died a long time ago?"

"What are you talking about?" Jacob snapped.

"Uh. Nothing." She inched back a step.

The knight gulped. "This." He swallowed again. "This is the Blackhound's banner."

"What?" Der cried.

"Impossible," Carak muttered, shaking his head.

She felt her mind racing. "Sure, Pallens helped the elves banish the chemmen, but that was *before* the Blackhound. So why...?"

"I don't know, Der," Jacob whispered.

"I don't think they liked him either." Carak pointed to the eyes.

Jacob kept his gaze pinned on the flag. "I was there. I was part of the army that found this very banner flying on the citadel of Pallens. We didn't get there in time. We only found that one flag, and we burned it."

He remained standing there, unmoving.

Der whirled her back on the banner faster than she'd intended to and wandered into the forest of crystal bulbs again.

"The chemmen are certainly confounding," Carak remarked. "Do you suspect the scourge of the old empire had dealings with them? Before the fall?"

Jacob shook his head. "I wouldn't think so. Der's right, the Blackhound was human, so he wouldn't have been alive when they were banished." He broke his gaze away. "I don't know."

"I don't think it was the Blackhound who burned out those eyes," the dwarf said.

The knight's hands hung at his sides. "Timing's all wrong."

"Hey!" Der waved both arms over her head from across the room. "I found a sword!" She squinted—it was hard to see through the grayness, and it felt as if she were staring through water, but she had to examine it. "It looks kind of like those pieces of Pallens art in Riverfall." Her hands scrambled over the oval like paws on ice. "Um, the sign reads *rex*. That's Palls for dog, right?"

That broke whatever dark dream was still haunting Jacob. "No, Der, it means king."

"Even better." She squashed her nose against the crystal. The hilt was designed for serious warfare, but a gem—she couldn't tell in the grayness what kind—protruded from either side of the pommel. Twin streams of what looked like melted metal decorated the crosspiece in an endless trail, dipping into corners and complex loops.

No nicks or burrs marred the edge, which shone even in the gray light. The crossguard bore an emblem of a sword encased in a circle.

Carak's jaw fell so low that his beard scraped the floor. "That's a..." He tried again. "That's a..."

"A weapon of Pallens." Jacob's eyes widened in amazement.

Carak dropped to a knee. "In all my years, to see such a wonder."

Der shook her head. "But—but the Blackhound ordered all the weapons of Pallens destroyed. Everyone knows that!"

"That he did," Jacob said.

She stroked the oval. "It's not stealing, right? I mean, the chemmen must have stolen it first. So we're, like, rescuing it, right?"

The knight closed his eyes and shook his head. "We can't take it. Who knows what spells and traps the chemmen may have on these things? Oh, I wish."

She clamped her hands on the crystal bulb. "Sir, I'm not leaving it."

"Derora." Steel echoed in his voice.

Her face creased in agony, and as much as her eyes shone with defiance, she muttered, "Yes, sir."

Carak regained his feet. "It brings water to my eyes to leave such a prize." He hefted his axe in one hand and his torch in the other as he walked farther ahead into the darkness. "I wonder what other treasures this place holds."

Der kept her head turned toward the Pallens sword.

The knight's expression softened. "I used to do those things, and I've lost friends who've tried. It's just treasure, Der; it's not worth your life."

"Yes, sir." She narrowed her eyes but looked down.

"Something horrible will happen as you try to break that glass. Believe me, I've seen it all before."

"Yes, sir," she exhaled.

Carak hustled toward them, waving his torch. He beckoned. "How much do you miss the reds and blues? Come see!"

The back of the treasure room was set up as a workshop. On the table was a half-formed crystal bulb, and inside it, a slender, spiky crown.

And it was in color. The platinum and gems twinkled in defiance of the grayness. The sleek metal rose above the patterns into sharp tips. A massive, golden colored jewel rested in the center while sapphires, rubies, and emeralds wound the rest of the way around the crown.

Der sighed in relief, not in awe. Color still existed.

She pointed. The gold gem sparkled with green and brown hues within as she tilted her head. "Is color working right?"

"Sphalerite!" Carak burst. "And to see one so large!"

Jacob swallowed. "This is the crown of Indelleiria. Has to be. They must have stolen it when..." He dropped his eyes. Then he removed his gauntlets, reached his hands into the half-formed crystal, and pulled the crown free. "Damn!"

"What? What?" Der demanded.

"Nothing, I cut myself on the thing. It smarts." Then he lifted the headpiece aloft using only the pressure of his fingertips.

Der's amazement fizzled. "You said we couldn't take anything."

"This is different, kid."

"Why?"

"Because I say it's different." He led the way back to the hidden entrance. The other two followed closely, taking in the crown's color as if it were the only light in all of Darkreign. They crested the small threshold of the trophy chamber. Finally, the knight smirked. "Der, I remember being young, and you wouldn't believe the things I did."

"Good," she replied and stopped walking. "Then you know why." She spun and was already sprinting before she heard the knight's shout of protest. She darted through the bulbs until she reached the Pallens sword.

She balled her fist and kept running. She hit the crystal at full speed and the side of it shattered. The shards reflected gray light as they flew across the room.

The floor vanished. It was there beneath her feet and then, suddenly, it wasn't. Der flailed and latched onto the base of broken bulb with her left hand. She winced as the jagged crystal sliced into her palm, but held on.

She thrust her other hand up and freed the imprisoned sword. "Yes!"

From the safety of the entryway, Jacob glowered. Beside him, Carak goggled.

The knight exhaled like a bull. "What was your plan for this part?"

She tried to shrug, and when that failed, she waved the sword around. "This is the part of my plan where you rescue me."

"No." He turned his back and walked toward the hidden door.

Der's jaw dropped. "You can't leave me!"

The dwarf stood there, his head whipping between the two of them.

"Jacob!" She slipped down before she caught herself. Her arm was burning, and she could feet hot blood pulsing out of her cut palm, lubricating her hold on the broken crystal. Some of it dripped, and she never heard it hit any floor. "It's getting slippery here, sir."

She lost her grip, and for one horrible moment, she found herself plummeting into the abyss. Then her fingers snagged on the jagged lip and she bit down against a scream. Her little finger slipped free, and she could feel her ring finger sliding. "Jacob!" This time, all the pride had disappeared from her voice.

"All right, all right," he called. "But I get to kill you whenever I want."

Carak looked up at him. "Do you know what to do?"

Jacob frowned and backed up a few paces. "We need to think like the chemmen." He began studying the floor. "They wouldn't devise anything that could harm themselves without an easy fix. And, secondly, they're arrogant. They might believe that all intruders would be trapped."

"We couldn't find the door trigger."

"Let's hope this isn't the same." He found a break in the stone wall next to the edge where the floor vanished. "Ah-ha."

He reached into the opening and toggled the switch.

Der's grip finally slid too far, and she slipped free. She felt only the air beneath her as she stretched her left hand back up at the crystal bulb but missed it.

Her butt smacking the solid floor interrupted the drop. She blinked. "Huh?"

Carak jogged over to her, but Jacob marched, still cradling the crown. The knight growled, "Now we really need to go."

The dwarf snatched up her arm and started tying a cloth around her palm and fingers. She hardly noticed now that she had time to study at the Pallens sword. It was the exact size for her in length, width, and weight.

It was so perfect, and its heft in her hand reassured her.

Jacob shot her the look no soldier ever wants to see from an officer. "From now on, if you disobey an order, I will leave you. I am not joking. Do you understand?"

"Yes, sir." She didn't glance away from the Pallens blade.

He thrust out a hand. "Give it to me."

She tightened her jaw and hesitated.

"Der."

She pushed the sword out toward him, point down. He snatched it up, but the weapon fell from his fingers and clattered to the floor. Glowering, the knight bent to pick it up. The sword remained stuck fast.

Jacob scowled and attempted again.

Carak retreated. "Is that a magical blade?"

"No," Jacob grunted. "Just an extremely stubborn one."

Der leaned forward. "May I try, sir?"

"Fine," he clipped.

She wrapped her fingers around the hilt and swept it up.

The dwarf lifted both eyebrows. "Not magical, you say?"

The knight glared at the blade. "It doesn't matter, we have to leave. She can hold it, so she's got the edge on us there."

Der groaned.

"What?" he growled.

"You said—"

He snapped his fingers in front of her face. "Shut it."

"Yes, sir." She grinned as she pulled the sword back toward herself and swished it around. It was finely balanced. She experimented with a few moves. It felt like a dream. She paused, smiled, and then frowned. "All right, why did the chemmen have it?"

Jacob growled, "We can ponder these questions all we want with rosy glasses of wine in our hands under a blue sky, but first, we have to find somewhere where the sky is blue."

"We don't know how to meet up with the others," Carak pointed out.

Der grinned. "Let's cause a disturbance. They'll notice it too—or at least notice all the chemmen running—so they'll know where to go."

Jacob gave her a look as dry as the desert. "No. We're on our own. They're on their own."

"But—"

"It's cruel, but maybe this way we won't all die horrible deaths."

"We can't leave them behind."

Carak sighed. "Alas, the captain's right."

"So that's it? We're not even going to try to rescue them?" She cast her gaze up at the knight.

He shook his head. "Our only realistic chance of survival is to fend for ourselves. I'll wager you don't want to die."

"Of course not! But—but I can't leave Kelin or Thalon." She glanced at Carak. "Or the dwarves. Or

Fienan." She looked up at Jacob. "What about you? You're immortal and down here with us; aren't you afraid to die?"

"You're right. I don't want to die, but I also know how I don't want to live." She watched him give a grim grin. "If we get out of this alive and you get to choose between doing this again and farming, then you'll understand."

She shook her head.

"Let's go, come on."

Soon, they once again stood at the back of the blank wall. Jacob breathed, "I hope no alarm sounded when we came inside or during Der's stunt."

As he spoke, the hidden door swung open.

Jacob raised the hand with the crown in it to indicate a halt and slid the other down toward his axe. He freed it and held the naked blade steadily. They waited. Nothing happened. After two agonizing minutes of standing, he waved them forward.

They entered the corridor, and behind them, the wall swung closed.

A snigger arose from the darkness. Gray torches flared up on either side of the corridor, and Der saw the white flash of teeth as chemmen soldiers bared them. She brought the Pallens sword on guard.

Jacob boomed, "Carak, Der! Back to back with me!"

And the fight was on. She thought she counted four opponents, maybe five. She also found that the Pallens weapon glided across chemmen swords like a fish through water. Gray and white sparks leaped up her as steel screamed in agony. She retreated a half step. She didn't want to sacrifice the space, but it was that or perish.

A chemman in the back of the party flipped his sword to the side. All sound around them vanished as he thrust it through the neck of another storm-reader.

The world hung motionlessly. The chemman standing nearest to the one with the silent blade just stared. Jacob moved and drove his axe down through that stunned face. Der and Carak jumped forward, striking at their adversaries in their surprise.

Thistle grinned and slashed the blade again and again. In a matter of heart-stopping seconds, he was the only chemman who remained breathing.

Der laughed and felt like kissing her sword. It was amazing. She barely noticed when Carak charged past her.

Jacob caught the dwarf by his head. "No! This one's with us." Carak stumbled to a halt while the knight gazed at Thistle. "I think."

Thistle stared at the crown in Jacob's arm, but he said nothing.

Carak kept his axe between himself and Thistle. "An elf should know there are no chemmen traitors."

Jacob slipped between them, keeping his axe up. "Yes, I do, but as you saw, he took chemmen life. That's enough to not get an axe to the face—for the moment.""

Carak's eyes still bored into Thistle. "I don't understand. He's chemmen. It's a sin to them."

Thistle shrugged. "Then call me a sinner." He raised his gaze to Jacob. "Where is my son?"

"Unknown," the knight answered.

Der stepped beside Jacob as she stared at Thistle. "You told the chemmen when we came through."

"Because Thalon followed us. I acted to save him. There were already patrols searching for you because of the other traitor." He leveled his gaze at her. "I blame my son's behavior on your influence."

The sword in her hand sagged. "Er."

He lifted an eyebrow at her. Then he looked back at Jacob. "I found an escape."

Jacob narrowed his eyes at the storm-reader. "If you're leading us into another trap, I'm taking you out first."

"Fine." Thistle began to walk. "I have also learned something of value. The chemmen king and commander..."

"Dis and Vlade," Jacob muttered.

"They're the same person now. They share the same body."

"*What?*"

Thistle sheathed his sword. "There had been other savage experiments before the chemmen achieved immortality. Methods to salvage minds when bodies couldn't be repaired. And I don't think they know, but the other chemmen must."

"Good," Carak snorted. "Just one head to cut off then."

Der frowned. "Wait. You were there, with the king? Why didn't you try to end this war right then?"

"That would have been obvious," he replied.

"Yeah, the answer is obvious to me too."

"I'm no good to Thalon dead."

Jacob rolled his eyes. "Obvious, as in that's obviously trouble, Der. The king and commander can't go missing right now, or otherwise the chemmen may do what we don't expect. No, we need their leadership if we're still going to make this plan work."

"It's too far gone, sir."

"I hope not, or we've done all this for nothing." He turned to Thistle. "Where's this escape path?"

Thistle raised his hand down the corridor. "I will show you, but then I will find Thalon."

Jacob nodded.

"This thin spot is not far. However, I'm not sure where it goes, but the chemmen use spies and tree paths, so we'll probably end up near to at least one of those."

***

Several minutes later, they stood behind a torch-lit wooden altar, staring wide-eyed at the people in front of it. On the wall, the image of the doubled-headed serpent dominated the room. Animal, possibly human, intestines and organs were steaming on the altar. A man standing over them lowered his curved knife.

Jacob brandished his axe. "I hope we're interrupting."

CHAPTER FORTY FOUR

Caleb trailed his fingers across the windowsill in the guest chamber. Hundreds of the sword-flag flowers waved in the wind below. This narrow view looked too peaceful.

His brother stepped up behind him. Gladioli blooms were stuck behind his pointed ears, and he grinned at Caleb. He held a long stem in his hand like a sword and stabbed it into the air.

"If only our army were as numerous," Caleb murmured. "At least our enemies are here instead of spread over the countryside where we cannot control them."

The stem drooped. "We can't control them here, brother."

Caleb pulled a couple of the flowers away from his brother's face. "Come, we should see our fate." He turned and walked out of the room.

Lady Evelyn awaited them at the base of the vaulted tower's stairs. She curtsied. "My princes, it was just as we expected. They have arrived."

The last flower slipped from the younger prince's fingers. "It's really happening."

Caleb nodded. He stepped past the lady and marched up the stairs.

He pushed his head above the trapdoor and pulled himself up with only a grimace. Moonrise Castle's central tower rose twice the height of the rest of the fortress. Green shoots and buds curled around the ornate wooden railings and supports despite the icy wind. A stream from a fountain spiraled around the tower before disappearing into the floor. Alsalon followed him onto the tower.

"What's in here?" His brother squatted by a small wooden chest next to the trapdoor. He waved a hand over it and pulled it back as if it had burned him.

Caleb spun toward him.

Alsalon forced a grin. "Magic."

The older prince breathed out. He let his gaze fall to the valley floor. The chemmen army stood in formation behind the bunched and disheveled ranks of Sennha's cultists. In front of them were howling, bucking rows of calvar. Their cries carried on the wind up to the tower. Harnesses held them in check, but it wouldn't last. The leather already looked discolored against the strain of the animals.

The prince lowered his gaze to his army, hidden behind Moonrise's walls. They seemed so few, and instead of a fortress, the castle felt like a prison.

Their only hope rested in holding the walls that surrounded them. He looked to the sun; it was already losing its height, and his shadow was fast growing longer at his feet. He stiffened as the storm-readers' light crept through the valley and a fog emanated from it toward the castle, obscuring the chemmen army in grayness.

He steeled his jaw. So it seemed they had chosen to amplify the mist. And why not? It appeared they had victory in hand, so why not make it into a legend?

"You could be your father," a silken voice rose like an evening star behind him. Lady Evelyn stepped onto the tower.

He turned his gaze back to the fields below. "I can only hope that I carry a quarter of his character. He wouldn't have needed to take such a foolhardy risk to win a war."

"Perhaps not, my prince," the lady replied, "but he was unable to finish the last one."

***

Everyone was still staring: Der, Jacob, Thistle, Carak, and the cultists. The blood dripped off the nearest man's unmoving knife. Bits of liver clung to the blade. Der gulped, feeling the bile burning in the back of her throat.

They'd appeared through what looked like a stone wall behind the altar. A wooden staircase led upstairs from the cramped space, but there were more than a few cultists between them and the escape path. She found herself squinting against the overwhelming yellow light.

She sensed Thistle relax beside her, and from the corner of her eye, she saw him beginning to smile. He stepped forward, orange eyes alight in the flames.

One of them straightened his black robe and sauntered toward them. "We gave you as many soldiers as you needed. Now, the rest of us can continue our feast in peace."

Der's hands tightened on the Pallens sword as she glanced back at the guts on the altar. Jacob moved in front of her, keeping a straight face. She huffed and looked down, and saw her sword in color. She forgot about the cultists.

Her heart beat faster as she stared at it. She remembered what the prince had told her about Pallens using melted gems. The two lines dancing around the hilt and pommel had to be gems, one strand emerald, the other sapphire. The blade shone blue and gold in the orange torchlight.

Thistle snorted. "You call your men soldiers. They are weak."

The cultist's face froze.

The chemman took another step forward and pulled his sword free of its sheath. All sounds went blank as he spun it over and around his wrist, almost lazily.

The man in front of him tried to speak, but the sword voided his voice. Thistle stopped moving the weapon.

"Because of you," the lead cultist snarled, "our brothers were exposed in Second Acron. We had to flee."

"But we are leading you to victory over the elves. Something you did not dream of on your own."

"Of course, of course. But you promised to rid us of the king of Thealith, and now he's trying to rout us from his kingdom!"

"Because of your own stupidity when you let some children beat you in Duelingar."

"Hey!" Der blurted.

It fell on deaf ears. Thistle took another deliberate step forward. "That was not the only mistake you made." He leveled the weapon and stilled it. "You killed my wife." He thrust.

In silence, the cultist folded down onto the chemman's blade. His mouth gaped, his face raged red, and his chest deflated as he screamed with all his might when Thistle ripped the sword back. Yet, there was no sound. The cultist collapsed around the weapon.

The moment shattered, and the rest of the devil-worshippers clawed for their weapons, most of them jagged and ceremonial. Der leaped over the altar, the Pallens sword flashing against the torchlight.

Jacob rounded the platform. He sliced his axe across the chest of the nearest cultist, smashing the man's own knife into his ribs. He was dead before the axe cut into his body. Carak pushed his spectacles back up his nose, bellowed, and leaped forward.

Der grunted and waited for her opponent to attack. She blocked his blow, and when the momentum turned to her move, she not only riposted but kicked his knee out at the same time. He swore as his leg gave out, and he missed his parry. She stabbed his chest, the Pallens sword flowing like sharpened silk at her command.

Thistle, only a few steps in front of her, brought his bloody sword down repeatedly in silence. Der could see them scream, and she felt as if in a dream to see but not hear it. Jacob and Thistle made quick work of the rest of the cultists.

She looked around. The last one ran behind the altar. A web of red light erupted between his fingers, and she felt a rush of air sweep by her.

Jacob kicked the altar, crashing its mass into the cultist just as the devil-worshipper's spell exploded in his hands, sending wooden shards and guts flying out over the room.

Der breathed out, wondering what that magic would have done if the altar hadn't have taken the blast for them. She rubbed her ear; it felt like it was stuffed with something and she couldn't hear quite right.

She knelt to wipe her sword on one of the dead cultist's robes, but the blood simply slipped off the metal. She held it up and nearly dropped it in surprise as the nicks and burrs from the fight were healing themselves, leaving the blade as sharp and perfect as when she'd found it.

She grinned and thrust the sword toward the ceiling. "Yeah! You have made an enemy of me! On this blade, I swear that Sennha is my enemy, and wherever I find a follower of his—"

"Der," Jacob sighed. "Who are you talking to? They're all dead."

Her cheeks warmed as her face flushed. She ducked her gaze and it landed on what was left of the splintered altar, with a few wooden spikes still dripping from the slaughter.

Laughter fountained up. *Oh yes, child, come to me!*

She twisted around raising her sword, but the laughter had no origin. It was everywhere, in everything, and growing in intensity. The voice was as fierce and heavy as an angry ocean, and she was a single drop of water fighting against all of the sea's currents.

If this is how weak you've become, I bid you the grandest welcome to try again.

Der fought for breath. The air in the room seemed to be boiling now. She roared, "Fine, I will!"

The laughter exploded to deafening levels. *Your life isn't even worth being slain in my name right now.*

Then the sensation cut off.

She reeled for balance as Jacob hauled her to her feet. When had she fallen? She glanced down—she was still holding the Pallens sword at least.

He looked at her quizzically. "Fine-you-will what?"

She tried to focus on him. "You all didn't just hear—"

The wave receded and she realized she'd promised a god what she couldn't deliver.

And she had no idea *what* she'd vowed to try again. Or try for the first time, she corrected herself. She caught Carak gawking at her, but he looked away.

She lowered her sword as she exhaled. The knight was still staring as hard as granite at her, so she muttered, "Just...uh...remembering what the chemmen did to me and Kelin..."

He flattened out a grim smile. "If this was going to be a problem, you should have told me."

"Yes, sir..."

Thistle dropped to his knees, his sword silently falling beside him. He tumbled forward until his head hit the floor. His shoulders quivered, and a tear slipped down his cheek.

Der looked away and kept her mouth pressed closed. Jacob wiped his axe clean before sheathing it, ignoring Thistle.

She shuffled her feet, watching the knight.

The chemman's hand shot out and retrieved the sword. He rose to his feet as if pulled straight up by a rope. He spun. "Move."

Carak stepped aside.

"You're going back," Jacob stated.

"Thalon is all I have."

The knight nodded.

"But..." Der heard her own voice peter out. She moved to the side as Thistle pushed past her to the wall behind where the altar had been.

He extended a hand. It didn't pass through the wall.

He sheathed his sword, flattened his hands against the wall, and pushed.

He pressed harder, even shoving his shoulders and face up against the wall.

"It's gone," Der whispered.

"The explosion," Carak rumbled.

Jacob looked conflicted, but he shook his head at Thistle. "Your call, but we're leaving."

The chemman remained motionless.

Der tensed as the knight waved her and Carak forward. She and the dwarf tiptoed after him up the creaking wooden stairs toward a door. Jacob pushed it open with a foot, and the air smelled sweeter. He leaned back inside. "All right. Der, Carak, keep your weapons low. We don't want to frighten folks."

The three of them eased into a large avenue. Stars shone overhead, and only a few walkers strolled down the street. The giant knight bore down on the first people they saw.

Der felt a twinge of sympathy as a man and woman, who were holding hands, gripped each other so tightly that they both squeaked.

Jacob loomed over them. "Good evening, good evening. Um, do you mind me asking where the hell we are?"

The woman opened her mouth a couple of times before any sound came out. "Tenmar City."

The knight snorted. "Not bad." He turned to the others. "There's a tree path in their central square—only they don't know what it is, so we may cause a scene."

"Where is Tenmar City?" Der asked.

"It's the capital of the kingdom of Tenmar," the woman supplied, eyeing them as if they had arrived from the moon. "Magic users?"

"Far east and north of Thealith, Der," Jacob replied, ignoring the woman. "Well, lady, where is the central square from here?"

She just stared.

"We're in a hurry!"

The couple pointed down the road, too dumbstruck to speak.

Der started after the others but stopped and glanced over her shoulder. Behind, with aching slowness, Thistle trudged after them.

CHAPTER FORTY FIVE

"I don't like it here." Alsalon clutched his chest. Caleb watched him rub his arms together against the breeze as they stared into the fog from the top of the vaulted tower. He could make out the distant treetops of the forest beyond the field, but not much else. He could, however, hear the whinnying shrieks of the calvar. Beside his brother, Lady Eve waited with her hands clasped.

"Because we're trapped," Caleb answered.

Alsalon scowled. "It's rude to be so blunt, brother, especially now."

Caleb shrugged, finding politeness no longer a priority. His expression softened. "I don't like it either."

"And they're just waiting." Alsalon pointed to the field below.

Caleb cast a glance at Evelyn, who remained unmoving. He ran a hand through his hair. He balled a fist, and whirled toward the stairwell as he heard the commotion of feet hammering up the stairs.

Farallon and Amthros exploded onto the tower. The duke was trying to catch his breath. "I bring word. Fienan has returned."

Caleb gasped. "He has? Just himself?"

Farallon shook his head. "No. Fienan and the human, Kelin, with the half-breed boy and a couple of dwarves."

"Dwarves?" the prince repeated, raising an eyebrow.

"The boy is safe." A smile flittered across Evelyn's countenance.

"How did they get through enemy lines into the castle?" Caleb demanded.

The knight of Indelleiria's face was also flushed. "There *were* only a few enemy patrols behind the castle; they must've slipped through before the chemmen were in place."

"Any word on Der and Sir Jacob?"

"No. And the storm-readers may attack us at any moment."

Caleb frowned as the knight slid his gaze to Farallon.

The prince held his breath and nodded.

Amthros straightened his shoulders as he faced Farallon. "From what we know, my lord duke, you were the one who sent the word to the chemmen that brought them here."

"What?" Farallon paled and backpedaled.

The baroness retreated behind the knight. "No, the duke has always been favorable to us! I have sensed nothing wicked from him."

Amthros stepped forward, glaring at Farallon. "Our chemman prisoner informed us."

"And it is that chemman whom we cannot trust," Farallon thundered, balling his fists. "This is outrageous!"

"You thought that you should be king." Amthros's anger shone on his face. "That is why you launched the chemmen at our royal family's throats in the onset of this madness!"

"I did *nothing* of the sort! King Valladen was my dearest friend. I helped him and Thia build this kingdom!"

Caleb marched up to his duke and shoved him in the chest. "And then you marked them. That's why they couldn't run!"

Alsalon gasped and rapidly shook his head, but he pressed his lips together and dropped his gaze. Tears stained his face.

Caleb stomped forward as the duke retreated toward the trapdoor.

Farallon raised his hands. "No, my prin—my king! I loved the king and queen!"

"I don't believe you!" Veins bulged on Caleb's forehead and neck.

Lady Evelyn, hurrying to escape the press of bodies, tripped over the hem of her dress and tumbled forward, flailing to catch onto something. Her finger scraped Amthros's cheek as he whirled to arrest her fall, leaving behind a thin scratch.

"My lady?" The knight helped her to stand upright.

"I just felt faint, sir knight." Their attention swept back to the prince and the duke.

Caleb shoved the duke again with all his might. He pushed a third time, and the duke tripped backward over the stairwell. He tottered, but was too far over the edge, and he fell down the steps.

Caleb ran to the opening and screamed, "Guards, lock him away! And if he resists, throw him to the chemmen!"

Growling under his breath, he stalked back to the tower's short wall and gripped it with white knuckles. "Where in the corners of hell is Silver Dawn?"

"I was told at least a day out." Amthros grabbed his chest and grimaced.

Caleb narrowed his gaze at the knight, but he said, "Send the survivors of the raid to me."

Lady Eve tilted her head, "Are you cer—"

"I need to hear what they have to say."

"Of course." She nodded, closed her eyes, and hummed. Caleb felt the tingle of magic in the air. She announced, "They'll be sent up immediately, my prince."

Amthros pressed a hand against his chest. "Excuse me, my princes and lady." He ran for the stairs, and an explosive cough escaped from his lips.

Alsalon peered over the railing above the entrance. "A fine time for him to fall ill."

"Perhaps he's just nervous about the battle," Caleb deadpanned.

Moments later, Kelin, the dwarves, Fienan, and Thalon hustled onto the tower. Boison and Striggal each held a fat wooden mug in one hand.

They bowed, but Caleb was barely paying attention. He sniffed. "What's that?" He pinched his nose.

Golden-brown liquid sloshed over the sides as Boison gulped from the mug. "Drink."

Beside him, Striggal took a deep sip and said something that sounded like gravel rolling down a hill. Boison nodded.

Evelyn hid her suggestion of a smile behind her hand. "He says he's not stupid enough to fight chemmen sober."

"You can understand them, my lady?" Fienan folded his hands in front of himself.

"Of course. Also, they're concerned about the child's eyes, but the boy has been loyal so far."

Striggal downed the rest of his mug and rattled off words at a rapid pace.

Evelyn nodded and replied in return. She turned to Caleb. "They say Clan Heavyaxe will be our allies. They only regret they cannot send for an army before this battle, and they fear we might not win."

"He's not the only one," Kelin whispered. Caleb saw the human glance over the fields. The ranks of their enemies remained hidden in the mist, but the screaming of the calvar seemed to shake the stones of the castle.

Thalon peeked over the wall, and then he sat down and stared ahead.

"How did you arrive here in such haste?" Caleb snapped his gaze to Fienan.

Fienan bowed. "We were being chased by chemmen. I honestly thought we wouldn't escape."

"We got lucky," Kelin added.

Caleb scowled. "People don't get lucky, not in these situations."

Fienan dropped his eyes. "We did, my prince. We ran through a field of dead wheat and lost our pursuers there. And much to our surprise, they fled through a thin spot. I assumed they thought we escaped through it already and were continuing the hunt."

"They left it? Unguarded and open?"

Fienan nodded. "Yes, my prince. We waited until nightfall, and they had not returned."

"It took *forever*," Thalon interjected.

"We decided to chance it, and Amiery smiled on us. The chemmen had only left one guard for the thin spot on this world's side, and there was a tree path right there. We slipped through the ranks."

"How?"

Fienan shook his head. "They were still organizing. I think we were dirty enough to appear as cultists. We got to the rear of the castle, and our soldiers lowered a rope for us."

Caleb exhaled and glanced at Evelyn, who nodded, but then he swung his gaze back to Fienan. "Well, I pray you may be so fortunate again." He strode over to the wall. "You may rest instead of fight. You have been through enough."

Fienan bowed again. "No, my prince, we will defend this castle for as long as we are able."

"Good." The light slipped away from Caleb's face as rising storm clouds overtook the sun.

CHAPTER FORTY SIX

"Do you see through my eyes, Dis?" Vlade susurrated. "Do you see what glory we shall have?" He smiled at the sky. "There's a storm coming with us." He directed his gaze down to the fragment of the obsidian mirror he had taken great pains to break out intact.

"Or coming for us," a voice from the mirror snapped.

He glanced at the king's reflection, wondering if it looked as if he were talking to himself. Dis had been the one to show him their fate, and that information had cost him his sword. It should have been here with him, and he would make sure that his king knew what that loss meant.

He gazed out over the field. He was high on a rocky outcropping, overlooking his army. The wind was rising, and pushing out their magical mist.

The mirror continued, "Something bothers me, Vlade."

The commander smirked. "Don't worry, Dis, it's different this time. We've never had victory over the elves in battle before. You'll finally get to fulfill your father's pride."

Vlade's lips curled into a smirk as he looked out again. Their warriors had rolled onto the field, crushing the flowers beneath their feet.

He had spent so long building this force from the fragments of the chemmen after the banishment. Like forging a new, stronger blade from the melted shards of other swords, he had crafted this army better and had instilled it with the memories of how they had failed in the past. He had made a wasteland of their homeworld to do it, but he didn't care. Here was a fruitful world for the taking.

Over the ranks of the chemmen, beyond the mingling cultists, he watched the calvar lashing out against their leashes. He admired the beasts. They could charge the horizon and bite whatever they could, never being frustrated by tactics, timing, or patience. They were pure; they were free.

Even without his sword, here he was on the cusp of his victory. Vlade licked his lips. "We will break their castle like a flood."

The mirror snorted. "Or break like a wave."

The chemmen commander snarled and shoved the obsidian into his pocket.

***

Spike, Jacob's massive warhorse, cantered along the battlements. He whinnied as the lightning above him tore at the clouds like a battle itself. The armored figures on the wall stood motionless against the oncoming storm.

The wind calmed. Overhead, fractured electric radiance split the sky, and thunder chased.

Below, the calvar lunged and lunged. The leather straps holding them stretched too far. Some of the beasts broke free. Their handlers let go of the rest and ran for cover.

The calvar charged the castle, ruined harnesses streaming after them. They threw themselves against the walls and gate, ricocheting off but immediately attacking anew. They smashed at them again, over and over, wetting the castle with their own blood. Their hooves bit into the stone, scattering chips everywhere. The falling pieces came away larger and larger as they mined deeper into the walls and gate.

The cultists rushed from behind them, carrying ladders.

Up on the wall, the elves pulled their arrows free. The shafts lanced down at the mining calvar and cultists like steel rain.

But they were too few.

Ladders banged against the walls, and the enemy began to rise. Below, the calvar continued to tear, shredding through the flesh of the nearest cultists with total abandon, all while being peppered with arrows from above.

Above, Spike whinnied and galloped along the battlements. Once he reached the corner of the wall, he jumped. He soared down through the air but landed as gently as a leaf on the ground below. He whirled and buried his teeth into the shoulder of the nearest cultist before bashing the man against the castle until he stopped squirming.

Next, he slammed his hooves into the flesh of a calvar. Its skin, which had withstood arrows and stone, ripped open to him. He bit down on the back of its neck and squeezed. Bones crunched between his teeth as the animal screamed.

***

Up on the battlements, several cultists slipped off of their ladders, landing between the elvish archers. The first one up raised his sword at Salinienn's back just as the elf drew his bow for another shot at the calvar below.

An arrow took the cultist through the throat as the next nearest archer turned and let fly.

The man staggered forward, arms flailing, and collapsed onto the stones. Salinienn loosed three more arrows, and two other cultists spilled onto the battlements, dead. The third collapsed on the ladder, his body sagging onto the other climbers.

The elf kicked a ladder away from the wall and whirled back to shooting the calvar at the castle's base. Several of them had clubbed deep holes in the stone already. He reached into the quiver tied to his leg and patted it. Few arrows remained.

The storm-readers light crept all around him now, and the world seemed filtered through grayness.

Salinienn felt his body flinch and wondered why. His ears had heard a groan. He let his gaze fall.

A cultist he had killed stirred at his feet. He shot another arrow into the cultist's back and spun toward the next invader.

The body continued to push itself upright, clawing toward him. He stared, and the cultist raised his face and opened his mouth.

The elf gulped when he saw the other's eyes. They were sightless and fixed on a point not visible in this world.

The other two corpses he had just slain also unfolded themselves from the walkway. A gasp of panic died in his throat. He dropped his bow and yanked at his sword.

He swung the blade at the nearest undead warrior's head and found his voice. "The cultists! The chemmen have magicked them!" He felt hands, still warm, grappling at his legs.

More living cultists crested the battlements, and blades crossed with deadly music all along the castle. The cultists were no match for the elves' skill, but their numbers never decreased. The few elves on the wall fought brilliantly, but the cultists continued to rise over the walls of the castle.

***

In the back of the field, Vlade motioned the chemmen host forward. There was still a little risk, but he had waited long enough for this night.

CHAPTER FORTY SEVEN

Der, Jacob, Thistle, and Carak opened their eyes. Der blinked and rubbed her face. She was certain that her eyes had been open all the way, but all she could remember was shadow and then this dark, stormy forest. As they hurried between the trees, she held the Pallens sword in front of her, once again soaking in its colors.

"Is this Elloan?" she asked. Then she stiffened and froze.

She had never heard the sounds of battle before, but the clashing metal blended with the roar of soldiers into one unified thunder was instantly recognizable to her.

Their pace slowed as the castle and the backs of the chemmen legion came into view.

She thrust her sword into the air. "We have to save Caleb!" She charged.

Jacob shook his head at her.

After the next few steps, she was nose deep in the ground. She lifted her gaze to see what she had tripped over and caught a gleam of armor in the lightning. Hard eyes, like diamonds, glared from beneath a helmet.

She opened her mouth to yell, but someone else grabbed her from behind. The Pallens sword tumbled from her hand.

***

The calvar punched through the gate. The wood fractured and fell around them as they streamed into the castle and struck sparks with their hooves on the paving stones of the courtyard. The elves abandoned the space through several archways, and those on the battlements spun and released their remaining arrows inside.

Most of the cultists had turned to undead, and they did not stop their assaults on the defenders.

Behind them came the chemmen ranks. They funneled through the broken gate and stampeded into the courtyard.

***

Caleb ran his shaking hands through his hair. He moved away from the tower's edge and faced Lady Evelyn. "It appears we've lost." His hand strayed to the pommel of the sword.

She opened the wooden chest and withdrew a small, smooth bowl carved from a gigantic emerald. She extended a palm over it, and a single drop of water fell into it. Red candles rose out of the chest and planted themselves in a circle around her.

"You should meet your guards, my prince," she whispered as she set the bowl before her.

He tightened his jaw. Then he straightened his shoulders and bowed to her. "My lady, you are more valuable than I am this night. I will lead away any chase that may come." He disappeared down the twisting stairs.

Evelyn closed her eyes. Flames erupted from the candles, changing from yellow to moonlight white. They expanded until they became a wall of alabaster fire.

The radiance spilled over the sides of the vaulted tower, flowing like a flood. It touched the courtyard, filling the archways, and remained shining in them.

The battle's motion slowed as the brilliance blinded everyone. Several chemmen tried to retreat from the white fire into the center of the courtyard, but the press of bodies behind them pushed them forward into the light.

Their screams resounded over the castle walls.

Those fortunate enough to have ducked across the thresholds before the light had sectioned them off found themselves facing scores more elves hidden in the corridors and adjoining rooms off the courtyard.

Inside the courtyard, the remaining calvar took to new charging frenzies. They slammed into the white flames and wailed as they burned.

***

On the battlements, the undead collapsed as the white fire passed over them. The living remained unharmed.

A second rank of archers burst out of the towers where they had been hiding. Kelin chased after them, yanking the tarps away to reveal hundreds of arrows.

He dashed around a corner and crashed into Amthros. The knight grabbed his chest and collapsed on a pile of arrows. He snagged Kelin's ankle.

The human tripped and hopped to save his balance. He looked the knight up and down. "Sir, where are you wounded?"

Confusion twisted on Amthros's face. He struggled to form the words, "I'm not." Kelin watched his gaze narrow. "Where did all...arrows...come from?"

The human jerked his eyes back to the archers. One of them ducked to yank the cover off her arrows, losing valuable seconds in doing so. He tensed to dash. "I'll tell a surgeon where you are!"

As he ran, he checked over his shoulder to see Amthros push himself up to his knees and hands and crawl forward to a staircase. He tucked his chin down to his chest, rolled, and thudded down toward the belly of the castle.

The crashing of metal stole Kelin's attention. He whipped around and fought the urge to duck. He peeked between the battlements. In the courtyard below, amid the cloud of arrows, the chemmen had thrown up their shields and covered their ranks tightly.

In the back of his army, Vlade almost dropped the sword he'd been holding. He glared at the light spilling over its walls toward the field below.

"Good attempt, but I'll still send you all to hell." The chemmen still greatly outnumbered those trapped in the castle.

He heard the sound of metal scraping against itself behind him. Vlade tossed a glance over his shoulder. The trees shimmered against the storm's lightning and vanished.

Where they had been stood the knights and soldiers of Silver Dawn. The chemmen remained in the field in front of the castle and in the courtyard, but now with Silver Dawn closing in on three sides.

He watched from his perch as the first rank, mounted on horseback, lowered their lances at the backs of the chemmen army. Lightning flashed against their armor, but it was the knights who thundered forward.

They crashed into the chemmen lines. Those storm-readers spun to meet them, but the cavalry trampled the first rows. The chemmen soldiers forced themselves into formation, pushing back against the horses and lances. The battle was finally joined.

CHAPTER FORTY EIGHT

Der bounced from foot to foot. She had scooped up her sword right before Jacob had hauled her back to her feet. Ahead of her, she watched the soldiers marching, and she strained toward them. "We're going to miss it!"

Thistle folded his arms and leaned against a tree.

"What? Why not?" she gasped. "What about Thalon? What if they made it back?"

"I'm no good to him dead."

"But..."

He arched an eyebrow. "I don't think they'll ask which side of the war this storm-reader is on."

"Oh." She slouched. "Right."

Carak tugged at Der's elbow. "Leave him. He'll be safest here."

Jacob nodded, still cradling the crown in one arm. "It's a good thing you kept your elvish style clothes, Thistle."

The chemman shrugged. "Unlike the rest of them, I've learned to think for myself."

"Fine!" Der snatched the crown out of Jacob's hands and shoved it into Thistle's. "Can we go now, sir?"

The elf gasped. "Der!"

Thistle all but let the crown fly back into the knight's grasp. He stared at it as if it were poisoning him.

"Is that thing more valuable than saving lives? Isn't that what this battle is about?" She waved the Pallens sword toward the castle. "Let's go! Now!"

Jacob rolled his eyes. "Fine. Just get in a line in the back." He called as Der and Carak sprinted off toward the lines, "And don't forget to grab a helmet!" He snorted and glanced at Thistle. "Kids."

***

Carak kept pace with Der, his legs galloping twice as fast as hers, and she didn't notice. She hadn't heard what Jacob had shouted after them.

They slotted into place at the end of a line in the last row, and the dragoon soldiers nodded to them. Der found her jaw swinging open in awe of their skill, of the way they moved with shoulder-to-shoulder confidence.

As she watched, she realized the importance of staying in formation. If she stood here, that meant her shield partner was there, and she protected the person on her left with her shield. It all made perfect sense, and for the moment, she forgot that she didn't have a

492

shield. The warriors beside her towered over her, but she didn't give attention to that either.

As she glanced around, she saw that Silver Dawn boasted warriors of all major races, and all positioned so they were stronger for it. It so easily could have been a weakness, but they weaved it into a strength. The dwarves covered low for the taller warriors; their opponents' swords couldn't be both high and low at once.

She grumbled after a minute of straining on her toes. There was a clash and the sound of thunder, and suddenly, ahead of her, the roar intensified.

"Hole! They're driving through! They're driving through! Hole!" The shout carried down the ranks by way of many voices. She twisted to see chemmen charging through the Silver Dawn's ranks. And vanishing. They shimmered and disappeared.

It must be a thin spot to their world, she thought, and she saw that the dragoons were letting them go if they weren't attacking.

One wheeling chemman punched through and tackled her by sheer momentum. Her shoulders bit into the dirt as they both crashed into the ground, with him on top. She dug her sword into the storm-reader's lower leg—it was the only place she could reach.

Above her, Carak roared and pushed a finger up to adjust his spectacles. Then he smashed his axe down on her attacker's back.

Der scrambled out from underneath and to her feet. The axe still clung to the body, and the dwarf had to kick it out.

She gaped as she stared out across the field. She'd lost her place in formation, so she and Carak raced toward the nearest line. She admitted to herself that maybe more training wasn't such a bad idea after all.

More chemmen were running past, punching through the gap in Silver Dawn's lines.

She felt herself sliding along the edge of the chaos. She tried to call for support, but the roar of the battle overwhelmed her voice.

Briefly, she could see the trampled bodies across the field as she wobbled for her own balance against the rush of soldiers on both sides. Then she stumbled.

She rebounded off someone but she didn't have the space to fall. She heaved for breath in the press. She found herself fighting more for air than the enemy in the squeeze of bodies.

She jumped up as the pressure lessened. Silver Dawn was flowing into a new formation and surrounding the chemmen soldiers, funneling as many as they could toward the pathway between worlds. She kept her sword on guard and tried to keep in step.

More chemmen charged past, fighting those who impeded their way.

She hissed as the press of bodies pushed her forward like the unstoppable current of a river into the chemmen's path. There was no room for her to withdraw. A passing blade parried her sword, and she suddenly found herself on the defensive. She felt her enemy's experience through the bladework as she struggled to keep up.

Carak jumped beside her and went for the knees. The chemman jerked back a step and swung at the dwarf, and the storm-reader's sword got through his guard. Carak scrabbled away, his grip on his axe loosening. His free hand shot up to his throat.

Der stuck the chemman in the chest. "Carak!"

"Me beard! He cut me beard!" The dwarf's hair was thick until right below his chin, where it was sheared in a sword-straight line.

"Is that *all?*" She shoved the body off her blade.

Then the world dimmed as the storm-readers' light washed over the field and into the forest. Der squeezed her eyes and reopened them. The lightning above flashed white, and everything had faded to gray.

"Not again!"

***

Vlade cracked a smirk.

"Vlade!" Dis shouted. "Our army is run off or boxed in!"

"Then they can't run away from us," the commander countered through his crooked smile.

"We're fleeing!"

"There must've been a misunderstood order! We've trained for this for the last two thousand years. They have not." He stomped his foot against the outcropping from where he could overlook the battlefield.

"Let us leave before the fighting comes our way. We may try again, Vlade! This is not worth the cost of our lives!"

"That's your opinion."

"I don't even care about how my father cursed me anymore. Let's *go*—"

The commander slammed the mirror into a pocket. He snagged up his horn and blew out a pattern of sequenced notes.

What was left of his army responded immediately. They tightened into a square, ranks deep. Those closest to the castle held up their shields against any arrows and led the way. The chemmen infantry pushed through the breached gates of the castle. "We can hold it from there, Dis. Victory falls to us."

He grimaced in an effort to fight off another grin. The more sacrifice, the sweeter the victory.

***

At the height of the vaulted tower, a soft tune played on Evelyn's lips. Colors still glowed into the world here, above the chaos. She lit a slim orange candle in front of the emerald bowl. She sighed and inhaled deeply.

The baroness raised her hands above her head. Air rushed up the sides of the tower, funneling through her palms. Her dress and hair caught the current like sails.

Above the frenzied field, the castle quaked. Stones, loosened by the calvar, crashed into the plain below.

Wind exploded out of the tower and down the sides of the castle, and the wall of air struck the battlefield at a full sprint.

In the tower, Evelyn raised the emerald bowl and tipped it over the orange candle. The single drop of water slid down to the edge, caught on the rim, and then trickled out over the candle. It burned away before it ever hit.

The lady dropped the bowl and collapsed to her knees. "May I never do something so wretched again."

***

Der hung next to Carak as close as she could, but she also found herself shoulder-to-shoulder with a human dragoon soldier. She could see far enough uphill to witness the chemmen squeezing into the gate. She tensed to race forward. "If they all get inside, we're done!"

The soldier beside her snorted a chuckle. "Nah, we'll just lay siege to 'em. You're not with the order, are you?"

"Don't you know who's in the castle?" She realized how small she was. She looked up toward Moonrise. She couldn't save her friends from here.

The soldier was staring at her sword. "What the *hell* is—"

The wall of wind hit.

It pushed Der off her feet, and she was powerless to fight it. Behind her, it knocked Carak back, sending him rolling. Part of a tree collapsed onto his legs, but all she could do was stare. She couldn't even hear herself yelling. She craned her neck to look around, trying to find her bearings, and she was surprised to find that she wasn't upside down.

Then she blinked. She could see in full brightness and color again.

She wobbled back to her feet, sword in hand.

A female chemman exploded into her path. A hook slammed the Pallens sword down. Der ducked with it but still nearly lost her head as the chemman's sword, held in her other hand, whizzed overhead. She backpedaled but slipped against the dirt. She shoved her sword in the chemman's way, but the hook jerked it out of the way and disarmed her. Der kicked herself backward and tried to roll away.

The chemman followed with another sword slice. Der wrenched to the side and stuck her arms up to protect her head. The sword glanced off at a bad angle, but she still flinched as the blade cut her skin.

She kicked out against her attacker; the storm-reader sidestepped and thrust straight down at her.

Blades crashed. Sparks flew across Der's eyes as she scrambled back. She snatched the Pallens sword up from the ground and leaped to her feet.

She stared at the knight in heavy armor who had parried for her. She frowned; he didn't look like one of Silver Dawn's soldiers but instead a knight of Indelleiria.

The armored man drove the chemman back another step with his sword, easily parrying both of her blades. The storm-reader attacked widely with her sword. The elf dodged the crescent hook, but she trapped his sword in the same move, and he took a hard slap of her sword against his armor.

He retreated, and she hastened to advance. He did not even try to launch a counter attack. The chemman continued forward, her two blades whirling, a vicious grin growing.

Der recognized the trap only a second before the chemman's face melted into surprise. He'd baited her! She folded over his sword, weakly swiping with the hook. The warrior yanked the weapon back as the dying chemman collapsed to the ground.

He turned to Der.

She stared. "Farallon?"

"Who else, you idiot?" he yelled. "Where's their commander?"

She still just stared as lightning and thunder split the sky asunder overhead.

He marched after the chemmen. There weren't many left, but none were surrendering.

Der's gaze followed. Where the portal to Darkreign had been was a fallen tree, uprooted by the wind. Was that what the wind had done? Broken the paths between worlds?

She picked herself back up and staggered toward Carak. He looked out cold, but she could see his chest rising and falling.

She listened; the sounds of the battle had dimmed, and she felt rain pelting on her head and wondered if it was just starting, or if she hadn't noticed it until now.

"Caleb," she breathed. She turned on her heel and ran off toward the castle.

***

Hiding against the castle, Vlade spat and cursed. Sheets of water flooded down the wall and onto his head and shoulders. He cursed lightning, color, Dis, the princes, the dead elvish king and queen, King Midan of Pallens, arrows, elves, humans who pretended they were better than they were, dwarves, and on and on.

This was supposed to have been his revenge. His glory. His redemption for being banished. He was supposed to have his sword. He was supposed to rise above its original wielder to become the greatest chemman. This was his victory. He had breached the gates, and so easily! He shouldn't have had to use his secondary plan at all.

He hardly moved when the stones beside him groaned, and a small section of the wall, unmarred by the calvar's hooves, swung open. He raised his sword to the elf who had opened it, but the elf already looked dead.

CHAPTER FORTY NINE

Caleb thrust his head out of the window of his chamber. The rain soaked him, but he didn't care. He felt like he could fly. Alsalon quivered behind him, clutching a gladiolus to his chest. Caleb's tears mixed with the rain.

"We won."

The crown prince spun to find himself facing a mirror. It was the same one he'd stared into before the battle, but it looked different now. He scanned his reflection, and thought he looked a little older. Not in any physical signs but in other aspects, like the way he stood straighter.

"We should call this the Battle of Gladioli Fields," his brother proposed.

Caleb couldn't fight a smile. "Much better than Battle of the Pansies, which is what gladioli are."

A knock echoed. Caleb hesitated, but the door pushed open anyway. He exhaled as Jacob entered, holding a hand behind him.

"You survived!" he exclaimed.

The knight grinned. "It'll have to be something worse than a chemman to take me down. I have something that is yours." He brought the crown of Indelleiria around from behind his back.

Caleb felt his breath seize in his throat. He took it by his fingertips and held it up. "Where did you find it?"

"In the treasure vault of Darkreign, sir prince. Although accidentally, to be honest."

Fighting tears, the prince could only nod.

"Put it on," Alsalon suggested. He also smiled, and it was the first real smile that Caleb had seen on his face since the garden.

He glided across the floor and placed the crown on the windowsill instead. He shook his head. "No. I'm not..."

Jacob coughed into his hand. "Regardless, you should meet your guards. It is not wise for you to be alone."

Caleb scowled. "I respect your advice, captain, but I am exhausted of everyone telling me to do that."

The knight did not duck his eyes, but he kept his lips together. "You are in command."

Caleb turned back to the window. "And, as one of the ranking members of your order here, I'm certain you are needed in the field."

The knight bellowed a laugh. "They've got it well in hand. But I can take a hint." He bowed to each prince and then pulled the door open.

Amthros spilled into the room and tumbled over the knight-captain's leg. His features had shed their colors. Jacob rushed to stand between the fallen knight and Caleb. Alsalon also darted forward, but Jacob snagged him by the shoulder.

Caleb stuck out his hand. "No, my good captain. I want a word with him."

"Go ahead." Jacob stared at the other knight without moving.

The prince frowned. "I strongly suspect that those duties on the field must be urgent."

"Not as urgent as they were half an hour ago."

Amthros crawled to the wall and propped himself up against it. He groaned.

Alsalon covered his mouth with both hands. "He looks like the walking dead."

"Because he is." The older prince's glare hardened.

Jacob towered over the knight of Indelleiria. "What do you want here?"

Amthros seemed to choke on his own gasps. "I was told Silver Dawn was a day out."

"You were told wrong. Same with the number of warriors and supplies you saw in this castle."

Amthros swayed as he tried to push himself up. He muttered through cracked lips, "You...you haven't had victory yet...still time for justice at least..."

"Justice?" Alsalon repeated.

Jacob suddenly straightened. "Where's Eve? Lady Evelyn?"

Caleb replied, "She sealed all the paths to Darkreign up in the tower."

"She's by *herself?*" The knight-captain rose to the balls of his feet.

"Go to her," Caleb offered, letting a hand rest on his sword. "This man can do us no harm."

The captain looked between the prince and the door.

"Captain."

Jacob bolted.

Amthros pressed a hand against his chest and wheezed. "Did you poison me?" His wizened voice barely bled through the air.

Caleb squatted in front of him. "No. That would mean that we put something in. We took something out."

The knight fought to speak, but the confusion on his face was enough to ask the question.

"Your water of life. Lady Evelyn used it as the key when she locked away Darkreign. To open any path between our worlds now, one must have your water of life, wherever it has gone to in our great circle of a world." He sighed. "Your death will be far easier than what you gave many other good people. I don't know if there is an afterlife, but if you fail to discover oblivion, may your soul get what you deserve."

Amthros wetted his lips with his tongue. "But the chem—the traitor said—Farallon..."

Caleb watched him as he spoke, "To save his own life. You were right there; you could have denied

Thistle's words. You even tried to kill him before we escaped on the river. He later told us the truth. That it was you who betrayed us."

"Before...the raid?" Amthros rolled his head.

"Yes." Caleb ground his teeth. "It was you who truly marked the king and queen for death."

Alsalon shrieked, "Our parents! Our parents! You murderer!" He threw himself at the dying elf, his fists pounding.

Caleb hauled him backward. "Alsalon, no! He's already dying!"

The younger prince's voice had to fight through his sobs, "But he's why they're gone forever!"

"And we took his life for it! Get back!" Caleb flung his brother across the room by his waist.

A sound emanated from between the knight's lips like paper crackling in a fire. He was laughing. "Yes, I am a murderer. I have been for a long time."

"What do you mean?" Caleb whispered.

"The children. The storm-reader children we held as prisoners."

The prince narrowed his brow in thought. "Do you mean the storm-reader children that my father spared in Darii? You were defending yourselves."

Amthros trembled. "Didn't matter. They were *children.* We needed to pay for that sin. I needed to pay it."

"So you betrayed your own to an even worse evil."

The knight shook his head. "Didn't know what to do... They...wicked, but so were we. There was no balance..."

Caleb pursed his lips and tightened his fists. "You could have killed me and my brother whenever you wished."

"Wasn't your sin."

"Ah. Even though the chemmen wanted to kill us anyway."

"We had to pay for our crimes... I begged you not to come here..."

Caleb exhaled and straightened. "Well, in all this mess, we have you to thank for our victory."

Amthros creased his brow.

"We couldn't have brought the chemmen here without you. You were an invaluable source of information to them. We couldn't strike back against their scattered forces, and they had free run of the kingdom. If you hadn't told them that we were going to be here, they would have destroyed many, many more innocent lives."

"Because I told them..."

The prince nodded. "Yes." He stepped back. "But that just wouldn't be convincing enough. They needed to discover for themselves as well." He felt a smirk drawing across his face, and he couldn't imagine why when he was boiling with anger underneath. "So that's why Der and Kelin told them too—why they went on the raid. Two humans, mixed in this chaos, who had become pets of the crown prince and who had been previously tortured by the chemmen..." He felt his face tighten. "Well, the storm-readers would believe how easily they could give up some priceless information they accidentally learned." Caleb leaned forward. "And then there is the matter of Thistle. A chemman, supposedly married to an elf, with a half-breed son. But I'm certain his information was also believable to them in the end. After all, there are no chemmen traitors."

The knight's head tipped forward. "...you knew all along..."

"Yes, and we gave them exactly what they yearned for. Dis and Vlade needed to come here, didn't they? That being said, I gave orders to let as many chemmen as possible flee back to Darkreign. I am not like them."

Amthros gurgled.

Caleb rocked back on his heels.

The knight's voice seemed to come from a long way away, and his eyes no longer focused. "It's all right now. I think...we've paid our debt. My sin no longer weighs..." He closed his eyes and exhaled for the last time.

***

"Derora Saxen!"

Der stopped at Kelin's shout. She breathed out. They'd made it back.

He didn't jump at her, and instead remained sitting at the table. He looked exhausted. He, Thalon, Boison, and Striggal had made themselves at home in a dining hall full of empty tables.

Thistle followed her into the room. "Dad!" Thalon hopped up and latched onto Thistle's leg. The chemman rested a hand on the child's head.

Der grinned, still holding her sword.

"Pallens," Boison wheezed. He pointed at her. "Pallens!" He stared as if she had stolen it from his own hand.

Kelin slid right off his bench and onto the floor in surprise. "A Pallens sword? Wh—*how?*"

Thalon shook his head, and his eyes narrowed in confusion. "Na uh. The Blackhound—"

"He must not have found this one." Der pulled the weapon close to her chest. "Because it disappeared before he destroyed the empire. Probably."

"Carak!" Striggal stepped forward, searching. "What Carak? What Carak?"

"Where's Carak?" Der blinked. She glanced back through the door. "He's right here."

The other dwarf tiptoed around the corner, his eyes studying the floor intensely. His beard ended in a straight line below his chin. Boison and Striggal choked and broke into suspicious coughing fits.

Carak bunched up his face, turning cherry red beneath his skewed spectacles, and burst into tears. The other two dwarves ran up to him and began to share his sobs.

Der opened her mouth but never got the chance to speak. Kelin blurred in her vision as he leaped from the floor and yanked her sideways. He saved her life; a sword whistled through the air where she had been standing.

Vlade screamed like a wounded calvar and kept stabbing at them. Kelin and Der stumbled behind a table. The dwarves fought to untangle themselves. The chemman's sword caught Boison across his face, slicing through his nose and into his skull. The dwarf jerked to a stop, dead.

Vlade yanked his blade free and wheeled back on Der and Kelin. Der shoved Kelin to the side with her shoulder, bringing the Pallens sword on guard.

The chemman paused, staring at the sword with a curious expression.

"Thistle!" Der hollered. "Thistle!"

Carak and Striggal pawed at Boison's body. She heard one of them wailing in anguish.

Vlade seemed to hesitate as he locked his gaze onto Thistle. His head dropped toward Thistle's sword, and then to the boy quivering behind him. The point of his sword dipped. "There are no chemmen traitors."

Then he said, "I knew it, Vlade, I knew it. Your sword proves it."

"But...this...is impossible, Dis."

"No! You've—"

Der and Thistle lunged at the same time. The sound surrounding them deadened as Thistle's sword moved. Vlade slipped out of the reach of their weapons. He backed away from their onslaught, his sword strong and fast enough to counter both of theirs.

Thistle moved his blade higher and higher against the commander's chest. "Stay low!" he hissed.

Der realized his plan. If she attacked low on the chemman's body, then she would force his blade to be level with hers. She'd seen it in Silver Dawn's formation. Vlade would also have to defend high at the same time. She struck for his thighs, going as low as she dared without opening herself to an attack too much. Thistle thrust at Vlade's neck, but the commander's sword was in time to parry everything.

Thistle pressed his attack faster. Der strained to keep pace. She moved as rapidly as she could, but she couldn't match their speed.

Vlade's sword found an opening and licked along her arm. She thrust ahead and felt her sword pierce his clothing, but it caught on nothing substantial.

Thalon slipped around and lunged with one of his knives at the back of Vlade's legs. The long knife went deep into the back of Vlade's thigh.

The chemmen commander's sword swung around behind him and messed the top of the boy's hair.

Carak, Striggal, and Kelin brought up their weapons and advanced. But before they got close, Vlade rolled forward, smashing past Thistle and Der. She swung at his back, but he was already up and running. He was too fast and had gained several table-lengths despite his limp.

She leaped into the chase, but her foot caught against a table leg, and she fell onto the floor so hard that her chin split open.

Thistle hopped over her to continue the pursuit, but Thalon shrieked, feeling the top of his head. His hair was shorter in some places. His father nearly dropped his sword as he ran back to the boy. He swept up his son in his free arm.

Kelin raced across the dining hall. Carak scrambled to the other door, shouting, "Alarm! Raise the alarm!"

Kelin had reached the other end of the room and stopped. "He's gone! I don't know which way!"

"Doesn't matter," Thistle snapped. "Raise the alarm!"

Der grimaced, and her hand fumbled to stop the blood on her chin. "We gotta find Caleb!"

CHAPTER FIFTY

Caleb pressed his ear against the door. Along with the desperate shriek of the bell, the floor and ceiling pulsed with a fiery light. "Alsalon, get ready to run!"

"Where to?" The younger prince squeezed his hands together, his face shedding color.

"To the army! To anyone on our side!" Caleb's hand slipped to his sword hilt. How arrogant had he been to be alone now just because everyone said he needed not to be? He gulped. Had he endangered his brother?

The door exploded inward. Caleb froze. He couldn't move, even though he screamed at his hands and feet to respond. Finally, his breath fell back into rhythm. *"Who are you?"*

"Don't you recognize your death?" the chemman snarled. "I am Vlade."

"Vlade." He wondered if Amthros had told him where they were.

"I am Dis." The chemman limped inside, his sword point dragging along the stone floor as he stepped forward.

Caleb realized he was retreating, and he tripped over Amthros's corpse. He felt Alsalon's hands against his back as he stumbled. His brother's elbows rammed into his ribs as the younger elf tried to catch him from falling.

Alsalon yelled, "They're coming to save us!"

Caleb gripped his sword as he regained his balance, but he didn't think he could draw it in time.

"Yes, they are," the chemman replied in a calm voice that betrayed none of the wildness sprinting across his face. The prince noticed Vlade clutching a piece of mirror in his other hand. "Do you think they'll be quick enough to save your hides?" He swung the sword's tip up and jerked forward another step. "Your hides... I think I will skin you." The chemman's eyes refocused.

"No, Vlade, just kill them, and we can escape."

"I still need my victory!"

"Be silent; you will listen to me for I am your king!"

The storm-reader barked a laugh. "Now? Right now? You finally wish to order me around?"

"Yes, you've gone too far! Kill them and go, or we're both going to die!"

"What's happening?" Alsalon whispered, his breath hot on his brother's ear.

Caleb shook his head. His hand inched his sword free of its sheath. The chemman continued to stare into space. The prince lunged.

Vlade, or Dis, parried with snake speed, putting their sword in place like a divining rod.

Caleb tried to determine the rhythm of the fight. It changed instantly: slow-fast, fast-slow, slow-slow, fast-slow-fast. He couldn't figure out how quick the next thrust would be, and he nearly missed several parries as he weaved sideways to try to create more space. He knew he would already be dead if someone had not previously wounded the storm-reader.

The chemman dropped his point, dodged the prince's following swipe, and cut the elf on the knee.

Caleb crashed to the floor. The chemman raised his sword, and the elf barely brought his over his head in time. The storm-reader forced his blade all the way down to the top of the prince's skull.

Alsalon pushed himself off the wall, and Caleb caught the glimmer of light coming from his fingertips. Fire sparked between his brother's palms.

The chemman dropped the mirror fragment. Before it had even passed his waist, he grasped a knife from his belt and threw it.

The black mirror shattered against the floor as the chemman swung. The knife scraped across Alsalon's forehead. The younger prince yelped and stumbled into the wall next to the window. The light in his hands flashed away into smoke.

Vlade paused. "Where did you get that?"

Caleb took a fraction of a second to glance at the crown.

"I know I already stole it." He eased back his sword a fraction. "Oh well." He thrust.

"Run!" Caleb yelled, his sword flying to counter the chemman's blade as he pushed himself to stand. "Alsalon, run!" He threw his whole weight into his next attack, barreling into the chemman's blade. He beat aside the sword, but he riposted into nothing more than shadow. He parried wildly, but the chemman's sword cut his shoulder.

Alsalon dove through the open doorway. "Help! Help! Alarm!"

Caleb swiveled his blade around the sword, trying to cut underneath it, but to no avail. He couldn't land a strike. After a furious minute, the prince's sword flew free from his grip. It rebounded off a wall and landed on Amthros's body.

Caleb dodged the chemman's next attack to the side, banging his head against the inside of the windowsill. He cried aloud as he propped himself up, gripping the sill's edges. "Your army is run off or dead!"

The storm-reader's expression melted into a stiff smile. "It doesn't matter who perishes. The chemmen survive."

The prince stretched out a hand toward the crown. The gems reflected the lightning's unsteady light. "Even you? What if you die?"

"Even me." The chemman shrugged.

"Am I talking to Vlade or Dis?"

He shrugged again. "Does it matter?"

Caleb laughed. He pulled the smooth side of the crown to his chest and laughed again. He could tell by the chemman's face that the storm-reader was as surprised as he was. "You never understood immortality."

The chemman scowled and dangled the sword tip in front of the prince. "Oh, we do; it's the natural ascension of our race. Now we rule Darkreign, and soon, this world. There will be another chance for us."

While he laughed, tears slipped free from the corners of Caleb's eyes. "No, you don't. Being immortal is being an individual. And I refuse to believe you when you say it doesn't matter if you die—either of you—because you've been immortal too long." He cradled the crown. "And you killed my parents!"

The chemman smirked at the elf. "Yes, yes, we did. You know, they let us. No fight. No fun."

Caleb felt his saliva burning in his mouth and his breath singeing his throat. "And how many other people have you stolen from me?"

A figure appeared in the doorframe. Orange eyes focused on the prince. The newcomer held a black sword in his hand.

"Help us!" Dis screamed.

Caleb held his breath, but Thistle shook his head.

"That's my sword! That's *my* sword!" Vlade struck in an overreaching thrust. "You tr—"

Thistle parried the clumsy strike. The blades did not ring out. Caleb stared in amazement as the two began a furious dance with no accompanying music.

The chemmen leader dropped his point and scrambled backward. Thistle held the sword still as the other cried, "You're one of us, and you're saving an elf? You know what they did to us!"

"Not to me, Dis."

"But you're one of us! *There are no chemmen traitors!*"

"Then I'm not a chemman. I remember being human. And I bet you do too, somewhere in there."

The other chemman's face twisted. "*My* sword!" Even wounded, he held his own.

Behind them, Caleb pushed himself up against the wall, still clutching the crown to his chest. He watched the combatants in a daze.

Vlade disengaged his sword and slipped it underneath the black blade, swinging it back and forth before thrusting, while Thistle tried to parry each swing. He moved Vlade's blade to the side, but not far enough. The sword dug deep into his pelvis.

"No!" the prince yelled.

Thistle collapsed, dropping the silent sword. He clutched at his hip, and his chest heaved. The standing storm-reader spun to the prince and smiled.

Caleb froze.

The chemman jerked toward the black sword, then stopped. "Enough of this, Vlade! Kill them, and then we have to go! Can you hear me? You can make yet another one." The chemman glanced at the open door, but he whirled back to Caleb and sauntered forward. "You, boy, have been more trouble than you're worth."

He thrust.

Caleb jumped to the side.

"Hold still!" Then he screamed, "Dis, shut up!" The chemman lunged again, lurching forward while he argued. "Vlade, no!" But the storm-reader had fully extended his arm and blade, and the elf was inside his reach. Caleb rose and slammed the crown with its spiked points into the storm-reader's neck.

The chemman tried to inhale and staggered backward.

Caleb jerked the crown back and smashed it into the storm-reader's face.

The chemman sank to the floor. His torn expression contorted and softened as his body slackened.

Caleb wrenched the crown free. His heart was beating fast enough to explode, but his fingers weren't shaking as he rested the bloody thing on his head.

That white-hot moment churned with glory and vengeance, but it slipped away from him. He braced himself on the wall, reeling from sudden dizziness.

Movement exploded from the doorway. Jacob stood over the dead chemman, axe ready. More elves rushed to Thistle, who was writhing on the floor. "Not him!" Caleb's sight blurred as he sagged against the wall and exhaled. He forced himself to look up and see who had arrived. Distantly, he heard Jacob bellowing, "Did you have to run all the way from the courtyard? What took you—"

His voice faded as Caleb tried to concentrate on his vision. The knight-captain, Der, Kelin, Thalon, two dwarves—he blinked in surprise, one of whom must have decided that the beard was just too much—and several elven soldiers clustered in the door. Thalon dashed toward his father. Everyone else hovered away from him.

"Dad!" Thalon tripped over Thistle as he embraced him.

The storm-reader pushed himself up and winced. He wrapped an arm around his son, and Caleb felt a stab of loss. He'd never have that affection again. He whirled back to the others. "Is Alsalon safe?"

"Yes," Jacob replied immediately.

Caleb looked at Thistle. "Help him." He swallowed. "That's an order." He listened to his breath rattle in and out of his mouth. He looked up again. He stared. "Der, why do you have a sword with Pallens art on it?"

She met his gaze. "Caleb, why are you wearing a bloody crown?"

Thalon pointed. "It's...dripping..."

The prince lifted the crown from his head. He brought it to eye level and stared at it.

He caught Jacob's nod of approval at him.

"Caleb..." Der began.

The prince shook his head. "No, call me Edillon. I think I've earned the name my parents gave me."

CHAPTER FIFTY ONE

Dawn had chased off the storm. The downpour had washed away much of the gruesome effects of the battlefield, and the sun glistened on the remaining gladioli. The colorful sword-flags stood battered and ragged but still turned their heads toward the rising light.

Der shielded her eyes against the early light with her arm. She and Kelin had slept on the battlements. They hadn't meant to. They had taken a turn on guard like everyone else on the walls, and when that was done, they'd collapsed.

Her mind nudged closer to consciousness. Something lifted her elbow. She groaned and rolled over, falling back into bliss. Then her ears recognized the metallic scrape of someone moving a blade across the stone. Her eyes flared open, and she awoke with the force of a sitting person leaping to a full sprint. Blindly, she grabbed at whatever was there.

An elf jerked his arm out of her hand. "Don't fret, girl. The battle ended last night."

She stared at him until the trickle of memory flowed into a pool. Oh yes. Peyna, the physician from her first encounter with the elves. She grumbled. Carak and Striggal had gone off to do something with Boison's body. Jacob had started yelling at Spike, and the horse had started arguing back. That part was probably just a dream.

"Try not to move," the physician sighed. "Some of those cuts may open again the moment you stretch." He rubbed something into a fresh scar on her arm, still pink with pain.

"What's this?" She forced herself not to flinch away.

"Yarrow and cobwebs. They'll clot the blood."

She frowned. "That's what we use at home. I thought you elves would have some ultimate healing ointment or something. Like you did before."

"Of course we do," he snapped. "It's just that I'm saving that for those who need it. You don't. And that wasn't *an ointment* before. My surgery is art." He rolled his eyes.

She squinted in the brilliant sunlight. "Oh." She retracted her arm and tried to roll back over.

The physician snatched her shoulder. "No, stay awake. You can rest again after I'm done." She kept her eyes closed as she propped herself up against a battlement. She wasn't ready for daylight yet.

"Once again, you've been lucky." He held her elbow. The skin beneath his hand warmed, and the spectacular scrape and bruise disappeared. The surgeon sighed. "I don't know how when you're so stupid."

"I'm brave, not stupid."

"Well, if you're brave, then you are stupid. You can't separate the two."

She smiled. "Ah, but you can omit one."

***

"Did you doubt me?"

Jacob shifted his weight as Thistle stared at him. The elf ran a hand through his clipped hair and looked down at Thalon, who was clutching his father's leg. They stood in an empty, open corridor, but it wouldn't be vacant for long. He shook his head, but Spike, standing behind him, kicked his armored calf with a hoof. The elf exhaled. "Yes."

"I doubted you as well."

Jacob smirked mirthlessly. "Although, you were supposed to break us out of prison, not be the one who put us in there." He frowned. "But yeah, I know how deep the loyalty to Vlade and Dis ran; they made sure their people survived once upon a time."

The chemman snorted. "Vlade was far too trapped in his victory, and too passionate in the moment to be a good leader. As for Dis, well, he was never as smart as he thought he was, a very human trait. Neither of them were true chemmen either. Not sure if there is such a thing." He hinted at a smile and patted his son's shoulder. "But I think we should be going."

"Have you had that wound seen to?" The knight glanced at Thistle's hip.

The chemman nodded.

Spike coughed and raised a hoof. Jacob rolled his eyes. "Oh, all right. You know that you both are still prisoners of the Silver Dawn Dragoons. It's my duty to keep you as such, and to make certain that you are not mistreated and get fed and all that. But I'm busy after this battle. *Quite* busy."

"Busy making sure the lady's all right," Thalon quipped.

Jacob kept a straight face but flushed while beside him, Spike pawed the ground. The knight said, "I could just delegate some of my duties and have enough time to keep one eye on you."

Thistle placed a hand on his son's head. "He'll be good."

"He'd better be." Jacob turned but then paused. "I have to know. How did you escape the first banishment?"

Thistle held his gaze. "Because the water of life I have is Laurel's, and she had mine. Neither of us were fully elven or chemmen when the spell crashed down."

"I see."

Thistle shrugged. "Others may have found ways around this banishment if they weren't here at Moonrise. This one only sealed off Darkreign. It didn't remove the chemmen from this world, and there may be others elsewhere."

"We're aware. But Lady Eve and the prince did not have the resources that Valladen and Midan had."

Thistle nodded. "I hope they are out there." He continued as Jacob scowled, "They must change their ways to survive, and I want them to finally learn for themselves. And for the others in Darkreign, maybe now that they're free from Vlade and Dis, they'll become different. I wish I could aid them," his gaze dropped to Thalon, "but for now, I cannot. Unlike the rest of them, I choose family."

Jacob slapped Spike's massive shoulder. "Well, I'm leaving to check on my soldiers and I forgot to post a guard on the tree path for the next hour. My mistake."

***

Der sighed again and banged the back of her head against the wall they were leaning against. She and Kelin waited in the chamber outside Lady Evelyn's courtroom. She allowed a hand to fall to the Pallens sword; she had scrounged a sheath that fit it.

He rolled his head toward her. "Don't tell me you're moping because the war is over."

"Nah." She scowled. "But... I have this question. Ever since we left home."

He lifted an eyebrow.

She let the weight of her head rest on the wall and looked up at the ceiling. "And the only one I can ask—aside from being an evil deity—seems to be insane."

"Are you sure it's not you?" He frowned. "Being insane?"

"No." She stared at the ceiling. "I don't think so, at least. When this all began, when those riders came to town, I heard his voice."

Kelin said, "You never said the priest spoke to you."

"No," she whispered. "Not the priest."

He blinked. Then his throat wobbled, and after a moment, he belched out a laugh.

Der glared at him. "Do you think this is a joke?"

His laughter faded to chuckles. "No, but, well, it's just not as terrifying as it should be. And honestly, I'm not surprised because it's *you.*"

"I was!" She crossed her arms. "He called me his enemy. He has me confused for someone else, but what does that make me? And the second time he spoke to me—"

"*Second* time?"

Der stiffened.

After a moment, Kelin drawled, "What did his unholiness say?"

She forced her shoulders to appear relaxed. "Not much. But I have a promise to keep now. To try something that someone failed to do long ago that he seems desperately opposed to."

"But it was never you in the first place, as you said."

She shrugged. "Something still needs to be done. But..." She stretched her arms out in front of her. "Dark deity is gonna have to wait on me. I will claim my answers, but they need to be hunted, so I need to become a hunter."

"Der…" He shook his head at her, and what was left of any smile faded. "You carried me out of the burning forge. You carried me out of a chemmen dungeon, and now you've carried a lost king to his throne. You're a hero. It's what you've always been." He turned to fully face her. "So why are you chasing these dark dreams?"

Her brow narrowed and her expression become pained. "I have to know."

"Do you, really?" He inhaled as if to say more, but then he blew out a sigh and stretched. "Fine. That's your call, as crazy as it is."

"…Thanks?"

"As for me, I don't have any grand ideals or allegiances to pledge. But I know I can stand on my own now, and I am enough when people need help." He straightened. "And I can be the one to choose when to do it. I'm sorry, Der, but I'm not following you anymore. Especially if you're attempting to chase down a devil."

She raised her eyebrows. Without a word, she smiled at him and nodded.

He chuckled. "And I've been thinking that perhaps the world outside Riversbridge isn't so bad."

"Yes, and now that you've seen the world, you may return to your *village.*" Duke Farallon breezed into the antechamber trailed by several other elves. "If you don't want to wait for the snows to melt in the mountains, we can send you through the tree paths."

Kelin bowed his head. "You are generous, my lord."

"He just wants us gone." Then Der scratched the back of her head and pushed herself away from the wall. She lifted her eyes to the piercing gaze of the elven lord. "Um, your dukeness, I have to admit that, um, well, to you, I was wrong, and I'm sorry. And I'm also sorry that I wished that you were the traitor."

Farallon snorted and crossed his arms. "At least you now understand that you were wrong with every step you made for the duration of this emprise."

He and his entourage swept past them toward the court and opened the lacquered doors. Der frowned. "Hey. I apologized."

They ignored her and snapped the doors back into place.

Jacob emerged from around a corner, moving silently for a large man in plate armor. "Der, you must've eaten a bowl full of lemons."

Kelin chuckled. "She's fine."

"Good."

She shook herself free and glanced around. "Where are Thistle and Thalon?"

Jacob shrugged.

"What does that mean?"

"Don't ask is what it means."

"Oh." She deflated.

Kelin rubbed his neck. "Before this," he sighed, "the chemmen were just another campfire story."

"Sennha and his cultists weren't even that to us." Der frowned. "They're another problem. We need to—"

Jacob slapped her shoulder. "You need to get trained first." He tapped his chin. "Do you think you can be a warrior, Der?"

She fought to keep a stern expression but felt her pride swelling. Sure, her plan had been altered and had shattered apart like a falling star, but she didn't care. She had proven herself. "Yes. Why?"

He frowned thoughtfully. "Many fighters aren't warriors at heart. Both have the experience, but the thing that separates the two is the willingness to do it again." He took a step toward them. "If you were given a choice, would you make this journey a second time? You can't change how things happen: the torture, the deaths, the betrayals, the victories, and the defeats. Every wound made bright again and every bitter emotion resurrected, but this time you know how much those will hurt. Would you?"

Kelin closed his eyes. "No."

Der bore a horrified expression. Her voice was dredged up from the back of her throat as if she were dragging her tongue. "Yes."

Jacob's face brightened. "Then I might be able to arrange something for you. Maybe in a few years—"

"What?" Her grin became hopeless. "I mean, I'll already be eighteen when next summer comes around."

Jacob blinked. "And you went on that raid? At seventeen? That's too young!"

Kelin scratched his head. "You must've known this, sir. We are human."

"You children are way too young for this! When I started, I was...much younger... Damn, but back then it was gladiators, goblins, and brigands, never chemmen!"

She held up a finger in defense. "Most girls my age are getting wed."

The knight ran a hand over his face. "Marrying infants. What next?"

"Um. Do you want me to answer that, sir?"

"No." He clapped his hands together. "Well, my work here is done."

"Wait!" Der tensed. "You're not going to the coronation?"

"Der," the knight laughed, "that won't be for at least a century, and that's rushed for them. There's never been a coronation before, understand? But don't be mistaken, as of now, he is king." He straightened. "Meeting you two was an adventure, and I hope we cross paths again, Derora, Kelin, under more favorable circumstances."

"You're leaving?" Kelin asked. "Just like that?"

"Yeah." He nodded. "Best time, before all the ridiculousness starts." He waved a hand toward the court. "And we're moving our troops home." He turned but paused. "Der, you guard that sword." Then he started to march away and nearly plowed into the dwarves coming up the hall.

Carak hid behind Striggal as Jacob disappeared. Wisps of beard poked out from Striggal's sides. The first dwarf grunted. "Well met."

"Well met," Kelin replied, leaning to the side to peer around Striggal's body.

Carak stepped out, wearing his spectacles and a beard. It was silky and wasn't the same color as the rest of his dark hair. He even had strings tied to his ears.

Kelin and Der both slapped hands over their mouths, while Carak's face reddened to a bruised shade. Kelin flattened out his smile. "I'm glad to see that you're well. What are you going to do now that the chemmen have been vanquished and you're free?"

The dwarf shrugged. "Don't really know. Return to War'Kiln, I suppose."

"What's that?" Kelin persisted.

Carak's eyes lit up. "The great dwarven stronghold. Oh, its halls are glorious and much larger than these skinny elven buildings."

Der's eyes glossed over, but Kelin's came alight.

The dwarf waggled his massive eyebrows. "You are most welcome to travel there with us. Come, celebrate Candlebright."

"Oh, maybe. Midwinter's still awhile yet," Der said.

"I will." Kelin glanced at her. "I think this is the first thing that I actually want to do since this whole disaster began."

"Then you should." She grinned.

The lacquered doors opened of their own accord.

Inside the room, an array of flower petals flowed like a water fountain in the center, displaying an endless stream of colorful patterns. A simple wooden throne sat on a small dais under a glass dome that let in the daylight. Today, Lady Evelyn stood to its side.

Farallon and the duchess waited on the opposite armrest. Other elves streamed into the court. Lastly, Edillon and his brother entered from a far door. Alsalon sidled up beside Lady Eve just as Edillon took the wooden seat. He wore the cleaned, spiky crown of Indelleiria; it shimmered and seemed to carry its own inner glow.

His voice slid through the air like a smooth wine, "My thanks to you for coming here. Without all of you, neither my brother nor I, or our kingdom, would have survived. I know that lives have been lost, and we will never again meet our loved ones, but we stand here today in victory, not in defeat." He let his gaze settle on the crowd. "I am not a complete person. But I know who I want to be, and I want to take that journey with those in this room. You have earned my respect through blood, sacrifice, and faith in me. You have given me the belief that life can heal and can become better than it is today."

He raised a hand. "To whom we've failed to speak with since the Wars, the dwarves, I wish to extend a new hand of friendship."

Striggal and Carak shuffled forward and bowed.

Edillon intoned, "We cannot replace your friend. I am sorry for his death—as sorry as I am for one of my own. We both lost people, but we've regained something we've lost."

Carak bowed, his fake beard touching the floor. "Yes, your majesty, we have. We are happy to carry your invitation to the clans." He raised his head and melted back into the crowd.

Edillon's face remained commanding. "I need to praise Lady Evelyn of Elloan for closing the paths to Darkreign. My lady, there is no gift I can give you that will repay you."

She curtsied. "There is no gift you can give me that I require."

He nodded and turned to Farallon. "Thank you, my lord duke. I know I put you through much."

The older elf bowed his head. "Thank you for keeping your faith in me, my king. I ask that I stay by your side through the coming years."

Edillon smiled. "I would have asked it of you anyway, my lord." Then he turned back to the gathered people. "I also need to thank those who put themselves knowingly in the storm-readers' power in order to bring them to this battle." He looked around. "I do not see Sir Jacob, and that red armor can't be missed, so I would call forth Fienan and Salinienn."

The two elves stepped forward and bowed. Prince Alsalon handed each of them a ring.

"These rings will keep you warm, no matter how cold the world around you becomes."

They closed their hands over the treasures. They bowed and turned back into the mass of people.

"Kelin Miller of Riversbridge, please present yourself," Edillon commanded.

Trembling, Kelin ducked his face and slunk toward the dais.

Prince Alsalon came forward and offered him a single-edged, curved sword, hilt first.

Kelin grinned. "It looks like—no, it's not like the one I got in Riversbridge. That one looked like a child's drawing of this." He accepted the sword in both outstretched palms and bowed his head.

Edillon smiled. "This sword will break enchantments and is enchanted never to break itself. May it be worthy of you."

"Th—thank you," he stammered and retreated to the dwarves and Der.

Edillon smiled and passed his gaze onto Der. "What could I give the ever insolent Derora Saxen?"

She sauntered forward. "I don't know, Ed—majesty."

"You and Kelin gave me hope, and wisdom about both life and death. Thank you."

"You're welcome." She beamed.

He lifted his hand to reveal the handkerchief her sister had made for her all the way back in Riversbridge. It seemed over a year ago. The king opened his mouth to speak, but Der interrupted, "Keep it. It's dried your tears more than mine."

Edillon held her gaze. Then he smiled. "I accept your gift with humility."

She grinned. "Of course."

He raised a hand. "You've found a weapon of Pallens, so how about something to go with it?"

Alsalon thrust forward a small, silver necklace in his hand. She fingered the slender medallion and stared. He dropped its weight into her palm. It was the most perfect circle she'd ever seen, bisected down the center by the outline of a sword. It looked as if it could snap apart in her fingers, but it felt sturdy at the same time.

"This is the Dawn Sword." Edillon nodded to it. "Carenth's warrior symbol, and also the symbol of a warrior of Pallens. May you serve it well."

"Thank you." She smiled.

Alsalon reached for the Pallens blade. "My brother says we can give it a fitting home here in the meantime."

She rocked back half a step, and placed a hand over the crossguard. "So it sits on a velvet pillow like the rest of the Pallens stuff you have?"

Edillon's eyes widened. "You're going to use it?"

"Well, the chemmen took my other sword. Again." She cocked a grin.

He blinked in surprise. "Der—Derora, you can't carry the weight of the empire alone."

She tightened her hand on the blade. "It doesn't seem heavy."

"It was probably a paladin's sword!" Alsalon burst. He was grinning. "I've read all the stories."

Der's face flushed red and then white. "But paladins don't exist anymore. They all died with the empire."

"It's most likely not, children," Farallon grunted. Then his tone softened, "It's amazing enough in the fact that it's from Pallens. It should be protected and cared for."

"No."

She sighed. Edillon was still watching her, Farallon was scowling, and Lady Eve smirking. She shuffled her feet and raised the necklace in her hand. "Do you want this back then?"

Edillon pursed his lips. Then he shook his head. "It's a gift."

"Thank you." She folded her fingers over the Dawn Sword, bowed, and stepped back into the crowd beside Kelin.

Edillon raised his chin and cast his gaze out over everyone, pulling their attention to him. "As we've resurrected the Dawn Sword today, I am reminded of King Midan's words, 'I have never been a believer in the divine right to rule. One may gain a throne by divine appointment, but he can only retain it through his own wits and worth.' I think we've shown our wits and proved our worth on the battlefield. I have learned how this kingdom is worth more than one immortal's life, even a king's. I solemnly promise to be a ruler worthy of you, like my father and mother. Their leadership cannot be replaced, but we have learned from it. My parents, however, did not give their lives for this kingdom. They died for my brother and me. Throughout this adventure, I've learned..." his voice became a whisper, rippling through the air, "...that death, that which we have once again forgotten to know, is bittersweet. I still love my former king and queen, and I love this land that they built, and I will still celebrate this love, even though it is so painful to bear. My pledge is to always bear this burden and to always serve my kingdom."

Around the new king, cheers as loud as a storm echoed off the walls and thundered toward the sky.

EPILOGUE

People hurried like ants in the fields. They hefted bushels and scurried back to the village. The summer solstice drew nigh, so the new year approached.

Inside the village, the river flowed, the mill's wheel turned, and life plodded on. It had even been quieter than usual these past seasons. A sergeant had arrived in the early spring. He'd ordered the construction of a palisade and had trained the growing militia. But by now, he had already moved on to the next village to do the same thing.

Donley and his father were aiding the mayor's brother in building Riversbridge's first inn. The decision to build one was a hasty response to the arrival of a dwarven caravan. There had only been two wagons in it, but the dwarves sold metals and tools. No one could explain why they came. But they promised to return, and so the inn sprang up on the riverside.

Donley walked with Avice over the bridge. He often left his hand resting on the pommel of his sword just because he could. He felt like real military now. He glanced over at her. She blushed and looked away into the brown water.

She'd never blushed at him before. Not until the start of their trial marriage anyway. They still had most of the rest of a year to decide if this was right.

Movement caught his eye. Through the gates, he could see a rider approaching over a fallow field. His eyes watered at the shining armor.

"A knight," Avice breathed. "What next?" It had to be a knight, even if the rider was a bit shorter than imagination usually provided.

Don took a step forward, but she grabbed his arm. He shook his head. "It's my duty. I have to ask why he's here."

"We'll go together."

They met the knight at the town gate, where the stranger reined in the horse. Don craned his neck upward to look at the closed visor. "Uh..." His eyes slid over the knight's equipment. The mail was flawless as far as he could tell, and the saddle was inlaid with multi-colored embroidery that he was sure would make Avice cry. His gaze locked onto a sword hanging off the side of the saddle.

The pommel was imprinted with the black rose on a yellow field, the Saxen crest. He choked. "Wha—what happened to the owner of this sword, sir knight?"

Laughter answered him. "I'm no knight, Don." Der lifted off her helmet. "I just found a sword that fits me better." She patted an elvish sword tied to the other side of the saddle. "And this other one too, but it's all wrapped up. You wouldn't believe it!"

"Der...?" Don's voice called from a distance.

"You get off that horse right now!" Avice stamped her foot. The young woman nearly tackled Der when she dismounted. The majestic helmet fell to the ground like a bucket. "You've been gone so long!"

"You look so much older." Don blinked again, staring between Der and her horse. "Where have you been?"

She grinned. "You won't believe—"

"Where's Kelin?"

"With the dwarves—"

"Dwarves! So where have *you* been?"

"Got tangled up with the elves—"

"Elves!"

"And chemmen! There was this war—"

"War?"

"*Chemmen!* They don't exist!"

"Oh yes, they do. And there were magic swords and crowns and enchanted castles and dragoon knights—"

"Dragoons!" Avice yelped.

Der nodded enthusiastically. "The elves are still celebrating, and it's been three seasons!"

"Where's Kelin?" Don asked again.

"He went to the dwarves, to see their underground cities. I have a letter from him to his parents." She snatched her helmet up from the ground, lifted the reins of her horse, and started to guide him toward the village. She whirled around. "All right, the palisade was weird, but you're building an inn! And you, Don—" She thrust a finger at him. "When did you start carrying a sword?"

"I'm a corporal now, in our own militia." He grinned and patted his weapon. "I'm the best in town."

"We'll have to match blades." She smirked.

"We will. We'll see who is better now."

She looked at him with an expression akin to a certain knight-captain's. She raised an eyebrow. "Don't boast until you actually know how good you are."

Don blinked and exchanged a glance with Avice.

Der smiled. "I learned that one the wrong way." She locked her eyes on the bridge and began to lead the horse again. "I want to see my family now, especially my father." She glanced at Riodan's sword tied to the saddle before saying farewell and heading off.

She found Riodan in his wheat fields. Her father surveyed her as she approached. His voice was soft in wonder. "How did you...?" He straightened his shoulders.

"I delivered your letter." She grinned.

But he was still staring. "Whose service can outfit you with this?"

She shook her head. "I'm in no one's service."

"Then how did you afford such extravagant equipment?" His eyes narrowed. "That's elvish mail!"

"And a sword too. I brought yours back. I had to travel to a rotted-out castle in the Wild Lands to find it."

"The count, and the king, cannot afford such equipment without saving for decades."

"Lucky for me these were gifts then."

His jaw slipped open, and he shook his head. "Who could possibly afford to gift you with those? And what could you have done to deserve it?"

"I'm not exactly certain, sir, but I think it's because I saved the elven kingdom." She missed seeing his expression. She looked at the ground, remembering the years she'd spent farming it. "The elves tell it better, and I know the bards are coming. They would have been here sooner, but they take their time composing the music—in doing anything, actually. It can be acutely frustrating at times."

"Elvish bards?"

Der dug her hands into the embroidered saddle. "Yes. Um. I got Kelin and myself caught in the middle of a war."

"What? There's been no war."

"It wasn't in Thealith. It was in Indelleiria."

He stared.

"But the bards will tell the story better. They'll even sing it too!"

Riodan ran a hand over his face. Then he laughed. "If anyone else had said these things, I would not have believed them. I want to hear your story from you though."

She chuckled. "I'll go stable my horse and be inside then."

She led her mount into the empty stall next to the old plow pony. She leaned on the wall and watched the small, bleary-eyed creature chewing his grain. She smiled as she remembered how she imagined the old pony had looked. A year ago, he was a royal warhorse, but now, no matter how hard she tried, he was still an old dumpy plow pony.